Once Upon A Lie

MICHAEL FRENCH

Once Upon A Lie

A novel

Terra Nova Books

Santa Fe, New Mexico

Two people from two worlds—Alexandra Baten, Jaleel Robeson—united by fate, challenged by their struggles for justice. Their lives fill these pages—and move beyond them.

On Facebook
Alex: http://on.fb.me/1PKt1eH
Jaleel: http://on.fb.me/1TWERFo

And Twitter
Alex: http://bit.ly/1Xcmgqo
Jaleel: http://bit.ly/1TcGJWp

Library of Congress Control Number: 2015956142

Distributed by SCB Distributors, (800) 729-6423

Once Upon A Lie. Copyright © 2016 by Michael French. All rights reserved. Printed in the United States of America. No part of this book may be used or reproduced in any manner whatsoever without written permission except in the case of brief quotations embedded in critical articles and reviews. Send inquiries to Terra Nova Books, 33 Alondra Road, Santa Fe, New Mexico 87508.

Published by Terra Nova Books, Santa Fe, New Mexico.
www.TerraNovaBooks.com

ISBN 978-1-938288-65-4

For Patricia, Timothy and Alison.
And with special thanks to Jacqueline Spoonts.

"It's a strange world. Some people get rich and others eat shit and die."
>—Hunter S. Thompson, *Generation of Swine: Tales of Shame and Degradation in the '80s*

"I want to be an honest man and a good writer."
>—James Baldwin

Alex:
The Present

~1~

Sunday, July 6, 2014. My mother's car just pulled up across the street. The brunch is her idea—our private reunion after nine years. Her email insisted she has important news, but she wouldn't give details. All morning, I've distracted myself by rereading the memoir I can't seem to finish writing.

My book eludes its ending. Intuition says there's a missing piece, but I'm not sure where to look for it. Maybe Mom can help with that. The life of Jaleel Robeson, entwined with mine, is a complex wilderness. Colleagues to whom I've mentioned the project encourage me to keep writing. They don't know very much about the story, but they understand my temperament. Unfinished tasks nag at me like an empty stomach.

I take extra long in the bathroom, putting on eyeliner and lip gloss. After nine years, I still feel a need to make a good impression for my mother. A college professor should have her head on straight, but intelligence and insights don't always trump old patterns. A young girl looking for guidance and approval is an empty vessel quickly filled with her mother's points of view. Here I am, stirring in a chair in front of my makeup mirror, trying to look more attractive than I really am.

My mother has always understood the seductive magic of hair, makeup, and fashion. She lives in a stately pre-war building with a doorman on Park Avenue, and ranks shopping and Pilates at the top of her must-do list. Other than that, I endure an information blackout. Mom refuses to Skype or join Facebook, Twitter, or Instagram, and rarely does she send me emails. She never includes a photo or note with the birthday cards she snail mails. On the mother/daughter spectrum, there is little I would call ordinary about our relationship.

I cross the street, quickly assaulted by the New England heat and humidity. With its perfect symmetry, our campus of brick and ivy sometimes strikes visitors as a Legoland set. The school's gardening and grounds budget is probably what the French spend on Versailles. I stare at Mom's car with an Avis sticker on the bumper. Glare bounces off the back window, but I can still make out a trim, upright figure behind the wheel. My heart is a speedboat. As I approach, I can imagine her calm, take-charge smile in the side mirror, the smile I remember from childhood. The Good Mother.

The air conditioning is running as I scoot into the front seat. As she turns to me, she removes her dark glasses, a large gold "G" stamped on each temple. Her handbag is Louis Vuitton. She wears a designer top and jeans, a string of pearls, and what look like Jimmy Choo shoes. Blonde bangs peek from under a floppy straw hat. My snap impression of a woman in her early seventies is that she's still very pretty. When I look more closely at her eyes and mouth, I suspect she's partially found the fountain of youth at a surgery center.

"It's been a long time, Mom. You look great," I tell her.

"Thanks, sweetie." She gives my hand a squeeze. We don't hug or kiss.

"What a beautiful campus," she observes. "You're so lucky to be teaching here, Alex."

"I know. I'm grateful." I wait for a comment about my appearance or makeup. I'm in decent shape (swimming daily at the fitness center), but some weight shows in the usual middle-aged places. Mom's silence makes me churn.

"Things okay in New York?" I ask.

"Never been better." Out of nowhere, she bestows on me a look of great pride. "I opened your email just before I came, honey. Congratulations on becoming chair of the department."

"Thank you."

"It's about time they made you chair. I've read your C.V. to my friends. You're so accomplished."

"You told your friends?"

"The news of becoming chair? Why wouldn't I?"

I almost didn't send her the email. As far as I know, she's never made following my career a priority. Then again, she's always liked talking to others about her children's successes.

"Where shall we have brunch? What a treat that two busy people can connect after all these years," Mom says.

She doesn't act like our relationship is anything unusual. What's nine years? So what if we don't hug? Can't mothers and daughters be satisfied just being good friends?

Town is five minutes away. I scroll on my iPhone to a soup-and-sandwich franchise popular with students, an Italian restaurant where the wait staff wears ill-fitting red jackets, and an unpretentious bistro with fresh food and where you can hear yourself talk. I read off entrees from each menu. Mom chooses Bistro Louise because she loves lobster salad, the house specialty.

As we drive, my mother fills the silence with tales of New York. She has the energy of someone half her age. Mine is already beginning to flag. I'm distracted by a scene from an imaginary movie that whirls through my head for the millionth time: It's 1980. I'm nine years old, kissing Mom goodbye in her Mercedes, headed for my first sleep-away camp. Clutching a small carry-on, I run to the bus that reads "Camp Big Bear." I finally find an open seat among seventy girls. My stomach is watery. In my free hand, I carry Spencer, my worn, floppy-eared, stuffed rabbit. At my seat I wave to Mom like I haven't a care in the world. Her hand flutters back at me, more fingers than wrist. She's crying. Her tears are from happiness. She is known to tell even strangers that she is blessed with the perfect family.

Jaleel

~2~

He never needed an alarm clock. There had been a rooster in Jaleel's head as far back as he could remember, crowing faithfully at 5 a.m. without regard to school days or weekends. He didn't mind that friends laughed when he told them. "How can there be a rooster in your head?" one joked. "What do you feed it, Jaleel?" There was no point adding that he loved the rooster, because it never failed him, not even by a minute. Early morning, before the sky had a smear of light, was when his imagination jumped to places he was usually too busy to visit during the day or evening. In seventh grade, school was challenging when you always asked for extra credit work that kept you up late. But Jaleel wanted to be at the top of his class, and he saw no reason he couldn't do it if he worked hard enough.

Before his parents were fully up, he was usually on his bike, backpack jiggling with books, homework, a sack lunch, and a baseball glove that smelled of lanolin oil to play catch with the older boys before class. Statistics from the September 15, 1982 *Peartree Bulletin* sports pages filled his head: Robin Yount's and Eddie Murray's batting averages, and Guerrero and Schmidt too, and the ERAs of his favorite pitchers, Dave Righetti and Ron Guidry. As usual, he would be the starting pitcher in his coming Little League game. In big moments, when he needed a strike, he had somehow learned to keep his nerves at bay. You had to stay cool in the pressure cooker. Mental strength, his coach had told him—either you had it or you didn't.

On this morning he wasn't yet on his bike. In the kitchen, Jaleel's angular frame hovered over a glass bowl, stirring the blueberry pancake batter with a wooden spoon until all the bubbles disappeared. Then he sliced up some peaches, boiled syrup, and set the small kitchen table for three. He had rolled his mother's present in mauve-colored tissue, and tied it with a ribbon from the five and dime. By the time he heard her footsteps in the hall, the first spoonful of batter sizzled in the frying pan.

"Morning, mama," he said, looking up. "Happy Birthday!"

"My, look at all this!" Amelia declared. The large woman in a terrycloth robe couldn't stop admiring everything going on in her kitchen. "What mother could ask for a better gift than blueberry pancakes!"

He could feel her proud eyes on him. At twelve, he was tall and lanky—a beautiful reed bending in the wind, Amelia said—but lately, whenever he looked in a mirror, he saw wider shoulders and muscular arms to come. His narrow, contemplative face had a slash of a smile. Friends thought him quiet and studious, a black kid smart enough to mind his own business, to know his place in a small city in central Texas, in the middle of largely white Peartree County. Yet from childhood, his curiosity had flitted to other people, even those not his color, wondering about their business as much as his own. He noticed something new every day, keeping notes in his head, where no one else could find them.

"I have a real present for you," Jaleel made clear, nodding at the kitchen table.

As his spatula flipped the pancakes, he asked, "Where's Dad?"

"Oh, don't get me started. Sleeping in, like it was his birthday. That man—"

"Look on the table," he cut her off before his mother could get going. He had learned not to take sides in his parents' disputes. "Go on, Mama, open your present."

Amelia dropped in a chair and slipped off the tissue. When she unfurled the twelve-by-sixteen-inch color charcoal drawing, she just stared. Jaleel began to worry, until her head finally lifted. "This is the most amazing drawing you've ever done. So much detail. What an eye you have, Jaleel! You must have worked on it a long time." She paused, almost out of breath. "It deserves a special place in the house."

His sketch of downtown Peartree was from the perspective of someone ambling down Tenth Street, looking toward City Hall and a dozen foggy-glass storefronts where Amelia Robeson and her friends did their weekly shopping. He had worked on it all week, late into the night. Black people and white people were crossing the street but not together. Car and pickup truck tires pushed against the curb. Purplish clouds scudded along, hinting at rain. Amelia let her eyes dance again over the drawing as if she had discovered something mysterious, even profound, and certainly beautiful. In blue ink at the bottom, he had signed Jaleel Demetrius Robeson, September 17, 1982.

He expected the picture to go on the fridge with cactus and ladybug magnets, but Amelia, reading his mind, shook her head. When it moved so did practically every other part of her body. "I'm going to put it over the fireplace. A gold frame too. That's what it deserves."

There wasn't anything in the house that was framed, let alone in gold. "We can't afford it," Jaleel said.

"Don't you tell me that. Now you sound like your father. It's the most beautiful drawing in the world, and it's going over the fireplace."

He flipped the pancakes onto a platter, pleased with their perfect hue, while Amelia set two places at the table and poured them orange juice. In another minute, the pancakes were divided on a pair of white plates, slathered with butter, syrup and peaches.

"This is a birthday feast," Amelia declared as they began eating. "And tonight I'm going to cook your favorite dinner—fried chicken and mashed potatoes."

As his mother talked, telling him about her meeting with Reverend Johnson later in the morning, Jaleel's thoughts roamed to the future.

Teachers had said he was talented not just in art but also in writing, science, math, and history—and his grades told the same tale. Only a month ago, Reverend Johnson had called him "precocious" in front of the congregation. After the service, he had taken him aside and locked on the boy's soft gaze. "God has special plans for you, Jaleel. You don't know what they are. But I know that you are bound for greatness. Remember that, no matter how often life bites you like a mad dog." His rich baritone gave his words special conviction.

Jaleel never boasted about his talents, but he was happy when they were recognized by others. That made up for the mysterious silences of his father. His dad's rust-colored eyes were a particular puzzle. Jaleel could never read them with any more certainty than one could predict Peartree's weather. His father's eyes were so heavy and preoccupied (by God knew what) that they struck Jaleel as something purchased at a flea market, baubles of little value, something his Dad was stuck with and could never swap for anything better. He was stranded in life looking like nothing made him happy. Jaleel's mother mused that what kept Clarence going was his anger, which she told Jaleel was frozen inside him like a January night. He didn't totally understand—how could anger be a cold thing, and how did it keep one going? But he supposed his mother knew what she was talking about. His parents had been married for a long time.

"Gotta run, Mama," he said, his fork swooping down on the last bite of pancake. "I hope your day is special!" They hugged, and he took his bike from the hallway.

*   *   *

Jaleel rode straight home after baseball practice, with random thoughts popping into his head: a girl he liked in English class, his mother's promised dinner of fried chicken, homework that would keep him up late, but mostly Friday's baseball game. The last time he was on the mound, he'd struck out eight in a row. He had heard whispers of how well he'd do in the prep division of Babe Ruth when he turned 13. Jaleel wasn't so sure. He had a decent fastball and a great curve, but his sinker was like a drunk driver, as likely to hit a batter as sneak across home plate. If his parents had any money, he would have begged to go to a summer baseball camp, even for a week. He'd be stuck here instead.

Peartree was the county seat, a boom-or-bust oil town of eighteen thousand, a place to drive right through unless you lived or worked there. The only home Jaleel had known was the two-bedroom navy blue house with white trim on Elton Street. As he zigzagged over the street, he was proud that he lived in one of the nicer homes in a neighborhood of blacks, Mexicans and some Asians. To white people in Peartree, there was little difference between blacks and other minorities, his mother had told him. If you were poor, you were invisible—

that's all that counted. It was just the way the world was, Amelia said, though he knew she wasn't happy about it.

He carried his Raleigh up the porch steps, pushed on the front door, and wheeled the bike into the hallway. He could hear and smell chicken frying in the kitchen. He could also hear his mother's voice rising and falling with emotion. He peeked cautiously into the living room. His father was on the couch, his eyes fixed on a soundless television. Clarence was always tired after work, but at the moment his dad looked more than exhausted, like someone too weak or distracted even to stand. As she hovered over the stove, Amelia would glance at him through the open kitchen door. Her scolding voice wouldn't leave Clarence alone. It grated like a table saw through wood. Jaleel stayed in the hallway, out of sight, wondering what to do.

"Now look what you've done! In a fight with a man over some missing tool. A white man at that! Tell me how! Tell me how!"

His father didn't answer, so his mother spoke for him. "You got a bee in your bonnet to pop someone in the nose. What, did he insult you? You're a big man, Clarence, and you can hurt somebody. What are people going to think of us, you're so dumb you lose a job you've had for eighteen years? What could possibly be dumber than that?"

Amelia was suddenly in tears, crying from the humiliation, or worries about money, Jaleel thought. She was in tears on her birthday. He wondered if his father had even gotten his mother a card, and if that slight didn't feed her anger. He wanted to comfort her.

"You got in a fight with a white man. Well, that's something to be proud of, isn't it? Lord God, you think another job is just waiting around the corner for you? How you going to support your family!

"Wait till Jaleel gets home. What are you going to tell your boy when he looks you in the eye? He knows when something is up. What's he going to think of a father who lost his job—"

The tension was too much. Jaleel made himself step into the living room, hoping to bring peace. Be a diplomat, he thought. His mother didn't turn to see him, but his father acknowledged Jaleel with an opaque gaze. He suddenly pulled himself off the couch and tugged at his pants. He turned from Jaleel to study the woman who was cooking chicken and berating him.

"Hey, Dad, what's going on? You okay?"

Clarence's eyes stayed on his wife. Jaleel froze and watched his father. His mother bathed Jaleel in love, but it was his solitary father who most occupied his thoughts, like a difficult math problem, or a foreign language he couldn't read. Clarence had neither close friends nor open enemies. He was a responsible man who didn't miss a day of work on the rigs, nor complain if a day didn't go well. His only jewelry was a Timex watch, which he said he would give to Jaleel if he ever retired and didn't have to concern himself with time anymore. On occasion, he went to a downtown bar after dinner, but he didn't come home drunk—it was just something to do by himself. Some evenings, Jaleel read him books from the public library, mostly about World War II, when Clarence's father had served in the Navy and been stationed in Nagasaki after the second atomic bomb was dropped. Clarence would sit in the bruised leather rocker, listening, and while he never told his son to stop, Jaleel wasn't sure he was fully paying attention. Clarence, his mother said, had a wandering mind.

Sometimes, the two watched football or baseball on TV, sitting on the sofa together, occasionally commenting on the players. He wasn't sure what to say to his father, other than trivia. When it was Clarence's birthday, Jaleel simply wrote him a card, and his father, opening it, said, "Thank you, son." When he was around ten, he had asked his father about getting a dog—a German shepherd—and while Clarence had said no, that they couldn't afford the dog food or a vet, he had talked the longest Jaleel had ever heard him talk about anything. He said he once owned a mutt named Scoundrel, part-pointer, part-retriever, who was as faithful as a dog could be. When Clarence and his father hunted birds near the bayous not far from Baton Rouge, it was just the three of them, away from the hurly-burly. Jaleel was amazed. His dad had sounded happy telling the story.

"What's Baton Rouge like," Jaleel had asked another time. The French name—red stick—sounded exotic.

"Nothing to brag about, unless you're rich and got a nice place to live."

"You ever want to go back and visit, Dad?"

"No, don't think I will."

That was it. An exchange of a couple of sentences. Jaleel went off to his baseball game. He had given up asking his father to watch him play. There were three things in his father's life: his job, keeping the house in good repair, and tinkering with the family car. The '72 Chevy was always clean inside and out, and it ran with perfection.

"Clarence, I'm talking to you!" his mother's voice rang out from the kitchen in an octave of pure frustration. "Have you heard a word I said? What are you going to do? Where are you going to find another job?"

The next few seconds were like a car veering out of control, launching into a ditch or smashing into a utility pole. His dad moved toward the kitchen. He pulled from his waistband the small, silverish pistol he always kept in his dresser drawer. His large hand swallowed it like a toy. Jaleel murmured something that sounded to him like, "Whoa now." Amelia still had her back to Clarence. In the kitchen, the gun muzzle brushed a spot behind her ear.

"No! Dad, stop!" Jaleel shouted.

The gun fired before Amelia could turn around. It sounded like a bottle cap coming off a soda.

"Dad!"

Falling against the counter, his mother, despite her weight, was suspended at an angle for what seemed forever, held by the strength of an extended arm. Then gravity dropped her to the floor. There was no blood that Jaleel could see. His father's head twisted back to him.

"Run. Go away, son," he ordered. "Don't ever come back." The gun had lowered to his side. His eyes stayed bolted on Jaleel. "Do you hear what I say!"

"What did you do, Dad!"

"Go. Run."

"No!"

"You hear me?"

Jaleel suddenly thought that his father might shoot him too. A crazy man might go around the neighborhood and shoot everyone. But running was impossible. He had to take care of his mother, wrap something around her wound, and call an ambulance. She was lying still—playing possum, he hoped. Perhaps the bullet had only grazed her head. There was no blood he could see on the linoleum tiles. He closed his eyes, as he had done when there were monsters in his closet. When they opened, Clarence was still glaring at him. His arm was shaking, pointing the gun at Jaleel.

"Run, I told you!"

Jaleel's imagination was like a magician holding cards in the air. Pick one, any one, but make a choice. Do something.

"Run!"

As his legs moved him toward the front door, Jaleel glanced back to the kitchen and froze. His father had pushed the revolver to his own head, above the temple. He was staring at Jaleel, as if wanting to explain something. All Jaleel could hear was labored breathing. His father's eyes fluttered languidly, like someone finally at peace. There was another popping sound, and his father collapsed, right beside Mom, both on their stomachs.

When Jaleel rushed to them, he saw something dark seeping from Amelia's head, pooling by her shoulder. The left side of his father's face had a hole the size of a coin.

"No, no. Please God," he muttered.

He could barely understand the sequence of events. Could he have prevented this? He thought he might throw up as he made himself kneel by the bodies. He turned his parents' large heads, one at a time, and tried to find a pulse. His fingers trembled traveling from neck to neck. Nothing.

Impulsively, he lurched forward and kissed each on the forehead to say goodbye. His mother's skin was still warm. He tried not to feel betrayed or angry when he kissed his father—but how could he have done this? The revolver was still in his hand. Something that small, how could it do so much evil? He never wanted to own or shoot a gun in his life. After a moment, he took the Bible his mother kept on the kitchen counter, laid his hand on it, and made his promise to God.

~3~

Fifteen minutes after Jaleel called 911, a detective in street clothes and two uniformed officers arrived, preceded by the wailing sirens of their cars. The detective introduced himself as Roger Patterson. Jaleel gave his name and pointed to the kitchen. His heart felt as if it would burn a hole through his chest, but he managed to tell all three men, in a shaky voice, everything that had happened in the last thirty minutes.

After Patterson examined the bodies, he used the living room phone to call for an ambulance from the coroner's office, and then walked briefly through the house. He told Jaleel to sit on the living room couch. When Patterson rejoined him, Jaleel had already made some mental notes. In the detective's lapel was a Rotary pin. His revolver was holstered under his arm inside his jacket, and a gold-plated Peartree Police Department badge hung from his belt. His swept-back hair was the color of a worn-down quarter, and his cheeks an uneven, blotchy brown, as if he frequented the new tanning salon on Lincoln Street. The detective's face was expressionless except when he wanted to make a point or ask a question. Then his brow arched and his eyes coiled on Jaleel, unwilling to move away quickly.

The questioning lasted more than an hour. Jaleel heard the patrolmen opening drawers in other rooms, probably peeking under furniture too, exchanging whispers, while Patterson sat on the couch and wrote in his note pad. Everything Jaleel told him was the truth, except how he had knelt by his parents' bodies and kissed them goodbye.

He kept thinking of what his mother had said, how things had gone wrong inside his father years ago—something to do with that glacier of anger—and maybe nothing could have changed what had happened tonight. Still, he blamed himself for not stopping it.

His head perked up when Patterson asked how often he fought with his parents.

"I got along really well with Mom. My dad was kind of quiet, but we didn't fight."

Patterson cleared his throat. "Never?"

"My parents squabbled," he allowed, "but never with me."

"And they fought tonight? About what?"

He had already told the detective. His dad had lost his job, and his mother was angry about the stupidity of it, because Clarence had picked an argument with a white man, over something meaningless.

"Did he ever pick a fight with you, Jaleel? Did you fight back?"

"No, sir."

"Did he beat you, Jaleel?"

"No."

"Sure about that? Never with a stick or a belt? You know, black people discipline their children differently than white people."

"I told you, my dad and I didn't fight. He never hit me with anything."

"If you saw your father kill your mother, you must have been furious."

Jaleel's lips parted in dismay. Wasn't the detective listening? "I was scared. I thought he might kill me too. He was a big man, and he'd gone crazy. I started to run."

"Then why did you stay if you thought your life was in danger? Me, I would have been running like the wind—"

"I wanted to help my mother. I thought she might still be alive," Jaleel interrupted, as if that too should be obvious.

When the detective asked why his dad was carrying a gun, Jaleel told the truth—his father always kept a loaded pistol in the house. He suddenly remembered how he had picked it up once, maybe a year ago, out of curiosity, wrapping his hand around the grip.

"You saw your dad kill your mother, who you loved. That must have made you furious," Patterson repeated. "Me, I might have wanted to shoot my father. No one would blame you, Jaleel, if you felt that way."

He was exhausted but kept answering the detective's questions.

Often they were the same ones phrased in different ways. Patterson's eyes were always ready to jump on him if Jaleel contradicted himself.

"I told you, I didn't kill my father," he blurted out when he couldn't take it any more.

"We have to do autopsies, and forensic work, before any conclusions are reached. But if you tell me you didn't grab the gun from your father and shoot him, I should believe you. Right, Jaleel?"

He was too exhausted to respond. It must have been eighty degrees outside, and the house felt just as warm. The detective's face was shiny with sweat, making his botched tan look even more pronounced. Patterson suddenly sprang to his feet, fresh with energy that he might as well have stolen from Jaleel.

"You'll be staying at the county youth shelter tonight," he informed him.

"Why can't I stay here?"

"This is a crime scene now, Jaleel. Only police can enter."

The coroner's ambulance had yet to arrive. The detective had closed the swinging door to the kitchen, but in his mind, Jaleel could see his mother and father lying on the linoleum floor as clearly as if the door were open.

While Patterson stayed behind in the house, Jaleel followed the two officers to their patrol car. One was overweight and had a rash on his neck—the pattern of dots resembled a dog's face. The other cop chewed gum and kept peeking at his watch, as though he had somewhere important to be. For the first time, as they drove away, Jaleel broke down. He cried for his parents, for the fear of the unknown that bunched in his stomach, and for having no one to talk to.

He stopped his tears when an ambulance rushed in the other direction, without a siren. He stared out the rear window, hypnotized by a straw-colored moon in the denim sky. Where, he wondered, would they take his parents' bodies? The policeman in the passenger seat turned chatty, asking if Jaleel had any brothers or sisters ("no, sir"), grandparents ("no, sir"), or any relative who might want to take him in. Jaleel shook his head. His father had two sisters living in Michigan, but they never called or wrote, even at Christmas.

~4~

On his second night at the Peartree County Youth Shelter, Jaleel had been fidgeting in a chair in the small front office for at least an hour. He didn't have a watch but sensed it was after nine. The only window framed a summer sky of magentas, indigos, blacks, and distant glints of light. Detective Patterson had called the shelter to say he would be over shortly, but that was a while ago. A white woman named Mrs. Driscoll, perched behind a battered desk with a typewriter and stacks of files, walked over and handed Jaleel her copy of Saturday's *Peartree Bulletin*. She'd been absorbed in typing a report, but now she was more relaxed. Jaleel was entitled to know what the town was reading about his family, she said sympathetically.

"Thank you, ma'am."

He felt a spotlight glaring down as his eyes jumped to the front page: "Husband, Wife Shot to Death in Home." Every sentence was like a fist to his stomach. The writer noted that Amelia Robeson had been murdered on her birthday—how had the paper learned that? he wondered. A neighbor's quote made his parents sound like crazies. "It's those quiet, church-going folks who always surprise you."

Jaleel couldn't read more than a few paragraphs. He rested the folded paper on his knees because he didn't know what else to do with it. None of this could have happened, he thought, any more than his discovering a dinosaur bone or gold coins in some faraway cave.

Mrs. Driscoll asked if he was done with the paper.

"Yes, ma'am, for now," he whispered, suddenly feeling exhausted. He didn't offer to give back the newspaper.

"Nothing is going to change, no matter how many times you read the story. No sense keeping it around, honey, for my money. You're just in shock. But if you want to hold onto it, that's okay too." Her emerald eyes were filled with patience.

"I think we should forget Detective Patterson for tonight, don't you?" she said. "Why don't you turn in? You look like you're about to fall out of your chair."

His first night at the shelter, Jaleel had barely slept. His fatigue had seeped into his arms and legs now as he gazed through the half-open door to his right. The rows of sleeping cots were filled with kids he didn't know. They were mostly black or Mexican with a sprinkling of white faces. The shelter had separate male and female quarters. For boys, there were two dorms, a mess hall, rec room, basketball court, and a small library. Most books in the library were scarred with graffiti, and sometimes pages had been torn out. There was also a visitors' lounge, but it was usually empty. The girls' facilities were considerably smaller and separated by a hundred yards and a twelve-foot-high fence. Boys would scream across the void whenever the opportunity arose:

"Hey, you want to taste something sweet tonight?"

"When you get out of this shithole, call me. I'm Jacob."

"Honey, I want to marry you!"

The girls rarely answered.

"Mrs. Driscoll, may I go to church tomorrow?" Jaleel suddenly asked as he stood up. "And the library in the afternoon, if that's all right." He assumed that on Monday, he would return to school, no sense even asking.

"Honey, I'll have to talk to the director."

"Okay."

It was one thing to be denied entry to his house, but he saw no reason he couldn't go to the library or to church. One was quiet, the other noisy, but both were places where he could be himself. His English teacher had quoted him some lines about writing one's destiny in the stars. In the library, he had read about applying for scholarships to Princeton, Harvard, and other "Ivies." That was years away, but he had tucked the idea in the back of his mind and nourished it. To make a difference in the world, his teacher had added, one needed not just brains but also an imagination. You had to see the world in a way no one else had ever seen it. How can I imagine the world at all, he wondered, if I'm stuck in Peartree?

Jaleel drifted over to the dorm, padding across the linoleum floor to his bunk. The overhead fluorescents had been turned off, but some kids were playing cards by flashlight. The day had been a blur of chores—raking leaves, scrubbing bathrooms, sweeping floors—busywork that couldn't keep his thoughts off his mother and father. In late afternoon, everyone had to do an hour of exercise. There was no baseball diamond or weight room. Some boys sprinted around the inside of the fenced yard. Jaleel sat on the creaky floor of the gym, watching as others shot hoops. Kids left him alone.

"Hey, wazzup?" the black kid in the next bunk barked. He was on top of his blankets, his pillow doubled over to prop up his head, absorbed in an issue of *Popular Mechanics*. He had a silver penlight for reading.

Jaleel looked again. The bunk had been empty last night. The boy looked to be around seventeen, maybe six-foot-four or -five, the way his feet hung off the end. "You rob a fillin' station or something?" he said. "Look like your eyes ready to pop out of your skull. You on something? I can tell you about robbing fillin' stations, mind you."

Jaleel hadn't intended to tell anybody about his parents, but maybe if he did some of the pain would go away. "My father shot my mother to death, and then he killed himself. I watched the whole thing," he blurted out as he dropped onto his bunk. He showed the older boy the newspaper, as if proof was needed for something so unspeakable. The boy angled his neck to study the headline, then released a whistle, like, shit, that took the cake over a gas station robbery any day.

"Your dad killed his old lady? Right in front of you? She-it. Who got time to kill himself? Poor people too busy trying to stay alive. What's your name?"

"Jaleel Robeson."

"What kind of name is that? Jaleel."

"My great-grandfather's Christian name. He was an emancipated slave."

"Well, good for him. I'm still waiting to be emancipated, whatever that means."

"It means you're liberated. You're no longer a slave."

The boy's eyes fell on Jaleel with interest, as if he wasn't like the others in the shelter. "We're a do-nothing backwater town, and you just stirred things up to a boil, Jaleel. Don't get too many murders here."

"I didn't do anything," said Jaleel. He wasn't making an excuse. He was blaming himself.

The boy put down his magazine, arched his arm across his torso, and shook Jaleel's hand. "Marcus Worby, bro."

Other boys were beginning to stare, but Jaleel ignored them. "Why are you here?" he asked Marcus.

"When I came home from school one day, the family car wasn't there. My parents, my grandmother, my two little brothers, they weren't around either. . .vanished, like aliens kidnapped them. You know what I'm saying? The house was cleaned out, except for a ham sandwich in the fridge and some dirty clothes in the hamper. No money, no note. What, had they forgotten I lived here? I was the family troublemaker, but they left me behind like I was some kind of poison.

"You got some relatives to take you in, Jaleel?"

"No."

"Well, don't dwell on it. When you clear your head, don't look back. No time for that. Trust me. You think about taking care of number one."

Jaleel barely heard Marcus's advice. He suddenly remembered the two plots his mother had paid for in the Peartree City Cemetery. Who was going to bury them? He had saved $235 from his neighborhood chores, stuffing it in a glass jar in his closet. He doubted that would be enough. His dad's Chevy was worth something, but Clarence had mentioned taking out a loan on it. He had loans on everything—the house, the car, even the TV. But a proper burial and service were important. His mother had neighborhood friends, and many more at church. They would want to mourn her death together.

"How can I take care of them?" Jaleel asked.

"Take care of what?" said Marcus.

Jaleel brushed a tear away. "Never mind."

"You talking to yourself. Need to cut that shit out. Now, give me that newspaper."

When he handed it to him, Marcus shoved the *Bulletin* deep under Jaleel's mattress.

"You better get all that fog out of your head," he warned. "If you got no relatives, you're headed for a foster home. One after another. Get used to it. I been in five. Just got back from one this morning."

Jaleel wrinkled his nose. "Five?"

"I told you: I'm the one who makes trouble." He sat up, slipped off his T-shirt, and shined his penlight on his back for Jaleel to bear witness. The rash of fresh welts looked like he'd been stung by bees.

"You know how many people allowed to take a belt to a misbehavin' nigger? Foster families, they take you in for the county money, as long as they can stand you. You're nothing to them but a dog, and old dogs get kicked out for a new dog. Ask anyone here. So you best be careful."

"When they hit you, what did you think?" asked Jaleel.

He thought for a moment. "I wanted to kill them."

Marcus went back to his magazine. The sudden quiet pinned Jaleel to his bed. His heart felt like a swirling, dark mass as he lay on his back. He was feeling the anger, finally, that Detective Patterson had accused him of hiding. Like a boulder had dropped out of the sky, crushing his chest. How could his father have done this? Not just killing his mother but wrecking Jaleel's life too.

He got up and slipped off his clothes, then wiggled under the covers of the strange-feeling bed. It took all his strength to throw off the boulder and find the temporary peace of sleep.

~5~

After breakfast, Jaleel walked straightaway into the front office. Instead of Mrs. Driscoll, a young black girl lounged behind the desk, filing her nails with an emery board. He studied her nametag: Cindy Manning, PCYS Staff. She gave Jaleel a pouty look, as if he was interrupting something important, or shouldn't be approaching her at all.

In daylight, the desk looked worse than at night, some kind of punching bag that had been kicked, pounded, clawed, shoved around, and carved on. Jaleel asked the girl if Mrs. Driscoll had left him a note.

"Who are you?" Her chin jutted over the emery board.

"My name is Jaleel."

"Jaleel Robeson," she recited coolly, as if she knew the story in the newspaper, and that boys involved in crime were usually trouble at the shelter.

"You'll be with Battalion B," she said, returning her attention to her nails. "The work detail is posted on the bulletin board. There, in the corner." She didn't look up.

Battalion B sounded like he was in the Army. "I asked Mrs. Driscoll if I could go to church," he explained. "She said she'd ask the director."

The girl gazed up from her nails, as if Jaleel was dumber than a fence post. "No one goes anywhere on weekends. No exceptions. Besides—" She remembered something and shoved her hand into a drawer of loose papers. It took forever to tease out a dog-eared index card with fresh blue ink slanted across the top.

"Somebody left this for you," she said, reading the card. "Detective Patterson is coming. It says he'll be here by nine."

"He was supposed to come last night."

"So?" She put the card back in the drawer and returned to her nails. "Nine o'clock. That's ten minutes. You best wait right here."

Jaleel doubted that the detective or anyone else from the police department would show. But he dropped into the same chair he'd occupied last night, slinging his arms over his chest, waiting. He was angry that he couldn't go to the library or to church.

When Patterson appeared in a charcoal gray suit a few minutes later, Jaleel straightened up, surprised. The detective had a purposeful stride. He was accompanied by a patrolman carrying a fat briefcase.

"Good morning, Jaleel," he said in an easy manner. "Sorry I couldn't make it last night. You know how crazy things can get in my world."

He didn't know, not really, and he looked at the detective with an unsettling feeling.

"You want some coffee or anything? How about a donut?" Patterson turned to Cindy. "Got a donut for this young man? It's the weekend, girl."

"Sometimes staff brings in donuts," she told Patterson coolly, "but not today."

"I'm fine," Jaleel heard himself say, though a donut sounded tempting.

The detective turned his head from Cindy. "I'll see what I can do for you, Jaleel, when we're done here."

Unlike their meeting at his house, when Patterson was aloof and businesslike, his tone was relaxed, even confiding now, as if they were on their way to some kind of friendship. Jaleel didn't think they had anything in common: a white detective and a black kid he suspected of murder. He suddenly remembered his father ordering him to run, more than once, after shooting his mother. Maybe Clarence knew this was what would happen.

Jaleel followed the two men into an adjoining office. They settled into folding chairs around a metal table while Patterson made small talk. A window looked out to the grassy front yard, but it was hard to distinguish much. A flimsy, oatmeal-colored shade was drawn for privacy.

The officer opened his briefcase and removed a camera, a stamp pad, and what looked to Jaleel like a card for fingerprints.

"Why are you fingerprinting me?" he asked. "I thought you were here to ask some questions."

"I hate this SOP stuff as much as the next guy. It won't take long," Patterson said. The officer screwed a flash bulb into his camera. "Jaleel," the detective added, "would you stand against the wall for us?"

He had seen enough cop shows to know that a suspect had the right to ask for an attorney. He knew about his Miranda rights too, if they were actually going to arrest him. But Patterson hadn't said anything about that. On the wall were horizontal pen marks indicating various heights, all the way to seven feet. The top of his head reached five-foot-six.

The officer took a head shot facing forward, then Jaleel's left and right profiles. His eyes blinked each time the flash went off. Walking to the table, he extended first his right hand, then his left, fingers splayed. The officer guided Jaleel's fingertips onto the inky pad, one at a time, then the card, rolling each finger side to side in a separate box. Afterward, he gave Jaleel a Kleenex with a dab of solvent.

Jaleel went back to his chair. Patterson thanked him for his cooperation. "Hey, I just have one question for you, honestly. When I was looking around your house last night—"

"I want to see an attorney, please," Jaleel said before Patterson could get his question out.

"You're twelve years old, son. What twelve-year-old needs a lawyer? You told us what happened at your house was a murder-suicide. If that's true, why are you worried?"

He met the detective's gaze with a resolve not to back down. Patterson's eyes were not unfriendly—they shined like turquoise against his phony tan—but Jaleel felt something unmistakable under the surface. He didn't like black people.

"I want an attorney before I answer any questions," Jaleel said.

"I just wanted to ask how long you waited before you called 911."

He couldn't remember exactly. He thought it was right away. What difference did it make? "I don't know."

"Can you tell me, did you do anything in the house while waiting for the police? Did you move or touch the bodies, for example—"

"I didn't do anything," he lied, remembering how he had kissed his parents goodbye.

"I'd like to call my aunts too," he threw in. "They live in Detroit."

"Your aunts?"

"Yes, sir. My father's only living relatives. My mom doesn't have anyone."

"Got a phone number?"

"It's in the house. In my father's bedside table, in a small, green address book."

"The house is a crime scene, remember? Can't go in and tamper with anything."

"Yes, sir, but I still need their number. I have to give them the news."

The detective nodded as if he understood.

"Who's going to bury my parents?" Jaleel went on. He suddenly had a dozen questions. "They paid for two plots at the cemetery. They have to be buried properly."

"The city will take care of that."

"I'd like to speak to Reverend Johnson. He's my pastor. He can help with the burial." Maybe he can help me too, Jaleel thought.

Patterson picked at a hangnail on his pinkie. "Some things just aren't possible, son. You understand, right?"

"Well, when can I go back to school?"

"I think there're teachers who volunteer to come to the shelter. They hold classes in the library."

The detective swatted away his questions, one after another, like pesky foul balls.

Then Jaleel summoned all his nerve. "I guess I can find a phone book and start calling attorneys for myself."

Patterson's eyes widened as he climbed to his feet. "You're a determined young man, Jaleel. If you really want a lawyer, let me find you a good one. Give me till mid-week. Anything else?"

Jaleel looked away. He didn't believe the detective would do anything for him, including getting a donut this morning. All Patterson had done was lie to him. As the detective left the office, he gave Jaleel a goodbye clap on the shoulder before turning to the other cop and talking about their bowling league.

When Jaleel ventured outside, he learned that Battalion B's assignment today was sweeping the visitor parking lot and painting a picket fence with three brushes and one can of paint shared by nine boys. In total there were four battalions, each comprised of about twenty boys, supervised by an adult in a forest green uniform with a shoulder patch that read First Lieutenant, Peartree County Youth Shelter. Everyone had to ask permission for bathroom or water breaks, and return to his job in less than five minutes. Otherwise, work was tackled at a leisurely pace, as if nothing really mattered, and not even the staff truly cared what got painted, raked, or trimmed.

Talking was allowed in quiet voices. Jaleel tried to overhear as many conversations as he could. Between paperwork and interviews, the wait could be two or three months for a foster home to come along. For boys headed to the juvenile delinquency facility, getting a court date was even more elusive. There wasn't much relief from the waiting. Parents or relatives rarely visited. No one was allowed to exit the twelve-foot-high, chain-link perimeter fence without an adult, and you had to be back before dark. The public school teachers assigned to teach at the shelter didn't show up half the time. Phone privileges, courtesy of a single pay phone that was often broken, were from 4 to 5 p.m.—one hour for almost a hundred boys.

It wasn't until dinner that he found Marcus again. They sat by themselves in a corner. Jaleel asked where he'd been all day.

"Cleaning staff quarters. Good gig if you can get it. No one watches you there. Which is funny, because loose change and cigarettes are all over the place. They want someone like me to steal, so they can beat the shit out of me again." Marcus laughed. "How dumb do the assholes think I am?"

"Can I talk to you about something?" Jaleel said earnestly. "You're not going to tell anyone—"

"Let me guess. You don't like it here. You want to escape." Marcus smiled, as if knowing every thought rattling in Jaleel's head. "New kids are all the same."

"I'm not like everyone else."

Marcus looked him up and down, like someone scrutinizing a suit to buy, or one of the customized cars in his *Popular Mechanics* magazine. "I can see that."

They waited until after dinner to talk alone in the dorm, while almost everyone watched television or went back to the gym or shouted out to the girls. When Jaleel said he'd been fingerprinted and had his photo taken, Marcus only nodded. He said he'd guessed as much when he saw the detective and the other cop in the morning.

"Man, they fuckin' with you," he warned.

"What do you mean?"

"You know what I mean. I've escaped from this place three times, and three times they drag my ass back, but they can't do anything too serious with me. Robbing gas stations and boosting cars, shit, that's why half of us are here. They gonna stick you with a murder charge. Just waiting for the right moment to arrest your ass."

"I'm going to see an attorney," Jaleel vowed.

"You got a better chance growing wings and flying to the moon."

"It's the law."

"Suppose it is, most everywhere else. You're in Peartree. An attorney for a punk-ass kid?"

"Then I have to get out of here," Jaleel said, as if the conclusion was foregone. The dorm began to fill with bodies. He lowered his voice. "Why don't you come with me?"

"Why would I do that? In eleven months, I'm eighteen years old. Unless they want to put me in a real prison, the state can't keep me. I'm emancipated!" He laughed, like someone who'd finally outsmarted the system, if only by default.

"Then what? How are you going to make a living?" Jaleel pressed. "You have a high school degree?"

"I'll make a living just fine. In America, more folks get by on a smile and bullshit than they do brains."

Jaleel tried to think quickly. "Okay, I understand. Just show me the way out of here."

Marcus arched his brow. "You're not even thirteen. Which you gonna do, buy a bus ticket or steal a car? You even know how to drive? How much money do you have? Where exactly are you heading? Who's going to meet you?"

"I have a plan," Jaleel boasted, with the same certainty with which Marcus had proclaimed he had a future.

"Jesus, where have I heard that? Wait a day or two, think everything through."

"You just said they can charge me any time they want." He had

gone to the library dictionary and looked up "forensic." He wished
he had never touched his father's gun in the dresser drawer.

"I'm not going to wait," Jaleel said.

Marcus was staring at him, wagging his head. "You're a crazy nigger, nothing I can do about that."

"Will you help me?"

"You mean tonight, don't you?"

"Yes."

Marcus sighed. "I figured that. Get some sleep. We gotta wait till
eleven at least. That's the last dorm check."

"I won't be able to sleep," Jaleel protested.

"Suit yourself. But you'll need your energy. You'll be doing a lot
of running once you're out of here."

While Marcus closed his eyes, Jaleel pulled the newspaper from
under his mattress, stole a last glance at the headline, and marched
deliberately to a trash can. He never wanted to see the paper again.
He stayed in his clothes, pulling the sheet up to his chin to hide his
plans. It seemed forever before a man in a green uniform marched
down the dark aisle, sweeping a flashlight beam cursorily over the
bunks. Jaleel thought Marcus was asleep, but he sat up quickly when
the man had left and the door closed behind him. They listened to
the key turn in the lock.

Marcus pulled a screwdriver from under his mattress frame and led
Jaleel toward the bathroom. On his tiptoes, Marcus pried open a transom window across from the toilets. Then he boosted Jaleel's foot in
his cupped hands. Jaleel's fingers found traction on the window ledge.

"Thank you," he grunted, gazing back at Marcus.

"Keep your head. When you get out, there's a light above the gate,
so don't get too close. About thirty feet to the left of gate, that's where
you need to go. Here—"

He kept Jaleel's foot in his catcher's mitt of a hand as his free hand
reached into a pocket to retrieve his penlight. "A going-away present,"
Marcus said, handing it up. "Look for a small piece of red cloth tied
to the bottom of the fence. The chain-link is loose there."

"Who left the red cloth?"

"I told you, I saw the detective this morning. I knew what you'd
be asking me sooner or later. Live free or die, right?

"Just be sure you hide the cloth," Marcus added, "else they'll come after me. Nobody will miss you until the sun comes up. If I was you, I wouldn't stop until I was far away from Texas. Time's your enemy."

Jaleel began squirming through the narrow opening of the transom. He couldn't adjust his head to look back at Marcus. For a moment, he didn't think his shoulders would slide through. "Keep going, you got it," Marcus whispered. Jaleel kept wiggling his shoulders, right until a welcome breeze glided over them, then the rest of his torso. It was eight or nine feet to the grass. He torqued his half-freed body so that when he fell, he landed on his side, but nothing felt broken or bruised. He gazed back at the open window.

"You okay, Jaleel?" The disembodied voice comforted him.

"Yeah."

"Better get your ass moving."

"Thanks for everything."

"High school degree or not, don't count me out," Marcus had the last word, his voice jumping like a frog through the window. "Maybe our paths will cross again. Now go!"

Jaleel pushed himself to his feet, thinking how much Marcus's exhortation was like his father's. A solitary light on a tarnished pole shined on the gate. The darkness swallowed everything else. Jaleel turned on the penlight. The narrow beam of light found the red cloth tied to the fence, just as Marcus had promised.

~6~

His hand pushed up the loose chain-link, and he squirmed his shoulders under, then gripped tufts of grass to help pull his torso through. On the other side, the first thing he noticed was how much the night had cooled. He could have used a sweater. He untied the red cloth and shoved it in his pocket. There were no guards that he could see. In the distance was the flickering neon of a convenience store, next to a bar called the Owl's Nest, where his father had sometimes gone to drink. Sharp, angry voices suddenly collided in the thin air.

Jaleel slipped the penlight into his pocket and began running. He knew the town blindfolded. He steered away from the fight he thought he was hearing near the bar, and dashed through a couple of empty fields, down narrow alleys, and along side streets. Even where the bulbs were working, illumination from the street lamps was absorbed by the thick blackness. He felt invisible again.

When he reached his house, it seemed bigger than life, as if it had sprung out of the darkness like a mushroom pushing up through the autumn soil. For a moment he waited for his lungs to calm. Down the street, a dog bayed, stopped, and yelped again about whatever was on its mind. A few cars were scattered along the street. His dad's Chevy was in the driveway, its rear to the garage. Jaleel had never driven a car, but he'd watched his father on shopping trips—how hard could it be to push your foot on a pedal and steer? The transmission was an automatic.

His navy blue house was ribboned with wide yellow tape that flapped in a sudden breeze. He ignored the Do Not Enter warnings on the tape and scrambled up the porch steps. Summer evenings when he was much younger, his parents had lounged on a swing suspended from the joists. They had held hands while listening to music on a plastic-cased radio. Later, as his dad grew more withdrawn, Clarence became a sailor at sea, standing on the porch as if it were the prow of a ship, his chin jutting toward a dull, shapeless horizon. Jaleel remembered his mom trading gossip with the neighbors, and serving lemonade and vanilla wafers to his Little League team. Last summer, he'd made his own lemonade stand, picked lemons from a vacant lot, and pocketed $195 before fall arrived.

The front door was locked. The yellow tape kept flapping as he hurried to the door at the side of the garage. Inside, he seized a tattered moving blanket and wrapped it around his hand. The glass pane on the back door of the house broke inward, its shards falling dully on the linoleum like a handful of coins. Jaleel reached through the hole and turned the knob.

The darkness inside felt cold and dense. He turned on Marcus's pen light and went into the kitchen. The bodies were gone, but patches of dried blood, looking more black than red, were still there.

In his closet, the glass jar with his money was undisturbed. He stuffed the wadded bills in his pocket, and filled his backpack with a toothbrush, toothpaste, towel, soap, hairbrush, and a couple of books. In his mother's bedside table was an envelope with what she called her rainy day money, another $379. He thought of getting his aunts' phone number, but there was no point calling now. He remembered Marcus's advice: Forget the past; think only about tomorrow.

The charcoal sketch was on his mom's bedside table, rolled up in a rubber band. As much as the money and his father's car, the drawing was what had pulled him back here. One day it would find a gold frame; he would hang it wherever he lived. He spied his father's Timex on the dresser, hesitated, and slipped it on his wrist. An extra Chevy key was in the top drawer. He threw a sweater and some other clothes into a duffle, and stuffed food from the pantry into his small backpack until he could barely zip it closed.

Everything was stowed in the backseat of the Chevy. He turned on the headlights and adjusted the seat; there was no problem seeing over the wheel. Clicking his seat belt closed, he flicked the ignition key. The engine made an ominous grinding noise and stopped. The second time it whined to life. His father had kept the car serviced regularly, even when they couldn't really afford it. With a foot on the brake, he moved the gearshift from "P" to "D." The car barely budged, even as he removed his foot. When it slid over to the accelerator, two tons of steel bolted like a horse. The car jumped off the curb, barely missing a parked pickup but hitting the neighbor's garbage cans before Jaleel could brake. The Chevy stopped as a pair of the cans clanged down the street. He saw the neighbor's upstairs light switch on.

He steadied his nerves, and turned down the street. Crawling along side streets, he was careful to obey every stop sign and red light until he reached the outskirts of Peartree. On the interstate, he increased his speed to fifty, staying in the left lane. There were few cars; as they passed him on the right, some flashed their high beams in irritation. He moved to the next lane and turned on the radio, taking an exaggerated breath. No one was going to stop him. It simply couldn't happen. God wouldn't allow it.

Still, he worried. He didn't know how to change a flat. His father had never taught him much about anything, not even how to tie a tie or shave, let alone the parts of a car engine. The gas needle registered half full. Could he find an open station in the middle of the night?

He began to wonder if running away was the smartest thing. Detective Patterson might have forensic evidence, but he couldn't have any real proof that Jaleel had killed his father. If he had stayed at the shelter, maybe he would have ended up in a decent foster home, despite Marcus's warning. If the police caught him now, Patterson would say that Jaleel had run because he was guilty. What Texas jury would believe the story of a twelve-year-old black kid?

Come on, focus, he thought as he studied a map from the glove box. His plan was to travel northwest, cross into New Mexico, and ditch the Chevy. He would take a bus to Arizona or California. A big city like Phoenix or Los Angles was the place to lay low.

He would find a place to live, get a job, and go to school. He just hadn't figured out the details yet. Maybe he'd have to lie about his age to get work. How expensive were apartments? He had never been completely on his own. He hoped that inside him was a gyroscope, the kind he had read about, with an interior spinning wheel to keep him steady.

~7~

The Chevy reached Las Cruces a little before sunrise after a five-hour drive interrupted only to buy gas. Jaleel's earlier anxiety had been replaced by adrenaline, and then, somehow, serenity. He had stuck to the speed limit, slowly distancing himself from Peartree, and the night had been his friend. He hadn't seen a single cop. A mile off the interstate, he parked behind a Muffin House diner. The special—scrambled eggs, bacon, hash browns, and toast—cost him $3.75. He'd never had coffee but it was included. He added sugar and milk as his father always did. Eating at a restaurant had been a rare event for his family, but Jaleel knew to leave a 10 percent tip.

He walked to the Chevy feeling sated. It struck him as a miracle that he was in another state. Until now, the farthest he'd been from home was Houston to attend a church conference with his mother. The lights of Las Cruces as he had approached on the highway made the city seem smaller, but so much larger than Peartree. He could imagine endless places to hide here. In the diner, though, he'd seen a middle-aged man who looked as if he spent half his life in a tanning bed. The resemblance to Detective Patterson bothered him. He'd asked the waitress about the Greyhound bus station.

"Three blocks straight ahead," she replied, pointing to the boulevard outside. "Take a right, go two more blocks, and you're there, hon. Easy as pie."

From the Chevy, Jaleel grabbed his duffle, backpack, and the charcoal drawing carefully rolled in a pink rubber band. He had thought

about wiping his fingerprints from the car, but it was registered in his
father's name, so the police would figure it out. At the last moment,
he left the key in the ignition. Someone might steal the thing and
give him a little breathing room. Time was his enemy. Don't stop
until you get to the moon, he thought.

He learned at the ticket counter that two buses had just arrived,
one heading north to Albuquerque, then west on I-40 to Flagstaff,
Arizona, and ultimately Los Angeles. The second was on the southerly
route to Tucson and San Diego. He had six minutes to decide, and
tossed a mental coin in the air.

"Where are you heading, young man?" The ticket clerk had brown-
ish hair flowing down his neck and granny glasses, a ringer for John
Lennon. Jaleel expected he would speak with a British accent, but his
monotone was like a long, flat road.

"I'll be going to Los Angeles," Jaleel replied. "My grandmother
lives there."

"All right, would you be going near Union Station?"

"Yes, sir," he said, wherever that was.

"How old are you?"

"Thirteen." He thought that might be the minimum age for traveling alone without a permission slip from your parent.

"For argument's sake, let's say you're twelve. That cuts your fare
in about half," the clerk said. "Don't tell my manager," he added in
a low voice. "Ninety eight dollars and ninety-nine cents, please." Jaleel
gazed out the waiting room window to the two busses. Both had
restarted their engines.

As he prepared a receipt, the clerk asked for a name.

"Barry Birmingham, sir." He had made up the name in the car.
He knew that at some point, he would need new identification, and
in the middle of the night, coasting along the interstate, safe and invisible, Barry Birmingham had a special ring. It could have been a
baseball player's name. Number 42 for the Red Sox, batting cleanup.
The bat locked behind his ear, he waited patiently for the pitch. Inside
curve ball. He swung. Whoosh!

Jaleel dug out five twenties. The clerk handed back a ticket, the receipt, and a one-dollar bill plus a penny in change.

"Get on No. 6," he said. "Ever been on a Greyhound?"

"No, sir."

"Every three or four hours, you get to stop—buy some grub, a magazine, or just stretch your legs. It's about twenty-four hours to L.A. with the stops. You meet some unusual people on a bus, some you don't see anywhere else," he added, as if this might or might not have interest to Jaleel. "Have fun."

Jaleel carried his things to No. 6. The driver looked like Albert Einstein—bushy gray eyebrows and wild, kinky hair—which Jaleel thought was funny, as if the famous physicist had been reincarnated as a bus driver.

"Los Angeles, correct?" he asked, checking Jaleel's ticket.

"Yes, sir, Los Angeles." He suddenly felt mature and independent as the door swooshed closed behind him. The bus was half full. He found a window seat at the rear and stowed his things in the overhead rack. Walking down the aisle, he had tried not to draw attention to himself. At the same time, his eyes had been placing individual faces in his memory, like stamps on an envelope. A young couple holding hands, an old black man with a battered travel bag on his lap, two nuns in their long gowns, and Mexican laborers, the kind he saw all the time in Peartree. There were two Indians with bolo ties and turquoise bracelets. He wondered if everybody had someone to meet them, wherever they were getting off.

The bus lurched from the station with the sound of air escaping from its brakes. In the oversized mirror on the driver's visor, he watched Einstein rotate the steering wheel 180 degrees as the bus slid into the traffic. The gears shifted nimbly, and the whale gained speed. The engine thrummed beneath his feet.

Jaleel looked out the window for police cars. By now, he'd surely been reported missing. Detective Patterson would find the broken window pane at his house, and the Chevy gone—more evidence of Jaleel's outsmarting him. He wouldn't be happy.

The police wouldn't have a clue where he'd gone until they found the car. Maybe that would take a few days. Maybe they would forget about him and not even mount a search. Patterson might be too busy with other cases. No matter what, the boy from Peartree knew, he was never going to be Jaleel Robeson again. He was Barry Birmingham, age 13, born in Baton Rouge, Louisiana. Years ago, his parents had divorced, and now he lived with an aunt, Mabel Birmingham, a hair-dresser, in downtown Los Angeles. He attended private school, played baseball, and had lots of friends. His imagination kept budding with new details that flowered into the excitement of a fresh start. He was finally going to see the world!

Jaleel's eyes closed from fatigue. Hours later, when a glaring sun pried them open, he swore he had seen the same vista in a magazine: parched, brown land, scrub and piñon trees, arroyos dug into the earth, and buttes all around with near-vertical sides. He wondered what colors he would use if he had to paint this landscape. Everything seemed harsh and drab, even hostile. But there was something beautiful about the vista too.

The first stop was a town called Truth or Consequences. The Mc-Donald's near the I-25 exit had a sign reading, "Millions and Millions of Hamburgers Sold." Jaleel was the last one off the bus. He bought a large coffee with cream and sugar, enjoying the taste, and stayed clear of the other travelers until Einstein honked his horn ten minutes later.

Jaleel reclaimed his seat in the rear. From conversations he overheard, he knew some people were heading to Albuquerque, others to Arizona and Los Angeles. He was glad to be left alone. He felt his body levitating, as if the trauma of the last few days belonged to someone else, and he was suddenly perched on another planet, where he could see everyone below but no one could see him.

~8~

The bus was about to leave—Einstein had just closed the doors—when someone rushed up and rapped on the glass. As he boarded, the latecomer looked out of place in his navy blue suit and red tie. He was six-foot-four at least, and had a funny-looking plaid hat, topped with a pom-pom, angled toward his forehead. One large hand held a small leather suitcase, the other a rectangular briefcase. The man was tall and blond with sharp-edged features; his pinkish skin glowed with good health. Maybe an actor or model, Jaleel guessed, but why would someone like that be traveling on a bus? The man was in his mid- to late thirties, looking fit, someone very focused. Jaleel suddenly realized the bus was full. The man was marching down the aisle, toward the only open seat.

"Excuse me, sir," the stranger said politely, with a slight accent, "do you mind if I join you? I'm tall so I'm okay with aisle seats. Hard to stretch your legs on a bus, but I do my best. I remember when I was your age and height—there are conveniences to not being too tall." He sighed, as if resigned to his fate. After stowing his briefcase and suitcase in the overhead rack, he eased back in his seat and folded his hands over his lap.

"Traveling alone, are you?" he said as the driver wheeled the bus onto the interstate. "I'm not being nosey, am I? You look like someone who's shy. I've known a lot of shy people. I've worked with them, in fact. Some never want to talk if possible—they're afraid of the world—but others are eager to open up, if they only knew what to say. I grew up in

Holland, and no one in my family talked much. They were unhappy, fearful people. A pity, huh?" He directed the last comment to himself.

Jaleel was as disinclined to converse with a stranger as the new passenger seemed inclined to talk his head off. Jaleel thought of his dad's habitual quiet—what kind of fear had bottled him up? Fear and anger were two sides of the same coin, his mother had insisted. Jaleel had never been talkative either, but usually he was neither angry nor fearful. He was simply fixed on his own feelings and ideas, which leaped through his head at fast speeds and unexpected moments, making him happy with each new insight. Examining himself and his ideas took energy away from being social. He didn't see anything wrong with preferring his own company, though he wouldn't have minded a few close friends. It had been hit-or-miss in seventh grade, more of an outsider on balance, despite being a success in Little League.

His eyes darted back to the stranger, who was brushing a lint ball from his jacket, and humming a song. Jaleel thought that to continue being quiet might make it seem as if he was hiding something.

"I'm going home, to Los Angeles," he spoke up. The man stopped humming and looked at him. "I live with my aunt. We have a German shepherd named Scoundrel." Running out of things to say, he reached over and shook the man's hand. "My name is Barry Birmingham."

"Barry Birmingham! Well, then, C.M. Appleton," he responded. From his inside jacket pocket, he extracted his wallet, and then a cream-colored business card with an elegant, chocolate typeface. He presented it to Jaleel with a flick of the wrist, like someone opening a handkerchief.

Cornelius Mitchell Appleton

PO Box 13285, Grand Central Station, NYC
(212) 980-3488

Degree from Harvard Law School

Spiritually Awakened By Circumstances

Jaleel bracketed the card between his thumbs and forefingers, reading it twice.

"You might say that I'm a spiritual consultant," the man said when Jaleel looked up. "I help people find themselves at their deepest level, if that makes sense to you. Believe me, as you get older, it does. This is a task which can vary greatly from one individual to another."

Jaleel nodded as if he understood, but he had no idea what the man was talking about. Was he some kind of crackpot? How could "spiritual consultant" be a line of work? Was Mr. Appleton paid for this? Yet he had gone to Harvard Law School—that was impressive. Jaleel hadn't seen many business cards in Peartree, certainly none as fancy as this. Not to be rude, he tucked it carefully in his shirt pocket, like something important to be saved.

The man looked sympathetically at Jaleel. "Cornelius Appleton is a mouthful. Please call me Dirick. That was my Christian name in Holland. You know, I came to America with my parents when I was around your age. Your country so confused me at first, but I wanted to fit in. When I was sixteen, I saw the name Cornelius Mitchell Appleton in a newspaper column. It sounded so American. With my father's permission, I went to court to legally change my name."

Jaleel nodded again. The bus station ticket clerk had warned him about people he'd meet on a bus. He was determined to keep to himself, but Dirick was so unusual Jaleel couldn't keep his mouth shut. "Where did you buy your hat? I've never seen one like that."

"Do you like it? It's called a tam o'shanter. A Scottish bonnet named after Tam o'Shanter, the hero of a poem by Robert Burns."

Jaleel hadn't heard of Robert Burns, and he wondered what Scotland had to do with Holland. "Why don't you wear a Dutch hat?"

"The Dutch are boring. They don't dress with any flair," the man said, laughing.

"Where are you heading?"

"I have someone waiting for me in Kingman, Arizona. An apostle."

"What?"

"Oh, I can explain it to you later if you like. Long story."

"You always travel by yourself?"

Dirick's lips pursed, as if accuracy was important to him. "Most of the time. I have a girlfriend in New York. We go to Europe once a year. We like museums and good theater wherever we are. But mostly, I stay busy on the road . . . meeting people."

Jaleel had read about New York—the most populous city in the United States—with its five boroughs, subways, a theater district called Broadway, and taxicabs galore. He wanted to visit there one day. If he ended up at Harvard, he knew it wasn't far from Cambridge to Manhattan. "Is that where your parents live too?"

"My parents are deceased. A commercial plane crash outside of Chicago, thirteen years ago."

"I'm sorry," Jaleel said, even if the event sounded far way in Dirick's voice.

It was impossible not to think of his own parents. Unable to stop it, he felt his sadness begin spreading to other memories of loss. A close friend in grade school who had moved away from Peartree, a teacher who had collapsed and died of a heart attack, even a baseball game where he'd stupidly struck out with the tying run on third, swinging at a bad pitch.

"How about you, Barry? Where are you from?"

"Baton Rouge, Louisiana. That's where I boarded the bus. I was visiting my grandmother on my mother's side."

"I see. That's a long round trip from Los Angeles."

"I do it every summer."

"What school do you attend? Shouldn't you already be in classes? It's late September."

"I go to a private boy's school."

"I see. And what does your aunt do?"

Jaleel suddenly wished he had never started the conversation. Now he had to keep lying. He was already forgetting things he'd just said. "She's a hairdresser. She owns her own beauty salon."

"A private school. That's wonderful. I bet you're a good student. I can see your pride in learning, just by looking in your eyes. Are you an artist too? That's a drawing you have overhead, in the rubber band? Is it your work?"

"Yes," Jaleel said to both questions, surprised by Dirick's instincts. He was tempted to elaborate, but he'd already said too much.

"I'm familiar with Los Angeles. I have clients there too. Which part does your aunt live in?"

"Downtown."

"What's that like?"

"It's pretty nice. Houses with lots of grass and trees," Jaleel said. "My aunt's been living there for twenty years. I cut her grass for her."

"Is that so?"

He heard the skepticism in Dirick's voice. Yet it was different from Detective Patterson's. When he had told the truth about his parents, the detective wanted to believe that Jaleel was covering something up. When he gave Dirick a string of lies, the stranger seemed to understand there was an honest reason behind them. He wasn't about to call Jaleel out. Jaleel wanted to take his whole stupid story back, but what would he replace it with?

"Do you always take the bus when you visit people?" Jaleel filled the silence.

"Despite the lack of comfort and convenience, yes. I prefer it to trains or planes, or driving a car. I don't even own a car. I have a driver's license—but what's the need in New York? Buses are where I actually meet my clients. We become friends, and then I come to visit them. Never underestimate the bond that can grow between total strangers. Of course, none of us are really strangers. That's the whole irony, isn't it? We all have more in common than we like to think. It's a lack of trust that keeps us separated."

Jaleel wondered what he had in common with Cornelius Mitchell Appleton. Detective Patterson had also come on to Jaleel at the shelter as if they should be buddies. It didn't sound as phony coming from Dirick. Still, why should he trust any stranger?

In Albuquerque, a number of passengers departed and replacements came aboard, looking equally lost in their thoughts. Jaleel retrieved *Catcher in the Rye* from his backpack—a copy borrowed from a teacher—and a small bag of potato chips. He watched as Dirick opened his briefcase. Inside Jaleel saw the titles of intriguing books—about Buddhism and Japanese culture, twentieth-century Russian history, utopian communes in America. There was also a stack of pamphlets. He read the title: *The Zeitgeist Experiment: The Case for Economic Justice in America.* Cornelius Mitchell Appleton was the author. Dirick snapped the briefcase shut and returned it to the rack above their heads. Jaleel settled back with his book, wondering what zeitgeist meant.

As Dirick read, his features would bunch in concentration, at moments looking ferocious. His large hands held the book directly in front of his face. They turned pages quickly. His hands and neck didn't seem to tire from their rigid position. The first book—the one on Buddhism—was finished by the time the bus pulled into Gallup. Dirick took another from his briefcase. Jaleel thought he didn't dare disturb him. For the next three hundred fifty miles, only snippets of conversation passed between them. Mostly, Jaleel read, dozed, and woke to thoughts about his mother and father. Several times he stopped himself from crying.

~9~

The bus arrived at the Kingman Greyhound station at 6:45 p.m., eight minutes behind schedule. The driver killed the engine and opened the door, letting in the baked Arizona air. The sun was in retreat, just a smear of gold on the horizon. A silhouette of a greyhound dog—leaping through the air—was frozen over the building entrance. A hundred feet away stood a Jack in the Box restaurant. Cars moved through a drive-in lane in fits and starts, their radios blaring. Jaleel craved a hamburger and fries in the worst way, but he wanted to say goodbye to Dirick before he fed himself. The man from Holland was fussing with the contents of his briefcase in the overhead rack, reorganizing everything, too busy to be interrupted. Jaleel ambled down the aisle. He would say goodbye to Dirick outside.

He didn't spot the two men in state police uniforms until he was near the front. A shiny black car with a bar of lights across the top was parked partially out of view. The men stood on each side of the departing queue. The older cop had a paunch, a downcast mouth, and olive skin. His hands were tucked into his belt as he looked everyone over. The younger officer rocked nonchalantly on his heels.

Jaleel's stomach shrank into a ball. He shuffled forward, shielded for the moment by the five or six passengers ahead of him. He couldn't turn back and hide. They would search every row of the bus. His legs kept carrying him forward, like a swimmer caught in a current. Instinct told him to keep his eyes straight ahead as he approached the final step. The drop to the pavement felt like he was falling down an elevator shaft.

"Jaleel Robeson?" said the younger officer, laying a hand on his shoulder. It was a question from someone who already knew the answer.

The two cops seemed like giants. Neither was as tall as Dirick, but they were broad in the shoulders and chest, with necks that looked as long as a horse's. Their faces showed relief at having found the person they were looking for. When Jaleel didn't respond, the younger cop pulled him aside. Passengers gawked at the spectacle of someone who might be in trouble.

"My name's Barry Birmingham," Jaleel said.

"Birmingham, huh? Where are you from?"

"Baton Rouge, Louisiana."

"You ever lived in Texas?"

"No, sir." He was amazed that he was so calm.

"Peartree, Texas?"

"No, sir. Where's that?"

"Got some identification on you?"

It was possible that Detective Patterson, eager to contact as many police departments as possible, hadn't found time to transmit the photo taken at the youth shelter. A verbal description alone was questionable. He looked like a lot of twelve-year-old black kids. Jaleel pulled out his wallet. He had already stripped it of his library card and junior high ID, and the bus receipt from Las Cruces. There were a couple of twenty-dollars bills inside, with the rest of his money hidden in his shoe. He kept fanning through the wallet, pretending something was there if he just looked hard enough. He finally glanced up at the officers, shrugging in disappointment.

"Where's your bus receipt?" the cop with the big stomach asked.

"What?"

"Where did you board the bus, son?"

His shoulders twitched. "I told you. Baton Rouge."

The two cops nodded to one another, and the heavy one plodded toward the patrol car.

"Jaleel, we have an arrest warrant for you from Peartree, Texas," the other said. "My partner has to confirm some details. It will just be a minute." His reached for the pair of shiny handcuffs dangling from his belt.

Jaleel felt pummeled by the evening heat, as if embers were falling from the sky. "Those handcuffs can't be for me," he wanted to say, but the words got stuck in his throat.

He flinched when a hand dropped on his shoulder from behind.

"Officer, is there a problem?"

He knew the voice. He wondered how long Dirick had been listening. The Dutchman's neck craned over Jaleel's right shoulder, peering into the boy's eyes with disappointment. The tam o'shanter looked as if it might fall if his head angled any lower.

"What seems to be the problem, Barry? What did you do?"

"I didn't do anything. I was going to get a hamburger, like you told me to. These men think I'm someone named Jaleel Robeson."

"And who, pray tell, is Jaleel Robeson?" Dirick asked the cop. "I'm afraid this is a case of mistaken identity, officer. I am C.M. Appleton, and this young man is Barry Birmingham. He's in my charge. We're going to get a bite of food. Then we're going to get back on the bus. Then we're going to the wonderful town of Needles, California," he said with a laugh.

The confidence in his voice sounded to Jaleel like a golden-throated bird singing from heaven.

"We have a warrant for this boy's arrest. You have to back away, sir." The officer looked annoyed by the confrontation he hadn't expected. He kept holding the handcuffs.

"You mean you have a warrant for Mr. Robeson," Dirick corrected him. He put his briefcase and suitcase on the ground, as though willing to wait all night to clear this up. "What did Mr. Robeson do? Perhaps you can explain it all to me."

"Sir, I am asking you not to interfere. Unless you want to be arrested too." His voice was the opposite of confident. Not timid or doubtful but percolating with anger.

"What did Mr. Robeson allegedly do?" Dirick persisted, unfazed. "It is alleged, is it not?"

"It's none of your business, sir, but he murdered his father."

"Good god!" Dirick exclaimed. "That's almost too horrific to imagine. A child killing his own father! That would be patricide. Of-

ficer, you bring to mind some plays of Sophocles and Euripides. The
Greeks understood human nature at its most vile, wouldn't you say?
But this has nothing to do with us, I assure you. I've been accompa-
nying Barry since Baton Rouge. As I said, he's under my supervision.
I'm ultimately delivering him to his aunt in Los Angeles."

The reference to patricide and the Greeks confused the officer. To
Jaleel, he looked weary of the debate about who was who, or perhaps
he worried that he might explode and make the situation worse.

"Wait right here," he said tersely, looking at both Dirick and Jaleel.

The handcuffs still in his hand, the officer went back to the patrol
car. His partner was behind the steering wheel, half hunched over the
dashboard, talking into a handset.

"Take this, son," Dirick said, and like a baton, he passed on Jaleel's
charcoal drawing. "You need to leave everything else on the bus and
get out of here. You really are Jaleel Robeson, I'm assuming."

"I didn't murder my father," Jaleel said, his eyes flashing from the
patrol car back to Dirick. "I can tell you the whole story."

"You were a terrible liar on the bus. But I was sure there was a good
reason for it. I'd like to hear your story. Only right now—"

Dirick gazed around, as if formulating an escape plan. Jaleel had
no idea what to do. He held the charcoal drawing next to his chest,
like a talisman, something that was tied to his freedom, and that he
must never let go of. Dirick handed him another business card from
his wallet, with a phone number he quickly scribbled on the back.

"Walk into Jack in the Box, and then slip out the side door," he
said. "You'll find a pay phone several blocks east, next to a movie theater. Do you have a quarter for the phone? Tell the man who answers
that you are a friend of mine, and you're in trouble with the law. His
name is Randy. He'll pick you up in his truck and take you to his
apartment. You'll be safe. I'll meet you there."

Jaleel felt a couple of quarters in his front pocket, but he couldn't
make himself move. Wouldn't the police see him slip into the restaurant? To escape now would take the same luck he'd had leaving the
shelter. How long could anyone count on being lucky? Maybe he was
digging himself into a deeper hole. If he gave up here, it might not
be too late to claim he had been running from fear and grief.

"Jaleel, go!" Dirick ordered.

He studied the confident face of the man he had known for less than twenty-four hours. He was white, from another country, had a crazy business card, and wore an even weirder hat. Just because he'd spoken with conviction about the bond between strangers—

"Now!" Dirick's voice jumped a couple of octaves.

Jaleel walked quickly toward the restaurant, afraid to glance at the police car.

Dirick had sounded like Marcus, or his father, shouting at Jaleel to flee at a critical moment. The thought that he might consider Dirick his new father slipped into his head, only to fall back out. The idea was nonsense. He had no mother or father now. He was on his own. He could feel a thousand pair of eyes on him as he crossed the parking lot, yet when he finally gathered the nerve to look back, the two cops were in an animated discussion, oblivious to his escape. Dirick remained with his briefcase and suitcase on the pavement, as if ready to deal with the police when they came back.

Once inside the restaurant, he slithered quickly out the side door. His heart whirred in his throat as he kept moving. At the theater, he glanced at the marquee: "E.T. the Extra Terrestrial." He pulled out the business card, shut the phone booth's accordion door, and dialed the number Dirick had given him.

The permanent kink in the cord made him stand close to the black box. The phone rang several times.

"Hello?" The voice on the other end fought off a yawn.

"Hello, sir, my name is Jaleel. Mr. Appleton told me to call you. He said to tell you I'm in trouble. The police are looking for me, and you need to pick me up."

Jaleel's ragged breathing emptied into the receiver without a response. Maybe he'd dialed the wrong number.

Finally, the man said, "Where did you meet Mr. Appleton?"

"On the Greyhound bus."

"What does he look like?"

Jaleel included the tam o'shanter hat in his description. He wondered how many other tests he had to pass, but the man was apparently satisfied. When he laughed, Jaleel was stunned. How could he not realize that this was an emergency!

"I'm near the Rio Grande Theater," he said.

"All right. Good. There's a stationery store across the street—can you see it?—next to a narrow alley. Wait at the far end of the alley. You'll be hard for the police to see. Five minutes." The receiver clicked off. Jaleel had wanted to ask if the man had food in his house. It was a stupid thing to think about, considering the circumstances, but his hunger was ravaging him.

A battered pickup appeared a few minutes later. The driver cranked down his window.

"Well, hop in, Jaleel." It was the same voice he'd heard on the phone. The face was hard to distinguish in the darkness, but what Jaleel could make out startled him.

"Dirick is persuasive, but if he's trying to stall the police, he can't do it forever," the voice continued. "Come on. Get in."

Jaleel hurried over and settled cautiously into the passenger seat, strapping on his seat belt. The driver introduced himself as Randy Olson. Thinner than Jaleel, he wore jeans and a T-shirt with the word Nike across the chest. Randy had a welcoming smile, the kind first-time visitors got when they walked into a church. His features gave his face a pleasing symmetry—everything fit nicely, nothing out of place, except for the scabs and pustules scattered on his cheeks and forehead.

"Are you sick?" Jaleel wanted to ask, but he thought it might be rude.

"So, what kind of trouble are you in?" Randy asked.

Jaleel was quiet. He hadn't even confided his story to Dirick. "I can tell you later. When will Dirick meet us?"

"I suspect shortly. Are you hungry? I've got meatballs and spaghetti in the fridge."

Jaleel nodded. He could see the plate of spaghetti in front of him, even taste the sauce. Then he was back to staring at Randy's face. As they passed under a street lamp, the splotches looked like craters on the moon.

Randy had a toothpick in his mouth, swishing it from side to side. "I used to smoke," he said when he noticed Jaleel staring at his face. "Toothpicks and gum are my substitutes. You're too young, but believe me, when you get older, you might be tempted to light up. Peer pressure and all that shit. Resist," he advised.

Jaleel knew kids his age who already smoked. Even if he didn't want to be an athlete, he doubted he would even try it. Cigarettes stunk up your clothes, and there were studies from doctors that proved they caused lung cancer.

"You've lived here a long time?" Jaleel thought to ask.

"Born and raised in Tucson. I moved to Kingman after graduating from ASU a couple of years ago. Kingman's a hodgepodge to some people, lots of Navajos, trailer folks, and snowbirds. But a decent hospital if you get sick, which I am a lot." He added, as if it was one of the fringe benefits of living in Kingman, "People here leave you alone."

"I don't think I'll be staying too long. I need to get to L.A.," Jaleel replied. The pickup had drifted into a residential neighborhood where the tract houses looked a little like Peartree. He had begun to hate the idea of living in a small city. People might leave you alone, but they seemed to know your business anyway.

"Don't be in such a rush. If you're in trouble with the law, you should talk to Dirick. He's a pretty smart man. An important man," he added.

"What do you mean?"

"He does good things for people. I doubt I'd be alive today without him." They stopped at a red light, which lasted an eternity. "Did he talk up a storm on the bus? As much as you'd like to sometimes, you can never tell him to shut up. He doesn't listen." Randy laughed.

"What do you do for him? He called you an apostle."

"That's what he calls all of us who help spread his message. I don't know if that has as much meaning as simply calling me a friend. I see him as a friend."

The light turned green. Parted by the truck's headlights, the night had a purplish tint that reminded Jaleel of the early evening sky in Peartree.

"Did Dirick tell you about his parents?" Randy asked. "When they died in a plane crash, they left him and his sister a lot of money. But there was something weird about the circumstances—I'll let him tell you. Dirick likes dressing fashionably, but otherwise he lives as frugally as possible. I met his girlfriend once—she says it's a good thing she's in love with him, because otherwise, with all his traveling and crazy opinions, he'd be intolerable. But honestly, she's as eccentric as he is."

The conversation slipped away as the truck approached a six-story apartment building with an adjacent parking lot. Randy pushed a remote control on his visor. The electronic arm rose, the truck passed through, and the arm came down behind them. They went inside and took the elevator to the third floor. Randy had said he lived in a two-bedroom apartment, but when Jaleel entered, it looked as spacious as a house. Everything was new and shiny.

Randy warmed the leftover meatballs and spaghetti, and made garlic bread and a salad with diced tomatoes, green peppers, and cucumbers. Jaleel had second helpings of everything.

"Thank you," he said softly when he had finished. "Your salad was really good."

"Fresh, for sure. I try to eat healthy now. My kitchen beats the hell out of those fast food places on the bus route. I don't know how Dirick puts up with it all," he said with another laugh.

~10~

Jaleel's body screamed for sleep, but he refused to turn in. He worried that the police had arrested Dirick. Randy's phone hadn't rung—was that a good sign or bad? His eyes kept closing and opening as he settled in the living room, sometimes staring at an issue of *Time* with Ayatollah Khomeini on the cover. After reading a few paragraphs, he wondered what it was like living under a dictator. The United States was supposed to be a democracy, with guaranteed freedoms and rights. Jaleel guessed, from what little he knew about his bus companion, that Dirick didn't agree with that.

"Are you worried about Dirick?" he asked suddenly. Randy sat behind a desk with a large, silver stapler in his hand, assembling loose sheets of paper.

"He's too clever to have any real trouble with cops. Guessing he just got busy with something. Don't worry."

Jaleel walked over to examine Randy's work. Each page was single-spaced, a forest of words that Randy said Dirick called a manifesto. A pile of at least twenty of them—fifteen pages each—stood by Randy's elbow. Jaleel recognized the title page from the bus: *The Zeitgeist Experiment.* "What are you doing?"

"Dirick asks his friends to hand these out. He writes a new manifesto every month or two. It's the least I can do for him. Here—" he said cheerfully, bestowing a finished product on Jaleel. "Bedtime reading."

Randy insisted that Dirick wouldn't mind sleeping on the couch, so Jaleel drifted into the second bedroom with the manifesto. His room had its own bathroom. A hot shower pulled the ache out of his back. He was not too tired to at least start the zeitgeist pamphlet. Dirick wrote with passion about an America warped and twisted in its emphasis on money and power. But there was also optimism about the possibility for change and redemption. He was like an itinerant preacher in a Western that Jaleel had once seen.

*   *   *

Has to be a dream, Jaleel thought at first. Dirick's sweaty face loomed over his bed. He was dressed in a jogging suit. Light seeped through the curtained window behind them. Dirick reached down and nudged Jaleel's shoulder again.

"You awake?" Dirick asked. "Hungry, I hope?"

Jaleel kept squinting at the pink, sculpted face. For a moment he'd forgotten where he was. His sleep had been dead and dreamless.

"You made it," Jaleel finally said, relieved.

"The police were pissed off when I couldn't tell them how you vanished. I acted pissed at you too. It was all your fault, Jaleel!" He liked the way Dirick laughed, as if he didn't mind putting up with a runaway kid and unexpected inconveniences.

The smell of fried eggs and French toast wafted from the kitchen. When they all sat down to eat, Dirick and Randy wanted to hear Jaleel's story. He started at the beginning, with his mother's birthday present. When emotion choked his voice, he stopped until it passed. Dirick agreed that touching his father's gun in the dresser drawer was a mistake. By asking Jaleel how much time had passed between the killings and when he called 911, Patterson was probably thinking Jaleel had had time to hide some evidence. At least that's what the detective would tell the D.A. Dirick wasn't optimistic. There was no way for Jaleel to return to Texas without being arrested, and even if he was a juvenile, a long incarceration was a real possibility.

"Don't worry, what's done is done, Jaleel. None of this was your fault. We're sorry to hear about your tragedy. But let's discuss the future now.

"I visited some people last night, highly skilled, one and all. They're not criminals any more than you are, though the law would disagree.

They help illegal immigrants with visas, driver's licenses, social security cards. Do you know how many people come up from Central America and Mexico every year, illegally, hoping to escape corruption and poverty?"

Jaleel knew about Mexican workers in Peartree. They spoke Spanish, ate tortillas and beans, slept ten to twelve in one-bedroom apartments, and kept to themselves. He had never thought much about it, but he supposed they were mostly illegal.

"You're going to get a new name," Dirick said. "I had to make it up on the spot. The line for social security cards and birth certificates is as long as my arm. I need to take your picture this morning. Randy's got a camera."

"What's my new name?" he asked, curious.

"Edward Montgomery. Something neutral sounding. You were born in New York City, specifically Flatbush, Brooklyn, on December 1, 1968. You'll be fourteen in a few months—I aged you a little. It's a small thing but may help to throw the police off the scent. Your parents are Clyde and Elizabeth Montgomery. When they divorced, neither could afford to raise you alone. You didn't want to go to a foster home, so you ran away."

Dirick's piece of fiction was similar to the stories he'd heard at the shelter, and he suddenly wondered if most, like Marcus's tale, weren't absolutely true. "Edward Montgomery," he repeated. He was resigned to his new identity, but it felt weird, with so much change in so short a time. A few hours ago, he was Barry Birmingham.

"You have to think like a refugee now," Dirick advised. "First in terms of survival, counting only on yourself, getting by on your own resources. But you also have to behave a certain way in public. No matter what you really think of this country, you must act eternally grateful."

Randy's mouth lifted into a smile. "Here comes the soapbox," he warned.

"Wherever you end up," Dirick said, "you'll draw less attention to yourself not by hiding out but by being a part of the community. In school, besides being a good student, show that you're an optimist and a patriot. Be gung-ho. Americans love to see that in newcomers. It worked for me growing up in New York. Besides," he added, "there are good reasons for optimism."

Randy produced a Polaroid camera and took several close-ups of Jaleel. Dirick expected that the new documents, including a passport, would be ready in a few days.

"Why do I need a passport?"

"You never know when it can come in handy. Think of it as a safety net. When you're sixteen, get yourself a driver's license. You have to be bona fide. You have to fit in at all times. That starts with a paper trail."

Jaleel should leave Kingman as soon as the documents were in hand, Dirick said. No more buses, of course. Dirick knew someone who would drive Jaleel to San Diego. Another friend, he promised, would find him a menial job there and a small apartment, but just for a few months. In the long run, to be safe, Jaleel had to move on. Dirick would give him enough cash to jump-start a new life. Then he was on his own.

"If some major problem comes up, you have my card. I can't guarantee that I can help—I have a busy life—but I never forget my apostles."

"I'm your apostle?" Jaleel said, surprised.

"Yes, you are," Dirick answered, without explaining.

"Well, off to the hospital for a transfusion," Randy interrupted, as good-naturedly as someone departing for the supermarket. He promised to be back to fix everyone lunch.

When they were alone, Jaleel asked Dirick what was wrong with Randy.

"Doctors suspect there's a new virus in this country, started in Africa. Similar cases to Randy's are being reported to the CDC. Kaposi's sarcoma is one of the symptoms—those are the lesions on his face. Low blood platelet counts and weight loss too. There are some experimental drugs, but no one is quite sure how to treat the virus. Randy gets a blood transfusion every week. I'm afraid every time I see him that he's sicker than the time before."

"What's the CDC?"

"Centers for Disease Control. It's in Atlanta."

"Can I ask you a question? Why do you help people?"

"Wouldn't you do the same, if you were in my position?"

"I don't know," Jaleel answered honestly.

"I saw you reading *Catcher in the Rye*. Holden Caulfield's abiding hope was to save innocent children. I'd like to think you'll be an apostle for real change one day—it's in your soul to be that, Jaleel."

How did Dirick know what was in his soul? He sounded like Reverend Johnson. Jaleel didn't think he was capable of being an apostle for anything or anyone, not at the moment. But he remained in his chair, listening carefully.

"Once you make long-term plans," Dirick went on, "your life will take on a certain order. Just remember that your first duty is to survive. I would think most of the Earth's species do this with camouflage or concealment. You'll have to adapt to your new environment."

Dirick paused, as if searching for some final words, important ones that Jaleel could never allow himself to forget. "Fit in, but be prudent. Don't look for trouble. Don't take unnecessary chances. Turn your back on temptation. Do you understand?"

"Yes, sir."

"Any questions, Jaleel?"

He had more than a few. The one he came up with was hardly practical, but it seemed important.

"It says on your business card, 'spiritually awakened by circumstances.' What's that mean? What were the circumstances? Is that why you help people?"

"Indeed, it is," Dirick said, again without explaining, as if this was a mystery that Jaleel would solve on his own one day. Dirick disappeared to pack his suitcase.

After Randy returned, and they had lunch, Dirick announced that he had to be six places at once. He gave Randy and Jaleel each a hug. Randy seemed to accept the difficult schedule of a man he knew well. Jaleel coveted more time with Dirick, a man he didn't know at all but had already decided he trusted implicitly.

When he was left alone in the apartment, he gazed west out the window into a fiercely boiling sky.

Alex

~11~

If anyone had asked Marcel Proust how many hours he passed every day bathing in his memories, they wouldn't have been many more than I spend. In telling my story, here is the first thing I would say: I was born in 1971, but my life began much earlier, sometime in the '50s, when my parents were teen-agers, their attitudes and values formed for life, to be instilled in my brother and me like nails driven into green wood. Almost any historian will describe the '50s as the apotheosis of the American Century. With the nation fresh from victory in World War II, optimism and the economy spiraled to the sky, as inseparable as identical twins. Ike was President. Hula hoops were cool. Nat King Cole sang "Unforgettable" and "Mona Lisa." Huddled in their living rooms, my parents watched "The Adventures of Ozzie and Harriet," "The Twilight Zone," and "The $64,000 Question."

As I tell my students, the U.S. population in the '50s encompassed an upper middle class, a middle class, and a working class with modest aspirations. The very rich and very poor existed, but mostly on the periphery of consciousness, in newspapers, movies, and books. Harmony and serenity complemented our unfiltered optimism. There were no gangs with automatic weapons, no recreational drug epidemics, no hating your parents, no reason to imagine call centers in Bangalore. People thought: Why shouldn't the good times last forever?

Though they didn't know each other, both my grandfathers worked shifts for the Lockheed Aircraft Corporation in Burbank, California. Assembly lines at the mammoth factory sometimes ran night and day,

even after the war. Pay for semi-skilled labor was $3 an hour, $4.50 for
overtime. Their children—my parents—attended public schools. Summer camps and out-of-state vacations were unaffordable. At Christmas,
everyone got a couple of presents that didn't cost much. Members of
the working class seemed content if their diligent labor ultimately paid
off their mortgage, funded their retirement through Social Security, and
covered tuition for their children at a state college. If your finances went
awry, or you got sick, your family took care of you. If it wasn't from
love, it was duty that spoke. You were never abandoned.

Gloria Roslyn Adams is the name on my mother's birth certificate.
Her baby album, in addition to the requisite lock of hair and chron-
icles of first word, first step, first tooth, and favorite food, was filled
with testaments from relatives and friends. Everybody spewed like
geysers about her physical beauty, her even temperament, and her ef-
fervescent personality.

Mom's older sister by five years, Agnes, had a very different album.
She was plain-looking, had little personality ("such a quiet girl" people
wrote), and seemed to prefer her own company to having friends.
Had Agnes been the jealous type, she might have tried to suffocate
her little sister with a pillow, and no one would have been horribly
surprised. But it was the opposite. She was Mom's guardian and pro-
tector. Go figure.

I assume that my mother, lying in her bassinet, felt empowered by
the constant pairs of adoring eyes falling on her. It's in our DNA to
be drawn to beauty. The emotions stirred by it have inspired artists,
started wars, and left mountains of broken hearts in a tangled wake.
I've studied photographs of Mom in her high school and college year-
books, and plenty of casual snapshots with girlfriends and legions of
boys. As a teen-ager, she was tallish with tapered legs and pert boobs.
Add softly sculpted cheeks, a bow mouth, a perfectly proportioned
nose, and teeth so straight she never needed orthodontia (something
my grandparents couldn't have afforded anyway). Her eyes were
slightly far apart, an ocean blue in ambient light and a teal when
evening closed in. Even as an adult, her skin reminded me of a child's
pallor in a Renaissance painting.

She was a natural blonde—straight hair normally, curly at the
beach or after a rain. She said she hated when her hair got crinkly,

but that was disingenuous. My mother really didn't dislike anything about herself. Curls, when they happened, were something to twine her finger through as she listened to a boy (whose palpitating heart barely let his words out) sputter on about one subject or another. Mom was generally a curious person who valued learning from others. She was bright, if not always sure how and to what end her intelligence should be applied.

She could well have been a snob but was quite the opposite. Self-absorbed, to be sure, but she had a big heart and, if asked, helped any friend out of a jam. She even hung around people she didn't necessarily like, to make a positive impression on them. She couldn't tolerate being gossiped about. She hated that. She wanted to appear virtuous and beyond reproach.

She was elected tenth-grade vice president and eleventh-grade president. In her senior year, she was selected "student goodwill ambassador" to the office of the mayor of Los Angeles, a hazily defined honor that was still a big deal, according to her yearbook. A lot of honors came her way—trophies, plaques, laminated letters of commendation—all hung proudly in her room.

In her senior yearbook, under "dreams and ambitions," while other girls wrote "nurse," "school teacher," or "housewife," for my mother, it was "fashion model." *Vogue, Cosmopolitan,* and *Glamour* were stacked on her nightstand, next to her Bible, she told me. At UCLA, she registered as an English major, but after two years, she was lured to New York by someone's promise of fame at the Ford agency. Modeling proved to be an exciting but ultimately disappointing experiment. She had a couple of shoots but nothing jelled—there were so many other girls just as beautiful—and when she returned home, she had learned her lesson: Don't compete in anything unless you think you can win. Despite being tempted, she turned down several opportunities for screen tests at MGM. She also decided not to return to UCLA. She said something to me like, "after a while, those college classes seemed to add up to nothing, just another dead end."

In 1965, the year she turned twenty-two, she began taking classes at Cal State to earn her paralegal certificate. A year later, she was hired by an old-line Van Nuys law firm. It was a decent strategy for a very attractive woman looking for a husband. A weekend didn't pass when

Gloria Adams wasn't squired to an expensive restaurant, the Hollywood Bowl, or a weekend in Vegas. Strangely, she didn't end up with
a lawyer, not at first. She got engaged to a boyish pediatrician fresh
from his residency, and six months later, to an investment banker
named Sidney Calloway, a brute of a snob. She broke off both relationships for the same reason: My mother thought she was being
taken for granted.

She met my father in the fall of 1967. Louis Baten was three years
out of law school at USC, where he'd also been an undergraduate.
He had been spared the draft and the chaos of Vietnam because of
asthma, though one would never suspect a health issue from looking
at him. Mom later told me she had mentioned to friends that Louis
Baten reminded her of a panel of burnished mahogany. She was referring to his six-foot-three linebacker physique, athletic abilities,
tasteful clothes, and polished manners. If his authoritative voice didn't
catch your attention, there was the steep forehead and swept-back
black hair, prominent jaw, or penetrating smile. Charismatic was a
better description than classically handsome. His grandparents had
immigrated to New York from Hungary. They changed their surname
to Baten to honor a man who helped them after arrival on Ellis Is-
land—and never looked back.

My father's first professional job was with the Los Angeles Public
Defender's Office. One morning, meeting with an attorney at the
Van Nuys firm, he accepted coffee from a young, especially pretty
paralegal. Gloria Adams and Louis Baten quickly discovered the com-
monalities of their youth, from hanging out at Bob's Big Boy in Burbank to weekend trips to Zuma Beach in Malibu. Maybe, they figured
out loud, they had even run into one another somewhere without
knowing it. Eighteen months apart in age, they discovered they had
a friend or two in common. Phone numbers were exchanged. Just
like that, the stars began to line up.

After six months of dating, my mother had completed her list of
why my father would make a suitable husband, and began to feel the
blush of anticipation. Dad was judged by all to be ambitious, hard
working, knowledgeable, romantic, and, so critical to Mom, crazy
about her. He loved the way she dressed, her yellow Mustang con-
vertible, and the TV shows she gravitated to. He was also a church-

going man. He wasn't as handsome as many guys she'd dated, but it was a relief not to compete in the looks department. My father had so many strengths. Mom needed a couple of her own.

Of course, being a woman, she knew their future long before my father had a clue—when and where they would be married (the Methodist Church near where Mom had grown up), where they would live (some prestige community in Los Angeles), and how many children they would have (as many as needed to produce one of each sex). My mother's beauty was accompanied by a casual, go-with-the-flow attitude, but that was as disingenuous as her complaints about beach-frizzy hair. At her core was a deft and careful planner, sure of her instincts and of what she deserved from life. To marry a successful lawyer was the portal to a new world. I wonder if she gave much thought to being a parent, how even the best intentions can be upheaved, for different reasons, by two kids as challenging as Toby and I were.

In the early years of our family, before I turned eleven or twelve, I thought of her as the best of all mothers. She cried whenever I left for sleep-away camp. She attended every grade school play, even if I didn't have a line of dialog. When our Brownie or Girl Scout troop needed to raise money with a paper drive, Mom happily dragged me from neighbor to neighbor, seeing what we could scavenge.

Her beauty and social graces made her popular with almost everyone. I knew I would never have her looks or personality, but it didn't bother me because she made me feel that I was special. Whatever house we lived in, she filled my room with dolls, stuffed animals, books, and board games. When we shopped for clothes, I learned quickly what color combinations worked with my skin tone, and what accessories my mother considered stylish and tasteful. Mom made Dad and Toby feel special too, but I knew that I was a notch above. I was the first child, the only daughter, and from the beginning, I remember hearing Mom tell everyone how smart I was. Her soft-as-a-feather voice whispered in my ear the first thing in the morning, and was often the last sound I heard at night when she tucked me into bed. Her rhythm of contentment was our family's rhythm. In those early years, she made it easy to love and root for her.

~12~

When my parents were teen-agers, the San Fernando Valley wasn't yet an endless maze of stucco tract homes, apartment complexes, cedar-sided office buildings, and gallimaufry strip malls. On its way to becoming, yes, but between interlacing freeways and a score of small cities, Southern California still had ample pockets of agriculture, particularly fruit orchards and large swaths of land. Nature was a year-round event—purple mountains' majesty, a halcyon climate, and the beckoning Pacific that shimmered like tinfoil in the sun. When he designed and built his first theme park, in Anaheim in 1955, Walt Disney knew its success depended partly on climate. He called Southern California "God's Country." So did my father. He felt blessed to be there, even when the landscape began to lose its open spaces. When Toby, my younger brother, and I came along, he made us promise never to forget how lucky we were.

"Alexandra Roslyn Baten, you should cheer up," he declared just before we sat down for breakfast one morning.

I was six, and twisted my pouty mouth at him defiantly. We had just moved into a rambling, '50s split-level house on Whipple Street which was sorely in need of a general contractor. It was all my parents could afford at the time, because it wasn't only the house we were buying, Dad explained later—we also were investing in a very valuable neighborhood. On any map of the San Fernando Valley, Toluca Lake was an innocuous speck of unincorporated real estate, wedged between the much larger cities of North Hollywood and Burbank. Immodest in size but, like some medieval duchy, grand in its aspirations.

Toluca Lake had its own six-acre lake, built by developers in the '20s, a private golf club, and a semi-famous pharmacy—like Schwab's in Hollywood—where Red Foxx, Bob Hope, Jonathan Winters, and other celebrities bought their monthly stash of liquor and Cuban cigars, and for their wives or girlfriends, exotic chocolates and French perfumes. Former residents like Frank Sinatra and Amelia Earhart had their photos on the wall. To a child who didn't understand the cachet of celebrity, nothing seemed out of the ordinary. None of us made a fuss over Hollywood people or asked for their autographs.

Bob Hope's house was the only true mansion in Toluca Lake, occupying half a city block, yet the community's most prestigious homes were a mile away, ringing the lake. Abutting the eastern edge of the lake, Lakeside Golf Club had a par-72 course with not a single blade of grass out of place. The lush fairways were complemented by a clay-tiled roof, Spanish-style clubhouse; a pool that was almost Olympic-size; and a large parking lot (near the caddie shack) that was accessed by a short bridge spanning the jugular of the lake. A membership at Lakeside cost around $75,000. In those days, Dad had to get a loan. As with most private golf clubs in Los Angeles, only men could buy in, after a rigorous screening process. There were days when "the ladies" could play, and they had their own small tournaments, but club life centered on male friendships and business networking.

At the time there weren't many Catholics in Toluca Lake, fewer Jews, and I don't believe a single black person, except for Red Foxx and his family. Pride in country and community, belief in hard work, and a large net worth were the unspoken oath of entry. This happened to dovetail with white Anglo-Saxon Protestant values. Our community wasn't quite at the tony level of Bel-Air, or the more chic parts of Beverly Hills, but its winding, sloping streets were dotted with stately homes with emerald lawns and swimming pools of ice-blue water. Doctors, attorneys, bankers, businessmen, and television and movie people put down their stakes and rarely left Toluca Lake. We had a chamber of commerce but no mayor or city council, no schools, no fire, sanitation or police departments, and no pesky bureaucracies. Like loyal vassals, North Hollywood or Burbank served our municipal needs.

I couldn't fathom any of this at six years of age. All I knew was I was lonely. Moping through the kitchen that morning, I carried my stuffed rabbit, Spencer, by one of his long ears, twirling his body obsessively in a weird orbit. Dad came over and hoisted me onto his thick shoulders. He began whirling me around—as if I were Spencer—until I was giddy and laughing.

"We could all have ended up in Lower Slobbovia, Alex," he said when he finally put me down. "People would cut off their right arm to live where we do. So cheer up, sweetie," he repeated.

I nodded.

"And don't worry about making new friends. You'll find all you need. Just give yourself a little time."

In those days, my father was always right, just like my mother.

~13~

Six years later, when I turned twelve and Toby was nine, my parents moved into their dream home. The twelve-thousand-square-foot, two-story English Tudor sat over the eponymous Toluca Lake with a timeless, aristocratic bearing. The lawn rolled down imperiously to our private dock, complete with a twelve-foot rowboat (motorized craft were not allowed), which Toby and I used to fish for bluegill, or to jump in the water on muggy August afternoons. A pair of giant swans and no shortage of mallards paddled the waters. The lake's only drawback was the mosquitoes. Their larvae hatched in late spring, after seasonal rains, and the centuries-old cycle of new adults looking for animal blood repeated itself. Otherwise, nothing disturbed our tranquility and deep contentment. Dad had begun redefining "God's Country" as specific to Toluca Lake.

None of this upward mobility would have been possible had not my father, with a partner, taken the risk of starting his own criminal law practice. Friends advised him against it. Even my mother showed some reluctance. From the start, the office overhead in Beverly Hills was daunting, and gathering clients was a tedious process. My father, however, never questioned the move. His nature was to make up his mind, a process combining confidence with instinct, and never change it. He played golf the same way, picking a club out of the bag without overthinking, and then striking the ball dead center almost every time.

We had just purchased our Tudor when Mom wrote my father a love letter of sorts. I ultimately swiped it from his desk, hiding it in a

Moleskin journal that I had begun keeping only a few weeks earlier. Despite believing that God looked down on and protected us, something in me wanted hard evidence that we were a happy family.

> *"My dearest sweetheart, thank you, thank you,*
> *thank you! What a wonderful house you picked for all*
> *of us. It is so beautiful, Louis. I am never going to*
> *leave it. The world can freeze over. I don't care. This*
> *is where I was meant to be, and to raise our children.*
> *I want to be a perfect mother and wife.*
> *Love always, Gloria."*

My journal was not a typical diary. I wanted to write things about my family that I wouldn't necessarily share with anybody, along with ideas, crazy or not, that foraged through my head at increasingly frequent intervals. This seemed more exciting than blabbering about boys, hormonal girlfriends, and endless skeins of gossip. I wrote a lot about our new home, including how I found it difficult to accept that Toby and I were actually living here. Why did I deserve this luxury? Why did anyone? Who needed twelve thousand feet to live in? I don't know where my doubts came from—it was so opposite to my parents' temperaments—but sometimes, when a fever hits, nothing can break it.

Upstairs were five bedrooms, each with its own bath. The back two, without lake views, were for guests. Dad's study was just off the living room, a place to work in quiet, smoke an occasional cigar, and sip single-malt Scotch. The kitchen had been renovated by the previous owners and been featured in an architectural design magazine. A $10,000 crystal chandelier hovered over our dining room. The den was for television and Dad's poker games. But the most beautiful part of the house was the living room. Three parallel pairs of French doors opened onto a mammoth yard with a curved flagstone patio and rectangular swimming pool. The wrinkled, azure surface was like a David Hockney watercolor.

We hired a Beverly Hills decorator for the move-in. I watched trucks roll up to our house bearing richly upholstered sofas and chairs, Persian rugs, Asian antiques, and paintings bought from Los Angeles,

San Francisco, and New York galleries. It all seemed too much. The decorator, a bespectacled middle-age woman who liked to say, "Now this piece will be perfect right here," insisted on certain "elements" for my bedroom. I didn't care for them, but I didn't get a vote. I began to wish I was back in the Whipple Street house.

A home our size demanded that someone come in every weekday to clean, wash, iron, or shop, yet Mom insisted on doing certain tasks herself—cooking dinner was one. It was simply something a good wife and mother did. Toby and I took care of the dishes afterward, and on weekends, we had an hour or two of other chores. Mom explained that she didn't want us to be spoiled. I understood her thinking, but our whole family was already spoiled. Dad bought a new Cadillac DeVille for himself, and a new Mercedes for Mom, in alternating years. They vacationed in Canada, Mexico, or Europe. I was eventually enrolled, starting in seventh grade, at an exclusive, fifty-year-old coed institution called Valley Academy. Plaid, pleated skirts, and white blouses for girls, natty navy trousers with white shirts, blazers, and ties for boys. I hated wearing a uniform.

By the time I turned fifteen, I had acquired a restlessness and feistiness that questioned almost everything around me. At breakfast one morning, even though Toby and I were late for school, I wouldn't let my father hurry me off. I had watched a rerun of Perry Mason, my favorite television series, and wanted to describe the courtroom climax to Dad, to get his opinion.

"Alex, I don't mean to pop your balloon," he said when I finished telling him the plot, "but the show you love so much? It's basically bogus."

"What do you mean, bogus?" I challenged him. With breathless awe, I watched week after week as America's greatest criminal defense lawyer weaved his magic in the courtroom. I would gloat at the end of an episode when he exposed the bad guy that no one suspected, often sitting right there in the courtroom, and then his own client rightfully went free. The jury basked in Mason's brilliance just as I did.

"The premise of Perry Mason is flawed. A case is rarely solved in the courtroom, sweetie. You build your case before the trial, and then present it to the jury. Each side has a point of view, and tries to convince twelve strangers that it's the most probable scenario."

"And then the jury votes," I said righteously.

"Yes."

"Case solved!"

"Case settled, not solved. And not always even settled. There could be a hung jury, or with a conviction, an appeal if the defense believes the judge or the district attorney didn't follow legal procedures to a T. Even if a defendant pleads guilty, trying to get a reduced sentence, you're not one hundred percent sure who the bad guy is." He gave me a wink. "My apologies to Mr. Mason and his script writers."

I was stung by my father's words, but I couldn't argue. At Baten, Kleeb, and Donahue, Louis Baten was a celebrity in his own right. With the stamina to prepare for long and complex cases, and the wit to influence a jury, he had a remarkable string of successes. Along with Perry Mason, his dinnertime stories were my education in criminal defense law. Leaving the fate of the poor to the Public Defender's Office, BKD focused on those accused of extortion, racketeering, or insider trading on Wall Street, and sometimes high-profile homicides. The District Attorney's Office often claimed that criminal law attorneys were primordial ooze, crawling out from under a rock with their sleazy clients, Dad said, but it was those sleaze-balls who showered my father with gifts when they were acquitted. Who ever gave the district attorney a gift? he said half seriously. Dad's most impressive reward was a fourteenth-century Ottoman Empire bronze lion purchased by his client at a Sotheby's auction. It perched on his desk like a crown on a king.

I stopped eating my cereal. "But what about the truth?" I asked. "What if a guilty person goes free?"

"There's a standard—'beyond a reasonable doubt'—that juries have to apply before someone is convicted. But that's a far cry from the truth. The truth—something that is beyond all doubt—is harder to come by. Maybe impossible."

My father was the smartest man I knew, and maybe that's how juries worked, but I felt certain that the truth, absolute and indisputable, emerged at some point. It had to exist somewhere in the universe, if you looked hard enough, because life would be unbearable without some certainties. My father, however, lived comfortably in the shadows of the ambiguous.

I frowned. "Then I think the legal system stinks. What you're saying is, sometimes guilty people go free, and innocent people end up in prison."

"That's right."

"How many, in each group?"

"I have no idea. Statistically, about 13 million people are arrested every year in this country, mostly on drug charges or drunk driving. Maybe a couple of million end up in prison or jail. And a couple of million get released. The ebb and flow of the system. Mistakes are a fact of life. That's never going to change."

I slung my arms unhappily across my chest.

"Alex, it's important to say what you believe to be true. I'm just warning you that truth is often a matter of opinion. Laws and statutes can sometimes be interpreted in very different ways. Remember that. It will keep you out of unnecessary arguments."

"Okay, if you say so," I replied, not quite believing him.

I scampered away to grab my books, and joined Toby and Mom in the Mercedes.

"Have a great day. Work hard. Learn everything you can," said Mom, the cheerleader, when she dropped me at Valley Academy. She blew me a kiss and was gone.

After chauffeuring Toby and me to our different schools, Mom was occupied by her charity work, tennis league, golf lessons, or ladies' luncheons. Every day was befitting a prominent attorney's wife from Toluca Lake. She came back around three to take us to our after-school activities. I was in my last year in scouts. Toby labored at karate and baseball.

Toby's Little League coach approached Mom as we picked up my brother one afternoon. I listened as he gave her some bad news. At practice, not to mention in games, Toby was increasingly showing "anti-authoritarian tendencies and self-esteem issues."

"What do you mean, self-esteem issues?" Mom asked. She already knew about the anti-authoritarian stuff.

"When he gets to the plate, he strikes out deliberately."

"Striking out on purpose? I've never heard of such a thing."

"You've been to some games, Mrs. Baten, you had to have seen it—"

"Yes, but anybody can strike out."

"Not every time. Toby swings at balls that are halfway to China."
My mother was silent. "Maybe he finds baseball boring," she concluded.

"Maybe. Or he just doesn't like himself, or me, or the other players. I can't keep playing him, that's all I'm saying."

"You know, he's only twelve."

"Mrs. Baten, so are most of the other boys."

The next week, coincidence or not, Toby's sensei threw him out of the dojo for similar reasons. He didn't try. He didn't care. He was a demoralizing influence on others. Toby gathered his gi and personal belongings and stormed out, claiming he was being picked on. I understood his anger. The implication that he chose to fuck up, chose not to get along with people, that he criticized and whined and started arguments just because—that would have upset me too. But the truth was, he could be a lazy little shit, and he wouldn't be your first, or even second or third, pick as a friend.

Dad insisted Toby's struggles were a stage. He would outgrow his rough edges. My mother feared otherwise, or she feared her inability to save my brother, as she put it, "from going off the deep end."

For an upbeat perfectionist like Mom to be stuck with a dark-souled son was an unfathomable punishment. As a good and caring mother, she didn't deserve it, she told Dad. She was always reading how-to books on child-rearing, starting with Dr. Spock when we were infants. Her own method, if there was one, was to alternate between nurturing and handing down rules and guidelines. Don't drink more than one soda a day. Finish all the food on your plate. Don't ride your bikes out of Toluca Lake because some neighborhoods are dangerous. Call your grandparents on their birthdays. Do unto others. Turn the other cheek. Her edicts rolled in like steady waves, until you felt you were drowning.

On Sundays, at church, I would sense hundreds of eyes on us—a family to be admired for its togetherness, financial success, and faith. Mom and Dad took to heart every sermon and discussed it on the drive home. I got annoyed when the minister sometimes called me "Alexander" in the reception line. Mom told me it was an honest mistake and to let it go. "No problem," I said. "Next time we shake hands, I'll call him Harriet." Toby hated going to church, period. He carried a small writing pad in his jacket, and one Sunday, he began making sketches during the service. His favorite theme was Jesus being hung by a noose instead of on a cross, or Moses riding the Golden Calf through the parted waves of the Red Sea, and vanishing beneath them. Mom would confiscate the pad and plunge it into her handbag, making his blasphemy disappear.

Behind their bedroom door, I overheard my parents thrash out what punishment to hand down. Mom was much stricter than Dad. Toby suddenly had more weekend chores and less allowance. TV and phone privileges were suspended. Not that he had any real friends, but if he claimed to have them, he was told they couldn't come over. Toby absorbed the blows with tough-guy indifference. He thought his life was "Rebel Without a Cause," a movie he watched with the same devotion that I followed Perry Mason. Toby was just as handsome as James Dean. His angular face and large, china-blue eyes made you give him a second glance. He was the image of my mother.

Looks weren't enough to save him, however. The more frustrating my brother's behavior, the more hope Mom pinned on me. There came a point when Toby barely got mentioned in discussions with her friends. I knew that she still loved him, but she had a talent for compartmentalizing her emotions. I was suddenly the child who counted. I wasn't just a small jewel in a distant firmament but an incandescent star blazing across the heavens.

"Alexandra is going to be a doctor one day. Or maybe president of a corporation, or even a college," my mother started telling friends and neighbors. "Someone with her talent has many choices. I'm betting on doctor."

The biggest irony was not how her bragging focused attention less on me than on what a great mother she was, but that I decided, in pretty short order, I would go along with her wishes. I would become a doctor. I picked cardiologist out of a hat. I would be in a position to do some good for the world, I thought, imagining clinic work in Africa, or public health service at home.

When you're not a great beauty and don't have a personality like your mother, how do you possibly get noticed—except by being as different from her as possible?

~14~

Late summer, it suddenly dawned on my mother that my brother was about to start seventh grade and he wasn't prepared for a school like Valley Academy. The academic load and social pressure would overwhelm him without special support. She talked about getting Toby a tutor every day after school. Would that be enough? she asked more than once.

"Doubt it," I always answered.

"What makes you so sure?"

"Because I know Toby."

"We have to think of something."

"Sure. How about public school?"

"That's not what I meant, Alex."

My mother came up with her own idea. Toby would begin seeing a therapist, right away, to deal with his self-esteem issues. This would be done covertly. To my mother, seeking outside help reflected parental inadequacy. She called friends who she knew were in therapy, and told them she was "looking for a good therapist, preferably a psychiatrist, on behalf of an old college friend."

We settled on Dr. Sheffield, a severe-looking, frizzy redhead in her early sixties. She interviewed and tested Toby for a couple of hours. When she met with Mom a day later, her observations were more dire than those of the Little League coach. Mom told me everything. Dr. Sheffield believed this was not a simple self-esteem issue. She wasn't quite sure of a DSM category for my brother's condition: short attention span, unwillingness to make friends, tendency to be disruptive, needy of attention, and fear of conflict. Mom seemed freaked out the more she told me. When Dr. Sheffield suggested family therapy, she reluctantly agreed.

"There's nothing wrong with Toby," I said. "He's just different. What's wrong with being different? I don't see what family therapy is going to accomplish."

"Dr. Sheffield is an expert, Alex. We were lucky that she had a cancellation. She wants us all to meet the day after tomorrow. Your father can take off work early."

At the appointed hour, as Mom, Toby, and I waited in the reception area, Dad called to say he couldn't make it. A new client had just showed up at his office. The three of us Batens marched into Dr. Sheffield's sound-proof, somber-toned inner sanctum, where in the next hour I learned everything about my brother that I already knew. He sulked his way through the session, evading Dr. Sheffield's numerous invitations to speak his mind.

The following week, we had four more sessions, like this was life or death. Dad, busy at work, attended only one. I could read the irritation in Mom's eyes. He was too caught up in his own world, leaving her to bear this burden. Her legs were always tightly crossed in the sessions, as she nervously fingered the gold amulet around her neck.

After the last session, Dr. Sheffield walked us down the hall. Toby had escaped to the car. "What we're seeing here reinforces the results of the tests I gave him: Toby is a small-picture person. He likes being in a world that he creates and can control. He loves minutiae, getting caught up in details. Also, he mentioned he's always been engrossed in comic books. A rich fantasy life can compensate for social alienation, until the individual adjusts to the real world. Everyone has his own timetable. Let's see how Toby does at Valley. In the meantime, I'll keep seeing him alone. And make sure he feels he's a part of your family."

"Well, thank you for all your time," said Mom, realizing this was as much consolation as she was getting for now.

We drove home mostly in silence. As petulant and selfish as he could be, I felt sorry for Toby. I thought he would rather jump into a pit of snakes than continue with therapy, or attend Valley Academy. He would tell me years later that he always felt like a stray dog when he went to school.

The weekend before the semester began, per Dr. Sheffield's suggestion, I took it on myself to show more interest in my brother. Dad was in a golf tournament and wouldn't be back until dinner. Mom had just left for an exercise class, to be followed by shopping. After I fixed breakfast for us, I told my brother to put away his Spiderman comics.

"What for?"

"We're going on an adventure. We're going to explore," I said with some swagger. "Grab your bike."

"Explore what?" he said, suspicious.

"You'll see."

Unlike Toby, I was a big-picture person. I would soon be sixteen, ready to find my place in the universe. I had written a line from Carl Sandburg in my journal: "It is necessary for a man to go away by himself, to sit on a rock, and ask, 'Who am I, where have I been, and where am I going?'" My parents' early birthday present, a shiny, aquamarine Italian racing bike with lots of gears, waited in the garage to take me someplace special.

"Where are we going?" Toby demanded as we rolled our bikes to the sidewalk.

"I don't know. Just follow me."

"You don't have Mom's permission to go anywhere," he pointed out.

"Nobody has to know."

Toby made a face, like he was doing a huge favor just to accompany me. As we began to ride, I loved the feel of huddling over my handlebars, changing gears, pedaling madly with a breeze in my face. I led Toby down neighborhood streets until we hit Valley Spring Lane, an artery that paralleled a mile of lush Lakeside Golf Club fairways. For a moment, I thought I spotted my father and his pals in golf carts, but whoever they were, they didn't seem to notice us. The sky was bunched with cumulus clouds that looked greenish through the veil of Los Angeles smog. Toby's voice reached me at the end of every block. He was tired. The morning was getting hot. He wanted a root beer float.

"Take a chill pill," I yelled over my shoulder.

"Eat my shorts!"

We kept riding. Valley Spring Lane was a straight shot to Cahuenga Boulevard, the western boundary of Toluca Lake. Co-hang-ga, as it was pronounced, was a well-trafficked four-lane street—a kind of

Maginot Line in my mother's eyes. We were never to cross it in anything but a car. Exposed on our bikes, not only might we get clobbered by a careless driver but on the other side lay the terra incognita of North Hollywood. There were lots of smaller homes with unkempt yards, side-by-side stucco apartment buildings, and cars that would have been traded in years ago if they'd been in Toluca Lake. Drug pushers were rumored to live there.

When we reached Cahuenga, it looked more frenetic than usual. Cars and an occasional city bus streaked by on both sides of the double-yellow line. No one obeyed the 45-mph speed limit. Traffic gaps didn't come often. Part of me thought I should turn back. I didn't want to put our lives in jeopardy. But emerging into the blinding sun of adolescence, I felt new powers, tied to thoughts of freedom and invincibility.

I turned and cocked an eye on Toby. "Ready?"

"We're crossing here? There's no crosswalk. We could get killed!" He was almost having a panic attack.

"Just follow me."

"What are we going to do in North Hollywood?"

"I told you. Explore."

"Explore what?"

"I have no idea. That's the whole point of exploration—it's investigating the unknown. Are you ready or not?" I kept my voice calm, but my heart was starting to work its way into my throat.

"You're crazy!" he roared.

To prove my resolve, I rolled my bike off the sidewalk until the front tire pushed a foot or so into the street. A Ford pickup nearly brushed the tire. Toby stayed frozen on the sidewalk.

I watched as he abruptly picked up his bike, turned it a hundred eighty degrees, and pointed it homeward. For good measure, pedaling away, he threw me the bird over his shoulder.

Fine, Toby, chicken out, I was only trying to help you, I thought. At the first break in traffic, my legs churned madly. I reached the double yellow line and stopped cold. This wasn't much of a triumph. A car going in either direction could easily swipe me. Drivers ogled me but no one bothered to stop and let me cross. I'm going to be fine. I'm going to be fine. I'm going to be fine.

It seemed forever before a gap came. I was on my saddle and shot ahead. Three ohmygods fell from my lips before I reached the other side. A driver's horn blasted the air. "What's wrong with you!" he bellowed.

I glanced behind me to the other side of Cahuenga. Toby had vanished back into the comforting folds of Toluca Lake.

I considered whether I had lost all rationality. I was supposed to be in charge of my brother. I was trusted to be responsible. Instead, I had almost put his life in danger and then abandoned him, which made me feel guilty as shit. My regret sat on my shoulders like a chattering jay, but after a minute, it flew away and didn't return.

~15~

I rode my bike along the sidewalk, gazing down side streets off Cahuenga, narrow, nondescript arteries ultimately leading to the heart of North Hollywood. The small, weathered houses boasted good-sized cracks in their stucco or peeling paint. Warped roof shingles made me think a good downpour could be hazardous for the owners.

About five houses down one street, a young black man caught my eye. He was standing in a yard of uncut grass and dandelions, wearing jeans and a yellow T-shirt with Bob Marley's face on it, along with a Dodgers cap on top of a bushy Afro. Suddenly, he was staring back at me. I couldn't tell whether it was from idle curiosity or he wanted something. History might have turned out differently if I'd kept going straight ahead. Instead, like a true explorer, I moved toward the stranger with little thought of caution.

He looked about seventeen or eighteen, well over six feet tall with broad shoulders and muscular arms. In front of him stood a worn card table with two glass pitchers of a pulpy, yellow-gray liquid. Signs taped to the table read: "Fresh-squeezed genuine LEM-ON-ADE" and "12-ounce cup filled to the brim. 50 U.S. cents!" There was a folding chair to the right of the table, which he flopped in as I approached. Like some melodic bird in the forest, he began whistling with perfect pitch. His long arms stretched behind his head, fingers interlocked, as if he didn't have a worry in the world.

I stopped, staring at him and smiling awkwardly. Then I wheeled my bike around, heading back to Cahuenga.

"Good morning, young lady," his voice boomed after me. "Did I scare you off or something?"

Keep going, I thought, but seconds later I disobeyed myself. I slowed my bike and glanced back.

"Don't you want some lemonade?" he asked. I could hear a smile in his voice.

I stepped over a patch of broken sidewalk and moved in his direction. Something seemed off. You ran a lemonade stand when you were eight or nine, not seventeen or eighteen, and you sold your product in a prominent place with lots of pedestrian traffic. Both of his pitchers were full, suggesting that he hadn't sold a single drop. Because of the sun's glare, I couldn't see anything in the house behind him except a jagged crack in the upper pane of a bay window. There were no cars in the driveway. Was this where his family lived, or was the owner away and he'd opportunistically planted himself on the lawn?

"Say, what's your name?" he said good-naturedly. I stood a few feet away, clutching my bike should I need to escape. Light acne dotted his chin and one side of his broad nose. His eyes didn't budge from me, hinting at either great self-confidence or a lack of manners.

"You do have a name, don't you?" he persisted as I scrutinized his sign again.

"My name's Alexandra," I said, looking up. "Friends call me Alex."

"Sister Alex, would you like to taste the best lemonade in the Valley?"

"I don't know, to be honest."

"What do you mean, you don't know? You won't take my word for it?"

"Why do you call me 'sister'? Isn't that what black people call each other? Like, 'Yo, brother,' and 'Yo, sister'?"

I was nervous, trying to be humorous, but the way he laughed, maybe he thought I was just weird. "And you're an expert on black folks?" he asked, a smile floating over his face.

"My mom does charity work with underprivileged kids. They're some African-Americans in the group," I said, as if that might be relevant.

"Well, I can call you sister, and you can call me brother, and it doesn't matter what our skin color is. What matters is whether you're thirsty for lemonade—sister."

"I guess I am. But I don't have fifty cents."

"Say what?"

"That's what your sign says you're charging."

"I make deals for special people," he said. "Twenty-five cents for you, Alexandra."

"So I'm special, huh?"

"You bet you are."

I couldn't decide whether he was enjoying my company or was just a good salesman. Then I wondered if I was being duped. Maybe he wanted to sell me drugs.

"I don't even have twenty-five cents," I confessed, holding onto my bike.

"It's the weekend," he reminded me, "and you aren't carrying even a quarter? Look at that fancy bike, and the way you're dressed. How much those designer jeans cost?"

"I'm not carrying any money," I said truthfully, suddenly feeling stupid about it.

"Hey, Alexandra, I'm not going to deny you." He pulled himself out of his chair and raised one of the pitchers in the air. A plume of lemonade funneled into a paper cup.

He held out the drink. "You can pay me later."

I laid my bike on the sidewalk and took the cup in both hands. The lemonade was on the tart side, with a few seeds in it, but it was quenching. I emptied the cup in seconds, which I could tell pleased him. Several trees to the side of the house were still laden with good-sized lemons.

"What's your name?" I asked.

"Edward. Edward Montgomery. From Flatbush, Brooklyn." He extended his hand. It was the first time I'd ever shaken hands with a stranger who happened to be black.

"Edward, that's an interesting name for you," I said.

"It's not especially a black person's name—is that what you mean?"

"No. It's just that all the Edwards I know are kind of dull. And you seem to be the opposite. You live here?"

He glanced behind him, as if to see if the house was still standing. "Yep."

"Where are your parents?"

"My folks work every day."

"Even on weekends?"

"Got to. We're working class." He produced a private smile, meant to deflect further inquiries.

I decided Edward probably wasn't a drug dealer, but there was something that pushed my curiosity. "Where do you go to school?"

"I start my senior year in two weeks. North Hollywood High."

"North Hollywood High? That's what, maybe twelve miles from here? Your folks give you a ride every day, or do you car pool?"

"I ride my bike."

A twenty-four-mile round trip through traffic had to take at least an hour on a bike. Crazy, I thought.

"Are you going to college?" I asked.

"The Princeton admission office wrote me that I'll probably be accepted with a full scholarship, if I keep up my grades."

"Princeton? Really?"

His tone wasn't boastful. He was just answering my question, as if I'd asked his favorite band or movie. He had to have worked his butt off to get noticed by an Ivy, especially coming from a public school, I considered. Unless he was bullshitting me.

"So, what are your favorite subjects?"

"Favorites? Trig and physics. I like literature too. Especially biographies and fiction. But my passion is baseball. Know anything about the National Pastime, sister?"

I wagged my head. "Is that baseball? My dad watches it on TV sometimes. My brother played Little League."

"What position?"

"I don't even know. He wasn't very good at it. What's your batting average?"

"Almost .400. Sports writers have me as one of the top pitchers in the state too. Maybe I'll even make it to the majors . . . one of these days," he added quietly.

"You're a great pitcher and a great hitter? That's unusual, isn't it?"

"Babe Ruth did both."

"Show me your swing," I said playfully.

Edward cocked an invisible bat behind his shoulder and pierced the air with a full-throttle swing. His muscles rippled under Bob Marley's smiling countenance.

I bit my lip. I didn't know what impressed me more, the beauty of his strength, that he was a brainiac, or that he had a personality that yoked humility with swagger.

"So, ten years from now, will I be reading about you in the newspaper?" I said.

"Everyone's got to find his place in the world. No one said it's easy. Some people come from nothing, or they get bad breaks, but they still find a way to succeed. We're a country where you can invent yourself over and over, wouldn't you say? It's our zeitgeist." He paused to deliberate on his own fate. "Honestly, I don't know where I'll end up."

"What the hell is zeitgeist?" I prided myself on my vocabulary, but this was a new one.

"A German word. It means the essence of a particular country, or a period of history. You might say America's zeitgeist is that you have the opportunity to be whatever you want to be, if you're willing to work for it."

I couldn't argue with that. My father and his immigrant parents were proof. But I wasn't sure what Edward meant by inventing himself over and over. If he was telling the truth, he already had enough talents, he didn't need to invent anything. I was suddenly feeling inferior. The best future I could come up with was heart specialist in Africa, a dream that seemed as far away as Africa itself.

I was afraid Edward was going to ask what I was reading, where I went to school, and where I wanted to go to college. Instead, he asked what I thought about the AIDS epidemic which had probably started in Africa but now threatened to stretch around the world; the ongoing famine in Ethiopia, where politics kept outside organizations from offering much relief; and finally, the Hubble telescope which one day soon was going to explore pockets of deepest space. I answered each question the best I could but it was a struggle.

"When do you find time to read so much?" I asked.

"I'm up at five every morning."

"You're kidding. Me too. Or most of the time. I still don't read as much as you."

An older car suddenly purred up to the curb, its engine idling as Jaleel approached it. A middle-aged woman in a floral print dress rolled down the passenger window. Behind the wheel was a younger man with wire-rimmed glasses.

"Are you selling lemonade?" the woman asked, as if she hadn't read the sign.

Edward came alive with purpose. "Yes, ma'am. How many would you like?" He squatted beside the car, looking as if he wanted to rest his arms across the open passenger window but thought twice about it. "Both you and your husband thirsty?" he said, forearms settling on his thighs.

"He's my son," the woman said, "but I'll take that as a compliment. Yes, we'll take two lemonades please."

"Coming right up."

I waited until Edward had finished his transaction, putting the dollar the woman handed him in his front pocket, and watched the car putter away.

"Hey, you made a sale!" I said, pleased for him.

"I'll sell out before the day is over. I always do. A lot of traffic comes down this street—folks use it as a shortcut from Ventura Boulevard. I ask you, Alex"—he gave me a slice of a smile—"what's more American than selling lemonade on a gorgeous summer day?"

I thought the question was rhetorical until he put a finger in the air to make a further point. "Just being in this great country, that's what's special," he said. "Being free to sell lemonade."

Except possibly for my father raving about "God's Country," I had never known anyone so upbeat and patriotic as Edward. I reached down for my bike. "Well, I better get going, Edward."

"You take care of yourself. Come again if you're thirsty. My stand is open every weekend until I run out of lemons."

He pushed out his hand, and I shook it happily. I wasn't sure whether I believed in coincidence or fate, but in either case, I was pleased with the unexpected encounter. Edward had made me feel grown up—someone on his way to Princeton conversing on serious subjects with a fifteen-year-old.

I couldn't wait to find an excuse to see him again.

~16~

I rode almost half a mile until I reached an actual crosswalk, and this time I walked my bike across Cahuenga, like someone who had learned a lasting lesson. On the other side, Toluca Lake was quieter than ever, as if a lot of people slept in on Saturdays. I imagined "do not disturb" signs hanging from our lampposts.

When I got home, Toby was in his trunks, legs spraddled on a chaise by the pool, sunning himself. He was already the color of a coconut. Mom wasn't back. My brother's left eye rotated frog-like in my direction. "You were away long enough. What did you do?"

"I was gone all of an hour. I met a neat guy who was selling lemonade."

Toby squinched his nose. "That's all you did? Talk to a guy selling lemonade? How old was he?"

"Eighteen. He's African-American. Cool, huh?"

"He was eighteen and selling lemonade. What gives?"

Toby looked like he was thinking of how many black kids he knew. There was a handful at Valley, most from wealthy families, one or two on scholarship. At the golf club, all the waiters were black, but we didn't really know them.

"What did you talk about?"

"Baseball. Politics. Famines. Important things in the world."

His eyes shut indifferently, and his face tilted back to the sun. "I'm thinking of telling Mom how you almost got me killed."

"You're threatening me? I was trying to show you how much I care about you," I said, even if it didn't turn out that way. The little toad had no idea how obnoxious he could be. I might have punched him if I wasn't in such a good mood.

Mom returned with a trunk loaded with groceries. As I carried the bags in, Toby began hosing out the garage and raking leaves on the back lawn. A normal person would take an hour for those chores, but Toby reduced everything to eighteen minutes. That seemed to be his threshold of attention for anything, including homework. Half the leaves were still on the lawn when he told us he was done.

"Go back and do it again," said Mom.

"Why? That's what the gardener's for."

"Saturday chores are mandatory," she answered. "You didn't give your best effort."

"I got a whole bag full, didn't I?"

"You should have gotten two or three."

"Oh, so you're saying I'm lazy."

"Yes, I am saying exactly that, young man."

"Wait till I tell Dr. Sheffield."

"Get real, Toby," I said.

"What's it hurt to have a few leaves lying around? They're pretty to look at."

Mom should have picked up the phone and called Dr. Sheffield right then for a consultation, because she didn't know how to end the argument. Despite her role as the family disciplinarian, confrontation wasn't her strong suit. She was too thin-skinned. Even Dad, who adored her and did whatever she asked of him, could irritate her. I had overheard Mom complaining to friends on the phone that my father was a workaholic who was rarely on time for dinner and retreated to his study immediately afterward rather than spend time with her. On weekends, he was usually off with his buddies—golfing, ocean fishing, or duck hunting.

Tonight, although Dad once again showed up late for dinner, Mom wasn't troubled by anything, including Toby. Her spirits were high. In fact, they were in the stratosphere. Labor Day was closing in, the unofficial end of summer, and the date of our annual party. It was more than a party. It was a Cecil B. DeMille production, where practically every friend, neighbor, client, and colleague that my parents knew was invited. Mom loved international themes. She had made local history with "Romance in Paris" and "Moonrise over Machu Picchu." The parties got written up on the front page of the *Tolucan* and sometimes made the *Los Angeles Times*. They were talked about at the golf club for weeks afterward.

In addition to having our yard graced with set designs and costume-wearing guests, we always hired a ten-piece band. A dance floor was installed next to a cavernous tent, where caterers prepared a theme dinner. The nights never seemed to end, or so I was told. Toby and I were always shipped out to friends' houses because these were "adult parties." Afterward, Mom usually spent a day or two in bed, recovering. Elaborately planned and executed parties could take their toll.

"Honey," she said happily. "You and I have a special appointment on Tuesday, after school."

"What appointment is that?" I said with suspicion.

Her smile narrowed; she was disappointed that I hadn't figured it out. "You need a costume for 'An Evening on the Nile.' I've hired a seamstress, as well as a consultant—someone who knows Egyptian history."

"I don't go to your parties, Mom," I cut her off.

"You're about to start tenth grade. Don't you think it's time the world gets to meet our sophisticated, brilliant daughter?"

"What's that mean?"

"Think of this as your debut, Alex." She gave Dad a goading look.

"That's right, sweetie," he chimed in.

I shook my head, resentful that I was being tag-teamed. I had heard of cotillions, confirmations, bar mitzvahs, sweet-sixteens, and other coming-of-age rituals, but I thought I had escaped all that shit. I certainly never imagined that An Evening on the Nile would be my special moment. I would be paraded in front of my parents' friends, shake a zillion sweaty hands, and cough up some meaningless conversation. It seemed beyond pointless.

"Mom, unless it's Halloween, I'm not going to be caught dead in a costume."

"I was thinking that you could be a member of the pharaoh's family. A young princess, heir to the throne. I've been reading about the Middle and Late Kingdoms, and the lavish parties they had at temples in Luxor and Carnac. They were extraordinary."

I didn't know much about Luxor or Carnac, but I made a mental note to open our Britannica that night. I was pretty sure there weren't a lot of female pharaohs, except for Cleopatra. And I didn't know if she'd ever had a daughter. That was something Edward might have known.

"I'm not going," I spoke up.

"Sweetie, of course you're coming. You'll have fun!"

She said the last word like it was something unknown to me, as if I worked too hard and played too little. I couldn't possibly comprehend her point until I attended one of our Labor Day extravaganzas. I could see the expectation in her eyes. My view on life would be changed forever.

Toby shook his head. "You're so lucky, sis."

"Then why don't you take my place?"

"Twelve is too young," he whispered ruefully.

"Why do you have these parties anyway? They cost a fortune, Mom."

"Because everyone loves them."

"Because you love them," I corrected.

"So will you, honey."

"Come on, Alex, be a good sport," my father threw in.

I dropped my napkin on the table. "I'm not going. Period. Finito. End of discussion."

"Why don't you at least think about it," Dad said diplomatically.

"You're forcing me to go, aren't you?"

"No, I'm asking you to have an open mind."

It would have been no small event winning an argument with my father. He was harder to take down than Hulk Hogan. Clever courtroom lawyer that he was, his tone could shift from assertive to inquisitive to cajoling, keeping me off balance.

Silently conceding defeat, I asked, "Can I invite Joyce or Debora?" Joyce was my best friend.

"I don't see why not. Gloria, what do you think? Can't Alex have someone over?"

The idea hadn't occurred to Mom—I think she was planning on having me all to herself—but she hesitated and then said okay.

Upstairs, I gazed out my window to the lake, which seemed so black as to be invisible. Our lawn, gardens, and trees blazed with landscape lights. I tried to imagine what it would be like to have three hundred people milling and tromping about. An Evening on the Nile was a mere week away. My parents' voices drifted up from downstairs in a mumble, no doubt talking about party details.

I closed the door, grateful for the sanctuary of my room. In one corner—because I never had the heart to give them away—were my childhood dolls and stuffed animals. In another corner was a full-length mirror in which I could agonize over what dress or jeans and top to choose. A benefit of going to a private school like Valley was mandatory uniforms, even if I hated wearing them. You didn't have to decide what to wear every day. Posters of rock bands and movie stars hung across my fleur-de-lis wallpaper, along with a color photo of President Kennedy and his gorgeous wife, Jackie. On my desk was an IBM Selectric, a birthday present from Mom and Dad. A wickedly expensive designer chaise, intended as a suitable place to read a book, floated at the other end of the room. I never used it because my bed was far more comfortable.

Lingering before the mirror, I studied myself with fresh eyes: My Doc Martens, Jordache jeans, and some blousy, sequined top that Brooke Shields modeled in magazines began to strike me as horribly wrong. I had been wearing clothes selected or approved by my mother from time immemorial. Her voice could rise to unbearable decibels in my head whenever I touched a store clothing rack, as if I was just about to choose the wrong thing. I suddenly wanted my own look, whatever that turned out to be. Maybe I'd even start dressing down. The thought of being an Egyptian princess, even for a night, made my stomach ache.

I dropped on my bed with my journal. After rambling about our party-to-come, I drew a stick-figure sketch of me crossing Cahuenga on my bike, dodging streaking missiles. I likened myself to Columbus, trying to reach the New World.

August 29
Today I met a high school senior, an African-
American, named Edward Montgomery. I hope Mom
never finds out, because she'd have a cow and half.
Not that she'd care about his skin color necessarily,
but his family lives in a crumbling little house that

*looks ready to blow down in a good wind. She might
suspect his whole family is in the drug business. All
Edward sells, I'm convinced, is lemonade. He's very
cool. I love the way he thinks. He knows so much
more than anyone at Valley. Can't say exactly how or
when, but our paths will cross again. I'm sure of it.
Maybe we can even become friends.*

Perhaps a friendship was fantasy, but sometimes feelings that grab
you by surprise, that are the least likely to happen, are the hardest to
dismiss. I hid my journal in my closest, under a flap of loose carpet
which I covered with heavy boxes of old school papers. I wondered
what Edward had thought of me, or was I already forgotten as just
another lemonade customer?

It was hard to turn my mind off from Edward. Did he have brothers and sisters? What kind of work did his parents do? It had always
been one of my weaknesses, my reluctance to mind my own business.
I tried to solve puzzles that others didn't care about or gave up on. I
wanted to know all the secrets of the universe, no matter who or what
I had to disturb to find them.

~17~

Labor Day weekend sneaked up on us. Friday, as the humidity spiked, thick, brooding clouds spread across the Valley. By evening, a seven-hour downpour, unusual for Los Angeles in the late summer, began soaking every inch around us. The water in the lake rose more than a foot. When the clouds finally lifted, the heavy air clung to my skin. The storm had scrubbed smog-laden Los Angeles to the bone. You could see for miles. Just as the Egyptians believed in omens, said Dad, the break in the weather boded well for our party.

He dropped my brother at a friend's house where the boy shared Toby's obsession with super-hero comic books, returning to putter in his study. Our back yard began to bang and clang like a military operation. Mom, party commander-in-chief, oversaw ten men from Ogilvie's Entertainment Services as they erected a mammoth tent, strung lights, and installed a parquet dance floor near the pool. They brought in a fifteen-foot-high papier-mâché pyramid and a similarly sized sphinx, both electrified on the inside. Our guests would be arriving at the Temple of Luxor. A series of faux columns along the driveway gave evidence of the opulence of ancient Egypt. All day, florists and service people came and went. Finally, a van arrived from Lakeside Pharmacy. Two young men carried in a hundred twenty-seven boxes of liquor, wine, beer, and mixers to the back yard. Our RSVP list was three hundred twenty-six. Mom worried whether the liquor would hold out. Almost everyone was a drinker, and Dad alone, she half-joked, made up for the 5 percent who weren't.

"Aren't you excited, sweetie?" Mom turned to me as we surveyed the finished yard.

"It sure is different," I said dryly.

I could read her thoughts as she studied her handiwork. This would be the pièce de résistance among all her parties, the talk of the town for months to come. She and Dad had climbed their mountain of dreams to become who they were, one of the most talked about couples in Toluca Lake. Reaching the summit wasn't all about self-congratulation. Mom had already passed forty, and I'd seen her sneaking more and more glances in the mirror. It had to be slightly terrifying spotting the first dents in your beauty because you knew that around the bend were only more lines and sags. Perhaps she was thinking of tonight as a grand finale, before the new, less-glorious period of middle age truly began.

Then a small disaster struck, with the party only hours away. I didn't know when Mom discovered her mosquito bite. Maybe passing by a mirror, or her finger accidentally brushed the spot on her forehead, dead center between her eyes. In her bathroom, we looked together at the damage in one of those convex, high-magnification mirrors. The welt loomed larger than most bites. The ten plagues that Moses had visited on Ramses now had an eleventh, specifically for my mother. Her finger couldn't leave the bump alone. It seemed to be growing. She sat at her makeup table, pulling out tubes and sticks to apply.

I left her alone and walked outside, taking the steps down to our dock. A small battalion of long-legged mosquitoes skittered across the murky, opaque surface, as if they were guardians of what secrets lay below. I envied their effortless escape from the scene of the crime. I was stuck here—alone. I had made calls to five friends who I thought would never disappoint me, but they'd all endured their own parents' parties and wanted nothing to do with mine. What was the point of watching older people make fools of themselves, Joyce said. At best, it was mildly boring; at worst, someone jumped in the swimming pool or passed out on the dance floor or drove home so skunk-drunk that the police stopped them.

Around five-thirty, the servers, bartenders, valets, and tuxedoed band members arrived. My parents slipped upstairs. I was already dressed and waiting in the living room. My costume was relatively simple: a powder blue pleated linen skirt, cinched with a belt full of rhinestone, and a short-sleeved blouse. I wore a headdress befitting a member of the royal family, and sandals. I felt like a fool. At least I didn't have to wear a crinoline gown and white gloves. As debuts went, I was getting off light.

Mom had kept her costume a secret. My guess was she would appear as Cleopatra—one of the most beguiling, beautiful, and powerful women in history. She had supposedly broken both Mark Antony's and Julius Caesar's hearts, just by batting her eyes.

"Well? What do you think, sweetie?" Mom was suddenly in front of me.

My eyes darted first to the havoc wreaked by the mosquito. She had blotted out most of the bright red bump—you could still see it if you looked—but overall, it was eclipsed by her costume: a tight sheath dress of a glittering gold material, held up by two thin straps to expose her perfectly proportioned shoulders. The dress showed off her figure impeccably. It traveled down to her ankles, exposing feet wrapped in elegant sandals. A necklace of sterling silver feathers floated over her breasts. The most elaborate touch was a special Egyptian crown, called a *shuti*, I learned. It was made of ostrich feathers surrounding a six-inch-diameter sun disc, all balanced perfectly on her head. Her face glowed.

"I thought you might come as Cleopatra," I said.

"I was going to," she admitted, "until I studied pictures of her. We know she was full of guile and charm, but honestly, her beauty has been exaggerated."

"You look terrific," I said, which was what she wanted to hear. "Where's Dad?"

She twisted her head toward the stairs. "Louis, are you coming? You don't want the party to start without you, do you?"

When he didn't answer, I asked my mother how I looked.

"Gorgeous, sweetie. Absolutely beautiful. I promise that you'll remember tonight forever."

Pharaoh, a.k.a. Dad, tromped down the stairs. A faux leopard skin was draped over a bare shoulder and tucked into a bejeweled belt, where a lion's tail dangled at his side. A pleated skirt, stopping above his knees, was a soft goldenrod. Pharaohs didn't usually wear shoes, so Dad went barefoot. He wore a striped headcloth called a *nemes*, another pharaoh exclusive, and carried a gold-plated staff. He said he would tap the ground whenever he had a proclamation to deliver.

"Wow, impressive outfit, Dad. You should wear that to the office."

"Yeah, you think so?" He gave Mom a kiss. "Tonight I can pretend I rule the world."

"Louis, you rule the world anyway," she replied.

The three of us walked outside together in a grand entrance. Cecil B. would have been proud. A mild breeze, scented with our roses, drifted over the yard. Two dozen guests had already arrived. Some costumes looked more Roman or Greek than Egyptian. None were as elaborate as my parents'. I felt like I was in a period movie, as our lawn filled with time-travelers from Memphis, Athens, and Rome. The light in the deep end of our pool rippled like a reflection of the moon.

I was introduced to a couple of new associates in Dad's firm, Lakeside Golf Club members, people from church, Mom's tennis, tea, and philanthropy pals, and the owners of Lakeside Pharmacy, the King's Arms steakhouse, and Sorrentino's Seafood Grill. My parents had a wide swath of friends.

I already knew most of Dad's law firm associates. I was treated well at Baten, Kleeb, and Donahue for obvious reasons, and I'd been in a courtroom several times to watch my father arguing before a jury. Harding Kleeb was equally skilled. I sometimes thought that winning was more important to them than the guilt or innocence of their clients. My father's elaborate, careful strategies, relayed in our dinnertime conversations, seemed to give him a high.

When I told this to Dad one night, he laughed. "Most trial attorneys are adrenaline junkies, Alex. We love to gamble. And that's fine, as long as you win."

I clung to a 7-Up that Mom had handed me, and followed her around the party. I was in the eye of a hurricane, trying not to get swept away as I matched names with faces and answered questions about Valley Academy and where I would attend medical school. Mom started talking about Stanford, Harvard, and Johns Hopkins, as if everything was all set. People beamed at me—some with pride, others, who had less-ambitious children, with envy. My mother put her arm around my shoulder, as if I wouldn't be the success I was without her.

In addition to the sets and costumes, our food was genuine Middle Kingdom Egypt: slices of fatty goose, duck, goat, and quail; vegetable dishes like chickpeas and hummus; different cheeses; a melange of melons, figs, dates, and pomegranates. I heard some men grumble why couldn't the Egyptians have liked a good rib-eye.

The band began playing Madonna and Janet Jackson songs. Sometimes the Beatles and Stones crept into their repertoire. The dance floor was turmoil. Not just the sea of writhing middle-aged bodies but the pounding music as well, drowning out conversation. Soundless lips moved up, down, and sideways. No matter how fast the bartenders poured drinks, the lines of thirsty ancients grew longer. Someone crashed into the fake pyramid and snapped, "Goddamnit! Who put that here?" Everyone around him laughed.

"Hey, play something Egyptian!" someone shouted, and a Grateful Dead song suddenly filled the air. I didn't get the connection, unless, after incessant war or famine, a tired pharaoh was happy to begin his journey to the afterlife.

I never quite took my eye off my mother. Would I end up like her someday, a society hostess? I wondered. Part of me thought it wasn't remotely possible, yet another voice in me warned that it was a certainty. I would write in my journal that night that at least Mom didn't get drunk or make a fool of herself in public. She was the hostess who knew how to lay her hand lightly on someone's wrist, tilt her head in curiosity, or make her eyes crinkle in sympathy. She soaked in the compliments about her beauty, her family, and the party. Knowing how to be appreciated was just as much an art form as appreciating your guests, she told me once.

After a while, I drifted upstairs. I opened my window and marveled at the glaze of stars. Strangely, the conversations that had been soundless by the dance floor now rose above the music. I could distinguish individual words, but they weren't strung together to make any sense. My parents kept in their separate orbits, Dad roaming the pool area with his friends, whimsically banging down his pharaoh's staff, and Mom weaving through the crowd to make everyone feel welcome.

I lost her for a minute before her ostrich-feather crown bobbed up again. She was nearing a row of magnolia trees at the eastern edge of the property. Landscape lights played peek-a-boo with her figure. A man was by her side. They entered a realm of darkness and settled behind a tree, standing close enough to each other to be camouflaged by the trunk. At moments they moved and came into view but not for long. The man was slightly taller than my father. His costume looked ordinary—a wraparound skirt of some kind, with a tunic—as though not much enthusiasm had gone into it.

I pulled my binoculars from my desk. Even after I adjusted the lenses, the magnolia trunk still obscured them. The man's hands sliced the air, and he kept throwing back his head, what I could see of it, as if he was frustrated or angry about something. He took my mother's hand and pulled her deeper into the shadows. The binoculars were practically useless. Part of me wanted to rush down and find out who the hell it was.

But I stayed in my room, training the glasses back on the magnolias. Two or three minutes passed before my mother emerged from the shadows. She was adjusting the feathered crown on her head, and moving at a deliberate pace toward the pool. In no time she had a fresh drink in her hand, resuming her hostess duties as if nothing were amiss. I doubted anyone was sober enough to notice her absence.

When my gaze jerked back to the magnolia grove, a breeze tousled the branches. There was no other movement. I suspected that the man, whoever he was, had taken another route back to the party.

I opened my journal, and like a good historian, began recording everything I'd seen. Later, I slumped on my bed in a troubled state. The band stopped playing around midnight. I could faintly hear car doors close and engines whine to life. Downstairs, the caterers moved with the same relentless efficiency in cleaning up as they had when cooking and serving. Then they too were gone. Around two thirty, my tired parents moved languidly up the stairs, Dad singing the Beatles' "Love Me Do," making up verses when necessary. Mom said little. She opened my door but didn't come over to kiss me.

Sleep was hard to come by. I added a couple of sentences in my journal.

> *Part of me wants to give my mother the benefit of the doubt—you're innocent until proven guilty, as Dad has said many times. But why steal away with some man into a tree grove in the middle of a party? I can't tell Dad what I saw until I get to the bottom of things. He trusts all of us to the ends of the Earth.*

Mom was right. I would remember tonight forever.

~18~

When the fall term began the next week, our Mercedes was the first car in the parent parking lot. Toby sat motionless in the back seat, eyes half closed. He looked handsome in his jacket and trousers, though it had taken him multiple efforts to get his tie right. I shouldn't say motionless, I should say limp, like someone who'd rather go to the guillotine than enter his new school.

The next parent to appear in the parking lot was an elegantly dressed platinum blonde in a Buick, with her seventh-grade son in tow. Slightly overweight with pointy ears, the boy gazed out his window in awe at the campus. I gave him a sympathetic glance as I waited for Mom's plan to unfold.

Like a one-person welcoming committee, she hurried over before the newcomers were out of their car. I listened to her speech about the ins and outs of being a parent at Valley, which she called the premier preparatory school in the United States. Apologies to Andover and Exeter, and maybe a dozen other institutions, I thought. When Mom wanted to be friendly to a stranger, she had no rivals. My first day as a seventh grader, she had walked me into the administration building, getting whistles from upperclassmen. She flirted right back with them.

I had felt like her shadow, beyond humiliated. "Honey," she said, catching my look when we said goodbye, "what's wrong?"

"Please, please, please don't do that again," I said.

"Don't do what?"

"You know what. All that flirting shit."

"Sweetie, it's harmless. But if that's what you want, all right. Just don't forget that you and I are a team. We're best friends."

Now, team leader was at it again. She wanted my friendless brother to have a potential new ally out of the blocks. With a nod from Mom, as rehearsed, Toby climbed sluggishly from the Mercedes. I followed at a distance.

"Toby, this is Mrs. Winters, and her son, Steven. I think you two might have a couple of classes together."

Steven smiled and extended his hand. Toby looked at him blankly, nodded, and simply marched away across the parking lot. I stepped up and shook Steven's hand for my inconsiderate brother. Toby didn't even say goodbye to Mom. As I walked on, I heard her make an excuse to Mrs. Winters. Great start, I thought.

When I caught up with Toby, I told him he didn't have to be so rude. "Do you know how draining it can be for Mom or me to always cover your ass?"

"Then don't," he said simply. He suddenly stopped, looking around the campus in a fog. "Where do I go?"

"Jesus."

"Are you going to help me or not?"

I led him past a complex of classrooms down a brick pathway toward our athletic facilities, which kids mockingly called the Beverly Center for their size and opulence. We walked on toward the auditorium and science and theater buildings. Manicured lawns and specimen trees were everywhere. Our thirty-five acres included woodlands and a fishpond with koi. None of it seemed to impress Toby.

I walked him into the math and science building. "Your homeroom is 106, to the left. You okay?"

"Don't worry. I'm cool."

"Sure?"

"Yeah, I'm sure."

"I'll meet you in the parking lot at three. Don't get stressed out. It's only your first day."

He seemed to ignore my pep talk as he had Mom's master plan with the new boy. I took a short cut to my locker in the administration building, talking to friends I hadn't seen all summer. From nowhere, a secretary from the headmistress's office approached my locker. Her hand flapped at me like a flag in the breeze.

"Good morning, Alexandra," she said, friendly but business-like. "Do you have a minute? Ms. Graves would like to see you."

I followed her down the hall and into the headmistress's office, the inner sanctum of Valley Academy. What could possibly be wrong, or urgent, the first morning of school? Had Toby gotten into trouble in all of five minutes? Ms. Graves was scribbling in a notebook and didn't glance up, which gave me more time to be anxious. I took the chair in front of her mammoth desk. The walls were decorated with plaques and trophies, photos of famous alumni, and expensive art that was part of Valley's endowment.

The personal photos on her desk testified that Ms. Graves had been pretty in her day. She was about fifty now, and hadn't married until well into her forties. She was fond of saying that Valley's students— twelve hundred fifty of them, including the two hundred boarders— were her family. Her hair was in a pageboy, right out of the early '60s, and her conservative clothes rarely varied. Joyce claimed she was a lesbian. I didn't care one way or another. The critical thing was that she ruled Valley with an iron fist, and you had to be respectful.

"So, Alexandra, a good summer, was it?" Ms. Graves said, finally glancing up. She maintained the same peppy voice all day, like someone who loved her job and would never leave it. She pretended to know, with uncanny accuracy, what every student was doing at every single moment.

"Yes, it was a great summer," I said, forcing some enthusiasm. "Very productive." I had read about twenty books on different subjects, as well as the *Britannica* on Egyptian history.

Her eyes remained fixed on me, trying to determine something.

"Is something wrong, Ms. Graves?" I asked.

"Absolutely not, Alexandra. Tenth grade, so far so good?"

I shrugged. The first bell for the school year had yet to ring.

"I believe you're taking a foreign language," she said.

"Latin One."

"Good. Everyone knows an ambitious student by whether he or she takes Latin. *Faber est quisque fortunae suae.*"

I stared back.

" 'Every man is architect of his own fortune,' " she translated.

"Ah," I said, pleased to learn something new. It was a maxim that Carl Sandburg might have said.

"You know that Friday is Founder's Day," she came to her point. "We're expecting over five hundred alumni, from twenty-four states."

"That's an amazing number," I said, meaning it. Founder's Day was always a big deal at Valley. I thought of salmon swimming thousands of miles to return to their spawning waters.

"Alexandra, would you like to give the keynote this year?"

"The keynote?" My face was wreathed in doubt. An insane suggestion! Except for dopey cliches, I wouldn't have a clue about what to say to five hundred alumni.

"That's usually done by a senior, isn't it, Ms. Graves?"

"Not always. Sometimes it's good to show up-and-coming talent."

"I'm not much of a public speaker."

"I have this sense you're better than you think. You'd be making an impression in front of distinguished and influential people."

She quoted another Latin phrase that she didn't translate, as if I should look it up. It was accompanied by a glance that said I would be unwise to turn down her generous offer. She wasn't unlike my mother, full of expectations, refusing to be disappointed.

"How long should the speech be?"

"Five to seven minutes. We always hear the same thing, year after year. Feel free to be original. Just remember that most of our fundraising takes place this one day. You'd be surprised at the size of the pledges."

I didn't have a lot of time to think. So I submitted, swept along by my general ambition and the headmistress's flattery. "This is an honor, Ms. Graves. Thank you for trusting me with it."

I sprang to my feet, extending my hand to seal the deal.

~19~

When I announced the unexpected honor at dinner that evening, my mother was thrilled. She felt the Founder's Day speech would be something to put on my college applications, along with my being vice president of my ninth-grade class. I felt I had gotten elected for my outspokenness, in addition to being generally efficient, but there were endless after-school meetings that wore me down. Mom thought I should run for office again, but it wasn't going to happen. She reminded me she had been eleventh-grade president at her school—back when dinosaurs ruled the earth, I thought.

So that Toby didn't feel excluded, Dad asked how his classes were going. Did he have any favorites?

"Lunch," he said.

"Seriously?" Mom asked.

"Seriously."

"Didn't you like algebra?" said Dad. "You're pretty handy with numbers."

"No, I'm average. Anyway, I don't want to talk about it."

"Okay. What do you want to talk about?"

He dropped his arms over his chest and stared at Dad. "How about my birthday?"

"Sure. You know what you want?"

"A computer. An IBM ps/2 with a diskette drive, and a bidirectional 8-bit port."

Mom frowned. "What's a bidirectional 8-bit port?"

"If that's what you want," Dad said, "I'm sure you'll put it to good use."

"Totally bitchin'," Toby said.

I had little idea of Toby's interest in computers. I didn't know much more than Mom about the latest technology, other than that BKD secretaries were beginning to use large, bulky desktops. Dad and Harding Kleeb had computers in their offices as well, but I wasn't sure how much they used them. Most kids at Valley were still churning out papers on typewriters.

After dinner, I closed the door to my room. I was feeling a little daunted as my pencil skated across a legal pad. Twelve hundred students and five hundred alumni was not a small audience.

> *Greetings dear Valley Academy alumni and fellow students. It is my special pleasure this morning to welcome you to the fifty-third anniversary of the founding of our beloved Valley Academy . . . .*

I kept writing, my pencil trying to keep up with my thoughts. Ms. Graves had told me to be original. The next three evenings, I made repeated changes, wanting everything to be perfect, and rehearsed in front of my mirror.

"Sweetie, could I hear your speech?" Mom asked me on Thursday. "I might have a suggestion or two—"

"No."

"Why not?"

"Because you'll just gum it up."

She hesitated, looking for another angle. "Would it be all right if I came and sat in the back of the auditorium?"

"No parents allowed, unless you're an alumnus."

"Are you sure?"

"Positive."

I wasn't sure, but I didn't want to be jinxed. This was my chance to shine. I still couldn't think of my mother without flashing on her foray into the magnolia grove.

Friday morning, I watched bodies swarm into the auditorium. Valley Academy hadn't become co-ed until 1970, so the older alumni were men, all in suits and ties, looking privileged and prosperous. Many were famous in their professions. Shaking hands and hugging one another like returning war heroes, most gravitated toward the front of the auditorium.

Ms. Graves and important faculty members sat in chairs on the stage. They approached the microphone, one by one, with brief salutations. We heard that alumni had come from as far away as New York, Paris, and Rome. The alumni president, George Kincaid, owned one of the largest oil fields in Oklahoma. Valley graduates were doctors, lawyers, CEOs, politicians, journalists, diplomats, entrepreneurs, and actors.

I rose from the front row in the auditorium and went up the short flight of steps. My typed speech was rolled in my hand. An early case of nerves had been replaced by a strange calm, as I realized I had nothing to lose.

"Greetings, dear Valley Academy alumni," I began after I got behind the lectern. "My name is Alexandra Baten, and I'm in tenth grade at this incredible institution of learning." I heard my voice booming through the mike. The overhead lighting bothered me slightly—a glare bounced off my unfurled pages—but I could also see faces looking up in expectation.

"It is my distinct pleasure, on behalf of our faculty and my fellow students, to welcome you to the fifty-third anniversary of the founding of our beloved Valley Academy. Greetings one and all."

The headmistress and faculty began clapping behind me, and then the entire auditorium exploded with applause. I could feel my face glow. Of course, I was wrong to imagine the alumni were clapping for me. They were clapping for themselves, for the school, for Valley's undisputed legacy of achievement and greatness. Over the years, alumni had funded an endowment worth $180 million. A seven-year plan envisioned hitting the half-billion-dollar mark. We were the elite college preparatory school in the western states. We would never be as wealthy as some East Coast schools, but our finances were healthier than those of many small colleges.

"I know how important our alumni are to this institution. You are not just role models of character and achievement—as important as those are—but a source of financial strength. Your annual gifts help subsidize our tuition, teachers' salaries, scholarships, athletics, and special programs. We would not be the school that we are today without your unprecedented generosity."

The applause boomed around me like a sound barrier-breaking jet as I continued for another five minutes with earnest observations about our promising futures. Finally, I approached the heart of my speech.

"As I look out on so many proud faces this morning, I am going to ask each of you to do something very different with your pledges this year. Do not necessarily give your money to Valley Academy. Look around the world, look at the famines, earthquakes, floods, civil wars, and children dying from preventable diseases—look until you see something that moves your heart and stirs your conscience. This year we don't need a new gymnasium, library wing, or a field trip to Washington, D.C. If we do, there's plenty of money in our endowment. Everything pales compared to helping our fellow men and women. The courage of your convictions will be revealed. Thank you so much again for coming to this year's Founder's Day."

I was expecting Niagara Falls, a thundering cataract of applause that would turn palms and fingers to a blistering red. What I heard instead was clapping so faint that it sounded like horse hooves padding over sand. I scrambled down the steps and sank in my seat. No one looked in my direction. Ms. Graves almost sprinted to the microphone, thanked me briefly, and announced the day's program with an enthusiasm that would make everyone try to forget my message.

Joyce glided up to me after the assembly. Her dark, saucer eyes were burning in disbelief. "What, Alex, did you take a fucking insanity pill this morning?"

"I still don't—"

"How naive can you be? Feed starving children? Help earthquake victims? Are you nuts? Our alumni are supposed to give their money to us, douche brain."

Another friend came over and said that if I wanted to save the world, I should drop out of school and bike across the country to end cancer. I thought she was serious until her voice tittered at the end.

Minutes later, I was called to Ms. Graves' office. The oil baron, Mr. Kincaid, sat on the windowsill and fiddled with the blinds cord. Ms. Graves was on the phone with an alumnus in Nevada who had already heard the news. When she finally finished apologizing, Mr. Kincaid rose to his feet, arms akimbo. He frowned, like a coach trying to grasp why his team had played so poorly.

"Miss Baten, I'm sure you have a bright future. Ms. Graves speaks very highly of you." He forced a smile as he studied me. "Did you think to read your speech to someone before today?"

"No, sir."

His eyes jumped to Ms. Graves.

"George, I assumed she would have shown it to someone—if not me, then a teacher. Or her parents. If I didn't think Alex was trustworthy, I wouldn't have chosen her." Her head rotated to me. Someone had to take the fall.

"I didn't show my speech to anyone," I said, "because I didn't see the need. Ms. Graves told me to be original. She said that the alumni always got the same speech every year."

Mr. Kincaid burrowed his eyes into me, but his words were intended for the headmistress. "We don't want to get too hung up on this, do we? A letter of apology will put out the fire just fine. You agree, Ms. Graves?"

"Of course," she said. "I'll write it. It will be out by end of the day. Alexandra will sign it."

Mr. Kincaid's eyes slid to Ms. Graves, but this time he was talking to me. "Does that plan sound all right with you, Alex?"

"A letter of apology?" I said. "For what?"

Mr. Kincaid cleared his throat, looking puzzled. "You just suggested that our alumni not give a dime to Valley Academy this year."

"Just for this year, sir. I think there're more-pressing causes we could donate to. I personally plan to give to the famine victims in Ethiopia."

"You're an idealistic young woman. I understand and respect that. But we live in the real world."

I thought for a moment. What was the real world exactly? Was George Kincaid's universe more real than mine? "I'm not going to sign an apology, sir."

Ms. Graves removed her glasses and polished the lenses with a special cloth pulled from her desk. "What you were doing this morning, Alexandra," she clarified, "was suggesting a course of action. It wasn't a mandate to the alumni. We'll make that clear in your letter."

"Actually, I was doing more than suggesting. I believe I was ex-horting." Exhort was a word I had fallen in love with. Its enunciation hinted at its meaning.

"You were only speaking for yourself, not for the school—you'll at least admit that in your letter." Mr. Kincaid's patience was beginning to thin.

Ms. Graves came to her feet, appraising me anew. "You should go to class, Alexandra. We'll catch up later."

A mere hour ago, I thought, I had been Valley's model student. Maybe now, with my insubordination, Ms. Graves was considering suspending me.

I spent the day avoiding talking to anyone about my speech, but public opinion was conveyed through sideways glances and stifled laughter. There were anonymous notes stuffed in my locker through the ventilation slits. "Hey, smart girl, why don't you blow me like you blew your speech!" "Some people know how to embarrass themselves—you know how to embarrass everyone." "Eat shit and die, Baten."

The headmistress never did catch up with me. When Mom picked us up at three, Toby left me the front seat. After ten seconds of small talk, Mom asked how my speech had gone. I was silent.

"You didn't hear already?" Toby said. "I thought it was on national news. Sis laid an egg. Ended up in Ms. Graves's office."

My mother gave the rear view mirror a "that's impossible" look.

"You know those ads in *Time* where little Haji is begging for food? Or some woman in the Himalayas is barefoot carrying a refrigerator on her back—"

"Shut up, Toby," I said.

"That's where Alex wanted the alumni to go. To visit little Haji and buy him a mansion."

I reached over the seat and grabbed my brother's nose, squeezing it hard.

"Shit!" he yelled, pushing me away.

"Alex, look at me, please. Is that what you really said? In front of the whole school?"

I was glad I hadn't allowed my mother to come. She was about to have a heart attack in the car. "I said our alumni should think of all the problems in the world, not just helping Valley Academy."

"And Ms. Graves—"

"She wants me to apologize. In writing. To the whole world."

"If that's what the headmistress wants, that's what you will do then."

"I'd rather not," I said.

"You'd rather not?" Her brow jumped half an inch. "Alex, you're an honors student!"

"What's that have to do with anything?"

But I knew. Mom was wondering if I had lost my mind. What would she tell her friends about my future now? I was supposed to be the golden child. It was as if I had drawn a winning lottery ticket and, for reasons known only to me, decided to tear it up.

Dinner that night wasn't as unbearable as I'd feared, not at first. Dad took the news of my heresy with the same shrug he used to greet Mom's frequent reports on Toby. Maybe both of his children were rebels, admittedly with different styles, but it was not necessarily a bad thing in his eyes. Maturity wasn't possible without going through rough patches.

"You stood up for your convictions, Alexandra," he concluded, rapping his knuckles twice on the table, a gesture of approval.

"But she used poor judgment."

"In your opinion, honey."

"Why are you taking her side, Louis? Alex should have known that the last thing you do is lecture the alumni. Isn't that common sense?"

Mom was acting as if I was some kind of suicide bomber who had just blown up her future and turned family dreams into a pile of rubble. Indifferently, Dad slathered his meatloaf with ketchup and dug in.

If I had come forth at that moment with a "You're right, Mom, I should have showed you my speech," or "I'll apologize to the whole school," our family argument would have ended. Forgiveness extended. Feelings of mortification smothered. It was in my hands. But that's not what I did. I chose silence.

"Well," Mom concluded, "I think Alex should be grounded for the weekend."

"I'm being punished!" I exclaimed. I hadn't shoplifted. I'd given a speech.

"It's not punishment so much as a time-out for you to reflect, Alex."

"Reflect on what?"

"Alex, you're fifteen. You may not believe this, but the next five or six years will be rough. Rebellion is a stage we all go through. There will be temptations, and you'll make mistakes, like today. You just don't want to do something you'll really regret."

What was the really part? Drugs? Pregnancy? Jumping off a bridge when a boyfriend jilted me? Mom didn't trust my judgment. She wasn't going to make the mistake Ms. Graves did. What was I supposed to think of Mom's judgment, skirting off into the magnolias with her secret lover? I rolled my eyes at her and left the table.

I surprised myself by what I wrote in my journal that night. I didn't lash out too much at Mom. In fact, I did exactly what she asked of me. I accepted my grounding as a chance to reflect on the big picture.

Why did I recklessly ride my bike across Cahuenga Boulevard? Why did I write that particular speech for the alumni? Why wouldn't I apologize? Why did a person go to McDonald's and always order a fish filet sandwich? Maybe you ordered it ninety-nine times in a row, but the hundredth time, you decide on a Big Mac. Something changes your mind. You can't always explain it.

I remembered what Ms. Graves had told me in her office on Monday, when we were still on good terms. *Faber est quisque fortunae suae.* As small or large as your destiny might be, you alone were its driver.

~20~

No matter what time I go to bed, I've always been an early riser—a 5 a.m. field mouse exploring not just smells and sounds but also my choices for the day ahead. After being grounded, eating breakfast alone as the light gathered at the bottom of the sky, I dove into my Latin assignment. Mr. Hornsby had given everyone Hans Ørberg's *Lingua Latina*, which helped set the stage for mastering a dead language. There were no short cuts. You had to commit to memory verb endings, noun cases, and declensions. The best way is to make lists and study them endlessly, Mr. Hornsby suggested. I wasn't to worry about speaking grammatically correct Latin; that would come in our second year. That's when I would see the beauty of a world that no longer existed, he promised. I liked him for the dream in his voice, for making me feel like the past was always relevant.

I didn't call Joyce until eleven because she slept in on weekends. We had declared ourselves best friends in fifth grade. Her parents, both medical doctors, had moved to Toluca Lake from a small city in Oregon. She had a pogo stick body that was nevertheless strong and athletic. She was smarter than I was, especially in math and science, but she didn't work as hard, and her grades weren't as good. That she didn't give two shits about grades meant we weren't overly competitive. I liked her sarcasm and melodrama, most of the time anyway.

"You're grounded? What the fuck?" she said. "We were going to see a movie."

"You've got other friends."

"Yeah, and they've all got plans. Way to go, Alex."

"I didn't know my mother was going to have a cow over my speech."

"A letter is going out not just to alumni but parents. Ms. Graves is apologizing for you." Joyce paused. "Anyway, that's what I heard."

"Apologize for me? She can't do that!"

"Really? Last I checked, God could do anything she wanted."

I listened as Joyce had a shouting exchange with her mother, and then her bedroom door slammed closed. "How long are you grounded?" she came back on the phone.

"The whole weekend."

"Want me to sneak over?"

"No."

"You're probably throwing a pity party. You put on your headphones and listen to Alison Krauss."

"She's better than David Bowie. He sings like someone is squeezing his balls," I offered.

My insult to Joyce's favorite rocker was too much for her. She mumbled how hopeless I was and hung up. Mom came in my room around eleven. I was brain-dead from Latin. In an unsettled voice, she announced she was taking Toby to Dr. Sheffield.

"On a Saturday?"

"She's making an exception for us. I told her it was urgent. I'm scared out of my mind. Half the time, Toby shuts himself in his room and won't come out. I'm afraid of what he's thinking."

I rolled my eyes. "Mom, he's not going to hurt himself. He's thinking how much he hates being in a cutthroat school. I told you, he doesn't belong at Valley."

"He doesn't even try with his assignments. I've gotten calls from his teachers. But I'm not giving up."

She promised to be home around five, dropping Toby at a mall video arcade for a few hours after his session. Dad, as usual, was at Lakeside, due back by six. Would I put the pot roast in the oven at four, boil some artichokes, and make a Caesar salad? Mom asked.

Alone in the house, I fixed myself a sandwich—with extra mayonnaise, something Mom, in her most subtle way, discouraged. She would never say I was overweight, or needed to be vigilant about my diet, but soon after I got my first period and my body began to change, her messages had become more insistent. So and so in my class had the perfect figure, or the dress I wore just two weeks ago suddenly looked snug on me, or Christie Brinkley—Mom's favorite model—was a knockout in a bikini, and wouldn't I like to wear one too? Mom still wore hers. Screw that, I thought, staring at the sandwich. I tripled my usual portion of mayo. I still couldn't believe what Ms. Graves was doing to me. She was a malevolent god, punishing me for speaking the truth.

I slipped into my one-piece bathing suit and drifted down to the dock. Freshly cut grass competed with the smell of my suntan lotion. Mom denied it, but I wondered if my skin being so pale made me look like a freak of nature. For whatever reason, it took me twice as long to get a tan as it did for Dad, Toby, or my mother. I sat on the edge of the dock and splashed my feet in the murky lake. When I stopped kicking, the water turned glassy, joining the rest of our community in its monolithic stillness. Even the ducks paddled about this morning without quacking. I tore at my crust and tossed pieces in the water. A pack of bluegills devoured them one at a time.

It was after two when I got dressed and pulled my bike from the garage. The sun felt like a sheet of linen across my face as I traveled down Valley Spring Lane. I didn't worry too much about disobeying Mom. The purpose of my grounding was self-reflection, I rationalized, and that could mean exploration of all kinds.

After I crossed Cahuenga, two towhead girls jumping rope on the sidewalk waved at me, as if they'd seen me on my first visit. A block down, a black man with curly hair soaped his car from an orange bucket that read "Sears—Where America Shops." When I reached Edward's house, there were no signs of life except the undulating, uncut grass and a pasture of dandelions spiking ever higher. The lemon trees had been picked clean. I walked my bike around the house until it was out of sight from the street.

"Edward?" I called after I knocked on the weathered front door. When there was no answer, I pounded harder with my fist. The third blow was the charm. The ill-fitting door sprang open a few inches.

"Anybody home?" I called through the opening.

There were no sounds inside. I slipped in and closed the door behind me. Technically, I was trespassing, but I excused myself because I wasn't exactly a stranger.

Stale air hit my nostrils. I took into account the closed windows and gnarly looking, wall-to-wall shag carpet—turquoise blue with an orange border. The only living room furniture was a plaid couch and a pair of worn upholstered chairs facing one another, ideal for someone putting up his feet to read. On the wall leading to the kitchen was a gold-framed drawing of some town. A dozen weight plates, with a bar and clamps to hold everything together, shared the other side of the room with baseball bats and gloves. There was no television or phone anywhere.

The kitchen was bizarre. Half of it was missing, everything but a stainless steel sink, a fridge, and a small portion of a Formica counter—like a chain saw had cleaved the thing in two. Someone had also removed the upper cabinets and the stove. A two-burner hot plate, Mr. Coffee, and a boxy microwave were the replacements. The few dishes on the counter had been washed. There was no garbage anywhere. In the fridge I found fresh milk, orange juice, cans of soda, and some apples, asparagus, and cauliflower.

I pulled two quarters from my pocket and plunked them by the dishes. A yellow Post-it pad and pen were nearby.

Edward, I wanted to pay you back for the lemonade
at full retail!

I hoped he found it funny. Then I added an apology for barging in uninvited, underlining the word "sorry."

Something moved behind me. Before I could turn, a blur of orange leaped onto the counter, startling me. The large house cat and I studied each other for a moment, then I let her smell my outstretched hand. When I scratched under her chin, the tabby turned her motor on. Her tail began switching like a metronome.

"Where did you come from, kitty? What's your name?"

Like my personal guide, she jumped to the floor and led me into a small room. The bed was covered by a powder blue spread, adjoined by an oval table with a gooseneck reading lamp, a half-dozen paperbacks, and a radio. Across the room was a large desk—scratched up metal office furniture—piled high with textbooks, a portable Smith-Corona typewriter, and manila folders. A throw rug warmed the beatup tongue-and-groove floor. The bathroom was spotless except for a trail of rust tears under the tub and sink faucets.

I went back to the paperbacks on the bedside table: Camus, Dostoyevsky, Bellow, Greene, Baldwin, Updike. I had heard of some of them. Dropping on the bed, I read the first three pages of *Rabbit, Run*.

I couldn't help myself from looking around. In the table drawer, I found the letter from Princeton that Edward had described. There were comments about his insightful admissions essay, and a reference to his SAT scores, 770 in math and 750 in English—almost dead perfect. I found a second letter, dated a year earlier, from an Atlanta Braves scout who wanted to interview him. He hadn't bullshitted me one ounce.

Toward the bottom of the stack, underneath unopened utility bills, was a photocopy of a California driver's license and social security card, along with a passport issued in 1982. A birth certificate stated that Edward Montgomery was born Dec 1, 1968, in New York City. He'd be nineteen in a few months, I calculated, which was old for high school. Had he dropped out for a year to earn money, or maybe traveled somewhere? I checked the passport. It hadn't a single stamp inside.

In Edward's closet were several pair of pants, mostly khakis and jeans, a few dress shirts, some T's, a blue blazer, a pair of slacks, and a tie. There were Nike sneakers, some baseball shoes with cleats, and a pair of dress shoes. An inexpensive calendar was tacked to the inside of the door, opened to September, showing a gold sunset over a pristine lake. The caption said Lake Louise, Alberta, Canada. I looked at the earlier months. Each day had been crossed out with a black line, like some kind of countdown.

In the living room, my eyes jumped back to the gold-framed color drawing. The storefronts were highly realistic. Elite Dress Shop. Hoover Drug Store. Fraker & Sons Garage and Service Station. The people on the street were white, black, and brown. The artist's name, in blue ink, had been all but rubbed off.

~21~

I waited on the couch for fifteen or twenty minutes before Edward floated past the bay window. He was walking his bike, an old-fashioned, fat-tired Schwinn with a basket between the handlebars. He whistled contentedly as he entered the house, pushing his bike ahead of him. When his eyes landed on me, time seemed to stop.

"White as a sheet" can't technically apply to a black person, but staring at Edward, that's what I thought. Back from baseball practice, I assumed, he was in shorts and a V-neck shirt with cut-off sleeves. North Hollywood High Huskies was blazoned across the front. I had the same fantasy as on my first visit, Edward smashing a ball out of the park, or blowing a fastball by a batter. Yet, in another sense, he looked anything but powerful. He was in too much shock to find any words. The ebullient, confident man I'd met selling lemonade was missing.

I thought of spilling the truth, that I had come to pay for the lemonade, but that suddenly seemed an inadequate excuse for a break-in. Or to give him the deeper truth, that I wanted to get to know someone older and smarter than me—that might sound even crazier.

I rose self-consciously from the couch. "Hi, Edward. The door wasn't locked. Sorry if I startled you."

It took him a moment to respond. "You just barged in?"

"The door wasn't locked," I said lamely.

"There's a lock. It's just broken." His eyes jumped around the room to see if I had disturbed anything. "I don't get many visitors."

He added, "Your parents know you're here?"

"What difference does that make?"

"I get this feeling you do a lot of things without telling your parents. How old are you?"

"Fifteen," I said with a certain pride.

"You came over this afternoon just because you felt like it?"

"I owed you fifty cents. It's in the kitchen. Or don't you remember?"

He steered his bike toward the barbells and weights, balancing the frame against the wall. "I remember. I think you should leave now, Alexandra."

I was happy he remembered my name. I started toward the door, when he said, "You've got something of mine?"

I looked at him, puzzled, and then I glanced down. *Rabbit, Run* was clutched in my hand.

I put the book on the couch. I told him I didn't realize I had it. "You don't think I'm a thief, do you?"

"Ha! Why would a thief come here? Not like there's a Van Gogh on the wall. No thief would take a book." His tone had softened. "You can borrow it, if you want."

"Really? Okay, I will. And I'll return it right away."

Edward's eyes were poring over his living room again, more from embarrassment than suspicion. "Place is a mess," he apologized. But for a house suffering from a half-torn-out kitchen, Salvation Army furniture, dents in the walls, and cracks in the stucco and windows, it was as tidy as it could be. Nothing warranted an apology as far as I was concerned.

When the tabby reappeared, Edward picked her up like a small child, one arm supporting her butt and the other wrapped around her chest. She looked happy to be held.

"What's her name?" I said.

"Monster. She eats every meal like it's her last."

"My mother doesn't let my brother and me have a pet bigger than a hamster. Too messy, she says." I took it upon myself to drop back on the couch. "You sure it's okay if I borrow your book? I've never read anything by John Updike."

Edward laid the cat on the carpet and moved a chair to sit across from me. A second later he jumped up as if he suddenly thought he should be a better host. He returned from the kitchen with a Coke for each of us.

"Thanks for the quarters," he said, giving me a quick stab of a smile.

"Sure. How did baseball practice go?"

"Is that what's really on your mind?"

I shrugged. "I don't know."

"Ask me what you really want to ask," he came to the point. "If I don't answer, I don't answer. You had a good look around, I'm guessing."

I nodded. "What happened to your parents?"

If Edward had had a talent for hiding his feelings, he would have used it. Instead, his eyes slipped away, as if there was a flotilla of ships sailing through his memory, ready to drown him in their wake.

"It's okay if you don't want to tell me anything. Honestly, I don't mean to pry. I had this crazy idea we might become friends."

"Friends. You and me?" There was astonishment in his voice. "I've got plenty of friends at school."

"I'm sure. I get it, sports and academic star." I cleared my throat. "I just thought I'd ask. You said you don't get many visitors."

"I like my privacy."

"So you're not going to tell me about your parents?"

"I like my privacy," he repeated. "No parents, no brothers or sisters. Just my books."

I got to my feet, before I wore out my welcome.

"So I guess I shouldn't worry about you," I couldn't help tossing in.

"Me?" he laughed. A gleam of confidence sprang into his eyes. "You've read *Tom Sawyer* and *Huckleberry Finn*, haven't you? Well, I'm Huck Finn. I always get by."

"Well, thanks for the Updike book. I'll be going."

"You said you wanted to be friends. What did you want to tell me?"

My brow shot up in surprise. "What do I want to tell you?" I suddenly had no idea. My mind had gone blank.

"Friendship is a two-way street. Or is everything private for you too?"

I dropped on the couch again, happy to be given a second chance. I started with yesterday's Founder's Day speech and the big stink it caused, which had surprised and hurt me, I admitted. Edward clapped, and smiled again.

"You're a master of your universe," he declared.

"Whatever that means. Almost everyone thought I was an idiot. I was afraid I'd get kicked out of school."

"You have ideals. I like that. You know the writer James Baldwin?"
I said I didn't.

"He's one of my favorites. And here's my favorite quote of his: 'You think your pain and your heartbreak are unprecedented in the history of the world, but then you read. It was books that taught me that the things that tormented me most were the very things that connected me with all the people who were alive, or who had ever been alive.'"

Edward went on about Baldwin. I quickly learned about a black, gay, chronically broke author whose honesty and need to write sustained him against poverty and discrimination.

"I guess he never lived in Toluca Lake," I quipped. "Just as well. He would have been bored to tears like me."

"I wouldn't know. I've never been there either."

"You haven't even seen the lake, Edward? That's the one cool thing." I added, "My dad calls Toluca Lake 'God's Country.'"

"God's Country," he repeated, like someone taking notes. "A river shall run through it. Maybe that's your lake, metaphorically speaking."

"What are you talking about?"

"The *Book of Genesis* says 'And the Lord God planted a garden in Eden, in the east, and there he put the man whom he had formed. And out of the ground the Lord God made to spring up every tree that is pleasant to the sight and good for food. The tree of life was in the midst of the garden, and the tree of the knowledge of good and evil. A river flowed out of Eden to water the garden . . . .'"

I wasn't shocked that someone so well read could quote from the Bible, but Edward spoke in a tone that made me think he also went to church regularly.

"My parents think we're the luckiest people in the world to live where we do."

"You have a nice house, do you?"

"Yes."

"Nicer than mine?"

He chuckled. I laughed too. Sometimes things just click, out of the blue. I continued to sit there, describing not just our English Tudor overlooking the lake but also my ambitious, socialite mother, my struggling brother, and my hard-working, criminal defense attorney father. Our annual Cecil B. DeMille parties got special mention.

An Evening on the Nile had been our most lavish effort yet, I said. Every year, Mom clipped newspaper articles from the society pages and taped them into a scrapbook. I rambled on about Lakeside, our all-white, no-Jewish-members-admitted golf club which, like the community itself, was full of self-regard.

I had no idea what Edward was thinking when I described my life. Did he think I was a spoiled nerd? All I did was study. I'd been a klutz playing the violin, was average in sports, and if looks were a report card, I added, I'd be lucky to get a "B."

"What's that supposed to mean? You have pretty eyes, Alexandra. And a terrific smile when you're not brooding."

"Me? Brood?"

"Takes one to know one."

He wasn't flirting, though part of me wished he would. When I glanced at my watch, I almost panicked. Mom and Toby were due back.

"Thanks for the company. Maybe you can come over to my house some time," I said after he walked me quickly to the corner and I jumped on my bike.

He was suddenly gazing through the blur of Cahuenga traffic to the calm corridors of Toluca Lake as if seeing something that I didn't.

"You take care, Alex."

"As soon as I finish *Rabbit, Run*, I'll be back."

His eyes swept over me. "Maybe that's not such a good idea. You can keep the book."

"What are you talking about? I thought we were going to be friends."

"I'm not sure your parents would approve of where I live. It's our little secret, okay?"

"Okay. Our secret. But I don't care what they think. Good-bye," I said as I started to pedal away.

"Bye now."

I was home in less than ten minutes. When Mom and Toby finally walked in, they were talking about my brother's session with Dr. Sheffield. Toby seemed as diffident as ever. I caught Mom frowning as she peeked in the oven.

"Alex, when did the roast go in?"

I apologized for getting a late start on dinner. Latin verb declensions had gotten the best of me, I lied. In the end, my lateness didn't matter.

Dad wasn't home until after seven. He fixed himself his favorite single-malt Scotch and drifted into the study until the food was ready.

That night before climbing into bed, I jotted a thought in my journal.

> *September 10*
> *I think I figured out Edward's housing situation. My*
> *father mentioned the rash of foreclosures around the*
> *country, people losing their homes due to bad S&L*
> *loans. Lots of homeowners were walking away from*
> *their mortgages but not before venting their anger.*
> *How else did Edward end up with half a kitchen?*

Mom came in to kiss me good night. I was immersed in *Rabbit, Run*. It took her a minute to get around to what was on her mind. She would terminate my grounding early, she bargained, if I would take Toby to the club tomorrow and just hang by the pool.

"He can't find someone else? I have a history paper due Monday."

"You know how hard it is for Toby to make friends."

I did know. The "loner" label was a death sentence at Valley. Toby was already getting bullied.

"You can make a difference," my mother said. "You may not know it, but your brother looks up to you."

I found that hard to believe, but Mom seemed desperate. I said okay, as if I could solve any problem in the world.

"Thank you, Alex."

In the soft light of my room, my mother's eyes shined with hope. I'm sure she was thinking that tomorrow might be the start, once again, of turning Toby's life around.

I went back to "Rabbit" Angstrom. Besides Updike, I was already thinking of what Edward and I would talk about when I returned to his house. How had he become homeless? Were his parents still in Brooklyn? What other secrets did he have? For the first time, I thought, my life had turned really interesting.

~22~

I must have been four or five when I first became aware of Charlie Diggs. He always seemed to be hanging around with Dad. At our house, he would smile and say hi to me, and I would stay hi back. There was no deeper connection. I would eventually learn that he was a successful commercial architect who owned his own firm; a not particularly handsome but very charming and somewhat intense man; a gifted athlete in a number of sports; and someone, like my father, who made friends easily. He was also a stylish dresser, confident, and competitive—traits not dissimilar to Dad's. The two not only had enough respect for each other not to be rivals, they also ended up best friends. They even looked similar with their deep foreheads and strong jaws.

The two graduated from the same class at Reseda High School and promptly enrolled at USC, where they pledged Delta Upsilon. They partied, double-dated, and took up golf together. Later, Charlie introduced my father to duck hunting. There was something about sitting in a duck blind in freezing temperatures, waiting for the sun to clamber into the pale sky, that built camaraderie, Dad insisted.

My father and Charlie were best men at each other's wedding. First, Dad and Mom tied the knot—July 20, 1969, by coincidence the day Neil Armstrong stepped on the moon. Two years later, Charlie and Julia took their vows after meeting at an Arthur Murray Dance Studio, teaming up as strangers to win a competition. The two couples were inseparable before I was born: dinner and movie dates, weekend getaways to San Diego, and one summer the four vacationed in Acapulco. Julia—a petit woman with a sunburst smile and an eager, pleasing laugh—never got into public arguments with her husband, but if you watched their body language, you felt a chasm between them. Except for the moments they were Fred Astaire and Ginger Rogers, Charlie was so far above Julia in elegance and confidence that I came to think of her as a barnacle clinging to the hull of a stately yacht. Dad agreed. He said Charlie and Julia were like a person wearing brown shoes with blue socks. Mom felt superior to Julia as well, but she still considered her a close friend. As couples went, despite the differences, the Batens and Diggses were best friends.

I didn't think much about that closeness until the week after my Founder's Day speech. After picking us up at school, Mom dropped my brother at Dr. Sheffield's and dashed home with me. The housekeeper had called in sick. Mom hurried to put in a load of wash and organize dinner. Her focus was usually like a laser beam, but on this afternoon, there were perhaps too many details to keep track of. Mom spaced out that I was in the house. When I picked up the kitchen phone to call Joyce, I overheard her talking from her bedroom extension.

"No, no, you're not listening," the man said in an upset voice.

"I am listening," my mother insisted.

"She nags me, day and night, about her biological clock."

"I thought you two agreed you weren't having children."

"We did agree. Isn't that the point? She doesn't even realize when she changes her mind."

"Julia is my age. She's too old now, or almost," my mother confirmed.

I practically dropped the phone. Mom was talking to Charlie Diggs!

"That's why she's panicking," he said.

"I'm sorry she makes you miserable."

"Why can't she be more like you, Gloria? You've always understood me. You know, I'm not out to make trouble. I just want to be happy. Don't you too?"

"Of course," she said, catching her breath.

"Louis doesn't know how lucky he is," Charlie added. "Jesus, what you have to go through with him. He should treat you better, Gloria."

"I know," she said.

"Does he know how much I love you? Why can't you get up the courage and tell him?"

I wavered between repulsion and fascination as Charlie continued. Julia was drinking too much, getting short with her friends, and making a drama out of the smallest thing. Couldn't Gloria see that? (Yes, Mom said, she could). It got damn lonely being married to a woman who was so oblivious to his needs that he might as well be single again. He was thinking a lot about divorce again. In fact, he'd been talking to a divorce attorney. He couldn't keep living this way.

"Oh, Charlie, poor Charlie," my mother responded whenever his voice fell silent.

Oh Charlie, poor Charlie, I mimicked silently. Moonstruck by my mother's personality and beauty, bathing in the soothing waters of her sympathy, you were a lucky man, indeed, when Gloria Baten flirted with you, let alone had emotions for you.

"Can we go someplace to talk?" Charlie finally asked.

"Of course," my mother answered.

When he named a rendezvous spot for the weekend—the lobby of a small hotel in West Hollywood—I clicked off. Mom was still on the phone when I burst into her room. She knew instantly that I'd heard everything. Charlie was still talking as she hung up.

"Mom, what are you doing! What's going on!" My face was hot and cold at the same time.

All she could do was stare back helplessly, like a ghost haunting her own life.

"Don't lie," I said. "Have you been having an affair with Charlie?"

"No, of course not." Her voice was subdued but it didn't shake. Her gaze didn't waver.

"Don't you love Dad?" I demanded.

"Yes, of course I do, sweetie."

"Then what's wrong with you? You acted like lovers on the phone. Charlie is Dad's best friend. And you're friends with Julia."

"I'm really sorry, honey."

"Sorry? That's it? Sorry for what?"

"I shouldn't have taken Charlie's call. He's just lonely. It was all innocent."

"You took his call? I didn't hear the phone ring, Mom."

"I meant, I shouldn't have called him back."

"How often does he call?"

"I don't keep track. The calls don't mean anything to me. This is just how men behave. They're babies. One day you'll understand. They like to be pampered. Look at your father—"

"But you're married to Dad. You and Charlie slipped off into the magnolia grove at the party. I watched you. I'm supposed to believe that was innocent?"

"We kissed. That's all."

"For two minutes," I pointed out.

The phone began ringing again. When I went to grab it, Mom laid her hand over the receiver, like a bomb that would explode if I picked it up. It seemed forever before the ringing stopped.

"Promise me you'll never talk to Charlie again," I said. "I mean never. Next time you see him, tell him your friendship is over. And if you dare show up at that hotel lobby—"

There was no cover from my flailing words. Mom took the blows like the punishment she deserved. Her body seemed to shrink. I felt great power over her. Until she spoke again.

"All right. I promise. But you have to promise me something too, Alex. You'll never tell your father about this."

"Are you insane? I'm not going to promise that."

She knew I felt great loyalty to Dad. He had a natural, easygoing authority that I willingly followed. Unlike Mom, he didn't judge me. "I can't promise that," I repeated as Mom stayed silent.

"He wouldn't understand, Alex."

"That's not my fault."

"You'd only end up hurting him, and our marriage. You're right, I should never have agreed to meet Charlie. It was bad judgment. It won't happen again. You have my word."

Mom collapsed her hands over her face and began to cry, as if she wanted to be consoled. I felt sorry for her, but I didn't feel like wrapping my arms around her in forgiveness.

"I'll think about it," I said, and left the bedroom.

That night, my father was oblivious to any disturbance in the universe. The dangerous afternoon that I had lived through got shoved aside by family routine. My mother served Dad a thick slab of prime rib, and we sat around the table to hear about his day. He was like the color commentator at a football game, describing how he'd won an acquittal for his client.

The name Charlie Diggs came up only once. This Friday, Charlie, Dad, and their friends would be caravanning to a private, two-thousand-acre waterfowl preserve near San Diego. Charlie had suggested the trip weeks ago, Dad said. There'd be ten altogether. I was confused. How could Charlie beg my mother for a secret rendezvous and at the same time be planning an outing with my father? Then I figured it out, I hoped. Mom had already called Charlie and broken up with him.

Toby and I cleared the table and put the dishes in the dishwasher. From the living room, I could hear my father falling into one of his romantic moods, sighing, whispering to my mother as they dropped onto the sofa. A minute later, the stereo came alive with the Beatles' *Rubber Soul* album. Dad's favorite song was "Norwegian Wood." He could slow dance to it, and John Lennon's lyrical voice was like a snake charmer's flute.

As I watched my parents begin dancing in their stocking feet, I remembered how Lennon had been shot to death some years earlier as he and Yoko entered their residence at The Dakota in New York City. He had been killed by a wackadoodle named Mark David Chapman, whom Dad said he would never defend, even if he were the last criminal defense attorney in the world. There were some acts of evil that my father would not countenance, despite what a district attorney might claim.

I kept spying on my parents from the kitchen. Dad was smooching Mom's neck, moving unselfconsciously from her shoulder to her ear. The mystery of passion caught my attention for its unpredictable timing. My parents danced for over an hour that evening, until I began to think the alarm bells that had gone off in me earlier were false. I didn't need to say anything to my father. My parents were in love. Not even one of Toby's comic book superheroes could break that bond.

-23-

Friday afternoon, after Mom had picked me up from school, two station wagons arrived in front of our house. I peeked out the front door. It was hard to make out the faces clearly. The driver in the second car pressed on his horn.

"Come on, Louis, get a move on!" he shouted through his open window. I spotted two golden retrievers in the cargo bay of the first car.

My father had been preparing for the weekend since coming home early from work. Duck hunting was no small deal. Shooting the birds was one thing, plucking, dressing, and preserving them in ice chests another. You needed several changes of clothes in case you got wet, which seemed always to happen, and a lot of provisions, including food and booze. Half of Dad's gear was already stashed outside the door.

My father kissed us goodbye, bending toward each of us awkwardly, as his autoloader was cradled in the crook of his elbow. It was a 12-gauge Remington 870 with a 26-inch barrel, which was long, but the discharge was easier on the ears than from a shorter barrel. The autoloader also had a more-gentle recoil on the shoulder than a standard break-action gun, and a 12-gauge was lighter than a 10-gauge. Like most duck hunters, he used bismuth or tungsten shells because they were nontoxic and you wouldn't contaminate the duck's meat. I was far from an expert, but Dad had let me peer into his gun safe—a three-by-five-foot steel fortress tucked into its own hallway closet downstairs. Inside were a couple of shotguns, several pistols that he occasionally took to a firing range, and a Weatherby

Mag for hunting deer or moose. Like learning to play poker, guns were part of my home schooling. But one day, when he asked if I wanted to join him at the shooting range, I said no. Guns made me uneasy, and the idea of hunting ducks, or anything that was alive, was a turnoff.

I followed Dad outside to the second car, lugging an ice chest in my hands, half-smiling at the men, all of whom I knew from either our summer parties or Dad's poker games. I counted nine, including Dad.

"Where's Charlie?" I asked my father.

"He just called. Came down with food poisoning at lunch."

Dad gave me a mock military salute, as if he was going off to war, and levered himself into the car. The caravan peeled away, a weekend of male camaraderie waiting to happen. In the kitchen, I found Mom doing housewifey things. I was sure she already knew about Charlie from one source or another. Could he actually have food poisoning? Mom gave no hint of having the same anxiety that was bubbling in my stomach. After she picked up Toby from Dr. Sheffield's that afternoon, the three of us had a quiet dinner.

Saturday morning, as usual, I was up early. By the time my mother got to the kitchen, I'd fixed her and Toby eggs and bacon.

"Wow, great eggs. Thank you, honey." Already dressed, Mom sat across from me looking ready for a photo shoot. Not a hair out of place, her blue mascara darkening her eyelashes with perfection. She asked about my plans.

"Homework this morning with Joyce. We're going to the mall after lunch. What are you doing?"

Toby had run upstairs to get dressed. He had an all-day field trip to the Los Angeles County Museum of Art. After she dropped him off at school, Mom said, she was obligated to a tennis round-robin and a couple of hours at the public library, where she sometimes worked as a volunteer. She would pick up Toby after his museum trip and be home by five.

"Did you call Charlie and tell him everything was off?" I interrupted.

She squirmed in her chair, as if she'd been expecting my question. "Yes, I did." She emphasized each syllable, annoyed by my lack of trust.

"You swear?"

"Come on, Alex—"

"When did you call him?"

"Last night. After Dad was asleep."

"Who told you he had food poisoning?"

"Your father mentioned it."

"It feels really shitty that you and I are sharing this secret," I said.

"It's over now, honey. Please stop harping on it."

"I hate Charlie Diggs," I volunteered before we heard Toby clomping down the stairs. He was already complaining about the field trip—that it was wrong, even unlawful, to force a school activity on a student on a weekend. He said he was thinking of hiring Dad as his attorney.

"Are you ready?" Mom said to him. "It won't be so bad."

"Yeah. Right." Toby's eyes peeled away, like acts of torture were up to interpretation.

I was glad he was ignorant about Charlie. If he knew, I thought, he'd wig out big time.

When Joyce came over, we studied for a geometry test, and later her mother drove us to the Beverly Center to join a million other teen-age mall rats. Our primary mission was to have manicures. Afterward, we shopped for nail polish and eyeliner. I blew my allowance on scads of makeup I'd never tried before. My mood wavered between excitement over creating a new look for myself and wondering about Mom. Despite what she'd told me about Charlie, I wondered if she could give up the relationship so quickly.

When she arrived home with Toby, my brother was in good spirits. At dinner, he described what he'd seen at LACMA—Kandinsky, Monet, Picasso, and Matisse, among others—and said he wouldn't mind going back. Mom sprinkled in small talk whenever the conversation lulled. I mentioned creating a new look for myself, said I'd spent over a hundred bucks on makeup. Mom didn't raise an objection. Weird, I thought, because she was always weighing in on my appearance.

The lake and our pool were pelted with rain that night and into Sunday morning. I wondered how Dad was doing in the icy waters of a duck blind, deepening his friendships. I stayed in bed half the morning reading *Rabbit, Run*. Mom knocked on my door and asked if I would help Toby with his homework. My mouth opened in disbelief.

"Seriously?" I said.

"Just get him started on his Civil War paper."

"I'm busy. You should get him a tutor. Full time, if you insist he stay at Valley."

"Then everyone in the neighborhood would talk."

"About a tutor? So what? Let them talk."

Then I asked what she did yesterday.

"Oh, you care about that, more than you do your brother?" she said. "I didn't see Charlie, if that's what you're insinuating."

"You swear?"

"Alex, you don't have to keep making a federal case out of this."

Mom took an exaggerated breath, then turned and walked away. I didn't believe her. I felt like screaming, or getting on my bike and visiting Edward, or moving in with Joyce for a month or two. Yet half an hour later, I was in my brother's room, reading to him about Lee surrendering to Grant at Appomattox.

When Dad returned from his hunting trip late that afternoon, I greeted him with a hug, like he'd been gone way too long. Over dinner, he reported that his gang had bagged a hundred thirteen ducks, thanks to the Goldens who swam through cold, scummy water to bring in the booty. Dad's personal haul was twenty-seven, more than anyone else, though one or two kills were amicably disputed because the fowl were struck by more than one shotgun burst. Plucking feathers and scooping out innards occupied their afternoons, along with plenty of alcohol, no doubt. The men cooked dinner over a campfire and told endless stories.

Dad briefly instructed us all on the art of "aiming in anticipation." A bird came into your field of vision, he said, and you subjectively calculated its speed, the impact of the wind if any, the distance between you and your target, the trajectory and speed of your shell, and then . . . .

"Boom!" he said, his arms imitating a rifle and his index finger pulling the trigger.

The only emotion I felt was pity for the ducks.

"Can we talk about something else, Louis?" Mom asked.

"Why?"

"Because the rest of us have lives too. Toby went on an art field trip while you were gone."

"I know, Gloria." My father turned to Toby. "Tell me everything, son." Toby rattled off the names of more artists that he liked. Mom only half listened, no doubt thinking how hard it was to get a word in when Dad took center stage, which was virtually every night. Her irritation nibbled at her like termites inside the beams of a house. No matter how good a mother or wife she was, how well she ran the house, or how famous her parties, it was my father who usually got the limelight. Charlie Diggs was her sanctuary.

After dinner, I had a visit with Dad. His study was lined with bookshelves on three sides. He was a devoted fan of crime and espionage fiction, history, political science, biographies, travelogues, and even pedantic tomes on psychology, no doubt useful as he argued before a jury. The fourth side had an expansive view of our front lawn lit up at night, and immaculate rows of bedding plants closer to his study.

"What are you up to, Dad?" I sidled up to his antique mahogany desk. He was scribbling on a writing pad.

"Getting ready for a trial." He looked at me over the glasses hovering on the point of his nose.

"Well, you'll win. No one can hold a candle to you in a courtroom."

He smiled. "How's school? The whole flap over your Founder's Day speech, that's faded, hasn't it?"

"Pretty much." I didn't add that my ghostwritten apology would always bother me, and what had really faded was the die-hard loyalty I once felt for Valley.

I stuck around, admiring the lines of the ancient bronze lion on his desk.

"Something on your mind?" he asked.

"Oh, I don't know. Are you okay?"

"You mean my health?"

His asthma inhaler, a small device in a green casing with a canister of Albuterol inside, always sat on the corner of his desk. He kept another in his car. He didn't need Albuterol often, but asthma attacks could be unpredictable.

"I mean in general. You and Mom, are you pretty happy?"

"Things are fine, sweetie. Never better. Why do you ask?"

"I don't know," I said. "I love you." And I kissed him on the cheek.

September 16
*Alex, what a wimp you are. Why can't you tell Dad
about Charlie? Just because Mom asked me not to
doesn't mean I can't do it. Then again, how can my
father be so clueless? A smart attorney who seems to
know everything can't tell which way the wind is
blowing? Is it just arrogance? I would bet anything
that Mom is lying about Charlie being out of the
picture. If I ran the six blocks to the Diggses' house
right now, I'd probably find him reading a love letter
from Mom. Don't ask me how I know. I can just feel
my mother inside me, stirring around, scheming,
wanting freedom from Dad, just like I was once
inside her, fifteen years ago, wanting my freedom.
I think that's what most women want down deep,
just as much as they want a relationship.*

    *But I have a bigger question about Mom. How
should I feel about her? A parent who betrays her
daughter's trust, what loyalty do I possibly owe her?*

Jaleel

~24~

After saying good-bye to Alex, Jaleel walked the familiar half-mile to a hole-in-the-wall taco stand. It sat on the corner of Cahuenga and Riverside, offering a $3.95 all-you-can-eat rice, beans, and taco plate but only on Saturdays between two and six. Bob's Big Boy and the International House of Pancakes offered better fare, but they were beyond Jaleel's budget.

The amiable owner seemed to have been expecting Jaleel when he strolled in. "Edward, you've got a bottomless stomach. I should ban you on Saturday afternoons, before I go broke!"

Jaleel returned the wave—five vertical fingers spread as wide as possible, his hand shoulder height. "Javier, your food is so bad, who else is going to eat it?" They laughed together.

He filled his plate and sat at a table near the window. Two young mothers, smiling conspiratorially about something, pushed their strollers along the sidewalk. He envied how carefree they were. His last encounter with Alex kept weighing on him. He'd never met anyone so persistently curious—or just plain nosey. Who breaks into a house to leave two quarters for a cup of lemonade? Even more surprising was that he had allowed her to stay. He'd encouraged it. Something about Alex had gotten under his skin. He knew her well enough to predict she would be back. An underage white girl in a black man's home—a squatter at that—was worse than dumb. Dirick would say it was suicidal. Don't go looking for trouble, the Samaritan had warned. Turn your back on temptation. Stay out of peril.

He felt on edge at the moment but not exactly in peril. Nothing consequential had happened with Alex, just an innocent discussion about politics, books, sports, and school. He had listened with interest to her stories, and said goodbye to her on the street. He liked Alex because she was bright and idealistic, and she was sympathetic to him. A baseball star and Princeton-bound senior usually got more envy than sympathy. Unlike everyone at school, Alex had picked up on his loneliness right away.

He had said goodbye to Dirick in Kingman six years ago. God had been looking over his shoulder, he liked to think, as he drifted from a housing project in San Diego to living briefly on the street to a cheap apartment in Burbank and finally migrating to North Hollywood, where he stumbled on an abandoned, foreclosed house which the bank seemed to have no interest in reclaiming. He was always afraid someone would come and kick him out, but he'd been there for three years. He needed his luck to hold just a little longer.

At school, no one knew much about Edward Montgomery's personal life, other than that he was born in Brooklyn, an only child, and lived with his hard-working parents. It was a slightly different story than Dirick had originally concocted for him, but the key to adaptation and survival was improvisation. His demeanor at school—friendly but not too friendly—came with a deflecting sense of humor. He made everyone aware that he had a weekend job, and when he wasn't working, he studied like a fiend. Occasionally, he found his way to a weekend party, just so he would fit in. Because he was an academic whiz, teachers didn't insist on parent conferences. His baseball coach didn't either, as much as he liked bragging on Jaleel. Girls flirted, but interracial dating wasn't common, and the few black girls in his class, while some were pretty, didn't appeal to him.

He found it miraculous how easily he flew under the radar, though there'd been some uncomfortable moments. The high school registrar made him fill out paperwork that he'd peppered with lies. On his Princeton application, he'd faked his parents' signatures on a bogus financial statement that let him qualify for a scholarship. Sometimes people in the street gave him long, strange looks, as if someone of his size and race might belong to a gang. When he got his driver's license, he was relieved that fingerprinting wasn't required.

He'd gotten only one letter from Dirick, mailed to the P.O. box that Jaleel had sent him. Randy had passed away, without too much suffering, Dirick wrote. The Samaritan had paid for his hospice care. The AIDS epidemic was gripping the world, and Dirick was trying to raise awareness that it wasn't just a homosexual or drug user's problem. His ragtag band of apostles continued to pass out his mimeographed sheets. Jaleel wouldn't have minded receiving more letters, but he knew the man who had saved his life was busy trying to save lots of others.

He went back to the serving bar for more tacos, ate until full, and pulled a five dollar bill from his wallet as he approached the cashier. He had never opened a checking account or applied for a credit card. Utility bills were paid with money orders. His mail went to a post office box in North Hollywood. Until Alex showed up, he'd never had a visitor at his house. Neighbors knew he was a squatter, but they minded their own business, as if they had their own problems to deal with.

When he returned home, Jaleel found his bedside table drawer ajar. He had no secrets there, so why should he worry about what Alex might have found? He had tried to deflect her questions in the living room, yet he hadn't kicked her out. Part of him liked having her around. He envied her for having a family. Valley Academy and Lakeside Golf Club were less to his liking. The school sounded snobby, the club racist, and Toluca Lake a combination of both.

Still, he tried to imagine Alex living in a mansion with a pool and an actual lake below. She and her brother had their own rowboat—how cool was that! The parties their parents hosted sounded like they were out of *The Great Gatsby*. If anyone had a choice between living in Peartree or Toluca Lake, only a moron would choose a patch of dirt in Texas. But Eden was a dangerous place, he thought. He would never risk stepping into Alex's house, or meeting her parents. They shouldn't know he existed. When he saw Alex again, maybe the safest thing for both was to end their relationship. He had to keep his nose clean. He couldn't wait until he left for Princeton. A calendar pinned inside his closet door kept track of the days.

~25~

The next Monday, the *Los Angeles Times* predicted freakish weather for most of the city. Unseasonable rains were expected to continue all week, courtesy of a typhoon that had struck Japan like an uppercut. The storm clawed at houses and fishing boats on the outer islands, killing forty-three people before charging across the Pacific. The immediate consequence for Jaleel was no baseball practice. He showed up Monday, Tuesday, and Wednesday, but the coach canceled the workout as soon as the rain came. On Thursday, water fell in sheets all afternoon.

Autumn was football season, but Jaleel and other top players stuck with baseball workouts year-round. The Huskies were favored to win a league title in the spring, maybe even a city championship. High school sports writers always mentioned the pitching and hitting of Edward Montgomery. It wasn't just his reputation that motivated him. Nothing drove him more than the desire to work harder than anyone else. People spoke endlessly about the American Dream, as if it was something they were entitled to, like owning a house or landing a great job. Jaleel knew better: You just worked your ass off and hoped for a few breaks.

He negotiated the twelve miles back home through pelting rain. His backpack jiggled and flopped against his back when he couldn't dodge a pothole or his wheels brushed a curb. Wearing only a windbreaker, he was drenched as he reached his house. He spotted a fancy racing bike hidden behind bushes. He had known Alex would return, but so soon? He reminded himself again that he needed to end the friendship before the roots went deeper.

"Hey there," he said as he opened the door without quite focusing on Alex. She was standing next to his raggedy couch, arms dangling at her sides, her hair and face shiny from the rain. The Updike novel was in one hand. Her face was full of shadows. When she saw Jaleel, she laid the book on his chair as thoughtfully as she'd returned the two quarters on the kitchen counter.

"Would you like a towel, dry off?" he asked.

"I'm okay. Thanks."

"How are you?" he said, studying her more carefully.

"Okay."

"You upset about something?"

"I guess you could say that." She rubbed one eye with her thumb to keep a tear from descending. "Is it okay to ask you something? Something personal."

Alex never wasted time coming to her point. "Sure, sit down," he offered.

When she slid back on the couch, Monster appeared and snuggled next to her. Alex stroked the cat's back. Jaleel brought two sodas from the fridge and dropped into a chair.

"I liked the Updike novel a lot," she began. "The way Harry was caught between two worlds, the one he was supposed to conform to and the one inside him that said settling down and accepting his marriage wasn't going to work. It made me think of my own conflict."

"What are you conflicted about? Harry Angstrom had a whole lot of different issues."

Alex sighed, as if something might burst inside her. "I think you're the only person I can tell this to."

He wondered where the conversation was going.

"My mother is having an affair. The man's name is Charlie Diggs. He's my dad's oldest friend. What do you think I should do?"

Jaleel made a face. An affair—how messed up was that for Alex and her brother? But he didn't see how he could help. He needed to tell Alex to leave, now, for good.

"I'd go ask my friends, but what do they know?" she continued. Her eyes fell beseechingly on Jaleel.

"Ask them what?"

"It's just an idea I came up with. I don't have the courage to tell my father about Charlie, but I'm not going to let Mom destroy our family."

Jaleel locked his fingers behind his head as he listened to her idea. Without identifying herself, Alex said, she would warn Charlie to stop seeing her mother immediately, or she'd make sure that his wife, Julia, found out. But if Alex spoke to Charlie in person, she was afraid she'd get too emotional. The confrontation would also get back to her father, and World War III might erupt. She needed a go-between.

He was astounded. "Are you saying that you want me to talk to some man I don't even know?"

"No, not talk," she replied as if she hadn't explained her plan clearly. "You don't have to do anything. Except this—"

She pulled a sealed, letter-size envelope from her back pocket. It was wet along one edge from the rain. The name Charlie Diggs was typed on the front above his address.

"My letter's unsigned," she said. "I just need someone to deliver it."

"Why don't you?"

"Being anywhere near the Diggses' house creeps me out. And if Julia sees me dropping it off, she'll know who it's from. I have to be anonymous."

"Put on a stamp and mail it," Jaleel said. He wasn't going anywhere near the Diggses' house.

"There's no time. Tomorrow is Dad's poker game. Charlie needs to read the letter now—so he won't show up."

"You want me to put your letter in his mail box?"

"Is that asking too much?"

"It's really this urgent to you?"

"Yes," she pleaded.

This couldn't be happening, he thought. Something would go wrong. "Alex, I can't help you. I don't belong in your neighborhood."

"Why, just because you're black?"

"That's one reason."

"What are the others?"

"It doesn't matter, I'm not doing it."

"The Diggses' house is five minutes by bike. It's a large brick Colonial. Wait until dark. The mailbox is on the street. Piece of cake."

"No. This is a bad idea."

Alex looked confused and a little desperate. He was ready to tell her nicely to leave when something in him softened. She was only trying to keep her family together. The longer she remained on his couch, staring at him, the more his resistance eroded. He began to think of Dirick. Because of the Samaritan, good fortune had fallen on Jaleel. Didn't he have an obligation to help others? Wasn't that what it meant to be an apostle? It was just a five-minute bike ride in the dark.

He drew a breath, overriding his caution. "All right," he relented. "Just this once. Is that clear?"

"You don't know what this means to me."

Alex rose, gliding toward him like she was some ethereal wisp, an angel walking on air. She leaned over the chair and kissed his cheek. He was too surprised to say anything, and then she vanished.

Alex

~26~

Around seven-thirty, our doorbell began to ring. Dad was in the den conducting a last-minute beverage inventory. Some of his friends preferred scotch, others bourbon, some a specialty vodka or a foreign beer. In the middle of the room was a green-felt poker table, hauled in from the garage by Dad and Toby. His monogrammed poker chips ("LB" in a gold-leafed seraph script) were set in different-colored stacks in front of eight folding chairs. The initial buy-in was $1,000. On any given night, you could win or lose $20,000. A serious group. My father and Charlie had started the game six or seven years earlier, with little turnover. Some of the men had been on the duck hunt. Others were fraternity brothers from USC. Harding Kleeb, Dad's co-founder of their law firm, had entered professional tournaments in Vegas.

I had my theory about why some people, especially men, were attracted to gambling. It was certainly true of my father, and was reflected in his courtroom behavior. Having a defendant's fate in your hands—what more affirmed your cunning and guile than winning his or her freedom? It was the same narcotic tidal wave washing over you as winning a big pot in poker. I nodded whenever Dad told his poker stories, but I couldn't get any more excited than I did about someone shooting helpless ducks.

As the men paraded into our house, there was no sign of Charlie. I remained in the front hall, congratulating myself. Five minutes later, the doorbell chimed again. Mom stepped out from the kitchen. Charlie, bedecked in gabardine pants, Hawaiian shirt, and tweed sport coat with a handkerchief, strolled in. He greeted Mom with a quick hug, like old friends do. Then he ambled over not toward the familiar voices in the den but to me.

"Hey there, Alex. Good to see you." Charlie was his fraternity-likable self, with an unhurried smile and steady blue eyes. He pulled at his fingers, like someone taking off gloves.

"Hi, Charlie." All I could think about was my letter. Had Edward not delivered it? Or had Charlie read it, figured I was the author, and called Mom to powwow on what to say to me, to allay my suspicions? Sweet talk worked in a pinch.

"You're looking great, Alex. How's school?"

"It's okay, thanks."

"Your mom tells everyone you're another super-achiever, like your old man."

"Aren't you the same way, Mr. Diggs?"

"Come on, call me Charlie. I mean, how long have we known each other? Yeah, I guess we're all in the same club. Picked a med school yet?"

I shook my head no, wondering how long this pain had to continue.

"Med school, that's impressive," he went on in the silence. "Where do you think you'll go?"

"No idea. I haven't even chosen an undergraduate college. My plans about medicine might change."

What else had my mother told him? His hand grazed my shoulder, like a proud uncle. "Good luck with whatever you do, okay?"

Fuck off and die, Charlie, I thought as he slipped away to join the others.

My mother had returned to the kitchen. Her job was to provision the den with chips, nuts, sandwiches, cold cuts, and fresh ice. I watched as she assembled a platter of genoa salami, capicollo, sopressata, and prosciutto, as if we were all living in Italy. As much as she resented being in Dad's shadow, she made it worse for herself by trying to be perfect for him.

"I'll take it in," I said when she'd finished.

"Are you sure, honey? Don't you have homework?"

I didn't want her anywhere near Charlie. "I'm sure."

Amid the quips, baritone guffaws, and cigar smoke, I was barely noticed as I brought in the food. Cards and poker chips were being pushed back and forth across the felt table. Volleys of "raise you twenty!" and "see that and twenty more," crackled the air. I laid the platter on the credenza. Charlie was sipping his drink and frowning at his cards. His towers of chips were taller than anyone else's. My father seemed to be holding his own, but he was a clear second.

I knew what my father respected in Charlie, in any man—competence and loyalty—and I assumed that Charlie felt the same about Dad. But was there an element of competition, or envy, that got in the way? Despite the two being so equal in almost everything, Mom, no matter what I thought of her now, was much more of a class act than Julia. After Charlie and my father first demonstrated trust and loyalty to each other, did they have to keep proving those things over and over, or at some point, was everything taken for granted? In poker, you kept your emotions hidden. I wondered, watching Charlie, if everything hadn't become a poker game to him.

I left the fug of the den for the clean air of my room. Mom was still in the kitchen, polishing a sterling silver pitcher, a Christmas gift from Aunt Agnes—busy work. My stomach kept churning as I wrote in my journal. I was too restless to attempt homework.

When I slipped downstairs again, I suddenly saw Charlie step out of the powder room. He didn't notice me. Instead of returning to the den, he made a left turn into the kitchen. I crept closer, stopping just around the corner from where Mom was still polishing the pitcher, leaning slightly over the sink. Charlie came from behind and wrapped his arms around her waist. He pushed himself against her.

"No," she murmured without turning around. That didn't stop his lips from floating down her neck.

"God, I've missed you," he said.

"Me too."

I stayed frozen in the shadows of the hallway. Charlie kept kissing my mother. I heard my father's footsteps before actually seeing him. He approached from the living room, like someone on a mission, seeing but brushing past me without a word. I didn't know what had tipped him off. The loud voices and laughter continued from the den.

When things happen in microseconds, they are hard to sort out in your memory; the shutter speed is too quick. Charlie seemed to turn from my mother at the instant Dad entered the kitchen, yet one of those actions surely came first. Mom went back to polishing. Charlie strolled toward the fridge and opened it, as if to forage for food. He turned casually and looked up at my father, giving him a "hey there" nod. Dad peeled his eyes from Charlie to Mom and back to Charlie. Some silences are heavier than concrete.

"Alex, you should go upstairs," Dad said, suddenly glancing back to the hallway. I had never seen his face look so wild, almost stricken. He was used to gambling losses and sometimes a courtroom defeat, but he'd just suffered a different kind of blow, beyond calculation.

"Alex, would you go, please," he repeated without looking at me.

I took the stairs two at a time, grateful to be out of this mess, but at the same time, I had wanted to stick around. Nothing seemed real now except the boozy, oblivious laughter that kept rippling from the den. At the top of the stairs, I leaned over the bannister, peering down.

"What the fuck," I heard Dad say. He rarely lost his temper but I felt it coming on now.

"Calm down," Charlie said. "Nothing's going on."

"Nothing going on? Are you fucking my wife, Charlie?"

"Who the fuck told you that? You're just drunk."

"You're my best friend!"

"Who told you this shit?"

"No one. I'm asking you the question."

"Louis, you're drunk. I'm drunk. Okay?"

"Get out of here, Charlie. Leave my house."

"Louis, we've got a poker game to finish. What do you say, let's calm down and go back. The guys are missing us."

I heard a loud thud like someone had thrown or dropped something on the floor. I could imagine Dad's anger so clearly. His shocked face had come to life, his jaw trembling, teeth clenched.

"Hey, calm down," Charlie warned.

My mother had said nothing. Someone who disliked conflict probably still had her back to both men. This fight had little to do with her, she was no doubt thinking. A crazy, drunk friend had come out of nowhere and planted a kiss or two on her neck—big deal. In any case, she hadn't asked for the kiss. She was innocent. Surely that's what she would tell my father.

Toby peeked his head out of his room. I signaled him to go back inside and close the door. He made a face and retreated. I drifted down the stairs and moved closer to the kitchen. Charlie and my father had begun shoving each other. Incoherent shouting took over the house. Afraid of what might happen next, I hurried back to my room but left the door ajar.

"Oh, god, stop this," my mother finally yelled.

I braced myself for total chaos, but half a minute later, a switch got flipped. The house turned eerily silent, even the den. I assumed the poker game had ended out of embarrassment. Everyone streamed from the house with soft, slurred good-nights to my father, no doubt Charlie leaving with the pack.

The kitchen remained silent. I could imagine the humiliation on my father's face. To have your trust shattered had to feel like being tossed into a shark-infested ocean. He never knew he had marital issues until now, and soon all of Toluca Lake would be talking. I listened to my parents trudge up the stairs, one behind the other. This was different from the tired, triumphant silence of the Nile party. No one said good night to Toby or me.

I was as stunned as anyone. I lay on my bed with my headphones on. Johnny Cash's bass-baritone voice came to the rescue, for the moment anyway, like a gorgeous moon rising over our carnage.

~27~

The next morning, before breakfast, Toby and I were summoned by Dad to the living room. Mom was still in her silk robe—eyes red and swollen, hair pushed back into a bun, no makeup to hide the creases around her mouth and eyes. Dad was in jeans and a polo shirt, looking relatively fresh and determined. My parents sat on the sofa together, but their eyes didn't meet. I wondered how much they'd already talked. How could a couple not used to fighting be any good at working out solutions, especially over something like this?

What had tipped Dad off, my mother eventually told me, was what Charlie had left behind in his jacket, hanging from the back of his chair when he went to the powder room. A white linen handkerchief with special hand stitching peeked from the breast pocket. My parents had been shopping on Rodeo Drive in Beverly Hills months earlier. Mom had seen the handkerchief in a window and wanted to buy it for Dad. He smiled and said no thank you, it wasn't his style. The same hand-stitched handkerchief appeared in Charlie's breast pocket the night of the poker game. If I were my father, even if he was drunk, I might have made the same connection when he realized Charlie had been gone too long.

"What's going on?" Toby spoke first, scooching back in his chair.

"Your mother and I are having marital difficulties," Dad said without hesitation.

My brother twisted his jaw, like the whole notion was preposterous yet quite credible. "You mean this is about Charlie, don't you? Mom and Charlie were doing the deed?"

I looked at my brother. He was sharper than I'd given him credit for.

"Your mother told me everything," Dad continued, looking at Toby and then me. "It's painful for me to accept. However, it's officially over. I want both of you to know that. Did you suspect, Alex?"

"Yes." I felt cowardly again for not warning him earlier.

"It's okay. We'll all get through this."

The phone rang, maybe the fourth or fifth time that morning. We weren't picking up. News of my heresy on Founder's Day didn't spread as fast as Charlie and my father's shoving match. Another man in Dad's position would have been bewildered or traumatized, or consumed by anger. But in a crisis, my father's cool intellect took control, just as in court.

My mother, on the other hand, looked hopelessly, pathetically guilty, as much for being caught as for the affair itself. I should have felt good that everything was finally out in the open, but overall, I was miserable. How could this be happening to our family?

Everyone was suddenly staring at Mom.

"I'm sorry," she whispered, looking mostly at me.

"You're sorry? Where have I heard that before?" I shot back.

"That's all I can say, sweetie."

"Did you call Charlie this morning?"

"Yes. Dad listened to the conversation."

"Did Julia say anything?"

"Not to me. They have to work things out, I suppose."

Dad looked satisfied, but something felt off. Mom's apology seemed too glib, like a political dissident telling the tribunal whatever it wanted to hear. I knew her in ways that Dad didn't. She was a black belt in twisting, evading, and embellishing.

"She's sorry," Dad emphasized. "And I've forgiven her. We've agreed to start couples therapy, as early as next week. This may turn into family therapy," he advised. "Are you two prepared for that?"

Toby crossed his arms. "I'm not. We had family therapy with Dr. Sheffield, and you barely showed, Dad."

"This is very different."

"What are you implying? My situation wasn't that important?"

"Stop milking this, Toby." I shook my head.

"I need to know if you and Alex are on board," Dad said.

I told him "yes" in a clear voice. I would do anything to keep our family together. Toby finally nodded okay. Dad reached for Mom's hand. His grasp was firm, but the way Mom's hand slipped into his was more like a small animal burrowing in for temporary safety.

"All right, then," Dad went on. "We have a plan."

My father said he wasn't mad at me for keeping my suspicions about Mom to myself. He understood. He seemed to understand everything. It was certainly clear we all had a pact regarding the likelihood of family therapy.

When Dad left for an appointment at the office, Toby drifted upstairs. I followed Mom into the kitchen. She didn't say much. The defeat in her eyes seemed insufficient. She had been the cause of our upheaval. I wanted her penance to be more open.

She closed the kitchen door behind us, as if reading my mind. "I need to tell you something, Alex."

"Just don't ask me to keep another secret."

She was hurt that I couldn't see the obvious. "Who else am I going to talk to? I'm suddenly the laughingstock of the whole world."

"You mean Toluca Lake? You're not the first person to have an affair in the community. This doesn't have to be fatal."

"How am I supposed to face anyone in public? I can't go to church. I can't volunteer at the library. I can't even go to the supermarket."

"That's a ridiculous exaggeration."

She was too busy obsessing over being gossiped about to hear me. Then I felt another cold spot in my chest. I wondered if couples counseling, let alone family therapy, would really work. My sense was that my mother had been out of love with my father for some time, all the slow dancing in our living room notwithstanding. I wanted very much to be wrong, but I couldn't convince myself that I was.

"I need to tell you something, Alex. I love you and Toby. No matter what you think of me right now, I will always love you. But I'm leaving your father.

"I'm leaving your father," she repeated, ignoring my stunned face, "because I have no other choice. I mean, today. Right now."

"This is a joke, right?"

"No."

"Mom, twenty minutes ago you committed to therapy sessions with Dad."

"I've already spoken to my sister. I'm going to stay with Agnes in New Hampshire. I need some time for myself."

"You're flying to New Hampshire? You booked a flight already?"

"Yes."

"One way or round trip?"

"One way, for now."

"When did you speak to Agnes?"

"You ask too many questions, Alex."

"This was all planned? Before you agreed to therapy?" I was breathless. "You can't be serious, Mom."

"I know I've misbehaved, but there are extenuating circumstances. Living with your father has never been easy." She dropped into a chair like it was a church pew, ready to renounce her sins. But there was an asterisk. Everything had to be on her terms, in seclusion, with only her sister around. Her immediate family couldn't be near her right now.

"I've been thinking about things for a long time, Alex. Charlie asked me to run away with him several times. Out of loyalty to my family, I decided not to do it. Maybe that was a mistake." She angled her wrist toward her eyes, wiping away tears with the back of her hand.

"I don't believe this. You can't be leaving," I said.

"Your father is a very intimidating man. I feel I don't have a choice."

My respect for my mother, what was left of it, evaporated. I had thought of her as having her share of weaknesses but never as being a full-fledged coward. Since when did mothers abandon their families so whimsically? She was in a twenty-year marriage, and while far from perfect, a lot of women in Toluca Lake would have killed for it.

"I'll try to call your father sometime today," she promised.

"Dad's not going to understand. You know he'll be furious."

"I can't help that."

"When are you coming back?"

"When I'm feeling stronger."

"Who's going to look after Toby?"

"It'll have to be you, for the interim."

"Looking after Toby again? What's 'interim' mean?"

She didn't answer as she walked upstairs to give Toby the news. Fifteen minutes later, my brother found his way to the living room, but he didn't look particularly upset. He had a resigned, "so what?" smirk. Even if we'd never discussed it, he would admit to me later that our parents' breakup had seemed inevitable. He had sensed the gulf opening between them for several years. But there was a silver lining to the breakup, at least for Toby. One less parent meant considerably less hassle in his life.

Minutes later, Mom rolled a good-sized suitcase along the upstairs hallway, picked it up by the handle, and awkwardly carried it down. I was too angry to want to help. Her bleached-out eyes and swollen face had been transformed by makeup. I wondered if she'd secretly packed her bag in the middle of the night. A taxi suddenly honked from our driveway.

"You can't just run away!" I shouted as I followed her outside.

She stopped, turned around, and wrapped me in her arms, like there was nothing else she could do.

"Are you really coming back?" I asked.

"Of course I am." She kissed me on the lips as the driver loaded her bag in the trunk. "I'll miss you, honey. I just need some rest."

The cabbie wheeled out of the driveway and sprinted toward Valley Spring Lane, as I had done on my bike. My mother's disappearing didn't seem quite real.

When I called Dad at his office, he didn't pick up. I left a rambling message about Mom's departure. When he finally called back, it was almost three.

"Your mother did what!" he exclaimed.

"Didn't she call you?"

"Yes, but there was no coherent message. She sounded in a hurry."

I gave him the whole story, or everything Mom had told me. I didn't think anyone knew the entire story. At Dad's insistence, over the next week, I would retell him every minute of her last hour in our house, over and over. As if I had inadvertently left out an important detail that would give him hope and bring her back home sooner rather than later.

~28~

September 21

Not sure the point of all this journal writing. Not a bad way to record my feelings, particularly after Mom left yesterday, but writing about feelings rarely changes them. It's not a catharsis. Just the opposite. When I reread everything, I sometimes feel worse.

I listened in as Mom called Dad just before dinner tonight. She needed to be free for now, she said, which meant not being gossiped about like some evil person, or ostracized for her "sins," or smothered by my father's tyranny. She said Dad had always been insensitive and egotistical. Before he could get more than a few sentences in, she hung up. He did manage to ask if she was going to divorce him. She said no.

He smoldered all through dinner. His tyranny? he asked me, as if I was suddenly his only sounding board. Why hadn't Gloria once mentioned how she felt the previous twenty years? Was his tyranny her excuse for her infidelity? I didn't have an answer. If their Toluca Lake friends were already talking about Mom and Charlie, Dad predicted, they would also be talking about him. He didn't seem to care as much as my mother, but he cared enough. He had a reputation. I had never heard the word "cuckold"

*until he used it about himself. Toby kept saying
"cuckoo." I kicked him under the table.*

Starting Monday, my father drove Toby and me to school. Dad
didn't talk much, except to promise to be back around three,
which he always was, no matter how busy his work kept him. He
wanted to prove we could all get by without Mom for a while.

"You need help with anything?" Joyce asked me in the cafeteria
on Friday.

"With what?"

"Anything. What are best friends for?"

I told her I appreciated the support, but I couldn't think straight
at the moment.

"If anybody gives you a hard time about your folks—just let me
know."

"What are you going to do, deck them?"

"Maybe," she said.

"I don't understand my mother," I admitted. "Help me with that."

I gave her explicit details, realizing that asking for help was a two-
edged sword. Joyce was capable of giving good advice, but she could
also be a blabber. There were lots of divorces in our school, and kids
handled it, I said, so I couldn't explain why I felt particularly inept.
Maybe it had to do with being on top of the world one day, in free
fall the next, starting with my Founder's Day speech. Joyce responded
mysteriously that "the gods of long-term karma" were at work.

"Your mom always struck me as kind of reasonable," Joyce added.
"Why would she just get up and leave? Did she just go—" She circled
her index finger around her temple.

"She's no crazier than she ever was," I said, and wandered off to
my next class.

I tried calling my mother three times that week. Aunt Agnes always
picked up, chitchatted, and said Mom would have to get back to me.

"Is she okay?"

"Fine. Just needs some rest, dear. Talk to you later."

I gave up calling for a while. I tried to get used to life without her.
But seeing Mom's Mercedes in the garage, her clothes in her closet, or
just an empty kitchen made me lonely. I fixed Toby's and my lunch

every day, paid household bills (Dad entrusted me with the checkbook), and ordered liquor from Lakeside Pharmacy and groceries from Ralph's. Despite our housekeeper doing what she always did, I kept looking over her shoulder, as if I were Mom. Dad hired someone to prepare dinners for us seven days a week, but sometimes I insisted on doing it. He went back to playing weekend golf with friends, as long as Charlie wasn't around. Everyone understood that you didn't talk in front my father about that night. I hoped I never ran into Charlie again.

On occasion we ate out. One evening at the Tick Tock, a favorite family restaurant for all of Toluca Lake, the table next to us got too loud. I knew the people. The wife and husband had come to our Labor Day parties. We also saw them in church. Dad exchanged hellos as we strolled in, so you'd think they would have been discreet. But in the middle of dinner, it was impossible not to overhear them. Mom had been involved with several men before Charlie, the woman said. Mom's friends all knew and simply looked the other way. Gloria was cagey as the devil, the woman added, with a certain relish.

Dad threw the whole table a sharp look. The woman still didn't shut up.

"Come on, we're leaving," he said. He was upset enough to leave a hundred dollars on the table and not ask for change.

"I haven't finished my chicken fried steak," my brother protested.

"Get up, Toby," I said.

"Why?"

"Get up!"

I thought that my father, uncharacteristically, might grab my brother by his shirt collar and haul him out. Toby saved himself by quickly wrapping his entree in the cloth napkin and slipping out of the booth with it.

"Do you think that's true," Dad asked when we got home. I sat with him in his study. "Mom's had lots of affairs? Did you know that?"

"No," I said honestly. "Look, gossip is just gossip. Mom's out of her gourd right now. Best thing in the world is she stays at Agnes's for a while."

"You really think so?"

"Yeah. I miss her, like you do, but she has to get her shit together. Try not to think about her for a while."

His gaze took him out the window, to our flowerbeds and maybe memories of when we first moved in. The impeccable rows of geraniums and daffodils were the way Mom liked them. Her stamp was everywhere on our house.

"How could Gloria have done this to me?" For a second his face was a knot of anger and disbelief. Then it deflated, and all I saw was sadness.

I didn't know what to say. No matter what Mom had done, my father wanted her back. I wasn't sure how much he was still in love, but he certainly didn't want to let go of the marriage. Look no further than "The Adventures of Ozzie and Harriet," "My Three Sons," or "The Brady Bunch." Fathers, tireless providers, didn't jeopardize with a divorce the families they'd worked so hard to build and nurture.

On another night, when I was in his study again, Dad asked me, "What do you think of Charlie?"

"He wasn't my favorite of all your friends."

"My fucking best friend," he said.

"Dad, let it go."

"How long do you think her affair with Charlie went on? Gloria told me it was intermittent, whatever that means."

"I don't know," I said, but I suspected it had been going on for a while.

"My fucking best friend," he repeated.

If he wasn't going to get mad at Mom, Charlie was the only target. There was mounting fury at being deceived, or deceiving himself.

"Do you think I should confront Charlie?" he said.

"You already did at the poker game. Me, I pretend he doesn't exist now."

"But I want to know. I want to know every detail."

I could understand his search for facts. I had the same kind of mind. When things went against him, my father dug deeper. He couldn't help himself.

"I've got two tests tomorrow," I said. "I better get busy."

"When you call your mother, it's always the same thing?" he stopped me. "Agnes says Gloria can't come to the phone?"

"Yeah, she's resting or on a walk or reading a book."

"You really think she's coming back to us?"

"I hope so, but I have doubts." I was as candid as I could be. Dad opened his decanter of scotch as I left. No matter the pain, he refused to see a therapist. It was sinking in with me that I was filling that void. "I have doubts too," Dad said, his voice trailing me up the stairs. Pretty soon, Dad stopped ferrying Toby and me to Valley. He said he had too many clients to deal with, so he contracted with a high-end car service. Not that Valley was any more bearable for Toby with Mom gone, but suddenly having a chauffeur and a town car gave him some self-esteem. He was a BMOC. I would have preferred just taking a taxi back and forth.

A week later, I was wakened from a light sleep around two in the morning. Dad was trying to be quiet as he padded down the stairs. I slipped out of bed and gazed down from the landing. The light from the gun safe closet in the hallway spread over the carpet. I heard the heavy metal door squeak open. Dad stayed there for a good minute, moving things around in the safe. The heavy door closed, the tumbler spun again, and he went toward the garage. The Cadillac engine came to life, and he drove away.

I threw on a sweater and jeans, half-running the six blocks to Charlie's house. Except for the occasional parked car, the winding street was deserted. My mind wouldn't shut up. If I needed to, was I smart enough to know how to stop my father from doing the unimaginable?

His Caddy was parked between two lampposts across the street from the Diggses' house. Dad was in the driver's seat. I stood behind a giant sycamore, with a good view of the Colonial as well as Dad. Except for driveway landscaping lights, the property was masked by darkness. Moments passed and an upstairs window suddenly brightened. Charlie and Julia were marching back and forth, ghostly figures that appeared to be moving angrily. I wondered what provokes a fight in the middle of the night. Had my reclusive mother impulsively called her lover?

The upstairs light flicked off, and the house slumped back into shadows. My father didn't budge. I would have given anything to be in his head. I was afraid that he was intending to kill Charlie but somehow had thought Julia wouldn't be around. He continued to look at the house, studying it as if postponing his plan might work out even better. Maybe there were more details to consider. When it came to ducks, he was a patient, determined hunter. Another half hour passed—I was getting cold—before Dad drove away. Ten minutes later, I sneaked in our back door. The Caddy was in the garage.

"Where were you all day?" I said the next evening when Dad came home for dinner. "I called your office from school. Not even your secretary knew where you were."

"What were you calling about?"

"Nothing. I just wanted to be sure you were okay."

"I was at a client's office. Nothing to be concerned about. Everything's fine."

"Really?" I said, checking his tired gaze. "I heard you up in the middle of the night last night."

"I was puttering in the kitchen."

"Did you go for a drive afterwards? I heard the garage door open."

"I'm turning into an insomniac," he half joked.

He gave Toby and me a tight smile that signaled it was best to change subjects. Toby filled the void. If you had a personal computer as Toby did, there was a new thing called Internet Relay Chat, and my brother was all over it. I did the dishes and went to my room.

> *October 26*
> *Hand it to Dad. He doesn't lose his cool. I can't*
> *be absolutely sure what he's up to, but I'm getting*
> *nervous. I stared into his gun safe this afternoon.*
> *I knew he'd once put the combination on a yellow*
> *Post-it that was at the back of his desk drawer.*
> *Nothing seems to have been disturbed since the last*
> *time I looked, but that doesn't mean I should be any*
> *less anxious.*

~29~

The phone woke me early morning on Saturday, October 30. The sky was overcast and the air already hummed with the chorus of lawn mowers.

"Alex? Oh my god," Joyce began.

I came awake quickly. "What?"

"Did you hear?" Her voice seemed to explode in my ear. "Charlie Diggs was murdered in his house! In the middle of the night!"

She gave me as many details as she knew, mostly things she'd overheard from a police sergeant at the Diggses' house this morning. Around midnight, a neighbor had heard what sounded like two gun blasts coming from the brick Colonial. The North Hollywood police operator dispatched a patrol car. The police, after ringing the bell repeatedly, found that the glass on the back door had been broken. They let themselves in. Charlie's body was upstairs, near his bed. Fifteen minutes later, three more cars arrived, speeding down our quiet streets with flashing lights. Talking to the neighbor, the cops determined that Julia was out of town, visiting her mother in San Francisco. When they searched the house, Charlie's empty jewelry box was found on the master bedroom closet floor.

"What was the murder weapon?" I asked.

"One of Charlie's own shotguns. Apparently, he kept it in his closet."

The story was spreading through Toluca Lake like a virus, Joyce said. Everyone seemed to agree this was the first homicide in our seventy-year history.

"You should get over here," she added urgently.

"Where?"

"The crime scene, moron."

When I woke my father and relayed Joyce's news, his partially graying brows shot up, and his mouth pinched in deliberation. He sat up and said, "The bastard had it coming, don't you think? We should send the burglar a medal, or at least a thank you card."

"It's not funny," I said.

"Call your mother," he replied with mock urgency.

"Why are you treating this like a joke?"

"It's not a joke. But I hated the Judas, as you well know."

"Okay if I run over there? Joyce is waiting for me."

He was ready to say no, but he saw how excited I was. "Suit yourself. But don't be too long." He adjusted his pillow and turned on the morning news.

"Okay."

Despite his seeming indifference, I couldn't be blamed for wondering if my father was involved. He'd been acting funny for weeks. And I'd seen him stalking Charlie. What else was I supposed to think? But the very idea seemed impossible.

I walked to the Diggses' and met Joyce and two other friends. Four patrol cars and three unmarked sedans lined the street. Within minutes, more neighbors clustered on the sidewalk. Yellow tape had been strung around the house. Through an open front door, I could see plainclothesmen milling around, some carrying boxy briefcases. As if she watched Perry Mason too, Joyce announced that they were members of the forensics team.

For a community that spent its days and nights in taken-for-granted insularity, Charlie's murder had broken the spell. I heard neighbors chattering about hiring a private security patrol, and demanding increased police surveillance until the killer or killers were caught. If I heard the phrase "cold-blooded murder" once, I heard "it could happen again" repeatedly. Joyce's parents wanted her home with them for the weekend to be sure she was safe.

I strolled back to my house. Dad was in the kitchen, eating breakfast and talking to Toby about the shooting in a matter-of-fact tone.

"Fuck, what if those guys come here?" My brother's voice quavered as he glanced at me.

"Nothing's going to happen, Toby," said Dad. "You're safe. Calm down."

"How do you know?"

"I know."

"You don't know, you're just saying that. Were they drug dealers?"

"What would Charlie have in common with drug dealers?" I asked.

"Let the police do their job," Dad cautioned.

It suddenly struck me that I needed to call Mom. I doubted she'd been told because no one knew where she was hiding out. When it came to Charlie Diggs, Dad didn't care what I did. His wife's lover deserved the appropriate place in Dante's Hell.

"Do you want to talk to Mom?" I thought to ask him.

He seemed to think about it for half a second. "Gonna pass," Dad said, like the deadline to reconcile had gone and was irrevocable. He ambled off to his study.

Agnes picked up right away. I wouldn't let her brush me off this time. "I need to speak to Mom. It's urgent."

I could imagine my aunt's forehead wrinkling with doubt. "Why? What's so important?"

"It's personal."

"You can tell me, Alex, and I'll relay it to Gloria."

"No. I need to tell her myself. It's about Charlie Diggs."

Agnes surrendered when she heard the name, like it was the only password that would give me access to my mother. When Mom came on, I told her everything I knew. Toby was suddenly by my side.

"Oh, no," she said faintly before I could finish. Agnes, the biggest nosy-body of all time, was breathing into an extension. This was the first time I'd heard Mom's voice in six weeks. I had a dozen things on my mind for her, starting not with Charlie Diggs, as big as that news was, but whether she was ever coming back.

"How could this have happened?" she said, ignoring my question.

"The police think it was a botched burglary. Like the killer didn't know Charlie was in the house. Julia was in San Francisco."

"Oh, my god," she whispered, still processing everything, and then broke into sobs.

"I'm sorry," I said.

"You should get off the phone, Gloria," Agnes broke in.

"Mom, Toby is right here. You need to stop crying and talk to him. He thinks our house isn't safe."

"Mom, is that you?" Toby said, taking the phone from me. I stood next him so I could overhear.

"Hi, honey, Are you all right?"

"What the hell, I don't know. Charlie Diggs could have been murdered by any kook. I could be next."

"Alex said it was a burglary. We have an alarm system in our house."

"Half the time Dad never turns it on. Someone crazy could break in tomorrow."

"You don't really believe that, do you? You're just being dramatic. Anyway, you've got Alex and your father to protect you."

"You're not here, so how would you possibly know?" He tossed the receiver to me in disgust, and drifted toward the den television.

"What really happened, Alex?" Mom asked. "You're not telling me the whole story."

"I'm telling you everything I heard from Joyce and the police. Why don't you just come home and be with us? We'll figure it out together."

"Gloria Baten, it's time." Agnes's voice was like a nagging phone operator.

"I've got to go, sweetie." She still sounded incredibly upset.

"No, Mom! Talk to me!"

She hung up. Agnes advised me not to call back for a long while. The news I'd just delivered was going to set my mother's recovery back even more. I was sure my aunt already knew everything about Mom and Charlie.

I spent the next few days trying to keep Toby calm while playing detective in my head. According to the *Times*, the North Hollywood P.D. detective assigned to the case speculated that the intruder might have been waiting in Charlie's bedroom. There were enough blood, skin, and bone fragments on the carpet, bedspread, and walls that a forensics team had yet to determine if there'd been a struggle, or the victim was simply gunned down in cold blood. There was no official comment about possible fingerprints on the shotgun or surfaces in the bedroom.

I put down a timeline on my own legal pad. October 30 was a Saturday. Technically, the murder might have been committed a few minutes before midnight, on Friday, the twenty-ninth, or a few minutes later, on the thirtieth. Regardless, I was in bed, asleep, and I assumed Dad was too. I certainly hadn't heard him stirring around. According to a report from the Los Angeles County coroner, the only certain thing was that Charlie Diggs had been killed twenty feet from his bed, by two powerful blasts from a 12-gauge shotgun that obliterated his face. The murder weapon was abandoned next to the victim.

Feel like shit, I wrote in my journal that night, when I couldn't sleep. *Wish I was anywhere but here.*

~30~

Nothing happened the following week, other than stories about the police chasing down various leads and interviewing anyone in Toluca Lake who had something to say about the killing. A lot of people knew about the fight at the poker game. The burglary scenario was soon tossed out. It was just a cover-up, the police said. Everyone began talking about premeditated murder. The Crime Scene Investigation team was still combing Charlie's house for fibers and blood samples.

Overnight, the *Times* turned into the *National Enquirer*. Every morning I saw headlines like "Society Murder of the Year" and "Wealthy Victim Likely Knew His Assassin." People in Toluca Lake were described as Rolls-Royce-driving multimillionaires who dined regularly with movie stars and influential politicians. Charles Diggs achieved more fame in the way he died than for his architectural projects, golf and hunting prowess, or financial net worth. A reporter as well as the police got hold of the Diggses' phone records, showing that Mom occasionally called her lover at odd hours starting almost as soon as she left for New Hampshire. No one formally accused Dad of killing his best friend, but the police certainly seemed interested in him. He told me he'd gotten more than a few calls at his office. Dad was blasé, rather than irritated by the police queries.

At school, gossips had a fresh bone to sharpen their teeth on. I hung with Joyce and a few other friends whenever possible, as if they would offer me protection. Otherwise, I marched down hallways without making eye contact with anyone. Toby had started telling kids to fuck off. More than once, he was shoved around in a bathroom and left with a bloody nose. When he reported the harassment, the vice principal promised to investigate, but no one ever got suspended.

Two weeks after the homicide, two detectives, after calling ahead, appeared at our front door. One was in a navy suit with a red and black striped tie; the other, much taller, wore a blue blazer and tan trousers. He smelled of after-shave.

"Are you guys cops?" Toby asked when he opened the door and looked them over. "You've come to stay with us? Twenty-four-hour protection, right?"

I was right behind my brother. I didn't know if Toby was serious or being a smart-ass. I gave him a look, and he drifted to the back yard to begin raking leaves. With Mom gone, I was the enforcer.

Detective Lieutenant Joseph Hildenbrand of the North Hollywood Police Department showed me his ID and a badge from his front pocket. "This is Detective Sergeant Shier," he said, flicking his head toward his partner. "And you are?" he asked.

"Alexandra Baten, but you can call me Alex."

"And that was your brother?"

"Toby Baten. Sorry if he came across as a wise guy."

Shier looked about six-foot-seven or -eight, with the wingspan of an albatross, like surely he'd played high school or college basketball. His feet and hands belonged to a giant. He had the intensity of someone who was always on duty, figuring things out.

Hildenbrand was more relaxed, but he looked just as exotic, with his Mr. Potato Head features. Nose, eyes, mouth, and ears were rough-hewn appendages that didn't quite blend together. His thick black hair was swept back and parted down the middle.

"I think your father is expecting us," Shier said.

Hildenbrand seemed immediately at home inside. "Say, this is really nice," he said to his partner. They were looking out on our swimming pool, lawn, and the lake below. Staring at some antique lacquered chairs, Hildenbrand asked me, "Are those Ming or early Qing dynasty?"

I wasn't sure. Mom had picked them up in Beverly Hills. Dad, who must have overheard everything, suddenly strolled out from his study. Everyone shook hands.

"These are early Ming, detective," Dad answered pleasantly enough, and sat in one of them.

"What about that hutch," Hildenbrand continued, "next to the fireplace? Qing?"

"No, late Ming," Dad corrected him. "You're interested in antiques, detective?"

"My father's a dealer. I accompanied him once on a buying trip to Hunan Province." He shook his head, as if the experience wasn't what he had expected. "The Chinese are tough negotiators. They grind you down."

The two men scooted back on the couch. When Shier asked for a glass of water, I ran and got it, as if that would be my one role in the meeting and I could leave. Hildenbrand opened his briefcase, and was looking over whatever was inside when I came back.

"Okay if we talk to your daughter too, Mr. Baten?"

"I don't see why not." Dad looked like he'd been expecting the meeting for some time. He had his authoritarian voice on, hands folded on his lap, as relaxed as someone watching a movie.

From his briefcase, Hildenbrand pulled a couple of photocopied pages, followed by a plastic sleeve with the word Diggs taped along the sealed top. Inside, I quickly saw, was my original letter, the one left in Charlie's mailbox, along with its envelope. Dad and I were each handed a photocopy of the letter.

My father read it quickly. "Where did this come from?"

"Julia found it. Originally it was left in the Diggses' mailbox. You can see there's no signature. Apparently, since it was of a sensitive nature to Mr. Diggs, he hid it from his wife. She found it buried in a drawer, after his death."

"This person seems to know that Charlie was having an affair with my wife," Dad said, handing his copy back to the detective. The letter was six or seven sentences. I read it again, amazed, if not horrified, that I'd actually written it. At the time it had seemed like a good idea.

> *Dear Mr. Diggs:*
> *It is a poorly kept secret that you are in an intimate*
> *relationship with a woman who is not your wife. And*
> *you are best friends with her husband. This, of course,*

*should not be. You are committing a sin that I am
asking you to stop immediately, and stay away from this
woman at all costs before there are serious consequences
for everyone. I know you are a smart and caring man.
Please examine your motives and stop immediately.*
    A friend

"You didn't write that, did you, Mr. Baten." Hildenbrand phrased it as a statement.

"No, detective, I didn't."

Eyes fell on me. If my father wasn't the author, who else had a vested interest in ending the affair? My dad was probably wondering what else I hadn't told him, yet he didn't seem at all perturbed. Hildenbrand shifted his weight on the couch, leaning toward me. "Did you write this, Alex?"

"Yes, sir."

"May I ask why?"

"Doesn't the letter speak for itself?"

"There's a vaguely threatening tone to it," he said, which I could see now.

"I wanted Charlie Diggs to stop."

"How long did you know about their affair?"

"Two months ago or so, I overheard Mom on the phone with Charlie. That's when I first suspected something, though Mom denied it when I confronted her. I wrote the letter just before the night of Dad's poker game."

"Did you tell anyone what you were doing?"

"No," I lied.

"Why were you so secretive?"

"I was afraid of telling my father about something that was speculation. But in case it was true, I thought that if Charlie read the letter, he would stay away from the poker game. And he would end the affair altogether."

"But your father found out," Shier filled in, moving the narrative along.

"You have plenty of accounts from the poker night," my father interjected. "What you don't know is that my wife and I came to an un-

derstanding the next morning. Gloria confessed the affair to me. She
called Charlie on the phone from our bedroom, to end things then and
there. After she hung up, she told me how sorry she was. We agreed to
start therapy. As far as I was concerned, bygones were bygones."

"Really, just like that?" Shier asked. "Whose idea was the therapy?"

"Mine."

"What I'm trying to understand, sir, is the same day she agreed to
therapy, she packed a suitcase and left you."

Shier took a pad from his jacket pocket and gave us context. He read
off the date and plane flight of Mom's escape to New Hampshire. When
Hildenbrand had interviewed her twice on the phone at Agnes's, she
confirmed my attempted calls and said she hadn't taken them because
her emotional connection with Charlie was far from over. She didn't
want to involve me further. She admitted calling Charlie the morning
after the poker game, in front of Dad, and saying the relationship was
finished. But that wasn't being honest, she confessed to Hildenbrand.
She was afraid of my father. It was Charlie she was in love with.

I shook my head. I was so pissed that that was what Mom had told
a couple of strangers, even if they were police, yet had never confided
in me. All the chaos she'd caused, all the deception—why did I keep
hoping she'd come home? I was supposed to forgive her?

Shier asked my father if he knew what his wife's true feelings were.

"What do you mean, 'true feelings'?"

"It seems to me you're not accepting the fact that your wife wants
a divorce."

"The only time we talked—when Gloria called me shortly after
she left—I asked pointedly if she wanted a divorce. She said no. As
far as I know, we're still on for therapy as soon as she comes home.
Her sister, Agnes, told Alex that Gloria is suffering from nervous ex-
haustion and needs to rest. Whatever she confided to you, Detective
Hildenbrand, she may not have been in her right mind at the time."

"Until I hear from Gloria again, I have no reason to believe a word
that you've said," Dad summed up.

"Mr. Baten, the night of the poker game, you got in an altercation
with Charlie Diggs, isn't that correct?"

"Everyone's already given you the blow by blow, I'm sure. Why
wouldn't I shove Charlie around, in the heat of the moment?

Wouldn't you under similar circumstances? Later that night I calmed down. I remembered how deep our friendship ran. Charlie and I go back to a time when you were still in grade school, detective."

"You didn't want to kill him?" Shier interrupted, as casually as asking if there'd be rain tomorrow.

"No, I did not."

"Who do you think did?"

"I have no idea. If you're so focused on me, Detective Shier, if you believe you have evidence, why don't you make an arrest?"

The police and district attorney had great respect for my father and for Baten, Kleeb, and Donahue, Hildenbrand said. No one was rushing to judgment. I listened to their ass kissing with a straight face and wondered what they thought that would get them.

"Mr. Baten, did you have a key to the Diggses' house?" Hildenbrand continued.

"It's on my key chain. Charlie and Julia have one for our house. We've known and trusted each other for twenty years.

"The *Times* reported you thought this was a burglary," Dad tossed in.

"Initially. But there haven't been any burglaries in Toluca Lake for some time. To have one out of the blue, that would be unusual. Not to mention a burglar killing someone with two blasts from a shotgun. Can you alibi the evening of October 29?"

"I drove to a night driving range to hit golf balls. It relaxes me. Then I came back home, took a shower, and went to bed. Alex and Toby were in their rooms down the hall."

"Yes, sir. We were in bed," I confirmed. The truth was I hadn't kept track of Dad that evening. I remembered him putting his golf clubs in the Caddy and driving off sometime after dinner. That was the last time I saw him, I told Hildenbrand.

He turned to my father. "Anybody remember you from the driving range?"

"I don't know. You'd have to ask. It was nighttime, and the place was crowded."

"Mr. Baten, we have a body, a likely weapon that is still undergoing ballistics, and from you, motive and, very likely, opportunity. Would you come down to be fingerprinted and take a poly?"

"Be happy to be fingerprinted. I can tell you what I advise my clients about polygraphs. They're as useful as tits on a fish."

Our visitors popped to their feet. Hildenbrand pulled a search warrant from his jacket, and the detectives spent an hour wandering through our house. Dad, unconcerned, returned to his study. In the end, all I saw Hildenbrand take were a shotgun and shells from the gun safe, which Dad opened for them almost cheerfully.

"I thought you'd identified the murder weapon as belonging to Charlie," he said, watching Hildenbrand walk off with his shotgun.

"All we know for sure is the weapon was a 12-gauge."

"A lot of recreational hunters have those."

Hildenbrand also went through Mom and Dad's jewelry. He had a list from Julia of what was missing from Charlie's jewelry box. Nothing in our house matched up. Hildenbrand suggested he might impound Dad's Cadillac, as if a speck of Charlie's blood might be hiding on the seat or in the carpet. My father didn't back down. The police could take his car any time they wanted, he said.

I began to think my earlier suspicions about Dad were nothing more than anxiety speaking. If he said he was home in bed at the time of the murder, why shouldn't I believe him?

I stood on the front steps watching the two detectives slip into their car and hoping they never returned. I was feeling relieved, even superior to them, when Hildenbrand gave me a come-hither gesture from the curb. Dad had returned to his study.

"What is it?" I said, strolling toward his car.

"Alex, I forgot to ask you something." He borrowed his colleague's note pad and flipped through a couple of pages. His gaze traveled back to me. "The letter you wrote Charlie, you put it in his mail box yourself that night?"

"Excuse me?"

"If you want to answer this in front of your Dad—"

"No, I'm fine. Who else was going to deliver the letter but me? My little brother?"

"The night before the poker game, Charlie was working late at his office. But Julia was home."

"So?"

"She didn't see you. Were you on your bike?"

I nodded reflexively. Hildenbrand asked what kind of bike I owned.

"A Peugeot racing bike. I was there around seven thirty."

"Julia said that it was a man who came by, on an old-fashioned bike with thick tires. She caught a glimpse when he passed under a street lamp. Then he put something in her mailbox. She thought it might have been an advertising flyer, so she didn't go grab it."

"An advertising flyer, that could be. Charlie probably picked it up with my letter when he came home from work."

Shier cleared his throat. "The trouble is, the Diggses wouldn't have been the only house to get a flyer. Nobody else had anything in their mailboxes."

I shrugged, like, hey, beats me. "Anything else?"

"Not for now," said Hildenbrand. "Thanks, Alex. Nice to meet you."

I turned and walked back into the house.

November 13
I keep analyzing what happened this afternoon.
Not so much what the two detectives said as what
I told them. I hate lies, yet I told several about my
letter without batting an eye. I always thought I'd
be terrible at deception, if I ever had to use it, but
I was pretty good. Where does a skill like that come
from if you've never had practice, let alone you
despise yourself for doing it? Is it something I
learned from my mother without knowing it? I'm
never going to breathe a word about Edward. I
promised him that. Besides, he isn't relevant to the
investigation.

I crawled into bed, slipped on my headphones, and closed my eyes as I listened to the Rolling Stones. For a long time I thought about my father, all the shit he was going through. I wished I could help him. But maybe he didn't need it. It would turn out that a forensics team wouldn't find anything from his 12-gauge. The final ballistics test would confirm that whoever killed Charlie used the victim's own shotgun. There were specks of blood on the muzzle, but they belonged to Charlie. Forensics wouldn't find anyone's hand, finger, or shoe prints at the crime scene, other than Charlie's, Julia's, and a house-keeper's. The killer had done his work methodically and efficiently. Lying under the sheets, I let myself be distracted by raunchy lyrics and siren voices. I didn't have a boyfriend. Whenever I listened to the Stones, I got horny and imagined having one of them in bed with me. At the moment, I felt almost desperate to be held by someone. Yesterday, Joyce invited me to a Duran Duran concert at the Hollywood Bowl. Dad said okay, which was more than Mom would have done. I couldn't wait to go. Rock star gods walked the Earth knowing what every girl my age was feeling or imagining. I wouldn't have been surprised if Mick and Keith had been fucked a million times each.

~31~

Wednesday the next week, Toby and I stood by ourselves in the Valley parking lot, waiting for our driver. I had my head in a book. I didn't hear anyone walk up, but suddenly Detective Hildenbrand was in front of me, like a creature rising out of the mists. His gaze scanned the breadth of our campus, and then he gave his "this-is-amazing" smile, like he'd done at our house.

"Hey, Alex, how big is this place? Looks like a damn college."

"You've never been to Valley Academy? It's the Taj Mahal of prep schools," I said dryly.

Hildenbrand shook his head, taken by its size and opulence. "I haven't been to India. I was thinking Four Seasons. Do you guys get massages and Jacuzzi time every day?"

I thought he was envious. The Four Seasons didn't give five hours of homework every night, I replied.

"But you can't tell me you haven't got some nice amenities here. Where I went to high school, in Bakersfield, we had three drinking fountains and a vending machine."

"Where did you go to college?"

"I started at a junior college but finally got a degree from Northridge, in criminal law. Wanted to go to law school but it never happened."

"What are you doing here?" I came to the point. "Does my father know?"

Our town car rolled up. Toby, who was ignoring my discussion with Hildenbrand, jumped in the back. This was usually his happiest moment of the day, to be whisked away from prison by his own chauffeur.

"Whoa, what's this?" Hildenbrand said, studying our ride. It was Toby's idea that our driver wear a chauffeur's cap.

"My father's too busy to pick us up." I was about to jump in, when Hildenbrand raised his finger, like someone hailing a cab. "I just need a minute, Alex."

"I don't want to talk to you alone."

"We talked alone outside your house. One or two questions. If you don't want to answer, that's fine, I'm gone.

"I keep thinking about your letter to Charlie. You're sure you delivered it yourself?"

"That's right."

"We ran the envelope through the LAPD fingerprint lab. There were four sets of prints. One each for Julia and Charlie—they matched up with a couple of databases. Not sure about the other two sets. One is a partial, but we're doing our best with it. Maybe that's yours. Maybe it's someone else's. Can you come down and help us out?"

"You want to fingerprint me? You'll have to ask my father."

"We will, but we don't really need his permission. If we have reasonable suspicion of involvement in a crime, we can ask the D.A. to get a court order." His eyes floated over the campus again. It seemed to almost take his breath away.

"What are you saying?" I asked as his words hit me. "You think I might be involved with the murder?"

"Someone whose prints are on that envelope could be an accessory. We would certainly want to talk to him or her. Assuming you're one set of the mystery prints, who do you think the other belongs to?"

"I have no idea."

The toe of his shoe wiggled on the asphalt, putting out an invisible cigarette. The way the afternoon light attached to his face made me think of a craggy canyon floor. All those ill-fitting features looked like some kind of obstacle course.

I said goodbye and slumped into the front seat of our town car. I pretended not to see Hildenbrand waving at me. His finger was tapping my window before we had gone ten feet. The driver stopped.

"You know, I think you're right, Alex," he said when I lowered the window. "We shouldn't be talking alone anymore."

"Why's that?"

"I'm thinking about perjury charges. You should have an attorney with you next time."

I squinted at him. "Perjury charges?"

"Making a false statement under oath," he explained, as if I didn't know the meaning of the word. My father used it in his dinner stories all the time.

"I wasn't aware, Detective Hildenbrand. Am I under oath?"

"Not yet. Hey, you have a good afternoon, Alex." Hildenbrand, back to his intimidation tactics, watched as we pulled away.

There were messages on our answering machine when I got home. Sometimes we got anonymous calls accusing my father of being Charlie's killer, or queries from reporters, which I never returned, but today it was a couple of Mom's friends. They all wanted to talk to her. I was polite but evasive when I called back. I said she was fine and that we expected her home soon, period.

Around seven, when he arrived home, I served Dad his favorite scotch on the rocks in his study. I told him everything that had happened in the parking lot, Hildenbrand asking me who had delivered the letter, then warning me about perjury. My father seemed more annoyed than when the detectives had searched our house for a murder weapon, or talked with me on the street afterward. Like a lot of cops, Hildenbrand was clever and manipulative, Dad said, and he had no business accosting me at school. That was out of bounds. If it happened again, I was to call my father immediately.

"Okay," I said, feeling relieved.

"You know Harding Kleeb. You're going to meet with him tomorrow, after school. He'll be your counsel."

"I need my own lawyer?"

"If things continue to break the way they are, yes, definitely."

Harding Kleeb was a graduate of Harvard Law School and as East Coast a blueblood as one could find. As many times as our paths had innocently crossed at Mom's parties or Dad's poker games, we never spoke very much. I just knew my father had great confidence in the co-founder of his law firm.

"Why bring in someone new?" I said. "You're the best criminal law attorney in the city."

"You know that an attorney should never represent himself or his family."

"Right. But what's the sudden urgency?"

Dad said his next statement matter-of-factly, like a river that had to run its tumultuous course before it would ever calm down. "Honey, there's a chance the D.A. will bring my case before a grand jury."

"How do you know?"

He smiled. "I have friends in high places."

"But he didn't find anything in our house."

"He didn't, not that I know of. But that doesn't mean the district attorney is giving up."

Dad patiently explained that a suspect didn't have to be arrested to be the subject of a criminal grand jury probe. Sometimes, a grand jury met to find more evidence, which might ultimately lead to an arrest. Twenty-three jurors, plus alternates, would be picked at random from a petit jury list. By subpoenaing witnesses who wouldn't talk candidly to investigating officers, the D.A. would try to construct a much stronger case than the police had built so far, Dad said. It was all about turning up the pressure, he added. The grand jury might find probable cause to indict him for first-degree murder.

"No doubt, you'll be one of those witnesses, Alex."

"Me?"

"Don't look so worried."

"But I am. I'm worried for you."

"The District Attorney's Office would love nothing more than a headline about taking on a well-known criminal law attorney. In fact, they're fast-tracking this case. I should be honored to be so important, huh?" He smiled.

"I'm worried," I repeated.

"Alex, the evidence against me is circumstantial. The grand jury will see that. Unless something new pops up, I won't be indicted."

"What new thing could possibly pop up?" I said. I couldn't imagine my father being arrested or going to prison. I'd already had one parent disappear on me.

"There's nothing to lose sleep over. Believe me."

As my father finished his drink, I thought of the ice cubes rattling in his glass as a pair of dice.

"Now," he said after a moment, "I need to ask you a question. Did you deliver the letter to Charlie's house, or was it someone else?"

"Why is that important?"

"Like Hildenbrand said, your letter had a threatening tone. If someone else typed it or delivered it—"

"I told you, I wrote it."

"But you didn't deliver it," he guessed.

I shook my head. "I was afraid of being seen by Charlie. I asked a friend to do it."

"Which friend? Joyce?"

"A new friend. His name is Edward Montgomery. We met a couple of months ago."

"You never told Mom or me about Edward. Is this a boyfriend?"

"Dad, no! He's just a friend. He's an African-American, a cool guy who happens to be very smart. He lives in a foreclosed house off Cahuenga."

"What do his parents do?"

"I don't know. Why do you care?" I was getting upset. "Can't I make my own friends without your approval?"

"You lied to Hildenbrand," Dad pointed out calmly. "At some point, soon, you'll have to tell the truth. Harding will help you put everything in the proper chronology."

"Including that just before the murder, you drove to Charlie's in the middle of the night, and watched his house for an hour?" I blurted out.

If my father was caught off guard, he didn't show it. His eyes remained as steady as a compass sitting on a map. "How do you know that, Alex?"

"I followed you on foot."

"Yes, then you have to reveal that to the police. Everything that you had actual knowledge of, that relates to the D.A.'s investigation, should never be concealed. To put your mind at ease, I was out that night for a specific purpose. I was deeply agitated about what Charlie had done, and I wanted to talk to him. I wanted everything out in the open."

"In the middle of the night?"

"When you can't sleep, and you want to get things off your chest, yes."

"Okay," I said, resigned to being grilled by Hildenbrand again. At least I'd have an attorney in my corner this time.

"I need to ask you a few more questions about Edward. Where does he live exactly, and where does he go to school?

"I don't want to tell you, Dad."

"Why not?"

"Because that's between Edward and me."

"All right. I don't think there's anything to worry over if your friend did nothing but deliver your letter. Harding can give you his opinion.

"I think I know what's really on your mind," he continued. "It's why you look so nervous right now."

"What's that?" I said, playing dumb.

"I want you to know that I didn't kill Charlie. I might have had that impulse at one time, when I was really angry. But I didn't act on it. I didn't do anything."

"Well, who do you think did?"

"Like I told Hildenbrand, I have no idea, honey. Life isn't a Perry Mason episode."

I felt better as I drifted into the kitchen to serve the dinner our housekeeper had pre-cooked. Toby took the grand jury news in stride. He seemed to believe not only in Dad's innocence but also in his omnipotence. Dad had convinced him he would manhandle anyone dumb enough to break into our house. I began to feel just as safe about facing a grand jury. With my father's firm representing me, I would be ready.

November 21
I didn't know how much the mystery of Charlie's
death had been eating at me until Dad addressed the
point head on. I'm beyond relieved by what he told
me. I'm even beginning to think Mom will come
home soon—a rising tide (of hope) lifts all boats. But
I'm also a born worrier, and besides my Latin test
tomorrow, Edward won't leave my thoughts. Dad
may not be concerned about him, but I am. The
whole fingerprint thing has me a little freaked. I need
to tell Edward about Detective Hildenbrand as soon
as possible.

-32-

The offices of Baten, Kleeb, and Donahue nested on the forty-second floor of a Wilshire Boulevard granite-and-glass rectangle whose sleek and graceful lines, I suspected, an architect like Charlie Diggs would have appreciated, along with BKD's mahogany-paneled offices and conference rooms. The carpeting cost $50 a square yard. The bathrooms were lined with Carrera marble. Anxious clients, for whom well-appointed offices suggested confidence and success, paid whatever it cost to keep them out of prison or from paying onerous fines.

There were four senior partners (Dad called them "rainmakers"), six associates, four paralegals, and eight secretaries, all working within a temple of hushed voices, well-reasoned strategies, and impressive courtroom results. My dad joked that for visiting clients, the most comforting sound was the paper shredder, or the words "privileged and confidential." Most of the company's cases centered on white-collar crime, allegations of illegal acts such as lying, cheating, and theft by executives or government officials. These cases often entailed wrestling matches with the FBI, a district attorney, or a suite of regulatory agencies. Among the partners, Harding Kleeb and my father also had experience in homicide defense.

When we met with Mr. Kleeb on Thursday afternoon, he rose from behind his desk and gave me a vigorous handshake. I didn't wince, but it felt like he'd broken a bone or two in my hand.

"You always call me Mr. Kleeb when we meet," he pointed out. "You're now officially my client. I prefer 'Harding.'"

His monogrammed shirt cuffs were accented by a polka dot bow tie and expensive-looking braces, as men like him always called them. His Savile Row pinstripe, I would learn from Dad, cost $4,000. He was fifty-five, six years older than my father, but without an ounce of fat. He ran half-marathons several times a year. The roundish face had dark, nondescript eyes that reminded me of little periscopes in the way they jumped from side to side, taking in everything around him. I was told he had a prodigious memory for cases, clients, and the law in general. In front of a jury, I imagined, he was someone who commanded respect and fear, just like my father.

"Here's a factoid, young lady. You're my youngest client ever. And according to your father, you'll be one of my smartest."

"I'm just testifying as a witness, isn't that right?"

"That's correct."

"My father said I shouldn't be worried."

"Not if you listen to what I say. But there'll be some challenging moments from the prosecutor. Have a seat, Alex."

I took the chair in front of Harding. "I want you to tell me everything you know about the events preceding the death of Charlie Diggs," he began.

He had a smile that barely broke the plane of his face. He didn't strike me as an emotional man, or as someone inclined to small talk. His fingers interlocked behind his head, holding it steady while his shoulders pushed back in his chair. I stared at his perfectly straight bow tie. I would learn that there was a symmetry and purpose to everything about him. Dad had taken a seat in the corner, watching us.

"Did you know Mr. Diggs well?" I asked Harding.

"I did."

"Weren't you good friends?"

"Not as good as your father and Charlie, but we golfed and played poker."

"I never particularly liked him," I admitted, "but I'm sorry someone murdered him. No one deserves that."

"I agree, but you have to realize that none of us are without enemies. Charlie had his detractors. We have an investigator looking into other suspects. You want to keep the bloodhounds busy."

"You think there's someone who hated him enough to kill him?"

"Anything is possible," Harding answered. "Charlie dealt with some overseas clients that I can assure you are not wholesome citizens. He got into arguments. He took risks with money. Everyone has skeletons, if you dig deep enough."

"What about a burglary?"

"That's possible too, despite what the police are saying now."

I would never have expected my father's partner to be objective— his first duty was to defend Dad, any way he could—but I sensed something deeper than simple lawyer-client loyalty. Charlie might have been my father's best friend, but law partners had an equally powerful bond, maybe deeper than a friendship. If a founding partner was being accused of murder, the reputation—the legacy—of the whole firm was on the line.

I told Harding about Mom and Charlie's sneaking away at our Nile party, Dad driving over to the Diggses' house in the middle of the night, and, in a few sentences, my relationship with Edward. It was impossible that my new friend had anything to do with the murder, I insisted. He was just a go-between.

"But that's not what you told Detective Hildenbrand. You said you dropped off the letter yourself."

"Yes."

"You have to tell the truth, Alex," Harding said, repeating my father's advice. "Otherwise, the police will think you might be protecting Mr. Montgomery from something. Are you?"

"No," I said, startled. "He did me a favor, that's all. Look, he's an honors student, on his way to an Ivy League college."

"Well, that's good to know. The simple truth is that Mr. Montgomery, at your behest, dropped off the letter because you didn't want Charlie or Julia to see you. Isn't that right?"

"That's right." I looked at Dad. He nodded, as if we were all on the same page.

"I'll set up a meeting with the D.A. and Hildenbrand. I'll tell them you were so disturbed by the murder that you weren't thinking clearly about the letter.

"However," Harding added, "innocent or not, it's my strongest advice that you not be in contact with your friend Edward again."

"Why?"

"The less you have to say under oath about Mr. Montgomery, the better. You don't want anyone thinking there's some possible conspiracy between you two."

I was dumbfounded. "What conspiracy?"

"If for some reason the police begin to focus on Mr. Montgomery, it's enough that you two are linked by the letter. The more times you visit him—"

"The D.A. has no reason to be suspicious of Edward," I broke in. "I just told you, he's an honors student . . . ."

"With every unsolved homicide, there's a whirlwind of emotion. Not everyone might believe that a fifteen-year-old could write that letter, or that you wrote it alone. They'll want to know more about Mr. Montgomery. Your father told me he's African-American. How did you two meet? What do you have in common?"

"We met over a cup of lemonade. We've become friends—"

"For both your sakes, put Mr. Montgomery out of your thoughts. You're not to meet with him again, Alex. Am I clear?"

I smiled tightly. "Of course. I understand."

"You saw your father parked in front of the Diggses' house, in the middle of the night, several days before the murder," Harding resumed. "If asked by the prosecutor, you must say exactly that," he echoed my father.

"Won't a jury think Dad was stalking Charlie?"

"You followed your father because you were concerned about his well-being. Any loving daughter would be. He was under considerable stress, with Gloria abandoning him and his emotions still bruised about the affair. But nothing happened that night, other than the victim and his wife getting into an argument, which both you and your father witnessed from the street. Then you watched your dad drive home. You followed him on foot. Isn't that how it happened exactly?"

"Yes."

Harding assured me my father was innocent. Everyone at the firm knew that. So did his friends. Harding said he was not going to plea bargain with the D.A. He wanted a full and total exoneration of Louis Baten. He wanted an apology from the D.A. A loving father and devoted family man, a church-going man, a pillar of the community—

and the D.A. wanted to frame this exemplary citizen for murder? Outrageous, Harding said. But innocence was a fragile and perishable thing, he added. You could never take it for granted. You had to fight for it. Harding repeated what my father had advised me, that I was not to talk to the police again without having counsel present.

We said goodbye. Harding promised he would be coaching me some more. My father stayed behind to do client work. One of the firm's associates drove me to the North Hollywood Police Department, where I was to be fingerprinted. Harding wasn't fazed by this, or by any other obstacle to winning my father's exoneration. He was a man who seemed to fear nothing and was certain of almost everything.

~33~

The first Saturday after Harding warned me never to see Edward again, I rode straight back to his house. It was my third visit since the *Times* had first reported Charlie's murder. There was a new tidbit in the paper almost every day, including that a muscular black man had been seen riding his bike through Toluca Lake a few nights before the murder. I dreaded the meeting Harding was setting up with the police, the one where I was supposed to come clean. Despite being urged to tell the truth, I still hadn't made up my mind how much I was going to say.

Today's front page had left a pit in my stomach. Just as Harding and my father had known, a grand jury was being convened to gather more information about the murder. Detective Hildenbrand was still leading the police investigation, but because progress had been slow, the Los Angeles County District Attorney's Office, which prosecuted felony crimes in an area that covered four thousand square miles, was getting involved. The pressure for an arrest and conviction of someone kept ratcheting up.

When I reached Edward's house, I peeked in the living room window, spotting Monster first, then the bicycle, but no Edward. My two previous visits had ended in frustration. I didn't know whether Edward wasn't home or was hiding inside, but he never answered the door. I couldn't blame him for being angry or upset with me. A new lock had been placed above the door handle.

I began rapping on the door with my fist. "Edward! Please open up!"

When I sneaked another look, I saw a shadow dart between the living room and the bedroom.

I knocked repeatedly, as if that might indicate true urgency to him. "Edward!"

A voice suddenly snapped back. "Go away, Alex."

The anxiety in my stomach came to a boil. "I can't. I have things to tell you."

"Like what?"

"I need to explain."

"I can't take chances like this. There's too much risk. You got me in enough trouble. Go away please," he barked.

I began rattling the handle, like an insistent ghost that needed to be seen and heard. Finally, I listened to the click of the dead bolt. The door opened enough to expose a young man's head and shoulders. I barely recognized Edward. He was the ghost. The anxious, exhausted face looked past me, up and down the street, as if the police might be following me.

"May I come in?"

When he didn't say "no," I sidled past him, beholding a living room more disheveled than on my last visit. It was dotted with a pile of laundry, scattered books, a table with dirty dishes, and recent copies of the *Times* on the couch. I dropped next to the papers. Edward studied me without offering even a soft drink.

"What is it?" His eyes said that the sooner I departed, the happier he would be.

"How could I know the letter wasn't going to work?" I said. "How could I know Charlie would come to our house and get in a fight with Dad? The next day, Mom packed a suitcase and ran away to my aunt's. The more Dad learned about her and Charlie, the more secretive he became—"

"—and then he blew Charlie to kingdom come with a shotgun," Edward filled in, as he fell into the chair across from me.

"My father didn't shoot anyone. He's innocent."

"I haven't been to school in more than a week. I can't focus. I don't sleep. I'm sure teachers are already wondering about me—I've never missed a day until now. There'll be questions soon."

"Just pretend you were sick."

He seemed annoyed that I didn't get his point. "Every day I wake up sick with fear. What's your dad feel when he wakes up? I bet he's got ice water in his veins."

"He's innocent," I repeated.

"How naive can you be? Louis Baten is not just a likely suspect, he's the only suspect. His best friend was having an affair with his wife—who had a stronger motive than your father?"

"No one we know of, but that doesn't mean a suspect won't come along."

"Yeah, me," he said sullenly.

I didn't know how to calm him down. I grew agitated too when I came to the point of my visit.

"Detective Hildenbrand asked me who delivered the letter. I lied and said it was me. But I can't do that anymore."

Edward looked at me helplessly.

"Charlie's wife saw a man ride up on an old-fashioned bike."

"It was night. Someone saw me?" Disbelief seemed to arc through him like a lightning bolt.

"There was a street lamp. Besides, the police have the envelope. They're going to find your prints on it, along with mine."

"My prints," he said, as if he'd never considered that.

"Don't worry. Harding said you'll be okay. I'll explain to the D.A. that I asked you to deliver the letter. You're totally innocent."

He slumped back in the chair, like I'd hit him with a board. "Who's Harding?"

"Harding Kleeb. My father's partner. He's going to be my lawyer."

"Why do you need an attorney? I'm the one who's going to get screwed."

"Why? Your fingerprints aren't on file anywhere, are they? You've never been in trouble—"

Edward seemed to be disappearing in front of me. I sat with my knees together, suddenly worried.

"What's going on, Edward?"

"Why did you ever ask me to take that envelope?" he whispered, staring over my head as if addressing the universe at large. "Why did you ever come into my life?"

"I told you, I had no idea this would happen. I guess I was an idiot for not anticipating."

"Well, *I* did. I anticipated. I knew something bad was going to happen. I was just trying to help you. I'm the idiot."

His eyes burned with suspicion. "What exactly did you tell your lawyer?"

"I said you're a cool guy, and smart, and that you were an honors student going to an Ivy League college."

"You told him I was black?"

"He already knew that from my father."

"Living by myself?"

"I didn't say that."

"What did your letter to Charlie Diggs say?"

"It was dumb," I whispered.

"You told me you were going to be polite—."

"I tried to be. Sometimes things come out differently than you intend."

Every time his eyes flicked to me, he had to see someone hurting, burning to be forgiven. But why would he do that? How was forgiving me going to help him? It wouldn't undo what I had done.

"Don't worry, I'm not going to tell the police anything more than I told my lawyer."

"It's too late," he whispered.

"What's too late?"

"Please, Alex, just leave." He was suddenly staring at the gold-framed drawing on the wall. I turned to look too.

"Are you the artist?" I asked.

"Why is that important?"

"Is that where you grew up? I know you said you were from Brooklyn. That's not what Brooklyn looks like."

"No more questions," he said.

"Why won't you tell me what's going on?"

He rose from the chair. "I have to call someone now."

"Who?"

"What does it take to get rid of you, Alex? His name's Cornelius Appleton. Remember that name when the shit hits the fan."

It was a strange name, unique enough to remember. Edward's chest heaved, like he wished he'd never told me anything. I walked over and wrapped my arms around his shoulders. My kiss wasn't one of passion, or even flirting. I didn't know what it was. His lips came to mine as much as mine went to his. I could feel his heart against my chest.

"They're going to come for me, you know that," he said, pulling back. The air escaping his nostrils had a futile, lost sound, as if both his lungs would empty and he would slump to the floor. "No, they're not. Everything's going to be okay. I'll be here for you." I felt like some empty-headed, chirpy cheerleader, yet I meant my words. His eyes shut, as though pondering whatever secrets he had chosen not to tell me. I was beginning to imagine that the person I was talking to had an entirely different life, and I had fucked it up more than I could possibly know.

~34~

November 24
Ms. Graves called me into her office this morning, just before Thanksgiving recess. She let the suspense build, shuffling papers on her desk before bringing down the hammer. Since my mother was "no longer in the picture," and my father seemed "absorbed in his own problems," she had to deal with me "on a critical family matter." It was best that Toby find another school, she said. Valley's academics were proving too rigorous, and socially, my brother had major challenges. She acknowledged there'd been bullying that wasn't his fault, but the problems were "deeper than that." If my father wanted to discuss the matter immediately, she would make herself available. Otherwise, this was Toby's last day. He needed to empty his locker and meet with his adviser.

I forced a smile at the news, which I knew had been inevitable at some point, just not now. The timing sucked. When I told Toby, his reaction wasn't too different from when he got the boot from Little League. A flare of indignation at being singled out as inadequate followed by relief, if not joy, at being free.

The next morning, when Aunt Agnes answered the phone, I told her that we had a new issue with Toby.

Mom came on the phone and listened to our latest setback at Valley. With the disbelief of someone who had been blindsided, she said, "Well, what am I supposed to do now?"

"I guess you can't do anything. You're a recluse living with Mother Superior. The question is, what are Dad and I supposed to do?"

There weren't a lot of choices. Home schooling was out. Walter Reed Junior High, a public school, was the closest institution of higher learning to Toluca Lake. Thinking ahead, I'd already made an appointment with the principal for Monday.

"You're so organized," Mom said when I told her. "Maybe public school will be okay."

"That's what I told you months ago. This is a blessing in disguise."

"Is Toby all right? I worry about his self-esteem."

"He's fine, considering."

"Will you look after him, Alex?"

"Will you please stop asking me that?" I was ready to blow.

"Who else—"

"Enough," I begged.

She asked how Dad was doing.

"Hanging in. The police questioned him about the murder. Dad and Harding say they aren't overly concerned. But there's going to be a grand jury hearing. This is far from finished."

I didn't tell her Harding was my attorney as well as Dad's, and that I was going to have to testify before the grand jury. I would rather confide in Toby's hamster than share anything more with my mother. I certainly wasn't going to tell her about Edward.

"What do you mean, they're not too concerned? Should they be?" she pushed.

"The district attorney wants to find probable cause to put Dad on trial for murdering Charlie."

There, I had said it, and was counting on a fierce meltdown from Mom. Instead, she declared, "That's ridiculous," like someone who didn't want to speculate on anything, about either Dad or Charlie, that could bring her more pain. She had no choice but to believe in Dad's complete innocence.

I asked once more if she was coming home. I wondered again why I wanted her back. She had betrayed Dad, Toby, and me. But the idea of a wounded family, listing like a ship with a large gash in its hull, was better than no family at all.

"I have to see what my doctor says, Alex." As usual, I heard Agnes rustling about in the background. "Honey, tell Toby I'll call tonight. What are you doing for Thanksgiving?"

"I'm cooking the turkey. Actually, the whole dinner."

"You can ask the housekeeper—"

"No, I'll do it myself. I've got to run. Goodbye, Mom."

Monday morning, our driver ferried Toby and me to Walter Reed Junior High School. Grade sizes were much larger than at Valley— and easier to get lost in, I hoped. We looked absurd being chauffeured to school, but the silent stares we received being dropped off in front of a weed-choked front lawn and a melange of scruffy, aimless students were harder to decode.

An older boy gave me directions to the principal's office. Kids watched Toby saunter by, whispering, as if anyone who got chauffeured to school had to be a celebrity, possibly a movie star, like Corey Feldman in *The Lost Boys*. My brother soaked it all in, like a good suntan, like anything might be possible at his new school. His good looks and "who-gives-a-shit" strut helped fuel speculation.

Mr. Tachet, the principal, introduced himself. He closed the door of his office, pointing us to a couple of chairs in front of a small desk. I looked back through the glass half of the door to the chaos of mostly boys pushing, laughing, and yelling in the hallway.

"Good morning, Mr. Ta-shay," I began. It was a French name, and I was careful to get the pronunciation right. I shook his hand, offering a big smile like my mother would have given. His office was a parody of Ms. Graves' accolade-covered walls—a graying white, dinged up, cramped room with tangled Venetian blinds.

The middle-aged Mr. Tachet had a pencil thin black mustache but thick eyebrows. I could imagine his receding hairline covered by a beret. Behind his desk, he was a fidgety finger-drummer, as if he had a million things to do and no assistant to help him.

"I'm Alexandra Baten," I said, trying to be quick. I explained that my mother was ill, recuperating back East under her sister's care, and my father was preoccupied with professional obligations. I was taking responsibility for enrolling my brother at Walter Reed.

"Your father is Mr. Baten, the attorney, the one who's been in the papers?" Mr. Tachet asked straight out.

"Yes, sir, he is. But he's innocent."

The principal didn't comment. I handed him a list of Toby's classes from Valley and a letter from Toby's adviser describing my brother as a motivated student but someone who "learns differently." He would benefit, the adviser said, from an environment with "less pressure and a more-standard academic load."

Mr. Tachet read the letter, nodded, and told Toby dryly: "Welcome to Walter Reed." There was no interview, no chitchat. It was a public school—it was almost impossible to be turned down. Mr. Tachet said a few things about W.R.—essentially, the dos and don'ts—and sprang to his feet.

"Your first period will be social studies. Room 101. Straight down the hall. Your adviser, Mrs. Dempsey, will catch up with you later, Toby. Any questions?"

"Yes. How much homework do you think I'll have?"

"The average seventh grader is expected to do one to two hours a night."

"Not bad. Do I have to take gym?"

Mr. Tachet nodded. "It's a requirement, not an elective."

"What's your cafeteria like?"

I could see Mr. Tachet wondering where this was going. "Why? Do you have special dietary needs?"

"Sort of. I like my hamburger medium rare and fries crispy."

"Hey, Toby," I said, "I don't think that's relevant."

"Relevant to who?" he countered.

The principal cast me a glance, as though asking if I might be part of this put-on. If I'd had one, I would have stuck a needle in Toby's butt cheek.

"Sir, my brother is just nervous. He has a weird sense of humor. When he applies himself, he's capable of doing well in most subjects. He wants to get into a decent college. We have great hopes for him." I stared at Toby. "Isn't that right?"

"Yes, mother."

Mr. Tachet's phone began to ring, and I could see a line outside his door.

"Wait, there's one more thing," Toby added, ignoring the morning chaos that was piling up. "You know the trouble our father is in. At Valley, I got beat up and bullied. Would it be possible if I could use another name here? You know, so everyone would leave me alone—"

I couldn't decide whether this was more of Toby's rambling humor or he was conniving something. Mr. Tachet, a very busy principal, actually took a moment to consider the request.

"What name did you have in mind?"

"Niles Burns," Toby answered.

"That sounds totally made up."

"Exactly, sir."

I expected Mr. Tachet to let out a guffaw and kick us both out of the office.

"Okay. I'll tell the registrar. Our little secret. Now you better get to social studies, Niles." He turned away to answer the phone.

Whether Mr. Tachet had a heart under his brusque exterior, or my brother was so goofy that the principal refused to waste another second on him, Toby was thrilled. He marched off to class. I don't think anyone saw me slip into our town car and vanish.

At the end of the school day, Dad showed up at Valley instead of our driver. Harding was in the passenger seat. The criminal grand jury, he said, was beginning in two weeks. It was time for us to prepare in earnest.

I gazed out my window. The aching blue line of the horizon was barely visible through layers of smog.

For the rest of the week, to minimize distractions, Harding and my father worked on the case from our house instead of their office. I got permission from Ms. Graves to skip several days of school. Harding started me with an overview. A grand jury always met in secret. Jurors' names were not disclosed to the media or anyone else. The proceedings were purposely one-sided, unlike in a public trial. Witnesses were not cross-examined by the defendant's counsel because there was no defense counsel—in fact, there wasn't even a defendant. And there wasn't even a judge, at least not in the courtroom. One was only likely to be called, Harding said, when a witness refused to answer a question and the prosecutor wanted to cite him or her for contempt. A criminal grand jury wasn't required to hear my father give his side of things. He was under suspicion for killing Charlie but hadn't been arrested, so his rights were limited. However, Harding said he was asking the D.A. to add Dad to the witness list because my father had relevant things to say about the police investigation. The D.A.'s office had promised to get back to us.

Harding kept hammering one point home with me. When it came time to take the witness stand—a process that could last all day—my answers had to be complete, concise, and consistent. There was to be no lying, exaggerating, distorting, embellishing or concealing. I was not to call attention to myself by deliberately provoking the DA. Did I understand? he asked.

"Yes, sir."

"The D.A. would love nothing better than to get you on perjury, Alex. That's how the game is played. A perjurer, threatened with prosecution, almost always turns on the target of the grand jury."

"I would never turn on my father." I said the obvious. The suggestion was almost an insult. Even if I wanted to damage him, I didn't know anything that would do it.

After they finished in Dad's study for the day, I would make drinks for Harding and my father. Once or twice I fixed them hors d'oeuvres. In a way, domestic duties kept me distracted. Before going to bed, I wrote in my journal about my case of nerves, which revealed itself one morning as a scarlet rash on both forearms.

The biggest surprise in those two weeks was Toby. Mom had called to wish him well at Walter Reed, but that had nothing to do with what I termed "the miracle." My brother's incarnation as Niles Burns exceeded even his own expectations. I thought he would tell kids that he was an actor in an upcoming TV series. Instead, he impersonated a young wunderkind, a consultant for an unnamed software company. One of his perks was to have his own driver usher him to school. Somehow, this was credible to twelve- and thirteen-year-olds. Niles told everyone he was an expert on DOS, the Hayes V-Series Smart-Modem 2400, and the hottest and most expensive computer on the market, the Toshiba T1200 Laptop.

Toby devoured magazines like *PC World* and *Computer Shopper*. He knew that though there were eight hundred thousand cell phones in the world, the day would come when there would be three or four billion—almost everyone would own one. A company called AOL, with its dialup modem, was about go to public. Toby insisted my father buy the stock, along with Microsoft, because, he predicted, their share prices were going to the moon.

It was suddenly hard to shut Toby up. At dinner, he informed us about the global reach of the internet, the importance of owning domain names, and the different operating systems of Apple and Microsoft. At school, to a growing corps of video game addicts, he explained everything about the Shadow of Mordor, Final Fantasy II, and Super Mario Brothers 3. For the more serious-minded, Niles Burns held informal after-school computer classes, because Walter Reed didn't have any. He charged everyone $10 per class. Either Mr. Tachet didn't find out or didn't care.

I congratulated my brother on his newfound success. Toby shrugged like it was no big deal. "You don't get it, sis. Reality is so simple. Just mind your business and do what you're good at," he assured me, like he was the guru for all wayward adolescents, including me.

Whatever I did in front of the grand jury, he added, I shouldn't screw things up by lecturing everyone on right and wrong. He was referring to more than my Founder's Day speech. He'd always thought I tried to impose my point of view on others.

"Look who's lecturing now," I said dryly.

When I called Mom and told her of Toby's transformation, I could feel her gloating through the phone. "Of course," she said, as she rewrote family history not for the first time. "Didn't I always say how successful your brother would be one day!"

~35~

That weekend, without telling anyone again, I rode my bike to Edward's. Three sedans that looked like unmarked police cars were in front of his house. I dropped my bike and sprinted up the grass.

The door was half open, so I just walked in. Four or five men were milling around. I guessed right away that Edward had split. His barbells, baseball bats, treadmill, and furniture were there, but when I peeked in his room, his clothes and books were gone—Monster too, I assumed, since the cat food had disappeared. The gold-framed drawing had been removed from the wall. I had no idea where he'd found sanctuary, or if he'd had help. Two cops were dusting doorknobs and table surfaces for prints. They would find mine there, but it didn't matter. Harding had already told Hildenbrand that I had asked Edward to deliver my letter, and that I'd visited his house more than once.

"You look surprised," Hildenbrand said when he spotted me from the kitchen. He was scrutinizing the empty fridge and drawers, the whole angry configuration of a half-torn-out kitchen. "Did you guys have a date or something? Did Jaleel stand you up?"

"Who's Jaleel?"

"Jaleel Robeson, from Peartree, Texas?"

I shook my head.

"I thought you two were friends. Wow. Guess he was holding out on you."

I tried not to feel too stupid, and wondered what else Hildenbrand had to tell me. He was enjoying his authority. I followed him to the living room and sat on the couch.

"Off the record," he said, "did you help him, Alex?"

"Help him what?"

"Escape."

"Let me call my attorney," I responded.

"No need. You really don't know?"

I was getting frustrated. "Don't know what?"

"Jaleel Robeson, a.k.a. Edward Montgomery, is a fugitive from justice. He's wanted for killing his father in Peartree, Texas. Six years ago, he escaped from a county facility and eventually made his way here, hiding in plain sight. He goes to a public high school and earns straight A's, becomes a great candidate for admission to Princeton. Give him credit—he shows grit and intelligence, not to mention infinite chutzpah." Hillenbrand's brow flew up as he glanced around. "Hell, how do you suppose someone lived in this dump?"

"He killed his father? I don't believe you."

"Ask the police in Peartree."

"I wouldn't believe them either."

I suddenly couldn't get Edward, now Jaleel, out of my mind. There had to be more to the story than Hildenbrand was telling. Jaleel had begun to open up our last time together. Remembering our kiss, I couldn't accept that he would disappear without letting me know. Maybe Hildenbrand had found a note for me and was keeping it.

"You okay?" He was picking up on my agitation. Hildenbrand was in off-duty attire: khakis with a blue and white polo shirt, and sneakers with a Nike swoosh.

"I'm fine."

"Come on, Jaleel must have told you a few secrets," he pushed. "If you think he's innocent—"

"You said at school that we weren't talking anymore. And you've met my attorney. He can get really pissed off."

"If I was really a hardass, Alex, I could accuse you of helping conceal a fugitive."

"That would be bullshit. I never knew he was a fugitive. All I knew was his name was Edward Montgomery and he was a senior at North Hollywood High."

"Just tell me how he survived. Someone had to help him. He was twelve when he left Peartree. How did he support himself here? We're trying to find an employer. Maybe someone at his school knows."

"I guess you'll have to ask around."

At the moment, I thought, I was acting beyond stupid. A fifteen-year-old, sitting in the house of a friend wanted for murder, was talking to a police detective who wouldn't hesitate to extract information any way he could. The smartest thing would be to say goodbye, grab my bike, and head home. Or just call Harding.

I didn't run away or call anyone. I was in some adrenalized, fearless state, not unlike the way my father could get. If somebody intimidates you, he told me once, you need to intimidate them right back.

"You should stop asking me questions," I said. "Everything I tell you will be hearsay. It's inadmissible in court."

"Actually, evidentiary standards are a lot lower in a grand jury hearing." He stood up and stretched, gazing around the house again. "Hey," he said, "I'm going to order pizza. Starved. How about you?"

"No, thank you."

He took his cell phone outside. After the other men left, I wandered through the house, looking in Jaleel's bedside table. It had been emptied of his letter from Princeton and everything else. His closet was bare too. Wherever he had gone, I hoped it was far away.

When the pizza arrived, Hildenbrand sat across from me in the living room.

"Are you sure?" he said, holding an oily slice in the air. We were alone. The front door was partly open for ventilation.

"I'm not hungry."

"Want to talk off the record, Alex?"

"About what?"

"People like you have the wrong impression of me. And maybe I can get to know you better too." He took a healthy bite of the pizza.

"That's what you really want, to get to know me better?"

It was bullshit, but I was too curious not to go along. He asked if I'd started prepping for the grand jury, joking that I didn't look nervous enough. He said my father was as an iceberg on the surface, but down deep, he believed Dad was an angry man. I said I'd never seen my father really lose his temper, except with Charlie the night of the poker game.

"The killer shot Charlie in the face—that shows more than losing your temper. And to shoot him twice? Is there a term for deep and abiding rage?"

"Temporary insanity," I said. "What's your point? My father isn't the killer."

"Consider, for a moment, that this killing had nothing to do with insanity. Consider simply that the killer has violent tendencies. Normal tendencies."

"You're saying that violence is normal?"

"In a lot of men, yeah, just as most women have a nurturing capacity. I'm speaking as a cop, what I've observed. For men, something lights their fuse, and the explosion has a force of its own. Even if they don't say so, even if they aren't even aware, men are drawn to violence. Movies, books, sports, even stories you hear from friends. The bloodier, the better—you know? Take me. I like shooting my firearm at the range, and if the occasion comes, at fleeing suspects. It feels good." He looked at me. "Off the record, right?"

"Okay," I said.

"I've hit my wife. More than on one occasion."

I didn't have a response, other than to wonder what other secrets he wanted to confess to a near stranger. I felt another urge to get up and grab my bike.

"Not proud of domestic violence, mind you, but it happens. I kind of explode. My wife and I go to therapy. There's hope for us, I think. But my point is, you wouldn't guess that behavior from looking at me—or your father—would you?"

"My father never hit my mother," I said. "I don't know of any violence in his past. I don't think he's even gotten a speeding ticket."

Hildenbrand went back to his pizza. "You're right. We checked. Your dad is so clean it's scary.

"Nevertheless, ask a psychologist. Violence is in the male DNA. It's how the cave man survived. He had his territory, and if someone intruded, what do you think he did? He didn't sit down and say, Hey, let's talk about why you're here. He picked up a weapon. You know, when your dad goes hunting, what do you think goes through his mind?"

"I wouldn't know. I've never been hunting."

"Your dad never showed you how to fire a gun?"

"He tried."

"Women rarely kill with guns; they're built differently."

"I don't know what your point is," I said.

"I'm thinking about Jaleel too. Are you sure he doesn't have a violent side?"

"I doubt it very much."

"You two have a special bond—a soulmate thing? Or maybe you just have a crush?"

"I'm not answering that."

"When you've been on the run for six years, hunted, scared, feeling vulnerable," he went on, "you are one pent-up dude. You are primed to explode. You're ready for unexpected opportunities. That could mean ripping off a very nice home."

"Why would a highly rational person like Jaleel do something stupid like that?"

"Besides frustration and anger, here was a chance for a black kid to steal jewelry and cash."

"That's racist."

"Call it what you want. My job is to get to the bottom of things."

"So now we're back to a burglary. If you think my father killed Charlie, why are you even speculating about Jaleel?"

"It's my job to track down all leads. I don't make the final decision. That's up to the D.A. and a jury."

He had finished eating, and locked down the cover with the leftover slices inside. Then he pushed himself off the couch as he checked his watch.

"My opinion is that your father murdered Charlie Diggs. But in case I'm wrong, I think if Jaleel killed his father in Texas, in a pique, he could murder a second time."

"I'd like to hear Jaleel's story of how his father died. I don't believe yours."

Hildenbrand's shoulders rose and fell at the great unknown. I followed him outside as he began circling the house, making one last check for evidence.

"Did you find anything for me?" I called, sitting on my bike.

He angled his head back, and a hand pushed his ear forward.

"Did Jaleel leave a note for me?"

"You're out of luck there, Alex. I would have given it to you if I'd found something."

"Cross your heart?"

"I would have had to read it first, but unless it was self-incriminating, it would have been yours."

In our off-the-record encounter, Hildenbrand had opened himself up. Hitting his wife didn't necessarily make him a monster perhaps, just confused. He was in therapy; he wanted his marriage to work. I wanted to give my adversary the benefit of the doubt, if only for the moment.

~36~

December 16
I got a letter from Jaleel today, by luck nabbing it
from the mailbox before anyone else did. He
confirmed what Hildenbrand had told me about
running from Peartree, except it was a different story.
His parents had died in a murder-suicide, which he
had witnessed after coming home from baseball
practice. His father had lost his job that day, and
gave in to a despair that Jaleel still didn't
understand. He didn't know which was worse,
witnessing an act of violence he should have been able
to prevent or being accused by a detective of
committing that violence. He apologized for not
telling me everything when we were together—he just
couldn't. He was with a friend now, though he didn't
say who or where. Maybe it's Cornelius Appleton.
The envelope had no return address. It was
postmarked in San Luis Obispo, but I knew that
didn't mean anything. It could have just been a town
he was passing through. I feel soooooo great that Jaleel
is okay for now.

I'm scheduled to testify before the grand jury
tomorrow—finally. I'm not the first witness, nor the
last. Despite the rash on my arms, I haven't been

really nervous until this moment, thinking what it will be like to face twenty-three strangers and a tough prosecutor. Only twelve of the twenty-three need to vote "yes" on probable cause to indict. The D.A., after interviewing my father, decided not to let Dad take the witness stand. Harding said it was because my father's years of famously charming jurors gives him an advantage over an unsmiling prosecutor. Harding is pissed about this, but it's the D.A.'s party and he controls the invite list. Harding said a lot would be riding on my testimony.

God knows he's rehearsed me. I'm ready to talk about events preceding the murder, my friendship with Jaleel, Charlie, and of course my family. The prosecutor, Hildenbrand, and individual jurors can chip away at a witness all day long. While everything in a grand jury hearing is confidential, I'm allowed to confer with my attorney if someone asks me a confusing question. Harding will be just outside the courtroom, in the hallway with Dad.

I slipped under the covers, wondering if I'd be able to fall asleep. Dad came in and kissed me on the forehead. He looked as stoical as ever. Alison Krause's voice poured like honey through my headphones, but music wasn't enough to put me under. I began thinking about Christmas, nine days away. We didn't even have a tree up in the living room. When it came to holiday decorations, Mom, as she did for our parties, made sure we were the talk of Toluca Lake.

I'd call a decorating service when I'm done with the grand jury, I thought. A repeat of last year's themes would be the simplest route. It might make the three of us feel like this year never happened. We'd be happily frozen in the past: a huge red velvet bow on our front door, winking frost-blue lights lining the roof, Frosty the Snowman, and Santa with his sled of reindeer streaking over our lawn. That's how I finally fell asleep, jumping back in time.

~37~

With forty-seven courthouses, Los Angeles County Superior Court was the largest court system in the United States. My father's case was being heard in the West District. The three of us had breakfast at a coffee shop, going over last-minute details. The DeVille was as quiet as church on our way to the court parking lot. We checked in at the clerk's office on the first floor, and took the elevator to the sixth. A deputy district attorney and several uniformed bailiffs were waiting in the hallway outside our courtroom. The doors were closed as the grand jury was already in session.

"Are you okay, honey?" my father asked. The three of us were alone for a moment. For a case as sensational as my father's, the media had been barred from the floor.

"I'm good. I'm okay"—which was not quite true. My stomach was in a rumble. I had imagined this moment for weeks, like I'd anticipated the morning I addressed the Valley alumni. Now, something was different. The stakes were far greater. My head ached. My legs wobbled. I looked away from my father to see the deputy D.A. beckoning to me to enter the courtroom.

"I can't," I whispered to no one.

Harding, who was bending over the drinking fountain, turned. "What's the matter, Alex?"

"I can't do this."

"Of course you can. You know this case backwards and forwards—"

"Excuse me." My gaze found the bathrooms, and I walked rapidly toward the women's room. In sixty seconds, I chucked my entire breakfast. Light-headed, I looked in a shimmering mirror above the sink. Blood had drained from my face. I was embarrassed, feeling as if the whole world had just witnessed my meltdown. I took a half-dozen deep breaths, washed my face and hands, and waited for my head to clear. If my mother had been around, she would have told me to put on fresh makeup too.

I walked back to Harding and my father, signaling that I was better, or hoped that I was. The deputy D.A. hadn't budged from his perch. He waved to me again, looking impatient. Dad's hand cupped my shoulder, to give me confidence. I walked into the courtroom and listened to the door shut behind me. The wood-paneled room wasn't any different from the ones where I'd watched my father at work, except now there was no defense table, no attorney to shout "objection." The judge's bench was also empty. There was a stenographer—a young woman with tinted red hair—to record everything. I counted twenty-five jurors in all, cozily settled in and around the jury box. Some nursed cups of coffee. The deputy D.A. introduced me to the jury foreman but only by his first name.

Though they resembled one another, I told myself that the witness stand was not the electric chair at San Quentin. I was going to be fine.

The Major Crimes Unit was administered by the chief deputy district attorney. Her name was Lydia Mason-Jones, and she was suddenly standing in front of me.

"Good morning, Miss Baten."

Her voice was as crisp and cool as a head of lettuce. She looked to be about five-foot-nine, all business in a blue tweed suit. Her posture was military straight, her shoulders wide, and her face, with the barest of makeup and small diamond studs in her ears, void of softness. That wasn't to say she wasn't attractive, in a way that super-confident and determined people can be. But she was also as intimidating as a samurai warrior.

"As prosecutor, I represent the people of Los Angeles County, investigating Louis Baten in the death of Charles Anton Diggs," she informed me. "Is there anything that you need clarified before we begin?"

"Do I address you as Miss, Mrs., or Ms. Lydia Mason-Jones?" I didn't know why I asked, other than nerves. I didn't really care.

"Chief deputy district attorney," she replied. It was a mouthful no matter what.

While she turned to a table to scrutinize her notes on a legal pad, the foreman, a diminutive man with glasses and thinning silver hair, swore me in.

In the witness chair, I straightened my back and looked Lydia Mason-Jones in the eye. The basics took a few minutes: age, address, school, family structure, extent of daily interaction with my father, where my mother was living now. With every answer, my voice worked its way up the confidence ladder.

"Miss Baten," she said, "do you remember what night and time the murder of Mr. Diggs took place?"

"October 29, around 11:50 p.m."

"How do you know that? Did your father tell you?"

"No ma'am. That was what was reported in the *Los Angeles Times*."

"Before the event was reported in the media, did you visit the scene of the crime?"

"I did. My friend, Joyce, woke me the morning of October 30, around seven thirty. I was shocked by the news. I went over to the Diggses' house. The police were there, along with a lot of anxious neighbors."

"What was your reaction?"

"Besides mourning the life of the victim, I was sad for Julia Diggs. I was sad for my parents as well. The four of them had been close friends forever."

"Your father and Mr. Diggs were particularly close, were they not?"

"Yes, I'd say so."

"Did your father seem shocked by the murder?"

"That morning, when I woke him in bed, giving him the news, I'd say he was surprised but not upset."

"Not upset? Could you explain that to the jurors?"

"My father and Mr. Diggs had been in a physical fight, in our house, about two weeks before. My father believed Charlie Diggs was having an affair with my mother."

"And was this true?"

"My mother confirmed that it was."

"And then your mother left your father. She flew to the East Coast, to stay with her sister. Is that correct?"

"Yes."

"Was your father upset by your mother leaving him?"

"Yes."

"What did he do or say to make you think he was upset?"

"He asked me questions about what I knew about Charlie and Mom. Her leaving took him by surprise."

"What were your other thoughts as you observed your father during this period?"

"I was concerned about his emotional state. I was afraid he was going to blame Mr. Diggs for breaking up his marriage."

"Isn't it true that several nights before the killing, in the middle of the night, you heard your father go into the garage and start his car?"

"Yes."

"What did he do?"

"He drove away."

"What did you do?"

I pushed my back into the chair. "I got out of bed, put on some clothes, and followed him."

"Where did you think he was going?"

"The Diggses' house. It's less than half a mile from our house."

"So you followed on foot?"

"Yes."

"What did you do when you got there, Miss Baten?"

"I hid behind a tree."

"What was your father doing?"

"Just sitting in his car. He was trying to get up the nerve to knock on the door and talk to Mr. Diggs."

"Really? In the middle of the night? Why did you think that?"

"My father later told me he was too restless to sleep, and he wanted to get things off his chest with Mr. Diggs. But he never got out of the car. As I was watching everything, a light went on upstairs, in the master bedroom. Mr. Diggs and his wife were having an argument. Apparently, my mother had called Mr. Diggs in the middle of the night. That would have really upset Mrs. Diggs."

I was corrected swiftly. "The jurors can reach their own conclusions about motive for the Diggses' argument, Miss Baten."

"You don't want my opinion on anything?" I asked. I could imagine Harding telling me to calm down.

"No. Not unless you qualify as an expert witness," she said with enough sarcasm to put me in my place.

Her eyes flashed on me and then turned back to the jurors. "Just before your father left for Mr. Diggs' house in the middle of night, Miss Baten, you observed him going into his gun safe, is that correct?"

"Not exactly. From the upstairs landing, I saw him in front of the hallway gun closet, and I heard what I thought was the safe being opened, and then things being moved around inside the safe. I didn't see him take anything out."

"Your father owns several rifles and shotguns, does he not?"

"I was told the police had determined that my father's shotgun was not the murder weapon."

"That wasn't my question."

"Yes, he owns some rifles, shotguns, and pistols."

"So he knew how to fire a shotgun. I understand he was an exceptional shot, a duck hunter. Is that correct?"

I told her she was right.

She picked up her legal pad from her table and scribbled something. "Mr. Diggs was supposed to be alone in his house that night. Did you know that, Miss Baten?"

"No."

"Julia Diggs has testified that she had been planning to fly to San Francisco that day, to visit her mother. She postponed her trip at the last minute."

"I wasn't aware." I stole a glance at the jurors. It was hard to tell what they were thinking.

"The police believe that your father was intending to murder Mr. Diggs that night, if not for the surprise of finding Mrs. Diggs at home. When you were hiding behind that tree, what were you thinking and feeling?"

"A lot of things went through my mind, but then my father clarified his motive when I told him I'd seen him."

The prosecutor strolled back to the table, opened a manila folder, and pulled out a sheaf of pages, which she handed to me.

"These are phone company records for the Diggses' residence. I want to call your attention to the calls I've highlighted in yellow."

I looked through everything and found one page with over a dozen incoming calls at all hours marked by the prosecutor. The phone number they came from was always the same: Aunt Agnes's house. I looked up.

"You can see that a call was placed to the Diggses' house not only the night you saw your father in his car but several other nights that week. Do you know if your father was aware of these calls?"

"I have no idea. He didn't tell me."

"Did he tell you at any time that he hoped your mother would return home and patch up their marriage? That's what he told Detective Hildenbrand she said."

"Yes. He asked me if I thought that was possible."

"What did you say?"

"I said I hoped so but I couldn't be sure."

"Yet your mother admitted to the detective that she was in love with Mr. Diggs and wanted to divorce your father. What did she tell you and your father?"

"I never heard that from my mother. She didn't come to the phone when I called my aunt's house. My father said that when he asked my mother the same question on the phone, just after she left our house, she said she didn't want to divorce him. She needed to rest, she said, and then she would be home."

"So which was true—your mother was coming home, or seeking a divorce?"

"That would be asking me for an opinion, ma'am."

The prosecutor just stared at me. She was losing patience with my being a smart ass. Maybe I had gone too far. I wondered nervously— what if she called a judge and said I was being uncooperative? Harding would have a cow.

"Your father is a criminal defense attorney, Miss Baten," she continued. "A very successful one. Someone who has to rely on his intuition all the time."

"I suppose so."

"His intuition must have been telling him about his marriage, despite what Gloria allegedly said on the phone. Did he talk to you about that?"

"There was so much said. It was a very traumatic period for us. To the best of my memory, he implied that no matter how hurt he was, he would never commit a murder where he would be such an obvious suspect."

With my mother, I wanted to add, you couldn't always be sure what the truth was, but that would have been an opinion, too.

I had no problem looking at the jurors for their opinion. Several nodded at my last observation. I could tell now that they liked me, maybe more than they did the prosecutor. She was like a runaway train, ready to plow over any obstacle on her path to winning an indictment.

When I told the chief deputy district attorney that I had a question for her, her chin jutted out impatiently. I was beginning to feel a larger swell of confidence, despite the risk of being out of line.

"How could my father, or anyone for that matter, manage to murder someone and not leave a trace of blood or a fingerprint behind? I understand that there was no evidence whatsoever."

"We've already had experts testify about this, Miss Baten," she said coolly.

She returned to her table, picked something out a drawer, and reapproached me. "Tell me about your relationship with Jaleel Robeson. You first knew him as Edward Montgomery, is that correct?"

"I only knew him as Edward Montgomery. We met several months ago. He was selling lemonade in front of his house. We became friends."

"As the jury already knows, Mr. Robeson is wanted for allegedly murdering his father in Texas. When did you learn that from Mr. Robeson.?"

"Only after he delivered the letter."

"This letter?" She paused to hold up the same plastic sleeve that Detective Hildenbrand had brought to our house.

"Yes."

"When you asked Mr. Robeson to drop this in the Diggses' mailbox, did you first tell him about your mother's affair?"

"I did. I said I didn't want to take the chance of being seen by Mr. Diggs. I didn't want a confrontation with anybody."

The prosecutor nodded. "The discovery of the affair must have been unsettling for you. It's not unreasonable to assume you wanted to remain invisible in your parents' domestic situation."

"As invisible as possible." Unless you lived under a rock, I might have added, you got dragged into your parents' mess no matter what.

"What did Mr. Robeson say when you asked for his help?"

"He didn't want to do it."

"But in the end, he did as you asked."

"Yes, as a favor to me."

"He rode his bike to the Diggses' house, and put your letter in their mail box. Mrs. Diggs saw a young man on a bicycle. The police assume that this was Mr. Robeson."

"If Mrs. Diggs says she saw a young black man on a bicycle, yes, almost certainly. Toluca Lake doesn't have a lot of black people."

"Julia Diggs wasn't able to identify the race of the individual, but Mr. Montgomery later told you that he did as you had asked him, didn't he?"

"Yes."

"Since you weren't there, Miss Baten, you have no idea how long Mr. Robeson stuck around the Diggses' house, or what he did afterwards."

"He didn't tell me anything about that."

"The police speculate that he took a good look at that very expensive house and got an idea in his head. Not at that moment, perhaps, but later. Something that told him to come back and burglarize the house. Did he at all hint at this to you?"

"Absolutely not."

"Are you sure?"

I barely kept my temper. "He was an honors student at his school. He was counting on going to Princeton. Why would someone like that jeopardize his future?"

"So let me understand, Miss Baten. You don't think your father could possibly murder Mr. Diggs, and you don't think Mr. Robeson could have committed the killing either."

"I think I've made that clear."

"I see." She touched the pen to her nose, and moved even closer to me. "Do you think it's possible your father saw Mr. Robeson riding his bike around the Diggses' residence?"

"You mean the evening he delivered my letter?"

"I'm talking about much later, well after your mother left your father. We've had witnesses testify that they saw a young black man riding his bike in the area of the Diggses' house, specifically on the evenings of October 23 and October 24. That would be approximately a week before the murder."

Impossible, I wanted to tell her. Why would Jaleel go back to the Diggses' house, or Toluca Lake? "I know nothing about that."

"Do you know if your father, simply driving home from work, saw Mr. Robeson riding his bike in the neighborhood, as others have testified?"

"He never told me that."

"Perhaps he heard other people say that they saw Mr. Robeson. The police believe that would give him a motive to stage a burglary after he murdered his best friend."

Her scenario was pure speculation—in my head I could hear Harding cry "inflammatory!"—but I was already in enough trouble for bending the rules as a witness to criticize the prosecutor. I sipped from a glass of water as she looked back at me.

"How many times after the murder did you and Mr. Robeson get together?"

"A couple."

"How many times did you discuss the homicide with him?"

I tried to think. Jaleel had brought up the topic. "Once or twice."

"He never told you what really happened?"

"He told me he didn't kill Charlie Diggs."

"And you believe him?"

"Yes."

"Who did he say he thought murdered Mr. Diggs?"

"He said my father."

"Your father?" She paused, letting my answer sink in with the jury. "You said earlier that Mr. Robeson was an honors student, likely to be accepted to Princeton. No doubt someone with character and integrity, certainly in your judgment. Did you believe him when he said the murder was committed by your father?"

"I said he was wrong. I knew my father was innocent."

"And how did you know that?"

"My father is a man of integrity."

"You're giving me an opinion again."

"I suppose so."

"Then in your opinion, who do you believe? Your father or your friend?"

I didn't answer. I understood what the prosecutor was doing. If she couldn't convince the jury that my father had been the killer, she was setting up Jaleel. Even if he hadn't been questioned by the police, let alone arrested—even if the jury I was facing would have nothing to do with Jaleel should he ultimately be indicted—the D.A. was stirring the pot.

"That's all I have for you for now. Thank you, Miss Baten. You're excused for a ten-minute recess. Please don't leave the room."

"I'd like to see my attorney. He's in the hallway."

Her head perked up. "That's your privilege. Go ahead."

I made my way out of the room, waiting for my pulse to slow. Harding pulled me to one side when I came out, and we spoke in rough whispers so the bailiffs couldn't overhear. I told him some of the questions I'd been asked, and my answers.

"I don't think this is going too well," I said.

"From what you've told me, you're doing fine. Just keep your cool, Alex, and don't sass the prosecutor. After you finish, our side gets a copy of your transcript. If the prosecutor was out of line with you, or any witness, then I'll go to a judge."

My eyes pointed at Dad as he walked over. "Before the murder, did you see Jaleel riding around the neighborhood after dark?" I asked him straight out.

"Yes, I think I did."

"Why didn't you tell me?"

He frowned as if the answer was obvious. "The less you know, honey, the less the prosecutor can pull out of you."

"What else haven't you told me?"

"Nothing. You know everything now. The prosecutor is going to keep irritating you. Just stand your ground."

"What about Jaleel?"

It was Harding's turn to look perplexed. "What about Mr. Robeson? I told you. He's not relevant."

"He is to me. He's on the run again."

"How do you know that, Alex? All the police told us was he vacated his residence."

"Just a guess," I lied.

Harding's hand dropped on my shoulder, like a master trying to calm his jittery apprentice. "You know how this works, Alex. Our only job—your only job—is to help your father establish his innocence."

I nodded, trying to feel better, but then my gaze darted to a figure striding down the hall with authority, toward the grand jury room. He avoided eye contact with me. A bailiff opened the door and Detective Hildenbrand entered with his briefcase swaying in his hand. The door closed swiftly behind him.

"What's he doing here?" I asked, feeling my stomach clutch. "You said the police always testify early in a grand jury case."

Both Harding and my father seemed surprised by Hildenbrand's appearance. Only the prosecutor was allowed to ask a witness questions.

"Maybe the police found new evidence," Harding allowed. Dad nodded but didn't seem especially concerned. "Don't worry about it, honey."

What evidence could it be, I wanted to ask, but my father had just said there were no more secrets. He had revealed everything to me.

"Keep up the good work, Alex," urged Harding. It was more like a command than a compliment, and I marched back into the jackal's den.

~38~

Detective Hildenbrand was standing next to the chief deputy district attorney, his briefcase open on the table in front of them, when I reentered the room. I tried futilely to see inside the briefcase. The two continued to whisper. Hildenbrand, in a gray suit and navy tie, looked rested and focused when he finished his chat and took a seat at the table.

I returned to the witness chair, locking my gaze on the detective. He met my eyes for a second and looked away.

"So far you've established in your testimony," the prosecutor began, looking more at the jury than at me, "that you have no first hand knowledge of the murder, but you believe your father is innocent of killing Mr. Diggs."

"That's correct," I said.

"He never confessed anything to you about that night, or said, 'keep this a secret,' or anything like that?"

"No, he did not," I said. I realized I might be lying. Two minutes ago my father had revealed to me he had seen Jaleel on his bicycle. He had been keeping a secret.

"Does your father suffer from asthma?" she suddenly asked with a disarming smile.

"Excuse me?"

"It's a simple question. Does you father have asthma?"

In our preparation, Harding had never brought up the issue of my father's health, nor had Hildenbrand or the police. "A light case," I said.

"How long has he had asthma?"

"I'm not sure. Since he was my age, I think."

"He was turned down for the draft, for the Vietnam conflict, because of his asthma, wasn't he?"

"I believe so."

"Does he rely on his inhaler when he has an attack now? Or when he thinks he'd entering a stressful situation, perhaps? Have you seen anything like that with your father?"

I answered that on occasion, in his study, I'd watched him push his inhaler into his mouth and use it.

"An inhaler like this?" the prosecutor continued, returning to Hildenbrand's briefcase. She raised a plastic sleeve in the air for the jury to note. The prosecutor marched over and handed it to me. The four-inch inhaler had a green plastic casing, with a canister of Albuterol inside.

"My father has one like this," I admitted, handing the plastic sleeve back.

"Charlie Diggs didn't have asthma. Nor does Mrs. Diggs. Yet this inhaler was found in the victim's bedroom closet the morning after the murder."

"I don't understand your point," I said, trying to think quickly.

"It's quite simple, Miss Baten. The police are wondering how an inhaler got into Mr. Diggs' closet. Did your father ever make reference to visiting Mr. Diggs' home and taking along his inhaler?"

"No," I said.

"We're going to be entering this inhaler as evidence, thanks to the work of Detective Hildenbrand, who's just finished his investigation."

"It looks like my father's inhaler but maybe it's not," I managed to say. "His duck hunting friends—Charlie's friends too—I know one of them has asthma. He could have left his inhaler behind and Charlie stuck it in the closet."

"Detective Hildenbrand has contacted twenty two of Mr. Diggs' friends. Three have asthma and use inhalers, but none with a green canister."

I knew the police had checked the inhaler for fingerprints. If they'd found my father's, we'd possibly already be in a murder trial. I returned the prosecutor's stare and said nothing.

My nemesis revisited her desk, opened a drawer, and raised another, smaller plastic sleeve for me to see. Attached was a large tag that read "Exhibit 12" in bold print.

"I'd like to show you something else, something the jurors have already seen, Miss Baten," she said as she moved toward me. The sleeve was small enough that I had to hold it close to my face to see anything. I was squinting at what looked like a single human hair. "We found this on Charlie's shirt, the one he was wearing the evening he was murdered. It's already been entered as an exhibit, as you can see. Detective Hildenbrand testified about it to the jury."

I shrugged "so what" and gave it back.

"There's a very sophisticated test now available to police labs, based on human DNA samples," she lectured me. "Forensic scientists can now analyze someone's hair or saliva, for example, to determine their molecular structure. The hair I just showed you has the same molecular structure as one that Detective Hildenbrand pulled from your father's hair brush in his bathroom."

I remembered Hildenbrand and his sidekick roaming through our house. My overconfident father had given them permission to search at will.

"May I ask a question?" I interrupted.

The chief deputy district attorney reminded me that I was a witness, not a prosecutor. My job was to answer questions, not ask them.

"I had presumed Mr. Diggs was in his pajamas when he was killed," I continued anyway. "The murder was in the middle of the night."

"He was not in his pajamas," she replied.

"Then what shirt was he wearing? Am I allowed to see photos from the crime scene?"

The prosecutor once more looked annoyed with me, but she dug through a manila folder on her desk and produced several black-and-white photos to hand over.

"Do you have a point to make, Miss Baten?"

I had a hard time looking at what was left of Charlie's face. I wanted to throw up again. But I recognized the shirt—Hawaiian, with wide lapels, images of palm trees across the front.

"Mr. Diggs wore this shirt at the poker game," I said, amazed but gratified by the coincidence. "Anyone at our house can confirm it. My father and Mr. Diggs shoved and pushed each other in the kitchen. Wouldn't it be possible that's how my father's hair got on his shirt?" It was something Perry Mason might have pulled out of his hat.

"Perhaps. Perhaps not. Detective Hildenbrand is still checking with neighborhood dry cleaners about when this shirt was last cleaned. The victim traveled quite a bit. It's conceivable that the shirt was cleaned in an entirely different city, after the poker game."

The prosecutor was strolling toward the jury members, more intent on convincing them than me.

I wasn't impressed. She was speculating. It seemed likely, if the only evidence the police had captured from the crime scene was a single hair on a shirt that most likely had not have been cleaned, and an asthma inhaler without fingerprints, that none of this sufficed to establish probable cause.

Hildenbrand, after exchanging glances with the prosecutor, closed the brass latches on his briefcase and rose from the table, but not without firing a look at me. This was not over, his gaze said.

I stayed on the stand for another thirty-five minutes. The prosecutor suddenly badgered me about Jaleel's personality, asking if I thought he was a violent person underneath the veneer of academic and athletic star. My thoughts flew back to my off-the-record talk with the detective at Jaleel's house. Despite his promise, Hildenbrand had probably shared with the prosecutor everything we discussed. I was furious. How naïve could I have been to take his word? At least I hadn't said anything incriminating at the house.

Some jurors had questions for me—softballs compared with what the prosecutor had thrown. When I got off the stand and joined Dad and Harding in the hall, they quickly asked how things had ended.

"Pretty good I think. The prosecutor wasn't very happy with me."

Harding gave me a big hug. So did my father.

"You and I, we're peas in a pod," Dad said, "tough under pressure." He whispered in my ear, "You'd make a great attorney one day, you know that, right?"

Except for weekends and Christmas and New Year's Day, the grand jury met every day for the next few weeks. My anxiety had its ebb and flow—like waiting for a final exam result—but my father remained calm.

On the twelfth of January, the District Attorney's Office conceded defeat, though not in so many words. It announced it was dropping its investigation of my father for now. Harding said the prosecutor was withdrawing her case rather than call for a jury vote and embarrass herself. There simply wasn't enough evidence. But Lydia Mason-Jones wasn't giving up, he warned. She would go back to Hildenbrand and tell him to dig deeper. If new evidence came to light, she could still go back to the grand jury, and if the evidence was really spectacular, the D.A. could charge Dad with murder. Dad told me he wasn't worried. From his years of experience with the District Attorney' office, he added, you could stick a fork in this case. It was done.

Harding called the associate publisher at the *Los Angeles Times*, a golfing buddy from Lakeside, to make sure the grand jury results were mentioned prominently. He wanted the whole world to known of Louis Baten's innocence. I did too. I was tired of being gossiped about at school, tired of living with so much tension. My mother had escaped to her sister's, leaving a mess behind for me to help clean up. That's what it felt like, and there were times I couldn't help seething about it.

Grand jury transcripts are sealed documents, and, like all witnesses, I wasn't allowed to talk about my testimony, other than to my lawyer. In private, however, I felt pride for saving my father from the treacherous currents of ambiguity and innuendo. Maybe now, I wrote in my journal, my life can return to normal.

~39~

January 15
Harding is planning a victory celebration at our
house, inviting all of Dad's good friends. Happy as I
am for my father, in the back of my mind, I keep
thinking about Jaleel. I haven't heard a word from
him since his letter. It's hard going to sleep sometimes.
How can I forget that I'm the reason he's on the run?
The D.A.'s office wants an arrest. I'm lucky that
Hildenbrand hasn't come back to question me, but I
couldn't tell the police anyway. If Jaleel had ridden
his bike back to Toluca Lake those two nights before
the murder, I'm as perplexed as anybody.

* * *

The BKD office manager, a woman whose efficiency dwarfed
even my mother's, helped me organize the party. I used Mom's
Rolodex to pick a caterer, valet service, and florist. The office manager culled the guest list to an even one hundred, and took care of
ordering the booze. I began to realize my father had even more
friends than my mother. Maybe that was one more thing that had
gnawed at her.

When I called to tell Mom about the grand jury results, Agnes answered, of course.

"Something like that was expected, wasn't it?" she said when I gave her the news.

Expected by my father and Harding, I admitted, without adding that there were moments when I was stiff with terror and thought the outcome could go either way. Agnes ended our conversation with a promise to tell Mom.

Friday night, my father's friends, supporters, and clients streamed into our house. It felt weird having a party without my mother around. Toby, flush with money from his computer classes, had invested in a Niles Burns wardrobe. I think he saw himself as a character in his own comic book. He liked nerdy polka dot shirts, jeans rolled up two inches at the cuff, and Mexican huaraches. He would be thirteen next month, and suddenly was acting a year or two older than his age. No longer a pain-in-the-ass energy suck, he was fun to be around. He liked being the entertainment, but in a way—it was hard to explain—at the same time, he seemed to be detached from people.

I wore my black cocktail dress and spent a long time on my makeup and hair. I wasn't much of a drinker at school parties, never more than a beer, but tonight I felt differently. I wanted, if not to get sloshed, to be more than a little buzzed. It wasn't so much in celebration as to make the evening pass swiftly. Something was bothering me. I was on my second vodka and tonic when my father noticed my drinking. I expected him to say something—it was a brazen thing for a fifteen-year-old to do, and surely Mom would have stopped me—but Dad was too happy, and grateful, to do anything. Harding and other members of the firm kept congratulating me, as if I was now part of a special club, and that my performance was a harbinger of the future. Maybe that's what Dad was thinking too. Mom was gone. She was no longer an influence. Why would I want to be a doctor in Africa when I could one day join a prestigious law firm and make a boatload of money?

I circulated through the living room and den, putting up with the cigar smoke and the rough, self-congratulating laughter of men. A dozen women had been invited, mostly lawyers and paralegals, but I didn't feel I had any more in common with them than with Dad's male friends. He was everyone's hero, and, free of my mother, the spotlight on him seemed incandescent.

Around eleven, the house began to empty. Toby went to bed, then my father, after giving me another big hug. I stayed up until the caterers had finished cleaning and the house looked as if it had never been stepped in.

I lay on my bed without my head phones, revisiting events of the last few months, scene by scene. I didn't even know what it was that troubled me, but when a premonition lingers, I can't seem to leave it alone. It was a little after one when I put on my robe and padded down the stairs in bare feet. In my father's study, I slipped behind his desk. I turned on his lamp and began moving slowly through every drawer. Hidden under a legal pad was a letter from Mom. The envelope was addressed to Dad at his law firm, postmarked just a day after she'd fled our house. The eight or nine sentences communicated what my mother had yet to make crystal clear to me—she wasn't coming home again, period. Her attorney would be contacting Dad with details about the divorce, including alimony. The tone was all business. I remembered her much-earlier letter to my father, when we first moved into the Tudor, the one I kept tucked in my journal. Mom, who fell in love with Toluca Lake and the lifestyle Dad provided, had taken an oath of eternal loyalty to him and her family. She was never going to leave this place, not in a million years.

I put the letter back, shocked. Not only did my father know of the divorce early on but he also kept Mom's letter around, practically in plain sight, as if to remind himself every day of his defeat. His best friend had not only been fucking his wife, Charlie had fucked over his marriage. Most of humanity ran from pain and humiliation, but Dad gravitated to them, for inspiration.

He had lied to Hildenbrand, and he had lied to me.

The double-deep drawer on the bottom was locked. I went to Dad's bookshelves and studied the many biographies and novels. Any exploring field mouse worth her weight knew every nook and cranny of her nest. The spine of Saul Bellow's *The Adventures of Augie March* was not quite aligned with its neighbors. Behind it, I found a small envelope yellowing at the edges. I took out the key and returned to his desk. I'd used it once before, maybe three years ago, in a private exploration when my parents were in Europe. I had peered briefly in the drawer, not disturbing the manila folders inside, then simply locked everything back up. Now, I unlocked it again, pulling the large, heavy drawer all the way out until its front lip rested on the carpet.

I found the same stack of manila folders with white and red labels, each identified in Dad's careful handwriting. No one could say my father wasn't organized and responsible: trusts and wills, property deeds, birth certificates, passports, insurance policies, a few bearer bonds, financial records—all important stuff to our family. In the rear corner of the drawer, I spotted a long, thin, silver key, notched with distinctive grooves, as if it opened something important. I hadn't noticed it three years ago. I held it up to the light of the desk lamp until it almost seemed to wriggle in my palm, like a small fish out of water.

Most people had secure hiding places for their secrets, like I did for my journal. The more toxic the secret, I believed, the more elaborate the disguise should be. But my father's hiding places were embarrassingly simple: the locked glove box of his Caddy and the bottom double-drawer of his desk. I'd seen a formidable floor safe in his Beverly Hills office, holding important client documents. Nobody could penetrate that without a couple of pounds of C-4. But at home, the lion's sanctuary went virtually unguarded.

I drifted back to the hallway. The snoring of my father, a man convinced he had outsmarted the district attorney and the entire LAPD, tumbled contentedly down the stairs. I opened my fist and beheld the silver key again. When I was asked on the witness stand about my father's midnight trip to Charlie's house, the prosecutor had screwed up. She should have asked more questions. My father's footsteps going downstairs had woken me. Leaning over the banister, I'd watched the closet light flow across the hallway, and listened to the clicking tumbler of the safe. The heavy steel door swung open. I couldn't see, but it seemed like Dad was moving things around in the safe. When I checked the next day, though, nothing had been disturbed. Every rifle, handgun, the boxes of cartridges—all were where they were supposed to be. If he hadn't removed a weapon, what was he doing there?

The safe stood almost five feet high and about three feet wide; its bottom lay flat on the closet carpet. I dropped to my knees, spun the tumbler as quietly as I could, and pulled the door open. My nose wrinkled at the smell of solvents. I took each gun off its rack and laid it on the carpet, wanting to be sure there were no hidden compartments behind them. Every firearm had been freshly oiled: two shotguns, including the 12-gauge returned by Hildenbrand, three hunting rifles, two handguns, and ten boxes of various caliber shells. I didn't know just what I was looking for.

The interior of the empty safe was lined with fine gray felt. I heard the dull sound of solid steel when I tapped on the sides. In a corner, at the bottom of the safe, a nub of felt was raised just enough to grip with my thumb and index finger. I peeled back the entire three-foot-square piece, exposing a metal lid hinged on top with a narrow keyhole in it. The mystery key with its intricate grooves was a perfect fit. The lock turned soundlessly.

I had no idea what I was looking at in the foot-deep cavity. I gingerly pulled out what I saw and unfolded it on the floor—some kind of weird suit with long sleeves, and pants with two ample pockets. I thought of a beekeeper's suit, a hermetically sealed cocoon, everything white as snow. I stared back into the cavity and took out a cloth hood with a Plexiglas visor, and a pair of booties and gloves of the same tightly woven fabric. The suit smelled of hydrogen peroxide.

Something began churning in me. I left everything on the floor and darted up to my room. After I returned to the safe, and did what I wanted to do, I folded the suit, hood, booties, and gloves back into their hiding place, locked the lid, and restocked the safe with Dad's guns. The exotic silver key was returned to the corner of the double-drawer, and the other key to its envelope and hiding place behind *Augie March*.

I tossed all night. Jaleel had been adamant that my father was the killer. He was far more objective than I could ever be. What would he have made of my discovery tonight? Lurching up in bed, I turned on my reading lamp—the dark had begun to scare the hell out of me. I pushed myself to think everything through. If my father had made up his mind to kill Charlie, he would begin by focusing on detail and preparation. He would use the Diggses' house key to let himself in. Hiding in the bedroom closet, even if it was hours before Charlie came to bed, Dad wouldn't mind the wait. He was anticipating the expression that would appear on his friend's face. Charlie must have looked at the figure in the funny suit, emerging from his closet with a shotgun cradled across his arm, like Dad was a wraith. But Dad's face would have been visible through the visor. Charlie would have had a few long seconds for his panic and disbelief to build—enough to satisfy my vindictive father. I doubt words were exchanged. In a couple of more seconds, justice was dispatched. The power and adrenaline Dad must have felt—the mighty sword of righteousness felling the wicked.

The special suit had done its job, shielding Dad from flying blood, flesh, and bone—while keeping his fingerprints, clothing fibers, and hair away from the crime scene. There would be no traces of gunpowder on his skin or under his nails. The booties had no distinguishing markings on their soles to leave telltale prints. I imagined he had taken off the suit and booties and gloves as he left Charlie's house, stuffing them in a duffel he carried as he walked back home under cover of darkness. The DeVille never left our garage. At some point, maybe while the police rushed to the Diggses' house, lights flashing ominously, he'd calmly washed the suit in hydrogen peroxide. That would have removed any traces of blood splatter, or any other clues, and then he'd resecured the suit in the cavity at the bottom of the safe. Why hadn't he ultimately burned or buried it? What if the police had returned for a more-thorough search of his safe? He probably thought the smell of oiling his rifles was strong enough to obscure any traces of the peroxide.

The only perfect murder, Perry Mason once said, is the one you commit in your imagination. God knew there had to be a million of those every year. But this one was conceived and carried out by my father, and it was as perfect as perfect could be.

I might have cried, or puked from revulsion, or maybe written something in my journal. Instead, I switched off the light and lay still on my pillow, not sleeping. Despite the murder, and the lies he had told me, I was shocked that my loyalty to my father did not easily fade. It wasn't dissimilar to my feelings about Mom. Their mendacity notwithstanding, I only had one set of parents.

~40~

I did finally have a good cry, the next night. Then came the wave of anger. My honest testimony before the grand jury had helped get my guilty father off the hook. How had I let Harding and my father play me? I had had my suspicions about the murder, but they'd been pushed aside, swallowed up by my trust. At the moment, I felt like Atlas holding up the entire world in my wobbly arms, about to collapse under its weight.

"What's going on?" Joyce asked on the way to gym class. "This is the second day in a row you screwed up in Latin. Since when does Alexandra Baten not do her homework?"

"I'm having my period," I said.

"Gag me with a spoon."

"Everything's fine. I'm having a bad week. Big deal."

"Look me in the eye," Joyce demanded.

I refused. "Nothing's wrong."

"Liar. I thought we were best friends."

"Drop it, will you?" I whispered, and walked off.

I had come this close to telling her. I even considered telling Mom, before realizing the damage would be immeasurable. I had to talk to my father first.

I chose early Saturday morning, before breakfast. Toby was on a sleepover at a friend's. Dad was due to play golf. He was behind his desk, as usual scribbling on a legal pad, his glasses dangling at the tip his nose. As if nothing in the world was amiss, I thought, studying him from the doorway. He was smiling at something as his favorite fountain pen skated across the page—maybe it was the miracle that he'd resurrected himself and his career. My mother was gone for good, along with most of the pain her betrayal had caused him. Gone too was the public suspicion that had dogged him and his firm. He was a new and better man. Some survivors don't just bounce back, they bounce higher.

"Do you have time to talk?" I asked, moving toward his desk. I didn't recognize my own voice.

He removed his glasses and put them next to his pen. "Sure, hon. What's up?"

I sat rigidly across from his desk. I had rehearsed. There was supposed to be small talk before I dropped the bomb, but I couldn't do it. My stomach was knotted so tightly that it hurt. "I know everything," I managed.

"You know everything about what?"

It was as if my mouth had been wired shut.

"Is this something about Charlie's murder?" he said carefully.

"Yes."

"What is it you want to tell me?"

"I think you know."

"Alex, be clear."

He was going to make me say it. "I know you killed Charlie."

"How do you know that?"

"After the party, I opened the gun safe. I found the false bottom. Why didn't you just burn the suit and we wouldn't be having this talk?" He had a distant, almost-amused look, like he was surprised but not that surprised. He knew my exploring nature. He didn't seem at all contrite or worried.

"You're not denying this, are you?" I said.

"No, sweetheart, not to you."

Knowing it was true was one thing, hearing him admit it, in the most calm, controlled voice, was almost worse.

"I'm sorry you found out this way," he said.

He picked up the phone, and found a substitute for his foursome at Lakeside. When he hung up, I wanted to ask what else he was sorry for. It seemed to me it should be a long list. He'd taken a life as coldly as swatting a fly.

"What way was I supposed to find out, Dad?"

"I wanted to tell you when you'd be old enough to understand."

"Understand what? That you were sorry you killed your best friend, and that made it okay?"

"I'm not sorry," he made clear.

"—or there were extenuating circumstances, or maybe you went temporarily insane?"

"No, I was always rational. I planned everything down to the smallest detail."

I wiped a tear from each eye. "Whatever it was you were going to say eventually, tell me now please. Because I'm freaking out."

"Does Toby know?"

I shook my head.

"Promise me you won't tell him."

"No," I said, remembering my encounter with Mom over Charlie. "I'm done promising anyone anything."

I was tired of being intimidated by my parents, yet even at that moment, when I was coming unhinged, I knew I couldn't turn Toby's fragile world upside down. I could never go to the police about my father either, as angry and devastated as I felt. I had thought about it all week, but I couldn't do it. Yet if Dad gave me a river of bullshit now, even one word that wasn't the factual truth, I was going to pack a suitcase and never come back home, just like Mom.

He rose and ambled into the kitchen, returning with coffee for himself and some orange juice for me. I didn't touch it.

He dropped back behind his desk. "Where do you want to start, Alex?"

"I want to know," I said, "how a rational person, with a conscience, finds justification for murder."

He put his lips to the rim of his cup, and took a sip. "Sometimes killing has nothing to do with a lack of conscience," he said. "In this case, it had to do with having one."

The room was swirling around me. "That's bullshit, Dad."

"You and I have discussed this, Alex. Throughout history, most societies have had laws to punish someone who takes another's life. It's how we maintain the social order. Without laws, there's only chaos. But there have also been cultures where killing someone who betrayed your deepest trust, slept with your wife, and tried to destroy your family, is not breaking a law."

"Well, why not shoot Mom too?" I said half-seriously. "She deceived us. She helped destroy our family."

"Every man should have his own moral code, no matter what the law says. I probably wouldn't have killed Charlie if Mom hadn't asked for a divorce. Charlie brought a plague on our house. He took from me the woman I was in love with, and had always been faithful to."

"Killing Charlie, you risked going to prison for life. You risked destroying our family beyond recognition," I shot back.

"All risks are calculated. I had a very high percentage of winning."

"And then you lied to me—"

He looked indifferent to my charge, as if lying was such an ambiguous, relative act, just like taking a life. I was staring at a stranger. To my father, everything was a point of view. In a courtroom, crossing the line between cleverness and deception came so easily that I bet he scarcely realized the first time it happened. Maybe it scratched at his conscience a few times before it became habit. Deception had come easily to me too, with Hildenbrand. The difference was, I didn't like it. I hated myself for it.

"Now what?" I said. "Do I forget all this happened? Am I supposed to forgive you?"

"Why do you have to forgive someone who was only out for justice?"

"That's what you call it? You're guilty of breaking the law."

"The law, as you and I have also discussed, is far from perfect. Should we have to obey imperfect laws?"

"Imperfect in your opinion."

"All right, Alex. Then whose opinion should I follow, if not my own? What would you have done in my situation?"

"I wouldn't have murdered someone."

"Do you really know the depth of hatred of which most people are capable? Right now, you're an idealistic teen-ager. That will change, I promise you. Anyone pushed hard enough by unforeseen and unjust circumstances—"

"Please stop," I begged. My father was turning Hildenbrand into a prophet.

My stomach turned watery as I rose. At the door, I looked back and our eyes connected. Dad seemed to know I wouldn't go to the police. We also both knew our mutual trust was gone. He would dispose of the splatter suit, change the safe combination, and find new hiding places for his keys.

I wondered if he knew how quickly the roots of my new distrust would grow. I was backed into the corner of keeping another secret. It was like a cold fist had wrapped around my heart, squeezing all the blood out of it.

I stayed in my room the rest of the day. Dad came and went in his Caddy. When Toby returned with his friend, their excited voices echoed from the hallway as they imagined a world of robots, wristwatch phones like Dick Tracy wore, and television screens the size of a sofa. I looked out my window at our manicured lawn tumbling into a motionless lake. It felt like a piece of heaven that had broken off and couldn't be reattached. I took my Kodak Brownie and grabbed some final snapshots—my room, our lawn and pool, the rowboat tethered to the dock, a smattering of ducks. I knew I wouldn't be living here much longer.

Two days later, the *Times* carried a new story about the unsolved Toluca Lake homicide. The district attorney's office and police had another suspect in their sights: an eighteen-year-old black male named Jaleel Robeson, a.k.a. Edward Montgomery, who, it was reported, was from Peartree, Texas, where he had escaped from a county juvenile facility six years earlier. There was a warrant for his arrest for murdering his father. He'd been last seen living in North Hollywood, less than a mile from the Toluca Lake crime scene.

Jaleel

~41~

Four days before Detective Hildenbrand first entered the dilapidated house off Cahuenga Boulevard, Jaleel had acted. After Alex's troubling visit, he'd walked five blocks to a pay phone at a Mobil station, extracted Dirick's frayed business card from his wallet, and punched in the 212 area code. The Samaritan's machine answered with a brief, noncommittal message. Jaleel left his name and said his circumstances were urgent. He wondered if Dirick was even around. Jaleel promised to call back tomorrow at the same time.

When he tried to sleep, it felt like fire was searing his lungs with every breath. His freedom was over if he stayed in this house much longer. He had $250 in a shoebox, but maybe that was enough to get out of L.A. When he'd become fed up with America, James Baldwin had fled to Paris on supposedly less money than that.

Jaleel reached Dirick's answering machine again the next afternoon. The Samaritan's new message provided a phone number in San Francisco. Hopeful, Jaleel called right away. The two spoke for twenty minutes. Dirick said he was working at a rescue mission called Our Lady of Sorrows, in the city's Mission District, helping the luckless get back on their feet. As Jaleel relayed everything that had happened in Toluca Lake, Dirick told him to pack his bags and leave L.A. as soon as possible. They would meet in San Francisco. He would find a room for Jaleel at the mission.

A Puerto Rican family who had often watched the muscular young man ride the sidewalk with a fat orange cat in his bicycle basket agreed to take care of Monster. Jaleel said that his mother, who lived in Oregon, was sick, and he didn't know when he'd be back. He offered them his bike too. The little girl hugged Monster as if they had bonded long ago.

He got busy filling two beatup suitcases with books, clothes, personal papers, and his drawing of Peartree, which he untacked from its frame and rolled up carefully. His mind kept spinning, wondering how his luck could have ended so abruptly. What kind of fate was that? Maybe in life you only had so much good luck, and once you'd used it up, you were on a high wire without a safety net.

He took a taxi to the Greyhound station, and bought a one-way ticket to San Francisco. On the bus, he was too distracted for anything but fitful sleeping. His pathway to Princeton, and a possible baseball career, were now dead ends. He hadn't even been able to say goodbye to school friends. Soon they'd be reading about an impostor—a killer—who had attended classes, eaten in their cafeteria, and played ball with them.

The only person besides Dirick who knew the truth was Alex. When the bus stopped along the way, he had mailed her a letter detailing almost everything. Should something happen to him, he wanted her to know his whole story. Still, he couldn't tell her where he was going, and his feelings about Alex were definitely mixed. She had been the cause of his troubles. Yet here he was, writing to her as if he missed her. Except for Dirick, who else did he have to confide in?

The Samaritan picked him up at the bus station in a wreck of a station wagon. The early December weather was made even cooler by a stinging breeze coming off the Bay. Dirick's trademark tam o'shanter hadn't changed, but the suit and tie had been replaced by tattered Levi's, and his blue work shirt could have used an iron. The chiseled, determined face was unaltered. Dirick looked fit and purposeful, maybe more than ever.

"Let me get a good look at you, my friend. It's been more than six years." He studied Jaleel under the feeble dome light as the decrepit car bounced rather than rolled over the streets. "What are you now, six-three or -four? You look like you could break down a door with one finger."

"Exactly," Jaleel said tartly. If you were black, muscular, and dressed in street clothes, he thought, it might not matter what your SAT scores were. You were a thug.

"Look at you, Mr. New Yorker, " Jaleel said, trying to find a lighter mood. "Finally driving a car."

"Only when I have to. How are you holding up?"

"I've been better." He eyes darted around the streets. "It's not safe for me to walk around, is it? Someone will recognize me."

"The police aren't looking for you yet, are they?"

"I don't know. When you're paranoid, anything can seem possible."

"It's easy to keep to yourself at the mission. Passers-by will think you're just another homeless man. Our Lady of Sorrows has simple rules. No booze, drugs, stealing, picking fights, or having women in your room. I'll tell everyone that I'm helping you find a job. We'll pick a temporary name for you."

It was nice to have a place to hole up, but after a string of addresses in six years, he felt he didn't belong anywhere. Who was he, anyway? Another new name was hardly an identity.

The station wagon approached three attached five-story row houses sharing gray paint and a state of dilapidation akin to Dirick's car. Our Lady of Sorrows was stenciled in red letters on a wooden plaque over one of the doors. The row houses and grim neighborhood looked nothing like the county shelter in Peartree, but they made Jaleel feel the same.

"Well, here we are," said Dirick.

"I fucked up. You warned me, and I still fucked up," he condemned himself as he got out of the car.

"You're tired right now, Jaleel. We'll figure things out in the morning."

"Figure what out?"

"I have someone for you to meet. He can explain. You'll be safe at Our Lady."

Jaleel took out his suitcases, studying the concrete stoop that served as the mission's entrance. The air had a bite, but people were clustered on the steps as if for a summer party. He saw spectral faces illuminated under a pair of porch lights. Black, white, Asian, Latino. Teen-age toughs, older guys with bleached-out eyes and gray stubble, and indiscriminate castaways like he'd seen on Greyhound busses. There were a couple of women in jeans and sweaters. You couldn't guess anyone's age because the faces were puffy from drinking and drugs, and one had a black eye. Some smoked cigarettes in a corner; others were telling stories.

Jaleel weaved behind Dirick through the obstacle course to the door. He kept his head down, refusing to return any looks. The lobby, once the foyer of an elegant town home, had no shortage of religious paintings: a preaching Jesus, a beatific Mary, and Christ on Good Friday and Christ on Good Friday nailed to a cross with the other criminals. Used furniture was scattered around. There were two couches by a fireplace bereft of logs. A few people were cheering a basketball team on a black-and-white television.

Dirick walked over to a desk and came back with a room key. Everyone seemed to know him.

"Meet you downstairs at 7 a.m. We'll have breakfast down the street." The indomitable Samaritan gave him a hug and was gone.

Jaleel's room wasn't large but there was a double bed with clean sheets, a closet to hang clothes, and his own small bathroom with a decent shower. On balance, it was an improvement over where he'd lived before. The window offered a view of the street. He cracked it open for ventilation. Cars and an occasional motorcycle roared past. Directly below were the same people on the stoop, the tight little circles of friendship that he envied but was reluctant to go near.

He showered and went to bed. Sleep was uneven, coming in pockets that never seemed to last more than two or three hours. He never dreamed about Alex, but often, when he woke, she was in his thoughts, like someone standing unexpectedly in the middle of a room. He couldn't exactly ask her to leave. Sexual desire, as ashamed as he was to admit it for a fifteen-year-old, had insinuated itself too. He would never forget Alex's kiss. There was something maternal about it, but the longer it dwelled in his memory, the more he felt its tingling intimacy.

In the middle of the night, he climbed out of his bed, familiarizing himself with every inch of his room. The street was now quiet, the stoop empty, the hallway outside his door deserted. He was grateful for the night settling in so peacefully. There was beauty in silence, he thought, as he stared out the open window.

He remembered the evening he'd delivered Alex's letter. There wasn't a sound once he crossed Cahuenga. The gravity of disbelief as he followed Alex's directions had pulled his bicycle through the winding streets. He'd never seen so many handsome homes. The ambient light was streaked with charcoal hues, and then darkness dropped like a window shade. House lights came on one at a time, sometimes making distorted rectangles on the manicured lawns. He wanted to reach out and touch the picket fences. He inhaled the scent of roses and the grass on the nearby fairways. What was it like to play golf? He was athletic—why couldn't he learn one day? He suddenly imagined not just living in one of these houses but owning it. The boldness of the idea struck him as ridiculous, yet if he went to a good college, and then graduate school, he had the intellectual gifts and determination to succeed at anything he wanted. Some day, some day. . . .

When he approached the Diggses' brick Colonial, he fulfilled his promise to Alex, turned around immediately, and pedaled home. No one stopped him. The only soul he saw on the streets was a woman sliding into her car and driving off. She gave him a look but nothing sinister. He had always feared Toluca Lake, thinking it full of distrusting white people, but at the moment, things felt okay.

He returned on two more evenings to this forbidden city—the sky was still light—doing the same thing each time. He steered his bike to the bridge that spanned the neck of the lake adjoining the golf club. A troop of ducks chased each other in the water. His eyes rose to the stately homes ringing the lake. From Alex's description, he guessed which was hers. When he negotiated the streets again, he studied the two-story English Tudor even more closely, with its sprawling front lawn and circular drive. She had once invited him to come over. The property hypnotized him.

Jaleel ended up back by the bridge, out of sight behind some trees. Cars drifted in and out of the golf club entrance. He couldn't pull himself away for the longest time. The gloaming air made him feel invisible, but the dream of living here one day was tantalizingly real.

As he looked out the mission window, a police car rolled by below. Startled, Jaleel shrank back and waited until it was gone. The quiet returned, and he moved back to his bed. Toluca Lake was a million years ago, he reminded himself. The Samaritan was right. Looking back was folly. He had been seduced by someone else's dream.

~42~

Jaleel woke at five as usual, read for a while, and was downstairs promptly at seven. He found Dirick rubbing his hands by the fireplace, where three logs were crackling with abandon. The warmth radiated through the lobby. Beside Dirick was a man with a good-sized paunch (two shirt buttons refusing to close), unruly brown hair, and intelligent eyes that suddenly swept toward Jaleel. Except for a desk clerk across the way, the lobby was empty.

"This is Rudy Tusk, my good friend and colleague, and a terrific lawyer," Dirick announced as the two men approached Jaleel. He shook the stranger's hand in silence.

"Nice to meet you, Mr. Robeson."

Jaleel felt the man's intensity—someone who prized efficiency and achieving results—as if he were a clone of Dirick.

As the three walked to the coffee shop, Dirick did most of the talking. Rudy had spent sixteen years in the Public Defender's Office before "retiring" to pro bono work. His background in criminal law had yielded strong ties with the San Francisco County District Attorney's Office. San Francisco was as liberal and open-minded as any city in America, Dirick said. The D.A. was Latino, and his office was sympathetic to minorities.

"I briefed Rudy on your situation," Dirick said. "He thinks that it's time you stop running. I agree with him."

Caught off guard, Jaleel said, "What's that mean—turn myself in?"

"Yes, with Rudy acting as your attorney."

"Are you crazy!" Jaleel shook his head. There was no way. He could be packed and on another bus in an hour.

"Don't rush to conclusions," Dirick advised as they took a booth in the half-empty restaurant. "Rudy has a good track record with people in your situation."

"There's no situation like mine," Jaleel corrected him.

"I grant you that. Consider this scenario: Louis Baten is not indicted. The police or D.A. ends up getting a warrant for you, and with Peartree still hanging over your head, how long will it be before half the world is looking for you?"

Jaleel had no response, other than to silently acknowledge the scenario. But for an incredible streak of luck, he should have been captured already. Yet he didn't regret running from Peartree. He hadn't trusted Detective Patterson, and listening to Marcus's stories of foster homes, which was the best outcome Jaleel could have hoped for, had filled him with more anxiety. The worst—and more likely—outcome would have been a long stretch in a juvenile facility, followed by adult prison. Try getting into an Ivy, he thought, after serving time for murdering your father.

"Let me ease your fears," Rudy said as if reading his thoughts. "I want to approach a friend in the D.A.'s office. I'll ask him to talk to his colleagues in L.A. I want you to write something for me—explain what happened in Peartree, and then Toluca Lake. Write as many pages as you want. Include every name, date, time, and place. Leave nothing out. Imagine you were standing before a judge and had only one chance to establish your innocence."

"And I'll be believed, just because I tell the truth?" Jaleel asked dryly.

"If I represent you, you've got a good chance. Dirick will help. He's only been admitted to the New York Bar, but he's versed in California statutes. We'll be your team."

"A good chance," Jaleel repeated, "but no guarantees. And the price of failure is steep. Don't leave out that part." He looked at Dirick. "You saved my ass once. I'll always be grateful. But to be lucky twice feels like long odds."

"I got three things wrong in Los Angeles," Jaleel said. "Wrong place, wrong time, wrong color. I was a fool to believe I had a future."

"You're giving up hope before we even start," Dirick said.

When his voice filled with conviction, the Samaritan was hard to ignore. Still, Jaleel had doubts. Once he committed to Rudy's strategy, there was no changing his mind. On the other hand, if he kept running, why couldn't he land on his feet again? Maybe his luck wasn't totally gone. He was resourceful, and he had learned from his mistake of trusting someone else rather than his own instincts.

When their food arrived, Jaleel was surprised by the depth of his hunger. He attacked his eggs and stack of pancakes.

Dirick said, "I have a story to tell you. I hope you'll indulge me."

Jaleel looked up between bites. It was as if he were back on the bus to Kingman, a captive audience, putting his fate in the hands of a man who read strange books and wrote even stranger essays.

"I've told you before that in America, it's never too late to reinvent yourself—no matter how much injustice you've suffered, how many times you've been let down, how impossible your situation. You can begin anew. You can overcome. But your belief in yourself has to be ironclad, your faith in a greater power unimpeachable. There is such a thing as moral gravity, Jaleel. It means you take responsibility for being a serious person—"

"You promised me a story," Jaleel broke in. "You're giving a speech."

Dirick laughed. "Sometimes I can't help myself."

"Are you saying you don't think I'm a serious person?"

"A serious person is someone who acknowledges he has the power to change himself and then goes ahead and does it."

Jaleel nodded. He was listening.

"Go on."

"I was twenty-five when my parents died in a plane accident. The loss devastated me, as it did my younger sister. She led a very protected life. We each inherited a significant amount of money, which might have eased the pain, if not for extenuating circumstances. Luckily, I had finished law school. I was able to go to work. And I worked very hard."

"Why would you go to work if you had money?" Jaleel asked.

"A logical question, with a simple but hardly obvious answer. My father, it turned out, led a double life. He was a successful and legitimate businessman by day but with an inclination to take imprudent risks when no one was looking. For every dollar he left my sister and me, he owed somebody else two or three. Within a year, there were

$2 million in judgments against my parents' estate. Sometimes my father borrowed money from criminals; others were friends that he simply fleeced. How could anyone owe $2 million and not bother to tell his family? That's an obscenity.

"After the plane crash, I began reading books about con men. Many begin their 'careers' by lying to their families. If you're good at deceiving people you're supposed to care about, finding other victims is a no-brainer. It took me the longest time to forgive my father, almost as long as to satisfy his obligations. I didn't have to pay them off—there was no legal liability—but I wanted to. Nothing could slake my bitterness toward my father—until it came to me: My hatred was not helping anything. Jesus said to turn the other cheek. It was a process, but I did it. That I was capable of forgiving my father was my spiritual awakening.

"Does my journey sound like it was easy, Jaleel?" Dirick asked.

"No," he admitted. This was a far more complete story than Randy had told him in Kingman. And, finally, Jaleel had been told the nature of Dirick's spiritual awakening.

"My father was an immigrant from Holland. He took advantage of the dream that brought him to these shores. When I look around, it isn't money or shady deals that attract me. I understand the bigotry that you and so many others have endured. That's precisely what interests me."

"What, you want to change the whole world?" Jaleel said, half smiling.

"No. I just want you to allow Rudy and me to help you out of your mess."

"And if you can't?"

"The power of innocence has to be considered here, Jaleel. Yours is like a castle on the hill, with high walls, surrounded by a deep moat. The armies of ignorance and self-interest cannot easily bring down a place of righteousness. The three of us can pull this off, if we work together."

They were nice-sounding words, Jaleel conceded, but that's all they were: words, images, metaphors. "Why are you so interested in helping me? You have a million people you could choose from. What makes my innocence so special?"

"When I met you on that bus, I didn't know the story of your parents, but I could feel a great upheaval inside you. I knew that suffering was ultimately going to make you stronger. I felt the Holy Spirit in you."

Reverend Johnson in Peartree had bragged about his potential too, in front of the whole congregation. Everyone had high expectations for him. He'd fulfilled none of them. Suffering, zeitgeist, evidence of the Holy Spirit—it was all bullshit. They had the wrong guy. Rudy was quietly finishing his breakfast, looking at Jaleel as if the next move was up to him.

"I'll be away for two weeks," Dirick said, "working with the Ohio state legislature, trying to humanize their foreclosure laws. Let's see how things stand with the grand jury when I'm back."

Jaleel could hear the fear bubbling in his stomach—couldn't they hear it too? When Rudy asked if he was on board with their plan, he promised to let them know when Dirick came back.

~43~

During the Samaritan's absence, Jaleel had chores to keep him busy. Christmas lights had already been strung in the hallway, and a tree hung with silver and red bulbs, but there was plenty of sweeping and dusting, washing sheets, working in the kitchen, and stacking firewood. Jaleel ventured outside the mission only after dark, to buy fast food, toiletries, or reading material. A 24/7 drug store carried the late morning edition of the *Los Angeles Times*. The Baten grand jury had begun. No one could say when there'd be a decision.

When he thought over Dirick's and Rudy's suggestion of writing down his story, Jaleel found merit in it. Someone had to record his history, he felt. Otherwise, it would be distorted by people who had more power than he did, who didn't know anything, or had their own agenda. It was his duty to be meticulously accurate. Maybe nothing would come of his effort, but he had plenty of free time to work on a draft.

One evening, after weaving his way down the stoop, he heard his name called. He slowed as he reached the sidewalk but didn't stop. He wasn't sure where the voice had come from, and less sure that he wanted to search for it.

"Jaleel, my brother, is that you?"

The man's voice was hard-boiled but playful, with an undertone of disbelief. Jaleel's eyes pivoted to a shiny new Mercedes, slowing as it followed him down the street.

"Jaleel!" the driver shouted, pushing his head out the open window. "That is you! Shit, brother, say hello! Don't you recognize me? What you doing in the city?"

They stopped at the same time, the pedestrian facing the driver of the Mercedes, one wishing this wasn't happening but the other excited over the vagaries of fate. The arc of a streetlight made Marcus look much older than Jaleel remembered him. He had to be twenty-four or twenty-five now but looked to be in his thirties. The prominent cheekbones, wide forehead, and high-top fade haircut jumped out at Jaleel like a character in a 3-D movie. His smile radiated prosperity and confidence.

"That you, Marcus?" Jaleel said cautiously.

"Damn right it's me. What you doing in my hood?" His deep laugh seemed to roll down the street. "Didn't I tell you our paths were going to cross one day? I just didn't know it would be here. You living at the mission? What's that about, brother?"

Jaleel wished he could think of a way to vanish. Marcus motioned him toward the car. "Get in, Jaleel. You're a sight for sore eyes. I've been wondering what happened to you after you slid under that fence. I wasn't sure you were going to make it. Then again, you had grit. I couldn't bet against that. Get in!"

"Well, here I am," Jaleel said quietly, summoning a smile but not ready to step into the car.

"I thought you might write and let me know what happened to you," Marcus said, more serious. "I was the one who got you out of that crap hole, remember?"

"I didn't forget you. But I wouldn't have known where to send a letter," he said apologetically. He suddenly remembered the night of his escape—twelve years old, Marcus boosting him up in his large hand so he could squeeze through the narrow transom and tumble to the grass outside. He'd been wrong to think the Samaritan was the only one who'd helped him.

"You cool? Things good?" Jaleel asked.

"Oh, hell yes. Come on!"

"Where we going?"

"You feel like eating the best steak in the city? A reunion like this requires some Dom Perignon. Or would you prefer a vintage Shiraz? The wine cellar in this place . . . incredible, brother."

Even if Jaleel said no, Marcus was determined to drag him to dinner. He slid into the passenger seat.

"Bro, what you been up to?" Marcus turned at the corner, and the Mercedes shot onto a main artery.

"Busy with school. I'm graduating in June. On my way to college."

"College! You do have grit. Where's high school?"

"Los Angeles."

His brow shot up. "So what the hell you doing at the mission?"

"It's a long story."

"Aren't they all, brother?"

"What are you doing?" Jaleel said.

Marcus's laugh seemed bottomless. "You serious? Look at me. I never graduated from high school, but here I am, wearing an Armani suit. I got six more just like it in my closet. What do you think I'm doing? I help my clients at the mission and elsewhere fulfill their needs."

"You mean, you're a pusher."

Dirick had told him the rules—no using drugs, among others. You were on the honor system. If you were caught, you got the boot, no second chances. That meant Marcus made a fine living off a revolving door.

"Crack, 'lutes, heroin, pot, mother's little helper—but I'm on the executive level, mind you. I got folks working for me. Don't want to get my hands dirty. Isn't that the American way?"

"I remember one of the last things you said to me," Jaleel answered. "Something about me not giving up on you. You were going to be successful one day."

"That's exactly what I said! How's that for the power of prophecy? For a kid whose parents walked out and all they left him was a ham sandwich, Marcus Worby is doing just fine."

They drove to Pacific Heights. The steak house Marcus chose had a Victorian decor with gaslight-like fixtures on red velour wallpaper. The maitre d' went out of his way to take care of them. But when Marcus ordered a bottle of champagne, Jaleel declined.

"What's wrong with you? Dom Perignon not good enough?"

"I left my driver's license at the mission," he lied.

Marcus smiled knowingly. "I get it. You told me about yours being a long story. No one's going to ask who you are. Not when you're with me."

In the end, they ordered two bottles of Dom, and two twenty-four-ounce Porterhouses with creamed spinach and garlic mashed potatoes. Marcus turned to Jaleel. "They never served that at the shelter, did they?"

"No." Enjoy it, he thought. He had never had a steak in his life. Now he was chewing on a Porterhouse and sipping from a $200 bottle of champagne, as if the past six years of mad, desperate scrambling were over. He had to remind himself his life was on re-do.

"Tell me what happened after I escaped."

"Patterson said I had 'aided and abetted' you. He was furious. He swore revenge on you. But no way I was going to turn on you, bro. Patterson could swear revenge all he wanted. When it was clear you weren't coming back, you got a reputation at the shelter—some kind of miracle man. Local black boy makes good!

"Now, tell me what you been up to," Marcus insisted. "I like long stories."

That was easy. All he had to do was think of the story he was writing for Rudy and Dirick. He didn't make it too long. Greyhound buses, meeting Dirick, tales of survival in different cities. He hadn't found his stride for a couple of years. Then came academic and baseball success, and hope of attending an Ivy League school. That had kept him going, he said. Jaleel didn't mention Alex and the murder in Toluca Lake—his ruined dreams.

"By the way, my name's not Jaleel anymore," he added. "And you never ran into me tonight. Okay?"

"Whatever you say, brother. I'm not going to ask again what you're doing at the mission, but if you want some help, any help at all, here—"

Marcus wrote his phone number on a napkin and stuffed it in Jaleel's jacket.

Marcus related his own adventures. Peartree County had released him from the shelter with the clothes on his back, a toothbrush and razor, and $25 in spending money. His debt to society was now paid in full, the officer at the door said. I owed *you* something? Marcus thought. What about what the fuck you assholes owe me! You stole five years of my life!

He had hitchhiked west, picking up work in fast food joints. A friend of a friend turned him on to a dealer in San Francisco. Not ex-

actly a dealer, a chemist who made Quaaludes and needed someone
to market his product. Marcus said he'd give it a try.

"You know the real secret of my success? I stay away from the bullshit. Everyone's always shoveling you a line. Money doesn't need explaining. It's as quiet as the middle of the night."

He pulled out his wallet and laid five hundred-dollar bills on the table.
Jaleel stared at the money like it was a pit of snakes.

"Hey, don't be afraid. It's nothing but a token of friendship. No
strings attached. Do whatever you want with it."

"If you want me to hustle drugs—"

"No way. That's not your style, brother. You're not a simple nigger
like me. You're going to get a Ph.D. somewhere and be famous one day."

"You prey on people to get that money—doesn't that ever bother
you?" Jaleel said.

"I don't prey on anyone. I got clients everywhere, and they're not
all poor. For one reason or another, their life is shit. They got one belief: If you stay insane, if you stay in a magical place, if you float in
space, you are never going to die. Because there's no afterlife. It's all
here and now. I'm giving them hope."

"Hope for what?"

"That if you stay high long enough, you're not touched by all that
pain you walk through every day."

"I've got a friend who wouldn't agree with you. He would say that
pain and suffering reveal your soul. They make your character."

Marcus shook his head. "You got that exactly wrong. Pain and suffering destroy your soul. I've seen it over and over in brothers. There's
nothing left to make character out of. Tell me about your friend.
What color's his skin?"

"What's that have to do with anything?"

"White folks can be real smooth. But it's just words. Even if they're
well meaning, even if they want the best for you, there's something
you can't trust about them. Not in the end, not when it comes down
to life and death."

"You say that because you got shafted in those foster homes."

"That's right. I got shafted. Nothing makes you a believer more
than your anger."

"I'm not buying that all white people are bad."

"Not right now you're not, but if the police catch you, you're going to remember our conversation tonight. See who's gonna help you when your ass is in a sling.

"Don't be a fool," Marcus added. "Take the money."

No, thought Jaleel.

"Take it, man. Get out of this country. There's an arrest warrant for you in Peartree, and it feels like something else is crawling up your ass too."

Jaleel's mind went blank as he scooped up the bills and put them in his pocket. When they'd finished dinner, Marcus drove him back to the mission. His old friend didn't pretend to be something he wasn't. He didn't chase things he couldn't attain. He didn't want to change the world. For Marcus, there was no illusion about finding God somewhere.

"You take care yourself now," Marcus said, dropping him in front of the crowded stoop. "Call if you need me."

As Jaleel bounded up the steps, some men make wisecracks about the Mercedes. "Hey, it's not mine," he replied quietly. He understood their envy. They had nothing. They had all suffered. They were stuck here. A few people like Dirick cared about them, but the rest of the world could give a fig.

Christmas was around the corner, he thought when he got to his room. What Jesus had started two thousand years ago was a revolution—forgiveness and redemption for even the most wretched. Jaleel had grown up in the faith, singing the hymns, smiling and nodding at the sermons. He had believed it all.

After his evening with Marcus, he wasn't as sure. Some people knew they were never going to be forgiven or saved, nor did they care. The people who ran Our Lady of Sorrows would tell you otherwise, but when Jaleel really thought about it, maybe there was no reason to believe in God. You were stuck in your miserable little place, no matter how hard you tried to escape or how much you deserved to be free. Deserved had nothing to do with it.

~44~

When Dirick returned to the mission after New Year's, Jaleel didn't mention his dinner with Marcus. For now, he pushed that evening out of his mind. Mostly he'd been focused on writing his story, starting with the afternoon he'd returned from Little League practice to find his mother scolding his father. The meetings with Detective Patterson were particularly vivid, the sense that he was being framed but couldn't do anything about it.

He borrowed a typewriter from one of the mission's staff and had a twenty-three-page draft for Dirick and Rudy by the fourth of January. They met at the coffee shop. Dirick said he was impressed with the clarity of the writing, but Rudy wondered why Jaleel didn't give more details about Alex.

"She's fifteen, a rich, white girl, a nice girl who was in my house a few times. It's enough to admit she asked me to deliver the letter, isn't it? We were friends, nothing more, but watch, I'll be accused of something sinister."

"And if it comes to a trial, Alex will take the stand to deny it," Rudy replied.

"Even so, once a prosecutor implies something—"

"I'd ask the judge to overrule. And he'll order the jury to ignore it."

"The damage will already be done."

"Let me be the lawyer, Jaleel."

"I don't want Alex involved," he insisted.

Rudy wouldn't budge. Jaleel's narrative had to be thorough and complete. Selective self-editing would allow the other side to pick apart his entire story. Dirick make the same argument. They were like a tag team, two against one, Jaleel thought. Reluctantly, he agreed, but he added a caveat.

"I mentioned your name to Alex," he told Dirick. "If she tries to contact you, please don't answer."

"May I ask why?"

"It's for her sake. All we ever do is get each other in trouble."

"Dirick promised to honor his wishes. Rudy said he would set up a meeting with his D.A friend as soon as the narrative was finalized and signed. Rudy planned on having Jaleel's signature notarized and they would call the document an affidavit.

"At some point we'll deal with Texas too," Dirick added. "We'll find local counsel to help us avoid extradition. We can argue convincingly that Detective Patterson railroaded you."

Jaleel wagged his head. "You make it sound so logical. What goes on in Peartree has nothing to do with logic."

He picked up a copy of the *Times* the next day. The D.A.'s office had decided not to pursue an indictment against Alex's father. Jaleel had anticipated that Louis Baten would go free, but not his own reaction. The exoneration was more than upsetting—it repulsed him! His hatred for an influential, high-priced lawyer he had never met was even greater than it was for the legal system that had let him go.

He remained on edge all week. Rudy's contact in San Francisco had a conversation with a Los Angeles assistant D.A., who agreed to review the affidavit. When Rudy heard back a day later, the response to Jaleel's story was the same: If true, the facts and circumstances were compelling. Jaleel fought off a laugh. What did compelling get you? Did Rudy and Dirick really think that the D.A. and Hildenbrand, who'd bet the ranch on Louis Baten's guilt, would want to risk losing a second time?

Dirick visited him early on a Sunday. Jaleel was alone in his room, dressed, staring out the window.

"I'm afraid we've had a slight setback," he said. Jaleel turned. Dirick looked as fresh and earnest as always, but there was a crease in his voice. "A reliable source told Rudy that Hildenbrand has three witnesses who saw you, at separate times, around the Diggses' house. One insists he saw you enter the house."

"That's bullshit!" Jaleel said, barely holding his temper. "I rode by on my bike! I never stopped! And no one saw me on the night of the murder. That would have been impossible. I was home, just like I wrote in the affidavit."

"I believe you, but we have to deal with all of this, even when it's circumstantial. I know the police don't have your prints from the Diggses' house—we would have heard already. But you need to turn yourself in and convince them that everything in your statement is true. Rudy and I will be with you every step of the way."

"Why can't they talk to me on the phone? You know what's going to happen if I go to Los Angeles."

"I can arrange bail."

"A judge will call me a flight risk."

"Bail is a question of dollars. I'll provide the money, whatever it takes."

"There won't be any bail," Jaleel argued.

"We can only do what we can do. The system requires patience. I told you that."

"Someone like Louis Baten gets a grand jury. Me, I go straight to a murder trial."

He saw more than a flash of impatience in the scrubbed, pink face. Dirick was disappointed in him.

"You have to stop thinking negatively, Jaleel. Faith is a willingness to endure."

"Right. Just don't tell me I'm going to find the blinding light of redemption in all this."

He turned again to the window, watching a pigeon swank back and forth on the sill. It could fly away any damn time it pleased. He remembered what Marcus had said about white people. They found words to make you feel good, and then they flew away. It was black people who didn't have wings.

"Before you surrender, Rudy will set conditions with the D.A. We won't tolerate a perp walk. No interviews with the media. Everyone will know you have an attorney, so I doubt police harassment will be problem—"

"I'd like to be alone," Jaleel interrupted.

"Rudy and I want to have dinner with you. We need to prepare together—"

"I'm tired."

"Then breakfast tomorrow."

"We'll see."

"Jaleel, look at me. You're not going to do anything stupid, are you?" His eyes stayed on the bird. He heard the concern in the Samaritan's voice, but it wasn't as strong as the fear roiling in Jaleel's stomach. The hounds of hatred wanted to chase him down and devour him, bite by bite. The isolation and helplessness he felt were as bitter as the night Dad shot Mom.

That night, he packed just one suitcase. Traveling light was never more essential. He rolled up his mother's drawing to put inside, which meant leaving almost all his books behind. He didn't mind. The mission could benefit from a decent library.

When he called Marcus, his friend wasn't surprised. "This is déjà vu, brother. You're on the run again. What about those college plans?"

"I don't know. Things are a mess," he admitted.

"You gonna be okay?"

"Pick me up in an hour."

Marcus dropped him at the Greyhound station. There was a night bus to Seattle, and from there, he'd take a train to the Canadian border. His outdated passport, belonging to thirteen-year-old Edward Montgomery, was useless. It might even get him arrested if Canadian authorities knew about the Texas warrant.

He'd have to count on luck again, Jaleel thought, like desperate people always do.

Alex

~45~

When I returned to Valley after confronting my father about Charlie's murder, I tried to pretend life could still be normal, at least at school. I attended classes, ate in the cafeteria, laughed with Joyce and friends, and flirted with boys. But a loneliness shadowed me when the day was over. I went right to my room and did homework. Toby stayed late at Walter Reed, giving his computer classes. Dad, tackling new cases with more energy and purpose than ever, was never home before seven. My mysterious mother had stopped taking my calls in New Hampshire, and lately not even Agnes picked up the phone.

The sudden silence of my mother and aunt, shuttered in a small house in the New England woods, convinced me they were up to something. It wasn't until the end of February that I was able to ask Agnes if I could visit in the summer. She promised to get back to me. Two weeks later, I had my invitation. The welcome mat would be out for the whole three months, she said. I was puzzled by her sudden willingness to have me, but the invitation was a godsend. I couldn't wait to leave Toluca Lake. Every night in bed, I listened to Alison Krauss sing "I'll Fly Away."

Since our confrontation, I had avoided my father as much as possible. Every time I strolled by his study, I would steal a glance at him and keep moving. He might or might not look up. There was nothing to read in his gaze, other than that we were still father and daughter in name. Besides long hours at work, Dad had returned to his weekend routine of golf, poker, and duck hunting. He had so many buddies that Charlie Diggs wasn't missed one iota. I wondered how they had stayed best friends for so long, because what was so special about Charlie? Dad had eight or nine men with whom he shared the same kind of camaraderie. Revenge taken, I thought, he could detach from his memories of anybody, as if the person had never existed.

That's why the divorce with my mother had been relatively quick, I realized. Money had little to do with his emotions; the alimony settlement was generous. With Mom out of his thoughts for good, he began to date regularly, telling me about the different women, as if I would be interested. I was grateful that he hadn't brought any of them home yet. But that moment seemed inevitable—so did marriage, in my view—and I didn't want to be around for any of it.

"Can we talk about something important?" I asked my father one weekend in late March. We were finishing up dinner. Toby was upstairs. When I looked in Dad's eyes, I saw a man who viewed himself as invulnerable.

"What's up?"

"I've given this a lot of thought. I'd like to transfer to another school."

His chin rose in surprise. "You're doing well at Valley. Why would you leave?"

"It just feels like time to move on, you know? I'll be sixteen this summer."

"Move on where exactly?"

"I'm in the process of applying to a couple of schools in the East."

He didn't comment, but I could imagine him thinking: "Really? Why? You don't want to keep living with me?"

"You're sure you want to do this?" he asked.

"If it's okay with you."

His gaze landed on me as if I was ten years old again, still under his protective wing, a rapt audience waiting on his approval. But he didn't seem to want an argument any more than I did. We had an undeclared detente. "Sure, sweetie."

"You're okay with paying the tuition at my new school?"

"Why wouldn't I be? College and graduate school too. You're the shining star of the family."

"Don't give up on Toby. He might eclipse all of us." I had come
to think of my brother as the Jedi knight of the internet.
"I remember how anxious Gloria used to get over Toby. Silly, huh?
He'll turn out fine," Dad predicted.
There was no other mention of Mom, other than when I said I
planned to see her this summer, before the school year started. Dad
seemed okay with it, as she was just a stranger now.
"You'll be coming here for the holidays, won't you?" he added. "I
don't plan on moving. I'd like us to stay connected."
"You'll be in a new relationship by then."
"Maybe. But Toby will still be here. And you'll always have your
room."
"Well, that sounds good. Let me think about it."
I smiled, keeping up my end of our pretend relationship. The
proverbial team of wild horses couldn't drag me back here.
"Better get to my homework," I whispered, turning away.

April 29
Worst moment of the day: I ran into Detective
Hildenbrand in the express checkout line at
Ralph's—awkward. He asked if I'd heard anything
from Jaleel. I wagged my head. Like I would ever tell
him about the letter I got? Hildenbrand said Jaleel's
attorney had promised his client would turn himself
in to the D.A., but at the last second, Jaleel
apparently got cold feet and ran away. He was
thought to be hiding somewhere in Canada. All news
to me.
Maybe some people are born escape artists,
survivalists, Houdinis. If Jaleel was on the run,
Cornelius Appleton must have helped a little. When I
called his number in New York, he never picked up. I
left my name on his machine several times. After all
the trouble I'd put Jaleel through, maybe there was a
feeling that I was bad news. All I wanted was to
know that Jaleel was all right. I didn't expect him to
forgive me. I didn't deserve that.

*Best moment of the day: I've been accepted as a
junior to St. Anthony's, outside of Boston. It's pretty
prestigious; over half the grads go to Ivies, MIT, or
Stanford. Ms. Graves wrote a nice letter of
recommendation, mostly because she was happy to see
me go, I think. Maybe I'm getting ahead of myself,
but I asked Dad to send St. Anthony tuition for two
years instead of just one. Joyce has told me stories
about second wives using all means possible to
separate a new husband from his children.*

The next thing I knew it was May, alternately bringing spring
gusts, rain, and sun-bleached skies, and then the month spooled into
a listless, smog-choked June. Just when time is moving like a tor-
toise—you can't wait for something to happen—it suddenly speeds
up. Valley was officially out on the fourth of June. I said goodbye to
my friends with enough hugs, air-kisses, and tears to make me think
I was an explorer heading off to a distant, uncertain shore. I made
Joyce promise that we would never lose touch.

"I expect big things from you, Niles Burns," I said that night as I
finished packing in my room. Toby was in one of his nerdy outfits,
including a pair of black, thick-framed glasses he affected.

"You're really leaving? When am I seeing you again?"

I was brushing my hair back, looking at him in the mirror. "I
don't know."

"That's not what you told Dad. You said you'd be home—"

"No, I said I'd think about it. Between you and me, don't count
on it. You'll go through the same thing one day. You just know when
it's time to leave and not come back."

"Is everything okay?" he asked, suspicious.

"Peachy. I'll call you when I get to Agnes's." I gave him my "don't
worry, you'll figure it all out one day" look. I felt bad for abandoning
him, yet I knew it was the best thing in the world for my brother.
Toby had made great strides toward his independence—and a func-
tioning identity, as Dr. Sheffield might say. He would move even
faster without me around.

He hesitated. "Well, say hello to Mom."

"I will." I zipped up my two duffels and backpack, and gave Toby a strong hug. My plane was leaving in the morning, a straight shot to Wonderland.

~46~

Aunt Agnes met me at the Boston-Manchester regional airport. We hadn't seen each other for eight or nine years—the last visit of my reclusive aunt to Los Angeles—but some people you always recognize. It's not that they don't age, but Agnes's features were as memorable as anything on Mount Rushmore—a mouth straighter than a ruler, no-nonsense honeybee-brown eyes, and a permanent furrow above her nose. Buttoned-down, self-contained, fastidious—a work of art in someone's permanent collection, just not mine.

She wore a cotton print dress and modest makeup. Rather than give me a hug, she shook my hand.

"Greetings, Alex." She assessed me with the same economy with which, I gathered, she viewed the rest of the world. I got a single, long glance—long enough to form not just an impression but an opinion. Mom had told me that once Agnes had her opinion, she usually found little reason to change it. I did reasonably well. "My, how you've grown, Alex. You're a striking young woman. And such self-possession—I can see by the way you carry yourself."

"Thank you," I said, thinking how unself-possessed I was feeling. "Lost" or "aimless" would have been a better term.

"Your mother is very proud of you."

"I wouldn't know. You hardly ever put her on the phone."

"Everything for a reason," she replied, without giving me one.

I asked if Mom was okay. I had expected her to come to the airport. Agnes said she was fine. It was a forty-five minute drive to the house, she announced, and if I was hungry, I should eat something at the airport. I grabbed coffee and a glazed donut for the road.

Agnes cultivated detachment and mystery not just by guarding my mother's privacy but also by maintaining long silences and—if by chance she spoke—choosing her words carefully. I imagined that she had a cache of friends fully as laconic and precise as she was. Joyce had warned me that people in New England could be weird; just read some Stephen King, she said.

As we drove, Agnes asked about Toby. I mentioned his reincarnation as Niles Burns, which she probably already knew from Mom, but I was hoping my aunt might break into spontaneous laughter and betray a different personality.

"Niles Burns," she repeated. "Where did he come up with that name?"

"I have no idea."

"Your mother says Toby was always a challenge until suddenly he wasn't."

"Yeah. He's doing a lot better now."

Silence. Agnes asked nothing about my father, as if the subject was off limits. My questions about Mom continued to get spotty responses. The sisters were five years apart in age and even further in temperament, but I would always believe they'd contrived a secret pact in childhood.

Once we were out of the hurly-burly of Manchester, the scenery opened onto squares of farm fields, foothills in bloom, and a mix of barns and simple homes with satellite dishes and window knick-knacks. It all seemed a little strange but a welcome relief from the hardscape of L.A.

"Here we are. Be prepared," Agnes warned as we drove into a gravel drive off the main road. I studied the pitched roof structure—the white siding with gray window trim, curtained windows, and a deck off the side of the house. Everything looked tidy and immaculate. There were no immediate neighbors. The solitude and seclusion didn't surprise me. It fit Agnes to perfection.

She offered to carry my bags, but I wanted to show I could be as self-reliant and independent as she was. I dropped everything in the hallway when I heard the noise. I was stunned. Impossible! I thought, listening again. There was a lull, and this time the baby's crying greeted me like an air raid siren.

Agnes gave me a look, like, hadn't I suspected something like this all along?

No, I hadn't.

Mom, as if back on stage in Toluca Lake, swept out of a bedroom in dramatic fashion. She was holding a newborn in her arms. I could see the pink, mewling face sticking out of its striped blanket. I had a ferret's nose for digging out secrets, but I was caught so flat-footed now that I mentally shook my head. Mom wore a beatific smile, as if pure joy was a language all its own. She came up and we kissed each other on the cheek.

Slowly, wheels began to turn, and a second shock wave hit me like an atomic blast.

"Is that Charlie's baby?" I said.

Mom was too busy laying the infant over her shoulder and burping it.

"Yes, it's Charlie's," Agnes replied. "She's a girl."

"How old?"

"Six weeks."

Mom had left our house nine months ago, as if fleeing a fire. I thought it was just from embarrassment over her affair, or because she was out of love with my father.

"I take it Dad doesn't know," I said. I dropped into a chair in the living room. Mom scooched back on the couch and began to nurse. She looked healthy, maybe a few pounds of pregnancy fat still to lose but quintessentially pleased with herself. Agnes brought us glasses of lemonade.

"What would be the point of your father knowing?" Mom spoke up. The baby's mouth settled comfortable around her teat. "It would only have made our divorce more difficult . . . more clashing emotions that I didn't need."

I didn't think my father would have cared at all. Mom thought she was still important in his eyes.

"What about Julia?" I asked. "How would she feel about you having her husband's baby?"

"Would she really care?"

"Telling Julia seems like the right thing to do. You never know. She wanted children in the worst way, didn't you tell me that?"

"She wouldn't want my child."

"Did Charlie know you were pregnant?" I went on. I couldn't stop myself. I had a dozen questions.

Mom answered obliquely. "I don't know if Charlie would have been happy about this, even if we were in love."

"So you didn't tell him, despite all those midnight phone calls to his house."

I figured she would have had to tell him eventually, had he not been killed. Maybe they would have raised their daughter together. That seemed like the right thing to do. Watching Mom, I could see how attached she already was to the baby.

"Why breathe a word?" Mom said. "Alex, you're the only one who knows besides Agnes. I don't need people who were once close friends spreading more gossip about me."

I couldn't look at Mom for a moment. When you're expected to keep secrets so twisted up inside you that it's sometimes hard to breathe, it feels like you're a punching bag. I don't know who hit harder, Mom or Dad.

I sipped my lemonade, still agitated, before I looked up. "Does she have a name?"

"Lucy Baten. Isn't she a beaut? Lucy was the name of my favorite doll when I was little."

From what I could see—a small pinkish blob suckling on Mom's teat—I couldn't comment on her beauty, other than that it was in the eye of the beholder.

I came to another critical point. "Are you going to put her up for adoption?"

"You're talking about giving away your half-sister," Mom responded.

I had already thought about this as we sat. A half-sister wasn't something to take lightly. While I didn't feel any bond with Charlie Diggs, I cared a lot about my new half-sister, starting with who was going to raise her. "You're going to take care of Lucy all by yourself?" I said. "What about a father in her life? I read that it costs half a million dollars to raise a child today. Do you know you'll be sixty when she goes to college?"

Mom lifted her eyes in disappointment, as if I was slow to understand what was truly important. Having a baby in her early forties, one that was in good health and so beautiful, cheating her biological clock, was a small miracle. She should be congratulated.

"Agnes and I have spoken with a lawyer," Mom reluctantly admitted. "Agnes thinks like you, that putting Lucy up for adoption is the only sensible thing. Only if we can find the right couple, I say. We've already interviewed several."

"Do you have to tell them about the parents' backgrounds? Like Charlie being murdered?"

I immediately wished I hadn't said that. I had hurt her. Mom's face darkened. "You don't think I know a few things, Alex? I still have a couple of friends in Toluca Lake. Some people think your father killed Charlie, but I don't believe that for one moment. I was married to Louis for over twenty years. He could be stubborn and difficult, but he's not a killer. Besides, the grand jury didn't indict him, did it?"

"No, it didn't." I said, biting my tongue.

"I hear there's suspicion about some young black man, but I was told he hasn't been located. Is that what I should reveal to the couple who adopts my baby? I don't think so. They don't need to know anything—except that Lucy is in good health and has exceptional pedigree. All that matters is Charlie's genes. He was a great man. Actually, he was a genius when it came to architecture. And you know what an incredible athlete he was—"

"Why didn't you just divorce Dad years ago and marry Charlie?" I blurted out.

"Because I already had a husband and a family."

"Toby and I would have understood a divorce. We would have adjusted. Dad too maybe, if you'd explained things clearly. And all the shit we would have avoided—"

"Hindsight is twenty-twenty, Alex," she interrupted.

"There's no point in having a debate about the past," Agnes came to the rescue. "Gloria brought a beautiful new life into the world, and that's a wonderful thing. All that's left is to find the right home for Lucy."

As Mom returned her doting gaze to the baby, Agnes showed me to my room. It was spartan and clean, with a view to a stand of birch trees and stacked firewood under the roof of a nearby shed. A Norman Rockwell tableau. I was happy to be here, I realized, the shock of baby Lucy and my mother's cluelessness notwithstanding.

~47~

For the rest of the summer, I took morning walks on a brick path through Agnes's property, then along a creek, down a one-lane dirt road, and onto a broad field that felt like the quietest spot on earth. It was an eight-mile round trip. I came to love the solitude, doing nothing but looking and thinking. Why I had been such a mindless activities rat at Valley eluded me now.

On my walks, I pondered going to St. Anthony's in the fall. I wondered if making new friends would be worth the effort, since I had only two years there. The school was coed. I'd be happy to have one or two girl friends, date some interesting guys, and call it a day. Focusing on my grades and SATs seemed more important. I hadn't lost my academic ambitions.

I also thought about Mom, that if it weren't for her sister's insistence on adoption, she might keep the baby, just to prove how good a mother she could be. And she was good when Toby and I were little. But the immediate past carried much more weight. Mom had been in a destructive affair, abandoned us, and committed other selfish acts. My half-sister deserved a better track record than that.

When the three of us were together for meals, I studied the relationship between Mom and Agnes. It seemed like my mother was the child and Agnes the indulgent parent, to a point. My mother acted out her fantasy of having a baby with her lover (who in Mom's mind was somehow still alive, it seemed to me), and my aunt didn't stop her or even comment until it was absolutely necessary. For someone who didn't have children, and had never gone to college or been married, Agnes was a cradle of common sense. For twenty years, she'd worked as a bookkeeper for a car dealer in Manchester, saving enough to have a simple house owned free and clear, and living off successful investments. Frugality was her eleventh commandment, followed by self-education. Her living room boasted a floor-to-ceiling bookcase—art, history, philosophy, travel, cooking, gardening—as extensive as the one in Dad's study. I picked through her books whenever I felt like it.

"I read everything I can, especially history," Agnes told me over dinner. "My favorite period is Hellenistic Greece. I wouldn't have minded living in Athens then, as long as the state wasn't at war."

"Agnes should have gone to college," Mom interjected. "She had far better grades than I did. Not to mention a full scholarship to Berkeley. She was at the top of her graduating class."

"College would have been wasted on me," my aunt answered. "Too many distractions."

"Mom and Dad looked upon you as the scholar in the family, Agnes. I was just the beauty that everyone ogled." I coughed in my fist.

"I had my reasons for not going to college," Agnes said.

"Like what?" I asked.

"I simply had a gut feeling about all that hoopla. I didn't like beer keg parties or football games or sororities. I wasn't a joiner. So much of college is about socializing and being accepted. I preferred keeping my own company, and learning on my own."

I was beginning to enjoy Agnes a little more every day. While Mom looked after Lucy, my aunt did all the cooking. The food was fresh and tasty. I wondered if she'd learned about preparing it from a book. She had the patience and time to acquire any number of skills.

"Have you ever been in love?" I asked her at one dinner. I didn't know where the question came from. Mom shot me a look, like I was being too nosey.

"I've had a fling or two, at the dealership, but nothing stuck. I don't think I'm enough of a romantic to make a relationship last. Or maybe I'm just too eccentric.

"It's a fact that some people think I'm a lesbian, and that would be fine if I were, but I enjoy male company. There's a bachelor neighbor that comes calling once in a while. I'm not interested in a long-term relationship."

"It's not too late," Mom threw in, as if no woman's world could be complete without a prince on a white horse.

"Actually, it's way too late, Gloria." She turned to me. The straight-line mouth became an upward curve. The smile carried to her eyes. "How about you, Alex? Have you fallen in love yet?"

Mom sighed. "She's not even sixteen. You're talking about puppy love, if anything."

Agnes ignored my mother and continued her line of inquiry. Was there a particular boy I was seeing? Was there someone I fantasized about before going to sleep? What had I discovered about myself in the process?

"There's this boy, an older boy, I'm attracted to in a strange way."

"Tell me about him," said Agnes.

Mom pursed her lips. I could hear questions ricocheting through her head before I even started. Where did you meet him, Alex? What is so strange about your attraction? Have you had sex with him? Why didn't you share any of this?

I saw no reason not to tell Agnes. My aunt was a resource, and a fount of wisdom, that I didn't have in my erratic mother. I wanted Agnes to know that in my impulsive way, I'd judged her incorrectly for years, and to make up for that, I now wanted her opinion on just about everything. I began to describe Jaleel as objectively as possible— a friend I'd made after crossing the Maginot Line of Cahuenga Boule-vard—but I couldn't keep the emotion out of my voice. My mother heard it too. She looked ashen. It wasn't just that I'd disobeyed her by crossing Cahuenga. It was when I mentioned that Jaleel was eighteen, black, and a fugitive from an alleged murder in Texas that her jaw fell.

"What else do you know about him?" Mom asked.

"He's tall and muscular, with a sense of humor that put me at ease when we met. He was essentially homeless but managed to get straight A's and played baseball at a competitive level. In some ways, we were complete opposites. In other ways, it felt like we were twins. Like we both get up at five in the morning . . . ." I started to laugh.

It was hard to stop myself. I'd given up journal writing after leaving Toluca Lake, but my emotions still needed an outlet.

Mom's eyes began blinking. "This eighteen-year-old black man, is he the one—"

"I would appreciate if you called him by his name," I said. "Jaleel Robeson."

She forced the words out, despite her shock. "Is he the one whom the police think killed Charlie?"

She was rigid, breathing through her nose, as if at any second she might come flying apart in a thousand pieces.

"Jaleel didn't kill anybody, Mom. The police need a scapegoat. He had nothing to do with Charlie's death."

"You calm down, Gloria," Agnes said. "Alex made a bond with someone special—two people from very different backgrounds. I think it sounds exotic, like planets colliding from different solar systems."

"I like that metaphor," I said.

Mom tried to pull herself together. Agnes seemed to be waiting for our discussion to find its way back to the subject of love. I had read somewhere that love was just lust with jealousy attached. It didn't feel that way to me. It was a much bigger mystery. Was it the same for everyone, or unique to each of us? Why did some people fall in love while others, like Agnes, didn't? In my analytic view of the world, I didn't know where and how love would fit into my busy life, only that I wanted it to. I wanted a family one day.

"Just knowing I could be attracted to someone like Jaleel was comforting," I went on. "Boys at Valley were pretty much the same. Everything was about getting into a girl's pants. Not that I wasn't tempted by sex. I flirted a lot, but I'm still a virgin."

I got a "Thank God" sigh from Mom, and then she said it was a good thing I was going to a new school—as if kids at St. Anthony's didn't have sex.

"To already discover the kind of person you're attracted to, that's a fortunate thing," my aunt said. "I wish I had let myself be more open at your age."

"Jaleel's disappeared, apparently somewhere in Canada," I said, trying to be philosophical. "I may never see him again. But I'm glad I had a chance to know him."

"Don't give up hope, Alex."

Lucy began to whimper from the other room, which turned into a cry of distress. My mother whispered "wet diaper," and hurried off. Agnes and I switched topics, to the unforgiving, cabin-feverish New England winters, and then local politics. New Englanders loved to talk politics, I found out.

When Mom returned, she still looked upset about Jaleel. I could read her ridiculous thoughts. This was the boy I was enamored with? A black kid from a backwater town in Texas? I would have known better had she raised me with more insight into how to evaluate men.

I got deeper into my daily routine of walks, reading from Agnes's library, and even helping with Lucy. I had no idea what a handful an infant could be. Mom kept asking how I felt when I held her, changed diapers, and endured the crying jags.

"Weird," I replied. "I want a kid one day, but I don't know if I'm cut out for it."

It was almost the end of summer before "the luckiest couple in the world," as Mom kept putting it, had been selected. The lawyers had finalized the paperwork, and arrangements were made to turn over Lucy to a 33-year-old Harvard-educated economist and his wife, who couldn't seem to get pregnant. The adoption was to be kept confidential. Mom had received $35,000 for agreeing not to make contact with the child again. Lucy was almost four months old now. I didn't rub it in with Mom how good I felt about the adoption. I did tell her that Lucy's perfectly round face and bow mouth qualified her as undeniably adorable. Her big eyes rotated back and forth at everything around her.

The morning Agnes was to drive Mom and Baby Lucy to the attorney's office, my mother refused to come out of her bedroom.

Agnes knocked firmly on the door. "Gloria, it's time. You've had all night and morning to say goodbye."

My mother stifled a sob. "I can't let her go."

"Everything has been signed, Gloria."

"I've changed my mind."

"You can't change your mind. You have a contract."

"I'll give back the money. I never wanted to do this in the first place."

"Gloria, you had months to think about this. You agreed on this family. They're terrific people."

"I'm sorry. I'm not giving her up." Echoing Mom's stubborn voice, a chair was shoved against the door from the inside, in case we were thinking of breaking in.

Agnes and I huddled. We could call the baby's pediatrician, whose judgment Mom trusted, or a psychiatrist, or our lawyer to tell the other lawyer there'd been a delay. But the more procrastination, we decided, the more entrenched Mom would become.

My aunt lowered her shoulder to the door and, with a strength that didn't surprise me, forced it open. I was afraid for what I might find. There hadn't been a peep from the baby. When my gaze found Mom, she was in a rocking chair, nursing Lucy with a bond that seemed unbreakable.

Coaxing the baby from her arms took more of Agnes's strength than breaking in the door. Suddenly empty handed, my mother fell into convulsive gasps, as if we had stolen something vital from her, and her life wouldn't ever be the same.

"Are you all right, Mom?" The original plan was that my mother and Agnes would both go to the attorney's office. Now, my mother was in no condition to do anything. Someone else would have to hold Lucy while Agnes drove.

"I'm okay," Mom claimed, still crying.

"Are you sure? I can stay with you. Agnes can find a neighbor to drive her and the baby."

"No, you go, Alex. You say goodbye to Lucy for me."

"Okay, then it's done," I sighed.

"You say goodbye to Lucy," she repeated, still with great doubt in her voice. "I love her to bits."

Agnes handed me the baby. I followed as she carried a bag with diapers and formula to the car. Carefully getting into the front seat, I strapped the seat belt around us. It was a half-hour drive, and the whole time I couldn't take my eyes off what had obsessed my mother. Unlike Mom, though, I wasn't feeling possessive about my half-sister. I just worried about diarrhea and projectile vomiting.

"It may take Gloria time to get over this," Agnes advised me on the ride back. The whole handoff had taken less than half an hour. The young couple was perfect—enthusiastic, polite, and grateful.

"Why?" I asked.

"She gets attached to her babies. Wasn't she the same with you and Toby?"

"I guess so," I said, remembering that I had doted on Mom as much as she had doted on me.

When we returned, Mom was in the kitchen fixing lunch for everyone. She didn't ask any questions, as if keeping busy would block out the trauma of giving up her baby. The house didn't feel the same for the rest of my visit. Not just because the baby smells and sounds were gone but also because of the uncomfortable silence that replaced them.

I had to leave for St. Anthony's the next week, but I thought more about my mother than I did my new school. Mom was busy packing too. She announced that she was moving to New York City. A new life awaited her, she said grandly. I didn't think she had any idea what was in store for her.

To celebrate my sixteenth birthday, Agnes decided we should dine at the best seafood restaurant in Manchester. She ordered wine for herself and Mom, a Coke for me, and we did a lot of toasting.

I took Agnes aside as we left the restaurant. "Is Mom going to be okay?"

"Gloria has to keep busy. When she was a model in New York, those were happy times. Maybe that's what she's thinking. And what better place to meet an eligible man."

I left New Hampshire a couple of days before my mother. She was distracted about the latest fashions in New York, how much new clothing she'd have to buy. It wasn't a great farewell—we had a quick hug as I fumbled some words about keeping in touch. It was easier parting with Agnes. We had really clicked that summer, and I wanted our new friendship to continue.

I took the train from Manchester to Boston, lugging my duffels and backpack containing almost everything I owned. I kept wondering how a family could once have been so close, only to lose its center of gravity. I would blame both my parents equally, but my mother's failings were more complex. She was an especially beautiful woman in her twenties and thirties who had come to resent the self-importance of my father. If they noticed Mom's discontent, perhaps other men, just as lonely as she, would have asked for something from her— sympathy, intimacy, or just the attention that they didn't get from their wives or girlfriends. It would have made her feel good to give them what they wanted. But maybe there weren't that many men, despite what we had heard at the Tick Tock. Mom would never have told me the truth anyway. I liked to think it was just Charlie, and true love. But that had been enough to unravel everything. It was like you woke up one morning and found your life was gone.

Jaleel

~48~

Vancouver's large mosaic of ethnic neighborhoods amid an over-all population of four hundred fifty thousand allowed Jaleel more freedom than he'd enjoyed since leaving Peartree. He disappeared among the cracks of low-income apartments, dimly lit coffee shops, and public transportation. A feeling of anonymity lessened his anxiety and clarified his ambitions. Let the Samaritan sermonize about redemption and forgiveness. Pie-in-the-sky for the poor and disenfranchised. As much as he respected Dirick, Jaleel was interested in spreading a different gospel. The United States, thumping its chest as the land of freedom and opportunity, seethed with hypocrisy. The disparity between the rich and poor widened by the day. Justice for all was a mirage. Wake up, people! he wanted to shout from the rooftops.

He had begun scribbling his first broadside on the train to Canada. Custom officials hadn't even asked for a driver's license, let alone a passport. Adopting yet another new name, he said he was visiting friends for thirty days. After filling out a three-by-five visitor's card, he vanished into a wilderness of possible new hiding places.

After six months, no agency, including the police, had checked up on him. Maybe they'd tried, but he was skilled at camouflage. As he'd done in North Hollywood, he paid cash for everything, and lived frugally. He didn't seek out friends. His digs were a one-bedroom, third-floor walkup in a large apartment building in a mixed neighborhood. A used IBM computer and printer were set on a simple desk, part of an ensemble of furniture gathered from thrift shops and garage sales. As always, he went without a phone.

The casual acquaintances he made in coffee shops and around the neighborhood, if they asked what he did, were told the truth: that he worked from his apartment as a tutor for high school students and those studying to take college admissions tests. He placed flyers around the neighborhood to solicit students. They came and went, paid in cash, and left him with plenty of time to write. Contacting Dirick and Rudy was tempting—if only to let them know he was safe—but he didn't put any surveillance trick past the police or the District Attorney's Office.

In his day-to-day existence, he felt contentment and self-sufficiency. The city of Vancouver didn't have the smog and overcrowding of the San Fernando Valley. Summer allowed for long, wood-shaded walks in Stanley Park, and if it rained, there were theaters, museums, and an aquarium to absorb him. People were neither overfriendly nor distant. Vancouver, and maybe most of Canada, had a "steady-as-it-goes" disposition. The ethnic mixture—Chinese from Hong Kong were the newest wave of immigrants—constituted a genuine melting pot. On the surface, there was much to like, but scratch down not terribly deep and Jaleel witnessed the same treatment of minorities he'd seen at home.

One day, he picked through a used book store until he found dog-eared copies of *The Fire Next Time* and *Go Tell It on the Mountain*. His original copies had been left purposely at the mission, for others to discover a great writer. Baldwin's novel of the early '50s, *Go Tell It on the Mountain*, examined the contradictory role of the Christian church for African-Americans. It was an example of repression and isolation, yet a necessary glue for the fragile black community. *Fire*, Jaleel's favorite, was written in the early '60s as the civil rights movement was shaping itself. Part of the book was a letter to Baldwin's fourteen-year-old nephew, on the hundredth anniversary of the Emancipation Proclamation. The author warned all Americans to attack the terrible legacy of racism—or else. Baldwin didn't shy from predictions of an apocalypse. You could give lip service to loving humanity, but that did little to stop something truly evil.

Jaleel's first modest pamphlet was only four pages, but he hoped it would prick the conscience of readers. In Kingman, Randy had called Dirick's work "manifestos." The description suited Jaleel's writing too—part insight, part confessional, part ultimatum. He chose a pen name—Poor Richard—borrowing it from Benjamin Franklin, and called his manifestos *My World*. He pinned them clandestinely on bus station kiosks, in laundromats, on library bulletin boards, and around college campuses—anywhere the poor, the exploited, or the idealistic might be found. He didn't want fame. His mission was to put his young life on display, to enlighten others.

> *I am the unforgiven. Every morning I wake wondering what I have done wrong, what I am to be forgiven for. I have hurt no one intentionally, stolen no one's money, broken no laws, sullied no reputations, and threatened no innocents. I am unforgiven, I think, for things I cannot help being. Brothers and sisters, I know I am not alone. We are all under suspicion for our religion, our skin color, or our political beliefs—or just the way our eyes shift in our heads, our lips purse, our hands dangle from our pockets. Our identities— our very souls—are threatened by the distrust and ignorance of the establishment. We must do something. When we're unforgiven for things we cannot or will not change, we bleed to death from hopelessness.*
>
> *I do not advocate revenge or violence. I advocate self-reliance, self-awareness, and the principle that racism is not simply about one man's irrational hatred of another but his self-hatred, doubting his own moral goodness and purpose. We must believe we are capable of transcending evil, of not needing to hide in the darkness or surrender to our basest fears. Rise up, brothers and sisters. If you've been the victim of discrimination, make your truth known. If you don't speak for yourself, who will? Silence is death. No brother or sister can be free until all of us are free.*

He published a new manifesto every couple of weeks. They were filled with tales of life in a central Texas town, of taunts from teachers and kids in high school, of sullen cops riding through Los Angeles neighborhoods looking to hassle you. He wrote that middle-class blacks turned a blind eye to racism, as if that would make it go away, or it wasn't a significant problem for them. But they needed to acknowledge that it existed for their less-fortunate brethren, and speaking against it was a moral duty.

The manifestos grew from four pages to eight, then twelve, as if his passion had just begun to find its voice. James Baldwin had recently passed away in France, writing less and less at the end. There were debates about his thoughts on racism in the '80s. Despite civil rights legislation in the '60s and '70s, despite protests, despite a few hard-won battles on the employment and education front, had things changed that much? Maybe the stain of original sin was stamped in our DNA, Jaleel wrote. Martin Luther King Jr. had talked about the moral arc of history, bending slowly, inevitably, in the right direction, but how patient did one have to be?

Living alone was nothing new for Jaleel, but keeping to himself was. In North Hollywood, at least he had school buddies. Making friends with students he tutored was too dangerous. Afraid of undercover cops, he stayed clear of all strangers if possible. He missed going to school, missed church, missed Alex's visits to his house. At times he felt like a rudderless ship drifting toward an endless horizon. His loneliness made him resentful. Why did he deserve this? He wondered what Marcus, Dirick, or even Alex would advise him. Sometimes he slipped into his father's head, feeling the bitterness and anger that had pushed Clarence into total isolation.

The apartment next to Jaleel's had been empty for months, but one day that changed. He didn't see the occupants or know their names, but he heard them. The couple waited to finish dinner before lashing out at each other. Husband and wife were equal opportunity screamers. Usually the fight was over money, but sometimes it was about their child, or an old grievance. The paper-thin walls were like loud speakers. The little boy could be heard crying, and a dog barked crazily. Jaleel's lack of sleep began to bother him. He couldn't write at his best when he woke every morning in a fog.

As he headed out for coffee one morning, the neighbor trudged ahead of him in his bathrobe, carrying a bulging grocery bag down the stairs. The clanking of empty bottles rang in Jaleel's ears. The man was twice as wide as he was and balding in back. Jaleel noted not only the unkempt appearance but the entitlement of his swagger as well, like he could do whatever he wanted. There was something thuggish about him. From the couple's nightly arguments, Jaleel knew he was out of work. The man seemed unaware of Jaleel until he emptied his liquor bottles into a bin on the street.

"Hey, blackie, what are you looking at?" he taunted, suddenly turning around. His bright blue eyes dug a hole through Jaleel. "Are you following me?"

"No, sir. I'm your neighbor. Nice to meet you. I wanted to ask a favor, if I could."

"What kind of favor?" His belly spilled out of the loosely tied bathrobe.

"The walls upstairs are really thin. When you and your wife get into arguments, it's hard for me to concentrate on my work, or to sleep."

"You listening in, getting into our business?"

"No, sir. I'm just asking you to keep your voices down."

"Your accent—you're not from here, are you? You're another immigrant who thinks he's got more rights than a Canadian citizen like me. Fuckin' nerve, boy."

"No, I don't think that."

"You're making trouble, you know that?"

The husband brushed past him with a dismissive scowl. Jaleel tried to push the encounter from his thoughts, and to hope he had at least made his point. But the nightly rows grew louder and longer. The little boy's high-pitched wailing was particularly unsettling. Did the man beat him? One night, for no reason, the brute began to pound on Jaleel's wall, purposely, like someone banging on a war drum.

He considered changing his apartment, yet as someone who had done nothing wrong, why should he have to move? Why capitulate to a bully? Jaleel asked the landlord to speak to the couple, or send them a warning letter to be quiet. He assumed that nothing happened. The fist-pounding on the wall grew more insistent. Enough of this, Jaleel thought after yet another sleepless night. He couldn't afford to have the neighbor call the police, yet didn't his manifestos insist that everyone stand up for himself, even if it put a person at risk? He was behaving like a coward, shrinking in a corner.

When he found a letter for his neighbor mistakenly placed in his mail slot, he decided to learn everything he could about Joseph and Marianna Hager. The father of a student he tutored worked in a credit agency that chased down deadbeats. Jaleel gave the student the couple's name, and promised free tutoring for the results of a thorough investigation.

I am filled with more than discontent this morning after a sleepless night. I am filled with anguish over my helplessness. In the middle of the night, my neighbor bangs on my wall and hurls curses at me, brimming with some unnamed hatred. He won't stop, even though I have asked him to. He doesn't even know my name, but it seems he can't exist without hating someone. Maybe he hates more than just immigrants and people of color, yet we are so convenient a target. I will tell him no more pounding on my wall or cursing me. I will tell him to take his hatred and if he must destroy someone with it, destroy himself. I will speak my mind. I will not be cowed. We must not run from our dignity.

After distributing his manifesto, he returned to his apartment and helped two young women prep for their college entrance exams. When he walked them to the door to say goodbye, he noticed that the Hagers' door was half open. He pushed his head in and called out "hello." Now was as good a time as any to confront the Neanderthal. When no one answered, he called out again. In the messy living room, his eyes jumped to the top of the television cabinet. A silver revolver gleamed in the window's light. What was a gun doing out in the open? He was dismayed. A child lived here.

He scooped up the weapon, hoping it was a toy. He found bullets in the chambers. After his father's death, he had sworn never to shoot or even touch a weapon. Now what? he thought. Leave the revolver and get out of the apartment, or for the sake of everyone, including himself, steal the gun? He kept turning it over in his hands, wishing he'd never come through the door.

"What you doing here, blackie? Breakin' into my home?"

Jaleel 's eyes jumped to the doorway. In a suit and tie, Hager hardly resembled the unkempt man in the bathrobe, but his small, pointy eyes fell on Jaleel with the same contempt and superiority, as if he had this black troublemaker right where he wanted him. Hager ran his hand over his partially bald head, like someone brushing back invisible hair, deliberating on his next move.

"I was just leaving," Jaleel said. "Your door was open. You should keep it locked." He didn't surrender the revolver.

"Here's what I'm going to do," Hager replied. "I caught myself a burglar in the act. And then you threatened me. With my own weapon. I'm going to take my gun back and shoot you between the eyes. It's all self-defense. Unless," he goaded, "you got the balls to shoot me first."

"I didn't threaten you, Mr. Hager. You left a loaded gun where your kid could grab it. That's what's wrong here."

"Oh, now you know my name, do you?"

The beefy man suddenly moved toward him. Jaleel raised the revolver, aimed, and pulled back the hammer. Hager stopped seven or eight feet away, with enough doubt in his eyes to buy Jaleel more time.

"I can see why you call yourself Mr. Hager. Your real name is Stephen Lyman, isn't it?" Jaleel said, using information his student had gotten him. "You've got a rap sheet. You've been in jail several times for failing to pay judgments. You might even be a suspect in the Bank of Vancouver robbery three months ago. That why you've been hiding out here with your ex and little boy?"

The volcano in Jaleel was moving from simmer to boil. "If I shot you this instant, would the police really care?"

"You're in over your head, pussy. I never heard of a teacher type who could pull a trigger."

"You don't know anything about me."

"I know a coward when I see one."

"So do I," Jaleel replied.

He took a decisive step forward, and watched as Hager stepped back.

"Here's what *I'm* going to do," Jaleel promised, barely recognizing his voice. "I'm not going to call the cops. I'm keeping your gun and going back to my apartment. I don't want to hear one more word of fighting, one fist slamming my wall, and if you ever hurt your child or even your dog, I'm going to come back and shoot you between the eyes."

The thug's lips dropped into a straight, sober line, as though some adversaries, even a black man who was nothing more than a teacher, needed to be taken seriously. He moved begrudgingly to one side so his neighbor could walk free.

Jaleel locked his door and dropped the revolver into a bedside drawer. In the cheap mirror above his bed, his face was a canvas of fury and confusion. He had written in his manifestos that he didn't believe in acts of violence, yet this afternoon, he had threatened a man's life. A worthless, scumbag life. He might even have pulled the trigger. Jaleel raised the revolver, aimed, and pulled back the hammer. Wouldn't the world have been better off without another bigoted asshole on the streets?

His urges vexed him. The line between standing up for himself and shying from violence was sometimes hard to see. He had been on the run for so long, maybe it was a surprise he hadn't exploded years ago. His rage had really started with Patterson, the detective in Peartree, and had grown in between with so many other injustices. James Baldwin had endured enough indignities to warn of outright war between the races. But this wasn't only about racism, Jaleel thought. It was about good and evil. He remembered his father, the one time he'd stood up for himself, against a man who'd swiped something from his toolbox. Jaleel understood Clarence more clearly now. It wasn't all his father's fault that his long-buried temper and self-loathing had provoked the fight. You could only be pushed so far. He remembered how his mother had humiliated his father that night.

The yelling and fighting next door stopped cold that evening. Jaleel waited for an explosion the following night, and the night after, but they never happened. The next morning, movers were hauling new furniture into the apartment. The tenant, a single, older man, told Jaleel that the Hagers had moved out in the middle of the night, dodging their overdue rent.

Jaleel said nothing and went on his way. You got off lucky, he told himself. He needed to be more vigilant guarding against temptation in the future. Unlike his father, he had to keep a lid on his rage. Late one night, he put the revolver in his backpack, walked to the end of a commercial fishing wharf, and hurled the gun as far as he could into a shiny, dark ocean.

~49~

A late night in September, with two dozen copies of his newest manifesto in his backpack, he took the city bus to the Burnaby campus of the Art Institute of Vancouver. On the east side of the city, Burnaby was too trendy, and too easy a place to be noticed, for him to hang around. But Art Institute students were interested in his message, judging by how quickly they picked up his manifestos. Next to the student union entrance was a metal rack holding flyers, magazines, and newsletters to be sorted through by the curious.

He was always careful to arrive after 10 p.m., when the student union was closed. A sodium vapor light hanging on a wall illuminated the rack. He pulled the stapled sheets from his backpack and wedged them in. Copies of his previous manifesto were gone. Some may have been discarded, but most, he hoped, had met a better fate. At some dropoff spots, he hung around from a distance, watching who was reading his work. They were mostly, but not always, young people and minorities. He was pleased that his voice was being heard across a broad spectrum.

Jaleel had moved away from the student union on his way to the bus stop when he noticed someone under a nearby tree, smoking a cigarette. The tallish woman, with a big head of crimpy hair, was in a pullover and wore what looked like Converse high-tops. She seemed to be studying him under the glossy, white moon. His mind took a quick snapshot: student, Caucasian, alone, probably harmless—but why so focused on him?

"You're the one who writes the rad political shit, aren't you? 'Poor Richard.' " Her voice startled him, snaking out from under the tree.

"Where's the fire?" she called when he began walking away. She followed Jaleel. "I just want to talk to you."

He stopped and studied her more closely. Her angular face was pretty. "Talk about what?"

"You are 'Poor Richard,' right?"

"Maybe."

"Your writing, your message. I like what you're saying."

Whoever she was, couldn't she see he didn't want to be bothered? His manifestos spoke for him. He looked around but couldn't see anyone else. Whenever she inhaled, the tip of her cigarette glowed like a rodent's eye.

"What's your real name?" she asked.

"I'm sorry. I have to go."

He began to walk briskly but she was quickly at his side again.

"Okay, not important," she conceded. "Poor Richard it is. My name is Carter Riggs. I'm a fine arts and lit major. Actually, I'm a professional student. Six years and counting. Better than living with your parents in Oregon, right?"

When Jaleel came to a halt, so did Carter. Her left hand cupped her right elbow as she smoked.

"Were you waiting for me at the student union," Jaleel asked, "or is this meeting all a coincidence?"

"A friend told me that you always came on a Saturday or Sunday night, at ten, dropping off your shit." She put the cigarette out with her foot. In the darkness, the moon left a streak across her high forehead.

"I read your stuff whenever it comes out. That last manifesto, you had a line that stuck with me. 'The obscenity of America is what goes on in its leaders' minds. Behind comforting smiles, bloodthirsty and vengeful thoughts.' Just wondering what the hell you're doing in Canada, if you're writing about America."

"I write about Canada too." Be careful, he thought. Leave.

"Just curious. I won't tell anyone. Were you in prison in the States?"

He shook his head at the woman's pushiness. "No."

"Then . . . are you on the run from something that you didn't do? Your writing is full of a very authentic anger. Powerful stuff."

"It was nice meeting you, Carter."

Jaleel began moving again, his long strides scooping up vast amounts of ground, but there was no shaking her. As they approached the bus stop, Carter pulled a matchbook from her pocket and scribbled something with a pen on the inside cover. "Well, nice meeting you too, Poor Richard," she said. He was relieved that the bus pulled up seconds later. She thrust the matchbook into his palm as he boarded. When he found a seat and glanced out the window, she was gone.

He opened the matchbook and saw "Carter J. Riggs 757-9904." Throw it away, he thought. Who needed this kind of temptation? He couldn't afford the same mistake he'd made with Alex. But after a moment, he slipped the matchbook into a pocket.

Two weeks later, on his way to the Art Institute, he wondered if Carter might be around again. After more thought, he wouldn't have minded a dialog about his manifestos, taking her out for coffee. But the student union was deserted. Disappointed, he ambled back to the bus stop under a lambent moon.

Soon things began happening that he had never anticipated. An independent weekly published a story on Poor Richard's *My World*, about how outspoken and insightful the anonymous writer was. A TV station followed up on the story, concluding that the author was a disgruntled former Cabinet minister in Ottawa. Another reporter identified a black political science professor at the University of Vancouver. Both men denied the reports. Others deemed Poor Richard, whoever he was, a hero in the struggle against government abridgement of citizen rights.

He realized he was becoming famous in a small, weird, and uncomfortable way. He began to fear that Canadian authorities might already know about Jaleel Robeson, and would make the connection to Poor Richard. He also worried about what might be happening in California. He had thought of calling Rudy or Dirick, but even if he didn't worry about wiretapping, they would be disappointed in him for running and try to convince him to come back. He was too paranoid to leave Canada.

"Jaleel, my man! How are you? *Where* are you?" Marcus said when Jaleel called him from a pay phone.

"British Columbia. Vancouver."

"Well, you made it, brother! Congratulations! I lose track, how long you been gone?"

"About eighteen months."

"Things okay? You need anything?"

"I've got plenty of work, I'm a tutor, but thanks. It's good to hear a familiar voice."

Marcus's carefree laughter raised Jaleel's spirits. "A brother is always a brother."

"Anything happening at the mission?"

"Like what?"

"People asking about me."

"I barely go there, but when I do, nothing, man. I haven't heard a peep."

"Listen, maybe I'll call again," said Jaleel, looking down the sidewalk but seeing nothing unusual.

"You do that. And look after yourself now. Promise me that."

Jaleel said he would, and scooted out of the phone booth.

He went back to writing his manifestos, having no lack of material. The cops he saw hassling kids over smoking weed or loitering almost always seemed to have skin color in mind. If arrested, what happened if you couldn't afford a decent attorney? If you were poor, who really cared?

With as much passion as he wrote, it was balanced now by a new caution. By late summer of 1990, he placed an ad in the *Vancouver Sun* classifieds: Seeking reliable personal assistant to help busy entrepreneur. Several people answered. When he winnowed the phone interview down to what he really wanted—a body to hand out pamphlets for a few dollars an hour—most hung up. But a philosophy major named Paljar, on a student visa from Nepal, seemed trustworthy. Jaleel was free to go back to living in the shadows.

He began to think of his writing as sermons more for the multitudes than simply like-minded dissidents and people of color. America, a country that had been founded on revolution, required a second one, he wrote. So did Canada. Democracy had become a hollow concept. If you didn't want it to disappear, take your country back from special interests and paid-off politicians. *Brothers and sisters—vote, demonstrate, challenge authority!*

He had finished a tutoring session one February afternoon when he gazed through the curtains of his window. Across the street were two men in a late-model sedan, in jackets and ties, both reading something. He couldn't tell if it was one of his manifestos or an ordinary magazine. He'd never seen them in the neighborhood. He watched carefully, but neither looked toward his apartment building. When he checked half an hour later, the car was gone. But the men were back in the same car the next morning, and the day after that.

He found Carter's matchbook in the back of a drawer. More than two years had passed since their meeting. Students moved so often that he wondered if her phone number hadn't changed too. Maybe she'd finally graduated, or was living with a boyfriend.

"Hello?" a woman answered after a couple of rings.

"May I speak to Carter Riggs?"

"Is this Phil Glotz, the T.A.? If this is about my Faulkner paper, I already told you, I need an extension." She sighed, as if tired of academia's bureaucracy.

Jaleel cleared his throat. "I'm not Phil Glotz, the T.A. You and I met at the institute a couple of years ago, at the student union. It was night. You were watching me from under a tree—"

"On my god. Is this Poor Richard?" she broke in. He could hear the sarcasm beneath her surprise: "I gave you my number, and now you're calling, a couple of centuries later? Let me guess, you need a favor. Or you're in some kind of deep shit—"

"I don't know about 'deep'."

"Well, what do you know?"

"I could use some help. I wasn't sure who else to call." He tried to keep his words to a minimum, his tone measured.

"I still read your manifestos. You're a celebrity now. Are the cops on to you for stirring up trouble?"

"I can't say."

"Okay, let's start with this: Who, exactly, am I helping? What's your real name?"

"You asked me that last time.

"If I'm the only person you know to call, I don't think you're in much of a bargaining position."

"What if we meet tonight and discuss things." He suggested a Korean barbecue joint a mile from his apartment.

"Okay. I'm not doing anything. I'll see you at eight. But come prepared," she added.

"For what?"

"To tell me why I should trust anything you say."

The streets were quiet as he drifted back to his apartment to change clothes. He saw that the mystery sedan had vanished, but he feared it would be back. Vacating his apartment struck him as urgent.

It was equally imperative that he keep writing, no matter how much jeopardy he was in. The liberation from ignorance and tyranny was a long war, because the oppressors always had the advantage. They smooth-talked the masses with lies and promises. Dirick had told him there was always a price to pay for refusing to give up hope. A fear of the unknown bunched at the bottom of your stomach 24/7.

~50~

He arrived early at the Kyo Norboo House, sitting at a booth with a brazier built into the table, Korean style. Delicious smells permeated the cozy restaurant. He tried to stay focused on who came in and went out. Carter showed up an hour late—maybe payback, he considered, for his two-year silence. Her kinky hair was now blonde and shorter, but her long legs still tapered from a narrow waist into Converse high tops.

"Well, here we are," she said, cocking her head at him with a puzzled smile. "You look exhausted."

"I'm glad you came." He hoped she would say that she was glad too, but Carter just bit her lip. "I never threw away your matchbook," Jaleel said. "I thought about calling you more than once. I looked for you at the student union whenever I returned—" He sounded desperate.

"You're really flubbing this, you know?" she broke in. "Why don't you just tell me who you are and who's hassling you?"

Her sinewy arms flopped impatiently on the table. He didn't know what context to put Carter Riggs in. They certainly weren't friends, and barely qualified as acquaintances. He supposed that at best, she was an ally. No matter what, he couldn't keep dodging her. There was no one else to turn to.

"You want the bottom line first?" he said. "My name is Jaleel Demitrius Robeson. I last lived in California."

"That's the bottom line?"

"Police think I've committed two murders in separate states."

Her dark eyes bore into him for the longest moment. "Two murders? That's impressive. And I'm supposed to take it on your word that you're innocent, as opposed to thinking you might pull out a gun or knife on me too?"

"I'm suspected of killing my father in Texas, and then an architect in Los Angeles, a man I never met. If I'd done those things, Poor Richard would be feeling guilt, not rage. I certainly wouldn't be risking my freedom by speaking my mind. You once asked where my anger came from. Now you know."

Her eyes were a blend of curiosity and sympathy. "So who did kill your father?"

"He shot himself, after he killed my mother."

Her face froze. "Wow. That's pretty heavy. I'm sorry." She turned quiet, digesting everything. Then she asked how all that connected to the architect.

"It's complicated. You like long stories?"

"If they're the truth."

After they ordered two Black Beer Stouts and thinly sliced beef to cook on the brazier, he gave her the details: his boyhood in racially conscious Peartree; escaping the county facility and fleeing to Los Angeles under an assumed name; excelling at baseball and academics in high school, creating a future for himself; then getting mixed up with a family in the wealthy community where the architect lived; and having to escape to Canada. Because he was innocent, he'd almost turned himself in, on the advice of a smart lawyer he'd met on a Greyhound bus, but at the last minute, Jaleel had changed his mind. Trust was hard to come by. It was easier to be a loner. He'd found a new life in Canada and didn't want to return to the States—ever.

"What are you, twenty-one or twenty-two? Quite a life. What's your encore?"

"I'm not going to stop what I'm doing. I want to reach more people. Right now, I need a place to crash. There's been an unmarked car outside my apartment."

He gave her an appraising look. "Do you still want to help, or have I scared you away?"

"I might know a place you can stay, at least for a while. It's my fatal flaw, always trying to help people. Then it ends up biting me."

"I won't bite. I'd be very grateful."

"I have a two-bedroom duplex, not far from campus. Don't get excited. We're not talking about the Ritz-Carlton."

"I can help with the rent."

"Don't worry about it. My parents cover everything, so far anyway."

When he asked Carter, as politely as he could, why he should trust her, she looked amused. "Look, I get your paranoia, but I took your phone call, didn't I? I showed up after two friggin' years. Maybe you'd like personal references too."

"What about people you hang with? Do you have a boyfriend?"

"If this is twenty questions, I could spend all night talking about men. I was over my last boyfriend six months ago. He turned out to be a loser." She went back to her beer.

"I'll respect your privacy," Jaleel assured her. "I won't get in your way."

"What will you do all day, write?"

"I hope so."

"I like great stories. Yours takes the prize. I'm attracted to people who take chances. What about you? Who are you attracted to?"

He was tongue-tied. He'd hardly considered the question, but he knew Carter wanted an answer.

"People who are kind, who care," he said honestly.

"What about people who want something back from you?"

Carter put down her beer, as if it was time to get serious. "This may not seem like much, or maybe it will. I want to be your editor for your manifestos."

"No, I'm not attracted to that," he replied. The idea of someone looking over his shoulder had all the appeal of a pencil thrust in his eye. "I wasn't aware that my writing needed help."

"You're a great writer, but lately your messages seem long-winded. I'm not asking you to be Hemingway, but sometimes brevity goes a long way."

"What qualifies you as an editor?"

"Look at my own writing if you want. What I'm proposing is, we could be a team. You've got the experience that makes the rage that makes the story," she said. "But for any writer, it's sometimes hard seeing the forest for the trees."

Carter hesitated, then dropped another surprise. "You know, you should be doing more than writing manifestos. Have you ever listened to your voice?"

He squinted, not understanding.

"The way you speak is hypnotic—hasn't anyone told you? You have this wonderful cadence, on top of a tenor voice. It's magical. Have you made a lot of speeches?"

No one had ever suggested he had public speaking talents, maybe because his focus had always been on academics and athletics. "I gave a couple of book reports in tenth grade," he joked.

"Sometimes I attend services at the Unitarian church near Stanley Park. The pastor is ultra-liberal. Women's rights, gay rights, affirmative action, death penalty—he's not afraid to speak out. He's led more than his share of public demonstrations. My atheist friends love him."

"Atheists in church?" Jaleel asked, entertained by the idea.

"Why not? They're some of the most ethical people I know.

"My point," Carter added, "is that Pastor Wyeth may give sermons about right and wrong, but he puts you to sleep some Sundays. Just doesn't have your speaking talent. He could use a backup."

Jaleel remembered Reverend Johnson in Peartree. When he made a dramatic point, it was like thunder rolling through the rafters. People listened, transfixed.

"I don't see how that's possible. I have to stay hidden."

"You just said you wanted to reach more people. Aren't some risks worth taking?"

When they'd finished, Jaleel paid the bill, and she drove him to her duplex. He slept fitfully in Carter's second bedroom, trying to orient himself to a new alliance. It wouldn't be the first time he had put his life in the hands of a stranger. It had worked with Marcus and Dirick.

The smells of breakfast woke him. An omelet and french toast were waiting in the kitchen. Carter joined him in her pajamas. Later, after a couple of phone calls, she convinced a friend to lend them a pickup. They spent the afternoon moving Jaleel's possessions to her place. He was relieved not to see the sedan with the two men in it.

Carter's duplex was on a side street in Collingwood Village, the heart of the institute's student housing. Maybe blending in there would be easier than he'd thought at first. Carter cheerfully integrated his furniture into her space, making his hand-me-downs look better than they deserved. The color charcoal sketch of Peartree went over his desk. He explained that he was the artist. It was a present to his mother the day she'd died. Carter gave him a sympathetic hug.

The dinner wine was Carter's selection, from a vineyard near Corvallis, Oregon. She'd been living in British Columbia on a student visa for six years, she admitted, refusing to be stuck in "claustrophobic, banal America." Her opinions made clear that she was a feminist, and believed in sexual and every other kind of personal freedom. She said she got impatient with the world for not catching up.

Her outspokenness reminded him a little of Alex, and even if Carter didn't describe herself as ambitious, he could see she was interested in literature and creative writing. When they finally slept together, he didn't have to explain that he was a virgin. She figured it out quickly, and liked having the advantage of being his teacher. Whenever she pushed her tongue into his ear, his body ached. The pleasure came like an ocean, alternately roiling and soothing him. Each time they made love that night, he could feel her pushing deeper into him, extracting more of his trust, making him more dependent.

In the morning, as the sunlight washed the walls, he felt reborn. He turned to Carter, studying her head on the pillow, and kissed her lips. He pushed the hair aside and kissed her on the lips.

"If you're the conqueror," he whispered, waking her, "I surrender."

"I'm going to make you into a great writer and a great lover," she murmured. Her eyes shut and she went back to sleep. It was difficult moving his gaze from her. His penis was hard again. It was way too early to know, but he could see himself falling in love. He took a shower, and studied himself in the mirror. His slender, intense face looked different. The glow he felt extended beyond his eyes, into his whole being.

When he glanced again in the mirror, he suddenly saw, beyond his image, a flat and parched desert. In the near distance, a wide chasm broke the line of the barren plain. On the other side were purple mountains, rising to the sky. If he were still drawing, this was the scene he would have created. Standing at the edge of the abyss—too wide to jump across—he waited for something to fly him over the void, up to the soaring mountains—a wind that would overcome all fears, all rage.

The world, he thought, could still be as wondrous as the dinosaur bone or gold coins he had dreamed about finding as a child.

~51~

"It won't hurt you to check it out," Carter nudged the next morning after fixing them breakfast. "When you were a boy, you said, you went to church all the time. It's Sunday. Aren't you at least a bit curious?" They sat across from each other in the kitchen, mugs of coffee rotating contemplatively in their hands. They laughed when they realized they were doing the same thing.

Carter was more helpful than he'd expected. Helping him move, cooking meals, and yesterday she'd made time to edit his latest manifesto. He'd reviewed her squiggly red lines and margin annotations. She was uncannily perceptive, he told her sincerely.

"Thank you."

She looked pleased as he made her changes in the final draft. He asked her what time the service was.

"We'd have to leave shortly. Do it for me," she said. "You'll get something out of it."

"Like what?"

"I told you, I want you to hear the pastor's message, and you'll see how you could make it better. Service is all of an hour. We'll sneak in and out, I promise!"

When they arrived at the simple wooden structure, its elongated roof rising to a peak resembling the prow of a ship, the pews were already full. The crowd was mostly students but also young families and a few old timers—an equal mix of Asians and whites, with a few black faces. Dress was casual. In Peartree, church had been more formal.

Even if almost everyone was poor, men wore suits, if they owned one, and women their best dresses, with a flower pinned on their lapel. Carter found seats for them in the last pew. The pulpit was next to an altar carved with bas-relief symbols. Pastor Wyeth led the congregation in reading from the Book of Common Prayer. All of five-foot-three, the minister was middle-aged with graying hair, his face serene yet carrying a lot of miles. That's what years of standing up for your principles could do to you, Jaleel thought.

His sermon focused on the history of racial injustice in Canada, starting with the Algonquian Indians and scores of other tribes. Under French and British colonial rule, discrimination and slavery became institutionalized. The irony that the aboriginals so quickly found themselves outsiders should haunt Canada for the rest of its days, Pastor Wyeth declared. He ended on a note of hope, though, mentioning Canada's new open-door immigration policies. The situation wasn't that rosy, Jaleel knew. Students could get a temporary visa that had to be renewed regularly. Otherwise, if you wanted to become a citizen, you had to open a substantial bank account to prove your net worth.

Overall, the pastor's message was strong, Jaleel felt, but Carter was right about his delivery. His scratchy voice seemed incapable of drama. Even a microphone didn't help.

After the service ended with the Eucharist, Carter clutched Jaleel's hand and marched him over to meet the pastor. She introduced Jaleel as "Thomas, my boyfriend," someone who cared deeply about social and economic issues, and who enjoyed speaking to groups. Jaleel almost died. At least she was careful not to tie him to Poor Richard. The pastor warmly clasped Jaleel's hand. Having Sunday guest speakers was common at their church. Perhaps Thomas would be interested? Jaleel smiled, flattered to be invited but promising nothing for now.

As Carter drove them home, he complained good naturedly, "I thought we were going to sneak in and out."

"I saw an opportunity to introduce you. Are you upset? You'll be a terrific speaker."

"Is that what my editor really thinks?"

"There is no doubt in your editor's mind."

"Why do you have so much confidence in me?"

"Because I know a winner when I see one."

He laughed cautiously, grateful but not certain he should believe her. Whenever he took an evening stroll for exercise, his thoughts meandered. How could a fugitive from justice possibly be a winner? Where would his life be in three years, or five or ten? When he returned to the duplex, his mood always changed. Carter handed him a beer or cuddled with him in front of the television. She made him believe that anything was possible. Some moments, it felt like he'd known her all his life. Weekdays, he was left alone with his books and typewriter. Carter stayed around campus until the end of the day, when she returned with observations about things learned in and out of class. They shared fixing dinners and cleaning the apartment. Weekends were allotted to movies, theater, or museums. They rarely argued over what to do.

After writing steadily for the next six months—each manifesto meticulously edited—he told Pastor Wyeth he was ready to address the congregation. He thought of the image he had first seen in the bathroom mirror, the parched desert with the wide chasm holding him back. It was time to cross it.

"What are you going to talk about?" Carter prodded over dinner.

"Let me guess, let me guess," she anticipated before he could answer. "Rodney King and police brutality? The LAPD beat him like a dead horse. The state has to prosecute those cops."

"Oh, they'll stand trail, and they'll all get off. Then there'll be riots, but nothing will change," he predicted, trying not to sound too bitter.

"You don't know what you're going to talk about? Is that it?"

"I know what I want to say in general. But details are everything."

"Just give me a hint, Jaleel."

"Maybe you should wait and be surprised."

She frowned. "You're not going to tell me? We share everything."

"I can't share this."

Carter turned away in a huff, as if being his editor entitled her to full disclosure. In bed, she barely spoke to him. He tried to make up with her in the morning. But she was stubborn.

Sunday, he donned his best jeans, a dress shirt, and polished black shoes. For the first time, he and Carter sat in the front pew instead of in back. Pastor Wyeth, as usual, called the congregants to read from the Book of Common Prayer. There were numerous community announcements and messages of welcome before he nodded to Jaleel.

Walking toward the pulpit, he felt the serenity of surrender. He had written about "the unforgiven" in his first manifesto years earlier, only to learn that the term had a deeper and more personal meaning. You could spend your life pretending to be in control, pushing away unpleasant thoughts and incidents, until the day finally arrived when that was no longer possible or necessary. You had to confront yourself. Your weaknesses had to be confessed, and then celebrated.

His typed sermon was in his back pocket, but he felt no need to reach for it. His eyes jumped over the restless faces staring back. How long could he hold them hostage with his story? Would they find it interesting and relevant? Even if people walked out, he was determined to finish.

"I have a story I need to tell," Jaleel began, without using the microphone. "It's about a twelve-year-old boy living in a small Texas oil town that was mostly white. That boy is me. My mother taught me to be careful around white people, but I didn't know the extent to which some people's cruelty could extend. I was sure if I minded my own business that nothing bad would happen to me. I knew, as my mother had told me, to be happy within myself, because that was my armor against those who led lives of anger and resentment."

Silence descended on the church. His listeners sat upright, like a jury waiting to make a decision.

"What I loved most in my life was baseball. I dreamed of playing it as a professional, because dreams are free when you're twelve. Still, I knew I would have to work hard to be successful. I wanted my father to be proud of my talent and to believe in my chances. He worked long hours in the oil fields. He was tired when he came home. On weekends, I asked if he wanted to watch me play. He often nodded yes, yet in the end, he was too tired or distracted to come. My mother said my father couldn't help himself. He lived in an internal world. She said he was full of anger, absorbed by it to what I now believe was the point of clinical depression. But occasionally, I saw love floundering in his heart, looking for a home.

"On September 14, 1982, laying my head on my pillow, I was too excited for sleep. Baseball fantasies swam in my head. Would I be a pitcher one day or an outfielder? Would I play for the Yankees or the Red Sox? My mother's birthday was the next day. I had worked all week on a drawing for her, and I wanted so much for her to like it. I gave her my present in the morning. She hugged me as if Da Vinci or Rembrandt couldn't have created anything as wonderful. I went to school happy with myself. Afterward, I had Little League practice, and then I rode my bike home."

For a second, Jaleel's knees wobbled. He could see his blue and white house in Peartree, his mother in the kitchen frying chicken, and Dad in the living room in front of the television, his eyes like tunnels.

"My father was already home. My mother was yelling at him from the kitchen. She was rarely angry, but that evening she was furious. Dad had lost a job he'd had for eighteen years. He lost it over a fight with a white man. It didn't matter who started the fight, not to my mother. We had no money in the bank to tide us over. We would soon be on the street. She kept yelling at my father, as if that would rewrite our fate.

"My mother's exasperation was the prelude to an avalanche of destruction. When Dad could no longer tolerate her shaming, he rose from the couch, scarcely looking at me, and pulled a handgun from his trousers. I suspect he was always going to use it on himself. He was already full of shame, but my mother made it worse. He walked into the kitchen and shot her to death.

"I watched all this unfold in horror. When my father turned his gaze on me, his eyes were sunk back in his head, as if he were already dead, or some things were too hard to explain for a man who lived in silence. When he finally spoke, he ordered me to run. I didn't know if my mother was still alive, and I wanted to help her. My father raised his gun at me, and in a coarse whisper, like someone running out of breath, out of time, out of everything that had ever sustained him, told me again to run. Then he turned from me and with his eyes fluttering with a kind of peace I'd never seen, he shot himself."

Jaleel felt his heart hammering in his throat. Eyes were pinned on him, keeping him upright. The sudden murmuring among congregants was like a rush of wind.

"Oh, brother, we're with you," someone called out.

"Amen. God bless you," said another.

"I've relived that evening a thousand times," Jaleel continued. "My parents' deaths led to a chain of events I couldn't have imagined. The police accused me of killing my father. I believe my father knew before he shot himself that this might happen. I could have run away as he'd ordered me or tried to wrestle his gun from him or done something to save my mother. I had many choices. I could have done any of those. But I did nothing but stand there in utter helplessness.

"For ten years I've been unable to forgive myself. At the same time, I have run from the evils of ignorance, bigotry, and stupidity. I have hurled myself against the wall of injustice. I have tried to put myself on the path of righteousness, to divine whatever fate God has for me, yet I've lapsed numerous times, giving in to my deep rage at myself and others. But I am here today, brothers and sisters, to ask you to forgive me for what I did not do that evening in my parents' house. No matter what we think or say we want from life, this is what really matters: to give and receive unconditional love. I ask for that love and forgiveness from you."

"You have our love and forgiveness, Thomas," a man in the back roared.

"Thank you for telling your story!"

"We ask for your forgiveness for our mistakes too."

There were more murmurs as he turned from the pulpit and proceeded back to the front pew. Carter seized his hand and held him close. Several congregants reached from behind to clasp his shoulder, while he could feel the gazes of others, embracing him with empathy and understanding. The wind of forgiveness had carried him over the abyss, to the soaring purple mountains of Eden. Remembering his father, he knew at all costs to guard this paradise from his demons.

~52~

Dirick had once told him that in America, it was never too late to reinvent oneself. As a young immigrant, that was what the Dutchman had done, and a second time too after paying off his father's debts. Poor Richard would never write another manifesto. Jaleel's first sermon had come from a private place inside him, with the unstoppable urgency of a hurricane. Dirick would be proud of him. He was becoming a serious person after all.

He wrote his second sermon in less than a day. The words flowed better when he didn't use a typewriter. He sat in the upholstered chair in Carter's living room, writing on a lined pad.

"Wow, that was fast," she said that night, looking over his shoulder at five pages of crabbed handwriting.

"Something inside me needs to get out."

"Do you know how lucky you are, to write that quickly? I'm a snail."

"The words come quickly, but the journey is slow," Jaleel said.

"Can I read your draft?"

"I'm not ready to show it to anybody."

"I'm not just anybody, am I?"

Not wanting another disagreement, he tried to explain. Unlike his manifestos, writing sermons was a very private journey. It was like descending into a cave whose pitch darkness had to be negotiated carefully, alone. You had to touch the surface of every memory. You had to try to understand the complexity of your moral universe, how it was formed and how it guided you. When he'd received forgiveness from the congregants, he knew he had the power to give it back, to everyone, even those who had hurt him the most. But the process required effort and patience. That's what he wanted to write and talk about.

"I want to see what you've written," Carter persisted. "I'm not just your editor, we're lovers."

"I know how much I owe you."

"Then I don't get it," she said.

"You'll hear it all in church, I promise."

"Sometimes you can be impossible," she huffed, and left him alone.

Over the next seven months, he gave a dozen sermons at the church, getting by on money he had saved, another contribution from Marcus, and the generosity of Carter. Suffering and deprivation were the passage to enlightenment, he preached. Strength of character was essential in the quest. The results could never be certain, but attaining even the smallest degree of self-awareness was important. "God is within us," he liked to say.

The radio shows and small newspapers no longer mentioned the anonymous author of manifestos. There was someone new to focus on, a young black man who was the opposite of the embittered Poor Richard. The lay speaker went by the name of Thomas, and was called a "seer" and "prophet" by some congregants. But there were others who had a different opinion when they called in to the talk shows. Jaleel was likened to Malcolm X or Stokely Carmichael, not Martin Luther King Jr. He was a wolf in sheep's clothing. He subverted the gospels. He made Jesus a secular figure. Or he was just an agitator and troublemaker.

"Subverting the gospels?" he said, bewildered, to Carter as they fixed dinner one evening. "The gospels are about the subversion of the old order two thousand years ago. Now it's time to question the new order. If Jesus were here today, that's what his disciples would write about."

Carter didn't seem to be listening, dicing a cucumber for the salad.

"What's the matter?" he asked, looking over.

"All this publicity, it's only a matter of time before some people figure out that you and Poor Richard are the same. You need to stop going to church for a while."

"I can't. I won't," he said quietly.

"Your friggin' ego has blurred your judgment, Jaleel. All this prophet bullshit."

"I never said I was a prophet."

"But people think you are, and you never tell them you aren't. It's too much for me."

"I used the word 'apostle' to describe myself. I told you the story of Dirick."

"Hanging around you all the time. Maybe I need a break," Carter whispered.

"I need you at tomorrow's service."

"You need me? Do you even know I exist?" She seemed to get more angry by the second. "Can you tell me the last time we made love?"

He didn't have an answer. When he walked over to kiss her, she pulled away.

"You're right about my ego. I need to be more aware," he apologized. "But I've been anxious."

He said he'd had a premonition for weeks. Something bad was going to happen to him. He didn't know when or where.

"What's going to happen? Are you playing prophet again?"

"I need you in church, that's all. It makes me feel more secure."

He went back to writing after dinner. Carter insisted on staying up with a book as he drifted to their bedroom. In the morning, he woke at five as usual. She wasn't next to him. Her side hadn't been slept on. Though Carter hadn't left a note, he sensed she was leaving him for good. Maybe his foggy premonition had come true. He sat for a while on the bed, conscious of his breathing and the feeling of abandonment he knew so well.

He got a lift to church from a student who lived down the street. Jaleel tried not to show his anxiety when he greeted people. Ascending to the pulpit, he looked in vain for Carter. It took all his strength to keep his concentration. Over two hundred people were looking back at him, and more spilled out the door, expecting a message of hope.

His rich tenor voice began to dart like a swallow from one corner of the sanctuary to another. No one stirred, not even children. He didn't spot the two men standing at the rear of the church until his sermon was almost finished. It was December, and they kept their coats on, as if they wouldn't be there for long.

Jaleel ignored the enthusiastic clapping that always followed his sermons. He told himself not to be afraid, and moved calmly toward the back. Almost everyone seemed to notice the two strangers at once. The slender cop looked unsettled, like he couldn't wait to do his job and get away from the crowd. The other, burly with a milky complexion, extracted handcuffs from his jacket.

"Jaleel Robeson?" he asked as he approached.

"Yes, that's me."

"Good morning, sir. I'm Detective Hoskin. We have a warrant for your arrest." His tone was somewhere between reserved and relieved. He pulled the warrant from inside his jacket and held it up.

"What am I being arrested for?"

"Violating immigration laws." The detective maneuvered around him, and pulled Jaleel's arms behind his back. The metal felt cold as it snapped around his wrists. Voices of astonishment rose around him.

"Hey, let him go," a young man with tousled hair shouted. "Your warrant's bullshit."

"You're the Gestapo," a woman echoed.

"His name is Thomas!" another man thundered.

Pastor Wyeth was suddenly at Jaleel's side, squaring his shoulders, ready for a fight. "Gentlemen, I'd like you out of my church. I'm going to call an attorney."

"No," Jaleel said. "I am Jaleel Robeson. Don't be alarmed. Everything will be all right."

He thought about giving a fuller explanation to the congregation. They deserved the most basic information. But the detective hooked him by the elbow and led him through the door, nudging people aside.

"Oh, forgot to mention, Mr. Robeson," Hoskin said with satisfaction as they reached an unmarked car. "There's a warrant for you from the State of Texas, and some people want to question you about a murder in Los Angeles. What a busy fella. You'll probably be extradited right away."

He pushed Jaleel's neck down, forcing him into the back seat. Before the door closed, half the congregation, including Pastor Wyeth, surrounded the car, jeering and taunting. Their fists pounded on the hood and windshield before the car lurched away.

Jaleel stared out the window. Maybe this was the real premonition he'd harbored. Now that he was in handcuffs, something about his arrest seemed inevitable. He had been on the run for ten years. The good news was that he was a different person from the boy who had wriggled under the fence of the detention center. No matter how many times you were reviled by words, or shoved into a police car, or threatened with extradition, it didn't matter. God was always inside you.

Alex

~53~

At St. Anthony's, I was able to focus on grades and my college boards in a way I never would have at Valley, distracted by living with my father. I felt lucky that Stanford accepted me. I wanted to be close to Joyce, who'd chosen Berkeley, as well as Toby, and I liked California weather.

Freshman year on The Farm was challenging—Western Civ, English, French, and Trig—but I had a perverse need to work myself to the bone. Perverse because you can want to be successful but you never, for reasons that elude you, quite enjoy it. Toward the end of the academic year, I received a call from two people I didn't know. Alfred Ralston and his wife, Stanford alums, were visiting the Bay Area and wanted to take me to dinner. They were part of an outreach program for freshmen, and Mr. Ralston had recognized my name on a list. He said he was a grateful client of my father, who had once rescued him from the clutches of the SEC. At first I said no. I wanted nothing to do with my father, even by association, and I was consumed with writing a paper for my Western Civ final. In the end, Mr. Ralston's charm, and the promise of a good dinner, won me over.

I met two energetic people in their late sixties at the Fairmont, a grand, historic hotel in the heart of San Francisco. The lifestyle of a retired investment banker didn't impress me as much as the humanitarian work the Ralstons had embarked on in Kenya. I had once thought of going to med school and being a doctor in Africa, I told them. The evening was pleasant enough as we exchanged stories about

Stanford. New buildings and departments were springing up like mushrooms after a rain, Mrs. Ralston observed. From its business and law schools to athletics and arts, Stanford was in an unparalleled renaissance. Mr. Ralston asked if I wasn't proud to be there, watching it all unfold.

"Of course," I said.

"You know, your father is someone to be proud of too." My host's smile expressed not just gratitude for knowing my father but also that I was the lucky one, being his daughter.

"Alex, I heard on the grapevine that you testified before the grand jury about that terrible murder in Toluca Lake—and you did a spectacular job."

Yes, I was the one whose silence when I found out the truth kept my guilty father out of prison, I wanted to tell him.

"How is your dad?" Mrs. Ralston asked. "We haven't seen him in a while."

"Never been better," I said blithely.

The questions kept coming, extracting more lies from me—how close my father and I were, how deep my respect for him ran, how beloved he was by clients. I gave answers the Ralstons wanted to hear, but with every word, I shuddered inside. Why was I covering up? Shouldn't I have said that my father had lied to me with the same cold-bloodedness with which he had murdered his best friend? I was someone who prided herself on exposing every dark crease and fold of the universe. Now I was hiding in them. I hated myself.

The spring quarter ended the first week in June. Joyce had rented a big enough apartment in Berkeley to invite me for holidays and the summer. Once I settled in, we developed a routine. We smoked a little weed, ate at ethnic restaurants, and went to movies, or readings at a cramped bookstore that smelled of burnt coffee.

The second week of July, Dad called out of the blue. Since I had left for St. Anthony's, we hadn't communicated more than a half-dozen times.

"Honey, I feel like we're strangers. You haven't been in touch," he began, as he did with every call.

"Sorry. You know what academics can be like."

"You're not coming home at all this summer?"

I hadn't been home in three years, always managing to root out a job somewhere and a place to crash. I told him I was staying with Joyce this summer. I had no plans to visit Toluca Lake.

"Well, I respect your independence, Alex. Everything good?"

"Yes.

"I have some news for you," he got to the point. "Big news."

"Yeah?"

"I'm getting married."

I wasn't surprised, but I knew he wanted an appropriate response. "Congratulations, Dad. Who's the lucky woman?"

He described an attractive, thin brunette, an intellectual property rights attorney whom he'd met at a bar association event. She was eleven years his junior. The new Mrs. Baten, nee Marjorie Orlonsky of Madison, Wisconsin, couldn't wait to meet me, he said.

"Put this date on your calendar, honey. October 8. It's not going to be too big a wedding. A resort somewhere in the Caribbean."

"Sure. I'll put it down. That's great."

A pain shot through my solar plexus. It didn't completely leave until a month later, when the gods decided to show me some mercy. Fancy Tiffany stationery, with Ms. Orlonsky's initials on the back flap, arrived at Joyce's apartment. My future stepmother had scrubbed the idea of Caribbean nuptials. A resort seemed too pedestrian for such an important occasion, she wrote. The three-day event would be hosted on a luxury yacht in the Gulf of Mexico off the Yucatan Peninsula, and whittled down to thirty guests. There was only so much room. She was so sorry that Toby and I couldn't be included.

"Thank you," I whispered to whoever in the heavens was listening. At the same time, the rejection stung. Who the hell was Marjorie Orlonsky? It made me think of how much importance I had lost in my father's eyes.

In my semi-monthly call to my brother, he answered "hello" in a cheerful enough voice.

"What's happening, Niles?" I kidded.

We talked for a while, and then I asked for details about Ms. Orlonsky. "*The* Ms. Orlonsky?" he said. "Honestly, she's pretty hot, and she's got a big personality, almost bigger than Mom's. Dad likes that type, I guess. Not sure what's under the surface. Glad to miss the stupid wedding."

"Me too. What do you hear from Mom?"

"She calls once in a while. Never says much, except that she's happy. Mom always has to be happy."

"Nothing else from New York?"

"Not really. Don't you talk to her?"

"No."

"How come?"

"I don't know. One of those things. Tell me about you."

With the exception of a math class or two, Toby reported that he wasn't setting any records. My brother wasn't fazed. He had made some connections in the software world near San Francisco, in an area called Silicon Valley. Any time he wanted it, he'd been told, a paying intern job was waiting.

"That's very cool, little brother." I was relieved. Real independence, at least financially, suddenly seemed within my brother's grasp. If he came north, I said, we'd be able to visit more often.

At least I had one person in my family to feel close to, two counting Agnes. Yet I could never tell my brother about the murder, I decided as we said goodbye. Nor about baby Lucy, whom Mom had conceived with Charlie, and wanted to keep secret from everyone but Agnes. Toby's life was challenging enough without whacky and disturbing distractions.

~54~

When I returned to Stanford in the fall, I developed a routine for Saturday mornings. The other six and a half days, I was busy being an overly ambitious sophomore, juggling eighteen to twenty credits a quarter. I'd elected a double major of history and poly sci, and a minor in psychology. I'd turned nineteen over the summer, and had no trouble seeing my future. After earning my doctorate in history, I wanted to teach at the university level.

My Saturday routine was to rise while it was still dark and walk at an aerobic pace from Branner Hall to the small stucco building that served as Stanford's student post office. Bay Area weather was designed to be confusing. In December it could be seventy one day, thirty the next. On this morning, I could see my breath cloud in front of me. The campus was a ghost town. Most students were sleeping off Friday night parties; others just slept in.

As the sun rose, I took in the impressive sight of MemChu—Stanford Memorial Church—the sandstone Romanesque anchor in the middle of the Quad. There was an exterior mosaic of the preaching Jesus, and panels of magnificent stained glass. Leland Stanford's wife had commissioned its construction after her husband's death. Students were welcome inside to pray or meditate.

Freshman year, I'd gone regularly to Sunday services, until one afternoon I emerged from a philosophy lecture shortly after my dinner with the Ralstons. God did not make man, said our professor, a stern-looking septuagenarian whose gray hair flopped over his forehead like a mop. Man had invented god, for political and social reasons. Religion was useful in establishing ethical codes and encouraging monogamy, but most everything else, he added, was "discretionary mumbo-jumbo." Every religion had its own rituals and mystery, laced with fear, to keep the flock from straying. My perception of the universe was suddenly altered. I decided I was an agnostic. This wasn't all my professor's doing. It also had something to do with my father—his criminality and my cowardice. If there were a real God, he would have shown me a way out of this wilderness of deceit. But maybe there was no way. Maybe there was no God.

At the post office, I peeked in the tiny window of Box 9035, spun the combination dial, and retrieved the usual credit card and magazine solicitations. Buried in the mix was a letter from my father's law firm, postmarked December 19, 1992. I stashed it in my jeans and proceeded to a coffeehouse half a mile away amid a grove of scented eucalyptuses. The place opened at seven, and on Saturdays, I was always the first customer. I ordered a brioche and a latte every time.

I wondered about my father's letter before opening it. He rarely sent mail, only for birthdays and Christmas, and never from his law firm. From Toby, I knew the October wedding had gone without a hitch, but a week or two later, settled into our English Tudor, my stepmother revealed her true colors. She began imposing new weekend chores on Toby and limiting the friends he could bring home. She had a stick up her ass as long as the 405, he said, and one evening, he simply told her to fuck off—this was his house more than it was hers. Dad wouldn't take his side, though. In disgust, my brother cadged a permanent room at a friend's house.

He seemed happy with his move, because the news kept getting worse on the home front. The new Mrs. Baten suddenly wanted out of Toluca Lake, as if every last trace of our family had to be purged. In November, our Great Gatsby-like estate, the pride and joy of Louis and Gloria Baten, the place to which I attached my strongest memories and where I wrote faithfully in my journal, the house that Mom promised never to leave, went on the market. When Dad called me, he never asked how I felt about the sale. He wondered if I wanted to comb through my room before everything was sold. I'd packed my journal and lots of photos before leaving for St. Anthony's. Nothing else seemed important enough to return for, not if it meant hanging out with Dad, or the stepmother I never wanted to meet. The house went into escrow after only two weeks on the market. I sipped my latte and opened Dad's letter. It was hand-written, as if he hadn't wanted a secretary to see it, or a record kept on the hard drive of a computer.

December 13, 1992
Hi honey,
> *Hope all is well on the Farm. Knowing your work ethic, you're probably blazing your way through every class. Congratulations. On the home front, Marjorie and I are planning to move into a penthouse condo in Beverly Hills. Change is good, right? In lawyerland, Baten, Kleeb and Donahue has never been busier— otherwise I would have gotten this letter out sooner. My friends think I'm getting to the age where I should be playing more golf, but that's hooey. I only have one gear—full speed ahead.*
> *I want to let you know that I received a call from someone at the D.A.'s office. Your young friend (not so young now, I guess), Jaleel Robeson, was arrested in Vancouver, after giving a sermon at a church. Not sure if you knew. There are plans to extradite him here quite quickly, and I wouldn't be surprised if he ended up standing trial for Charlie's murder.*
> *I know you had feelings for Mr. Robeson, but by now I'm hoping you've outgrown them. I'm advising you to stay neutral about Charlie's murder. I'm sure, as your attorney, Harding will give you the same message. Leave the past alone, Alex.*
Love,
Your Father

I wasn't sure whether the last paragraph was a plea to use my common sense, or a not-so-veiled threat of unspecified consequences. Would he stop paying my tuition if I got in touch with Jaleel? I wedged the letter into my pocket, walked briskly back to Branner, and closed the door to my room. I had grasshopper brain. How had Jaleel gotten caught after successfully hiding for so many years? Was he okay? What else had Harding and my father learned that they might not be telling me?

I found Dirick's number and endured his answering machine in frustration. I rambled a bit before ending my message.

"Please call me back, right away," I said. "If you don't already know, the police in Canada have Jaleel in custody."

~55~

Dirick returned my call the next morning. Sunday, I could hear the bells from MemChu pounding the air, as if heralding something good, even for a non-believer. Dirick immediately apologized for never returning my calls. While they were together in San Francisco, he explained, Jaleel had instructed him not to be in touch with me.

"But why?" I was hurt.

"After delivering the letter to Charlie's house, and your father about to beat the grand jury, he thought you and he jinxed each other. Better to go your separate ways." Dirick apologized again for his long silence before switching tracks. "Jaleel hasn't been in touch with me either. Tell me whatever you know."

I read him my father's letter with its threatening last paragraph. There were no helpful details about Jaleel, other than that the arrest had taken place in a church. Dirick agreed that extradition back to the States was a strong possibility.

"Well, the good news is that Jaleel is alive, and I hope in good health. But this is a pity. If he'd turned himself in when we asked, there's a good chance he'd be free."

"And now?"

"I know Detective Hildenbrand's and the D.A.'s mindset. The D.A. in Texas too. Jaleel's the guy who's always made them look bad."

"I'm concerned."

"Not to worry. For every problem, there's a solution."

"You're an optimist, I gather."

"Yes, I am."

He said he would call the police in Vancouver for the most current information. The more we knew, the more we had to work with in developing a strategy. I suddenly had no problem trusting a man I'd never met. Dirick's cleverness had kept Jaleel from being arrested in Arizona. Maybe he could perform some magic again.

"Jaleel told me you were an attorney. Can I ask you for some legal advice?" I said boldly.

"I have a friend who's a better attorney than I'll ever be, but maybe I can help. What's the issue?"

"I need to discuss it in person. Who's the other lawyer? Is he trust-worthy?"

"His name is Rudy Tusk. I would swear by him on a mountain of Bibles. Is this something relevant to Jaleel?"

"Yes. And to my father and me."

"Can you make it over to San Francisco?"

Dirick suggested a hole-in-the-wall restaurant near a homeless mission where he sometimes worked. Unless my legal matter was urgent, he asked if we could meet at the end of the week. We exchanged email addresses and phone numbers. He would call as soon as he learned something new about Jaleel.

The next morning, I was on winter break, packed and half out the door on my way to Joyce's when the phone rang.

"Good morning, Alex," the starched voice greeted me. "How are you today?"

It was impossible not to recognize Harding's voice. The pompous monotone provoked the same reaction in me as my father's letter. I had to stop myself from simply hanging up.

"Are you still there, Alex? I bring you news about Mr. Robeson, from a lawyer friend in Vancouver."

"My father already informed me."

"I have an update." I imagined Harding settled behind his sump-tuous desk, spinning around in his chair to stare at a panorama of Beverly Hills, the universe at his beckon. "Mr. Robeson is not going to fight extradition. In fact, he wants to come back here as soon as possible. His own decision. So far he's refused counsel."

"That doesn't make any sense."

"He told Vancouver police that if he was going to be charged with murder, he welcomed what the Sixth Amendment guarantees all Americans—the right to a speedy and public trial. The sooner he could tell everybody the truth, the more free he would be. "Those were his words," Harding made clear. He sounded concerned.

"Sounds like someone who has nothing to hide."

"Alex, think about it. He wants to turn the focus back on your father. Even if the grand jury failed to find probable cause the first time, it doesn't mean it can't reopen the case. What if Mr. Robeson persuades you to turn against your dad?"

Harding had proclaimed my father innocent a hundred times. In the sacred bond between founding partners, maybe there were no secrets. And confessing to your lawyer made perfect sense. Privileged and confidential, the whole thing.

"You know my testimony in front of the grand jury," I responded. "I said my father was innocent."

"I understand. You told the truth. But Mr. Robeson might try to convince you otherwise. You know, he had quite a following where he preached. You can't underestimate someone like that."

"I can make up own mind about things."

"Family comes first, Alex. Never forget that." He spoke in the same tone I had found at the end of my father's letter.

"Alex, you need to meet with your dad and me. Come in tomorrow. I'll have a driver waiting at the airport."

I said what I wished I had said to him years ago. "You're no longer my attorney, Mr. Kleeb."

"Mr. Kleeb?" he repeated. "Are you thinking of firing me?"

"I'm beyond the thinking part."

His eyes probably turned from the city vista as he began scribbling on a legal pad, reevaluating his strategy with me. He knew that I knew. Maybe my father had told him, maybe Harding just sensed it. What he didn't know was how I really felt about my father. Loyalty could be a fragile and whimsical thing.

"Fire me if you wish, Alex, but you might want to meet with your dad and me just the same."

"Why would I do that?"

"We don't have to go to war. Everything will be fine if you keep a cool head. Email me when you have your flight number."

Harding hung up first, only because my hand was shaking too badly to guide the handset to the receiver.

I thought about what I would have to go through in the next twenty-four hours. I booked a flight to LAX and emailed the time to Harding. My email to Dirick and Rudy asked that they drop whatever they were doing. We had to meet tonight, not Friday, I wrote. Events had taken a turn.

Tomorrow, I hoped, I would be at the offices of Baten, Kleeb, and Donahue at four thirty sharp, with my new attorneys. Never show up at a gunfight without your posse.

~56~

A driver met me at the Southwest terminal of LAX. I was whisked to the familiar edifice of glass and stone on Wilshire, took the elevator to the forty-second floor, and entered the penthouse offices of BKD. A backpack was slung over my shoulder. In jeans and a wool sweater, I could never be mistaken for a typical client. I didn't know the receptionist. When I gave my full name, it took a moment to sink in with her.

"You're the famous Alexandra," she said, almost gushing at the privilege of meeting me.

I squinted back.

"I should have been able to tell from the photos in your father's office. He's always talking about you and Toby. I've never met your brother either.

"Miss Baten, please have a seat," she added politely. She left her desk and moved briskly toward the suite of partners' offices.

I shrugged off my backpack and sat on a leather couch. Dirick and Rudy were late. Scrambling their schedules, I knew they'd be on a different flight. When we'd met last night, I wasn't sure what to think at first. Rudy was on the short side and paunchy, unshaven, and dressed like he shopped at Goodwill, like a distant cousin who hadn't been invited to the family reunion. Dirick was tall and poised, and wore his Scottish bonnet with a pompom. I warmed up to both men quickly, eager to get everything off my chest. The more I revealed, the better I felt.

"Well, hello there, Alex. Happy to see you. Thanks for coming." Harding approached in his expensive suit with braces and his signature bow tie. The voice was relaxed, if slightly preoccupied. His face and hair were a little grayer than I remembered, but otherwise he seemed as fit and intimidating as when we'd first met.

"How are things at Stanford?" he asked, sizing me up.

"Great. Busy."

"Your father says you're a history and political science major."

"That's right."

"That's one competitive school."

"Yes and no. Some kids are more serious than others."

"Alex, why don't we go into my office. Your father will join us in a minute."

"I'll stay here, if you don't mind."

"Why's that?"

"I'm waiting for my attorneys."

Harding was rarely cheery, never down, certainly never surprised. Even his smile lacked spontaneity. But I had struck a blow. His eyes made another sweep of me.

"You're waiting for your attorneys," he repeated. He let the silence give me a chance to rethink whatever crazy scheme I had in mind.

"That makes a total of five of us," I said. "I guess your office will hold everyone."

When we heard voices, Harding turned to watch two men entering the vestibule. Dirick, of course, was the more elegant of the pair. His suit wasn't half as expensive as Harding's, but he had the same air of intelligence and purpose. Rudy carried a fat briefcase as creased as his blazer.

"They're your attorneys?" Harding asked, straining to see if he recognized at least one of them. "What are their names?"

"Mr. Tusk and Mr. Appleton."

"What firm?"

The question was for my benefit, to let me know I'd hired some pigs in a poke. I didn't answer.

My father appeared and we kissed each other on the cheek. I could see his pride in me that the receptionist had implied.

Rudy and Dirick strolled over and introduced themselves, and we all went into Harding's office. The decor was similar to my father's—two groupings of pricey contemporary furniture flanking a large designer desk of some exotic wood rimmed with metal. The desk faced away from the view, but the vista was accessible with a half-rotation of the chair. Dirick helped himself to a glass of water from a stainless steel pitcher. Harding, making small talk, rearranged the furniture so each side would sit across from the other, buffered by the table in the middle.

"Alex, if you really think you need counsel, are these gentlemen familiar with the results of the grand jury hearing—and the checkered history of Mr. Robeson?"

"I relayed everything that I said to the grand jury, to the best of my memory." I resented the phrase "checkered history," as if everything that Jaleel was alleged to have done was true. But I kept quiet, saving my energy.

From his briefcase, Rudy retrieved two bound copies of Jaleel's lengthy statement and handed them to Harding and my father. I had read everything last night.

"I asked Mr. Robeson to write this narrative three years ago, when Mr. Appleton and I were urging him to turn himself in. I submitted it to a friend with the San Francisco D.A.. He gave it to some people in Los Angeles. It forms part of our argument for Mr. Robeson's innocence."

"So Mr. Robeson is your client?" Harding said.

"He was."

"But not now?"

"We're still trying to reach him."

"So you can't really be speaking on Mr. Robeson's behalf. You have no idea what he's thinking, or what his new counsel might say, if he has one. Maybe he doesn't want an attorney at all. The only client you can speak for is Alex.

"Of course," Harding continued, "Mr. Robeson should have an attorney. That whole mess in Peartree—"

"Anything that happened or didn't happen in Peartree," Rudy countered, "would be inadmissible in a trial about Mr. Diggs. Why don't we stick to the document in front of you?"

"Until Jaleel can speak for himself," I broke in, "I can tell you that everything he wrote about our friendship is accurate. Our conversations about the murder, his delivering the letter for me, his regret that I had pulled him into this mess—all true. Jaleel had nothing to do with Charlie Diggs."

"Of course he would say that." Harding looked dismissively at Jaleel's statement. My gaze floated to my stone-faced father. He wasn't giving the slightest hint of what he felt, as he'd done with Hildenbrand when he first visited our house.

"You should read Mr. Robeson's narrative very carefully," Rudy continued. "If there's a new trial, it will become an exhibit, and Mr. Robeson, and Alex, will testify under oath that it's totally accurate. It's clear that he had no interest in burglarizing a Toluca Lake home. He was only helping his friend by delivering her letter to Mr. Diggs. Mr. Robeson revisited Toluca Lake on his bicycle, fascinated by a neighborhood that was so different from anything he had known. But it was not on the night of the murder."

Harding steepled his fingers under his chin. "All you have is his word that he wasn't around. There may be neighbors who will testify otherwise. Mr. Robeson is a resourceful, highly intelligent, determined individual who had the capacity to plan, and execute, the murder exactly as it occurred."

"That description fits Mr. Baten to a T," Dirick couldn't resist. My father rotated his expressionless eyes to the Samaritan.

"We believe," Rudy added, "that with Alex's testimony, and new facts we're going to present—facts that were unavailable to Alex when she first testified—a jury might surprise you with its conclusion."

Harding dropped his large hands on his knees. "And what testimony, and what new facts, would those be, Mr. Tusk?"

"Why don't we let Alex speak to that?"

All eyes pounced on me. I took a breath. "I have absolute proof," I said, staring at Harding rather than my father, "that Charlie Diggs was murdered by your law partner."

"My law partner? You mean your father?"

I still couldn't look at Dad. "Yes."

"Absolute proof. Really?"

For the first time, scooting back in his chair, Dad looked both concerned and curious. To do real damage, he knew, I needed more than a recollection of his confession to me.

"What proof, Alex?" Harding pushed.

I suddenly remembered when Dad and I had watched a rocket launch from Cape Canaveral on TV. I kept looking at him more than the liftoff. There was a fascination in his eyes, as though he was wondering if the rocket was going to make it or explode into a million pieces. He was always calculating odds on almost everything—how he would do on the golf course, in a courtroom, at the poker table. Whatever card I was intending to play now, it had to be spectacularly good to beat him.

"You don't have any new evidence; you're bluffing," Harding declared. "In court, it'll be your word against Louis' impeccable reputation. You'll end up wishing you'd been swimming with crocodiles."

My former attorney, whose life of privilege had eased every bump on the road to incredible wealth and a sterling reputation, had a heart soaked in brine. I moved slowly to my feet, unzipped my backpack, and reached in.

When our eyes finally locked, I gave my father one last chance to say something. He was silent.

Where last-second impulses come from can be complex: your imagination, some instinct, or just the perceived need for self-preservation. After discovering the splatter suit in Dad's safe, I had raced upstairs for my Kodak Brownie as well as a pair of scissors. My pathetic little camera, which I had owned since I was eight or nine, was a bookend to the pre-digital age. But it worked fine that night while Dad slept. I took two exposures of the open safe, two of the cavity where the suit had been hidden, and five of the splatter suit at various angles, including a close-up of the manufacturer's label inside. When it became clear, after our confrontation in his study, that my father was likely to destroy the evidence, I developed the photos.

I handed one set to Harding and the other to my father.

"What's this?" Harding barely looked at the glossy prints.

"I have the date that Dad purchased it—ten days before the murder—and a copy of the credit card receipt that I dug out of his mail."

I reached again into my pack, and produced copies of everything, laying them on the table between us. My father stared at me. Harding stole a glance of the copies, and slid everything back to me with a disinterested flourish.

"So Mr. Tusk shows all this to a jury, Alex, so what? Your father purchased some crazy-looking garment. Maybe he was thinking dark thoughts, but that doesn't mean he acted on them. It's circumstantial."

"What about my testimony?" I said. "There are things I didn't tell the grand jury because the prosecutor didn't ask the right questions. This time I'm going to say everything."

"I grant you, if there's a murder trail, you'll make a splash, but to convince twelve people beyond a reasonable doubt? We'll take our chances."

My hand dropped one more time into my pack. Out came my own plastic sleeve, as if I were the prosecutor in the grand jury room. My little pouch contained a swatch of fabric the size of a silver dollar, extracted by my pair of scissors. Two spots of blood on the bottom of the left leg had been overlooked in my father's haste to clean the suit with hydrogen peroxide. Nor, I was guessing, had he noticed the hole I left behind when he eventually destroyed everything.

In silence, I held up a clear plastic pouch containing the fabric swatch. Harding and my father riveted their attention on something they couldn't believe existed.

"Five years ago, in its forensic infancy, DNA testing was often in-accurate," Rudy said, taking the evidence from me. "Today, I think a judge would consider this rock solid. Charlie's blood on a splatter suit purchased by your client, Mr. Kleeb—not a good position for anyone be in."

I waited for Dad to ask why I'd done this. Did I not understand his code of ethics? Was his lie to me so offensive that it tainted all the good he'd done for our family? How could I feel more loyalty to a boy I might have a crush on than a father who I had loved and idol-ized all my life?

He had tried to teach me that justice was largely a matter of opin-ion and persuasion. I was trying to show otherwise. He still hadn't spoken one word in the entire meeting. His eyes now carried him in-ward, maybe wondering when and how his life in paradise had hit such a snag.

~57~

No one left Harding's office. Dirick rose and stood next to the mammoth desk, his face angled toward the window. He squeezed his hands in his jacket pockets as he regarded the panorama of Beverly Hills. With the sun fading, I thought, the city's bloated magnificence looked in decline.

Harding stirred uneasily in his chair. "Where is this all going, Mr. Appleton? You want revenge?"

In our private meeting, Dirick had referred to Harding as a slick of oil polluting the waters of integrity. Now, I knew, he and Rudy were getting ready to drop a match on the ooze.

Dirick turned and sat on the edge of the desk, facing my father and Harding. "Believe it or not, our primary goal, gentlemen, is not necessarily to have Mr. Baten go to prison. Our main objective is to free Jaleel.

"I know Jaleel Robeson even better than Alex does. Actually, as I have no children, I sometimes think of Jaleel as my son. From the moment our itinerant paths crossed, I recognized unique qualities in him, even if I couldn't define them. He is a special young man, not perfect but innocent, I believe, of everything that's befallen him. It seems so obvious, the right thing for all of us to do now. To imprison Jaleel would not only mock his message of forgiveness, it would mean incarcerating an innocent man."

Harding was growing more fidgety. "What exactly do you want from this meeting, Mr. Appleton?"

"Mr. Diggs was murdered around midnight, October 29, isn't that correct?" Dirick said to my father. "Could you refresh my memory? Where were you that night, Mr. Baten?"

"He was hitting golf balls at a driving range. Then he went home to bed," Harding spoke for my father.

Rudy intruded. "I don't believe that. I believe, Mr. Baten, you were not at a driving range hitting golf balls."

"Don't answer, Louis."

Rudy's eyes fell on my father, but his words were directed at Harding. "At this point, Mr. Kleeb, wouldn't a plea bargain, so to speak, be in the best interest of all parties?"

"This is becoming childish," Harding scoffed. "A plea bargain? I don't see any point in continuing—"

"No, go on," my father said, stopping his partner. His voice was firm, but his eyes suddenly looked hollow.

"Mr. Appleton, Alex, and I have discussed letting you off the hook, Mr. Baten. If we can convey to Mr. Robeson that you have admitted your guilt, off the record, maybe he'll agree to refresh his memory too. You'll have to admit to deceiving Detective Hildenbrand. You were not asleep in your bed at the time of the killing."

I could almost hear Harding's teeth grinding. "What are we doing here, Louis? These con artists are trying to intimidate us. This is our firm, for Christ's sake."

"Mr. Baten," Rudy continued, "isn't it possible that the reason you lied to Detective Hildenbrand was that you wanted to protect Jaleel Robeson? You knew that while he was very much in danger of being arrested for murdering Charlie—a black, homeless teen-ager on the run from something he was charged with in Texas, desperate for money—he was in fact innocent. How did you know that? Because the evening of the murder, you drove over to his house. It's not in Mr. Robeson's affidavit, but it could have slipped his mind too."

"Why would I be at Jaleel's house?" Dad asked.

"Alex had told you where he lived, the story of how they met and how much she liked him. Any potential boyfriend of your daughter's, especially an older boy, an African-American, you wanted to check him out. You wanted to make sure Alex wasn't in over her head. So you dropped in on Jaleel, scared him half to death at first. You two talked until the wee hours. You ended up being impressed by Jaleel's intelligence and sincerity. Then you drove home, well after the squad cars rushed to the Diggses' house. You never saw the police, and they never saw you."

"Did we get any of this wrong, Mr. Baten?" Dirick spoke up. "You look full of consternation."

"What horseshit," Harding said. "You think anyone will swallow this?"

Dirick bit his lower lip, as if he'd been waiting to make our summary. "Actually, I do. No one lies with the conviction or pleasure of Louis Baten. In the prevarication department, he's the eight-hundred-pound gorilla. A monarch of liars. He makes his living from artful deception, just like my father did.

"Once we see a sworn statement from Mr. Baten about he and Jaleel spending that evening together," Dirick said, making the obvious even clearer, "I promise you that Alex's photos and fabric swatch will go away."

"This isn't law," Harding said. "This is blackmail and extortion!"

"Maybe you gentlemen need a few days to think everything over."

"I don't need to think over anything." As he spoke, eyes moved back to my beleaguered father. "You've made everything quite clear, Mr. Appleton."

"Louis, I refuse to allow you to say another word. Are you honestly thinking of trusting these people?"

Dad's gaze hung on me, like tired tinsel on a Christmas tree. That we were supposed to be peas in a pod, and I might be a partner in his firm one day—that lost dream seemed to crush him for a moment.

"You really want a confession?" Dad finally said to Dirick and Rudy. "All right. I knew Charlie was working late that night while his wife was away. I was over at his house just before ten, after Alex and Toby were asleep, and let myself in with my key. I hid in his closet and slipped on the splatter suit, except for the hood, because it wasn't easy to breathe. My asthma had been kicking up so I'd brought my inhaler along. That was my one mistake, leaving it in the closet. It fell out of my pocket. There were no fingerprints on it, though. On instinct I had wiped the canister clean before slipping it in the suit. As for my hair being on the Hawaiian shirt, that was from the poker game scuffle. The splatter suit protected me perfectly now as I waited patiently. I knew where Charlie's shotguns were, his shells, everything. I was ready to shoot him at any instant. When he came upstairs to bed, I slipped on the hood. He was startled when I walked into the bedroom, but he wasn't scared, even though I had his twelve-gauge cradled in my arm. He squinted at me and said, "Hey, Louis, what the fuck is this? Is this a game? Come on, man—" I didn't say a word. I let him stand there, until it sank in that I knew everything, and this was not a game. I wanted him to understand what he deserved for betraying our friendship and destroying my marriage. Ten or fifteen seconds passed. He just keep shaking his head, smiling even, until I raised the shotgun at close range and pulled the trigger. He fell to the carpet on his side, but my anger wasn't sated. I stepped closer and fired again at his face. That's how everything went down. I have no regrets. I did the right thing."

"Louis!"

"Harding, give it up," Dad snapped. "We're no longer in control. We have no options."

I didn't think of our "plea bargain" as a lie, or extortion, though clearly it was both. I considered it a cleansing. While I wanted the truth to come out to the whole world some day, more pressing was that Jaleel go free. The trade off was the only way to do it.

We spent another hour tying down details. Harding and my father would approach the district attorney to corroborate the story Jaleel would have to add to his existing narrative. Harding would cooperate with Rudy in filing any motions with the court. When Jaleel came back, all efforts would be made to have him released on bond.

The horse-trading wasn't quite done, though it took a different direction. Dirick insisted that just in case the new Mrs. Baten had ideas for spending her husband's considerable wealth, my father would immediately set up irrevocable trusts for Toby and me—$1 million each. The sum sounded huge to me, but it was all to cover our education, living expenses, and unforeseen contingencies for a few years. My father raised no objection.

As we left Harding's office, the last thing I did was to study my father's preoccupied face. My disappointment in him was hard to measure, but I knew it was a millstone I would always lug around. His look back was a lot clearer than mine. If there was anything for which he was really sorry, it wasn't the squandered dream of me following in his footsteps. It was the pain of losing a daughter.

"Goodbye, sweetie." He did his best to sound stoical.

"Goodbye, Dad."

It was the last time I would see him.

~58~

Momentum is a funny thing. Just when you think it's going one way, it has a mind of its own and takes you on another ride. Jaleel willingly allowed himself to be flown back to Los Angeles in handcuffs, accompanied by Detectives Hildenbrand and Shier with great pomp and circumstance, as if they'd captured Al Capone. They finally had a strong suspect, someone in the D.A.'s office told the media. But the next day, Rudy and Dirick posted a bond without too much difficulty and whisked their client away. My father and Harding, as we'd all agreed, met promptly with the D.A. with revisions to Dad's story. Avoiding the media required some luck. Dirick found a shabby motel in Santa Monica and registered Jaleel under a false name. I knew he was used to changing names, but how weird did this whole homecoming feel to him? All the machinations. Dirick said I couldn't see Jaleel. The three of them had lots of work, and there couldn't be any distractions.

I understood, but I kept wondering how Jaleel felt about me. We had been out of touch for a long time. He had never left my thoughts, but now that he was back, and close to freedom, I missed him even more. I ended up following the news at Stanford. Jaleel wasn't doing interviews, but his story leaked out. His Poor Richard manifestos and his sermons from the church no longer went unnoticed in the States. What kind of young man escaped from a murder charge in Texas and ended up preaching in Canada? He was a mystery. Talking heads filled the airwaves. For a brief time, the name Jaleel Robeson seemed to be

on everyone's lips, as if in America the more you tried to hide, the
more famous you became.

A month passed before I flew down to L.A., hoping finally to see
Jaleel. Dirick met me at Starbucks. Jaleel was still in the thick of things
and laying low, but the Samaritan had good news on a couple of fronts.
My father had withstood the barrage of disbelief from the police and
the D.A. about his alibi. Both he and Jaleel had been interrogated separately, more than once, and neither caved. Second, the Houston attorney Dirick hired to check into Detective Patterson's case against
Jaleel had been in touch. An internal investigation unit, working with
the Peartree County D.A. for almost a year, had announced its find-
ings. Patterson had been intimidating witnesses and cooking evidence
in cases stretching back fifteen years. Without any real evidence against
Jaleel, the Peartree County D.A. had decided to drop case.

I began to feel even better when we left Starbucks and Dirick
handed me a letter from Jaleel. I didn't open it until I was alone.

*Alex, hello. I want to thank you. Taking on your
father couldn't have been an easy task. Dirick and
Rudy gave me the details. To my thinking, you live in
a state of grace, what the Greeks called "heroic
virtue"—did we ever discuss that? Dirick also said
that you're at Stanford now. Congratulations! My two
years in Canada were trying, but in the end, a
blessing. I have a story to tell. When all this craziness
is over with the legal system, we'll get together, I hope.
Your friend, Jaleel*

I was relieved that he didn't hold a grudge against me, but I felt un-
sure that we would actually get together. On April 10, 1993, the L.A.
District Attorney's Office announced it was temporarily abandoning
its efforts to prosecute Jaleel, just like it had given up on my father after
the grand jury fiasco. With Dirick's permission, Jaleel began to give interviews. The whole country seemed interested. He seemed to be too
busy for me. Many cheered for a man whose last decade had been about
courage and defiance. But both Joyce and Toby told me there was out-
rage in Toluca Lake. Two prime suspects had gone scot-free. My father,

changing his story, was viewed with particular suspicion, as if he'd been the one to secretly work out a deal with the D.A.

The anger wasn't confined to Toluca Lake. The D.A.'s office was determined not to be embarrassed by its alleged ineptitude. Hildenbrand was ordered to recharge his investigation, interviewing more people, tracking down any new leads. "We'll keep looking for the killer or killers until justice is done, no matter how long it takes," the detective vowed on television. Hildenbrand looked composed as I watched, but if he'd punched a couple of holes in a wall from frustration I wouldn't have been surprised.

By the time Toby and I got together, it was the end of summer. I was back at school, so we met at a restaurant in Palo Alto. He wasted no time telling me he was dropping out of high school, though he'd promised Dad to get his GED. In the meantime, he and a friend were looking for an apartment to rent in Oakland. They'd mastered, entirely on their own, the tricky science of writing computer code. Screw high school, Toby told me—his future was in Silicon Valley.

"I'm all grown up," he declared.

"All grown up? You're sixteen." To his credit, he acted more sophisticated than his age, and he knew how to dress, both geek-style and conventional, depending on the occasion. Today, he simply wore jeans, loafers, and an open collar denim shirt. He had inherited Mom's sense of style as well as her looks.

"What are you thinking about?" he said when I remained quiet.

"Mom, at the moment."

"Why waste your time?"

"Because she's our mother."

"I spoke to her last week. What a trip! You can't trust what she says."

"Like what?"

"She's thinking of going to school and getting a teacher's certificate—in early childhood education! She said she loves little kids." His eyes twinkled. "She'll never do it. Too much work."

After my long silence with Mom, we had spoken a few times. I made the first call. She didn't mention going to school, but she did talk about the financial challenges of living in Manhattan, and how the men she'd dated so far were disappointing. She seemed to be floundering for the moment.

"Don't worry. She'll survive," I answered. "She always does." Our mother got by on luck and what she thought were a string of harmless lies. Even deserting her family, pregnant with Charlie's baby, didn't seem wrong to her. She was like someone who crossed a raging river by stepping on haphazardly positioned stones to reach the other side. It never occurred to her that she might slip. That's why she had Agnes, to keep her from falling.

"How do you think Dad's doing?" I asked.

"He lives for his work, then plays hard on weekends. I don't talk to that woman he calls his wife."

"What did you think about the murder? It's back to square one."

"What do I think? I think it's bullshit. I think Dad killed Charlie Diggs."

"What?"

"That sounds pretty fake, sis. You had to suspect Dad, too, even when you were testifying. You were just under his spell. Or maybe you were naïve, like asking the alumni to give their money away, or Dad was about Mom's affair. I'd blame the gene pool."

"Maybe I just had a heart, Toby."

"You used to tell me Dad was innocent," I pointed out. "What changed your mind?"

"Hey, I don't know positively that he's guilty, but if you asked me not to believe he killed Charlie, I couldn't. It's the kind of power trip Dad's capable of."

"Are you saying that if he did it, then it's okay? He shouldn't go to prison? Or Charlie had it coming?"

"I'm not saying any of that. Dad should be in prison if he murdered Charlie. But it's all moot now, isn't it? A new D.A. will come along and I bet Charlie's case will fade away. I'm glad your pal, Jaleel, didn't get the rap."

"You know, Mom thinks Dad is innocent."

"Self-brainwashing is her specialty."

I wondered what my brother would say about Mom having Charlie's baby. I wasn't going to bring that up any more than I would discuss what I knew about the plea bargain. Some things you share and other things you don't.

"Do you still talk to Agnes?" Toby asked as the check came.

"Once a month. I consider us pretty good friends."

"She's like your role model, huh."

"I could do worse."

My all-grown-up brother insisted on paying the lunch tab. He was the Phoenix rising from the ashes. The family member I'd grown up worrying about the most suddenly seemed the healthiest. He'd given up on Dr. Sheffield but begun seeing another therapist, who diagnosed him as fitting on the minimally impaired end of the Asperger spectrum. Even if I was minoring in psychology, I said I didn't know the term well.

"It's nothing fatal. I hate crowds, even small groups. Think of someone who functions best in a quiet room, without distractions, doing something he likes. Doing it well, hopefully."

He rose from the table to give me a hug. "Let's keep in touch, sis."

When I got back to Stanford, a week of rain was followed by cloudless sunshine. My friends got lazy about studying. I was such a bore that I turned down a weekend trip with friends to the city. Friday night, in the Stanford library, I counted twenty of us—out of six thousand undergraduates and eleven thousand graduate students—studying our heads off. "What the hell are you doing, Alex?" I thought, eyeing the other helpless souls. I couldn't get out of the groove of trying to be perfect.

I went to a vending machine for a Coke. When I returned, a young man was sitting across the table, looking through one of my textbooks. It took a moment for me to process everything. Jaleel was thinner, less muscular, the face more contemplative. His hair was cut short, and he wore simple black-framed glasses. Overall, his presence was a little like Dirick's, serene but mindful of everything. The last time we'd been together, at his house, chaos and desperation had ruled.

"This is a surprise," I said as he looked up.

When we'd first met, I remembered, Jaleel was full of swagger, determined to sell me lemonade. He had evolved. The way he scrutinized me now, maybe he was calculating how time and circumstances had changed both of us.

We walked back into the stacks, trying not to disturb anyone. I gave him a quick hug. He didn't reciprocate as much as I wanted him to.

"How did you find me?" I said.

His smile was the same, a quick sprint across his face, followed by
a knowing laugh. "For almost ten years, people were trying to find
me. I know the tricks. You just keep asking. A woman at Branner said
the most likely place to find Alex Baten on a Friday night—"

"Don't finish that sentence," I said, feeling my face warm. "Hey,
I'm done studying. Do you have time for coffee?" I sounded in control, but my emotions were a train wreck.

Tresidder, the student union, was open till midnight. We found
some book jockeys scattered around, along with normal couples not
trying to set the world on fire. We ordered a couple of lattes.

Jaleel roved his eyes around the large room, as if wondering what
it was like to be a student at a prestigious university.

"It's really good to see you," I couldn't help saying.

"Did you think I was ever coming back to the States?"

"I had no idea." I wondered again why he never wrote me. I understood his paranoia, but if he'd wanted to communicate, his letter
would have found its way to St. Anthony's. I might have written back
and tried to make him jealous. I had had my first serious boyfriend.

"I want to know everything," I said. "Start from whatever moment
is most important to you." For me, it was the one I darted across
Cahuenga on my bicycle and met Jaleel.

He began with his mother and father. Under Patterson's direction,
they'd been buried in a potter's field ten years ago. Once he was a
free man, Jaleel had called his church. Reverend Johnson promised
to help with the exhumation. His mother had paid for two plots in
the Peartree City Cemetery, Jaleel made clear, and that's where their
bodies should rest. Last month he made his way to Peartree. He'd
paid for two elegantly engraved headstones, and watched as they were
placed at the new graves.

His narrative jumped around. Life on the run in Vancouver
sounded harrowing. Jaleel did everything he could to keep a low pro-
file, but he was always looking over his shoulder. He had met a sympathetic, outspoken student named Carter, who let him stay with her
when he was at his lowest. He owed her a lot. She'd convinced him
to start speaking at the Unitarian church. They had fallen in love, or
at least he had.

"Do you still have feelings for her?"

"After living together for almost a year, she said my ego was getting too big. I couldn't disagree. Then she walked out, in the middle of the night. I never saw her again, but I'll always wonder if she was the one who called the police on me. In the end it didn't matter. I forgave her."

When it was my turn, I took even longer. He was sympathetic but didn't seem surprised by what I'd been through with my parents.

"So now what?" I asked when we strolled back to Branner. "I'm practically invisible, which is fine with me. You're a well-known name in the media. What are you going to do with that?"

"Not sure."

"Are your plans for Princeton back on track?"

"Princeton and Yale both reached out to me. I thought about the opportunities—and told them no."

I frowned. "I think that's a really bad decision."

"An Ivy League college doesn't interest me anymore."

"What about baseball?"

"If an athlete doesn't maintain his peak, no big league team is going to take a chance on him."

"You could get back into shape."

His smile jumped across his face. "I've changed, Alex. I don't want to play baseball either. It's just not for me anymore."

I couldn't quite grasp that someone with so much talent and ambition would so easily discard them.

"When I was speaking at the church, it was the happiest I'd ever been. I knew my past would catch up with me at some point, but that wasn't as important as connecting with people."

He said a New York publisher had contacted him to write a book. It was tempting, because he liked to write, but he wasn't sure he wanted to relive his past in print. The publisher kept prodding—the story of a fugitive from racism and injustice would make terrific reading.

"I hope you do it. That's another way to get your message out," I said.

At Branner, he kissed me on the cheek. I asked when we would see each other again. He looked at his feet, thinking, before returning to my eyes.

"I had no idea what it would be like to meet again, Alex. You've really gotten it together. You're grown up—"

It was starting to sound like a prelude to rejection. "I'm not that different," I said. "Not everything changes. I've always had feelings for you."

I threw my arms around Jaleel—like he was the most precious being in the world. He seemed surprised, but he didn't fight me. I remembered our kiss in his house.

"I love you," I said.

"You shouldn't say that." He pulled back, looking concerned.

"It's what I feel. I've never been shy about expressing myself, have I?"

My love for Jaleel wasn't from guilt or pity, or wanting to save him. I just cared about him, like I had cared for no one else.

A second later we began kissing, and didn't stop.

~59~

I wish I could say I remember every minute of the next six weeks, because they were the most memorable of my life. Their seamless intensity, however, transcend memory. I just know that they occurred, and they changed me, as much as anything, into a woman. I had to keep studying for finals, so I shuttled between library and classroom during the day. What I looked forward to—could think of little else—was meeting Jaleel every evening for dinner, and then passing the night in a Palo Alto motel room. Thirty dollars a night got you fresh sheets and a clean bathroom. You could call for pizza at two in the morning.

My first sexual experience was at St. Anthony's, but my first encounter with passion was in that cheesy motel room. The first time Jaleel took off my clothes and I watched him take off his, girlhood fantasies about Mick Jagger and Keith Richards melted like an ice cube in the sun. I didn't need to fantasize anymore. What's difficult for me to remember isn't the physical acts but my emotions. They were elusive, if not ethereal, the imprints on your soul that poets struggle to express. I couldn't come close to explaining their depth, except to say that I did something to his soul in return. We not only parched each other's loneliness, we also whipped our hearts into a frenzy.

"What are you thinking about?" he would whisper in the middle of the night. I would look lifeless, but he knew when I was awake.

"You, unfortunately."

"It's a curse, isn't it?" he said with a sly laugh. "What else is on your mind?"

"You know me. My whole life is constantly up for review."

He would stretch his hands behind his head, lying straight as a board next to me, staring at some invisible screen on the ceiling.

"Look, there you are, eight or nine, camping in a tent with friends in someone's backyard, telling each other ghost stories. You get so scared that you want to go home, but you don't tell anyone—you just keep biting your nails to the nub. You have to appear fearless.

"Ah, look at this one. You and Toby in your rowboat, fishing, and you're so fed up with him you can't wait to throw him in the lake, and finally you do. He pretends he's drowning, so you have to rescue him, which really pisses you off.

"Here's my favorite. You're taking a Latin test, but all you can think about is your Founder's Day speech, how you want to give the same speech over and over, with Ms. Graves tied to a chair until she acknowledges you're right."

"I was right," I interrupt. I drop my arm over his chest, kissing his neck. "What do you think about?"

"How you and I are from totally different worlds."

"That's one reason I want to be with you—I hate the world I come from. What else?"

"Scary stuff sneaks up on me. Getting off the bus in Kingman and those two cops are waiting. Or Vancouver, almost shooting to death a man who I had made into my enemy. I think a lot about my mother too."

"I have a question," I said. "Why did you ride your bike back to Toluca Lake, when you didn't have to?"

"I was spellbound. The lake, the fragrance of magnolia blossoms, the mansions. I picked out your house. I imagined how one day I might afford to buy one just like it. The demons of ambition got into my head."

We drifted back to sleep together.

If there was time in the morning, we'd have breakfast together and discuss our plans for the summer. It was hard to camouflage my excitement.

~60~

When finals were over, I returned to my dorm from an early dinner with Jaleel. As I began to pack, the phone rang. Harding Kleeb, the last person I expected to hear from, sounded like he was calling from a tunnel. He had some very difficult news, he said. My father had been making a routine summation to a jury this afternoon, standing in front of twelve people who as usual were mesmerized by his charisma and knowledge of the law. He had finished pounding home his points and started returning to the defense table when his hand clutched at his chest. He toppled to the floor, a witness said, like a building collapsing in an earthquake.

"Paramedics were on the scene in minutes, but they couldn't revive him. I'm so sorry, Alex."

It was the most sincere thing Harding had ever said to me. I was too shocked to process my feelings. I didn't even know where to start. I listened as Harding eulogized my father as "a warrior," a category that I had never thought of but probably should have. Dad had his code of ethics, a competitive nature, and an unending thirst for winning. He had died in battle. His stature was immeasurable, Harding added, waiting for me to agree. I couldn't find any words, except to promise to call Toby and Mom immediately.

The day of the service, the chapel at Forest Lawn in Hollywood Hills was mobbed. Mom, the great compartmentalizer, had elected not to attend, as Dad had died on another wife's watch. The woman I'd never met gave me a quick kiss on the cheek. She asked Toby and me if we wanted to speak at the service. Toby got overwhelmed by crowds, and I declined to participate as well. I would have ended up being too blunt. No matter the size of his accomplishments, my father's arrogance had allowed him to take too much for granted—his marriage, his best friend, and, most important to me, my allegiance. Toby and I sat in the front row and listened to others extol Dad. Ten of his friends spoke, all men. No one, of course, mentioned what Harding and everyone at BKD referred to as the Charlie Diggs "tragedy." My father was remembered for his "male virtues," like responsibility, professionalism, and hard work. As sexist as "male virtues" sounded, they certainly applied to Dad. He had been a good father in many ways. He probably had not lost his soul all at once, I conceded. It had been peeled off in thin layers, over time.

At the gravesite, I spoke to lots of people, many of whom I didn't know. I wiped away a tear or two as I listened to their stories of friendship with Dad. My stepmom didn't seem overly sad. She was too busy coordinating the reception afterward. I felt on the margins again. Toby and I weren't counting on being included in Dad's will, but at least we had Dirick to thank for setting up the two trusts.

I flew back to school the next day and packed my Volkswagen with everything I owned. Jaleel's publisher had offered to rent him a cabin in Big Sur, where he could write without too much distraction. The drive took me through Monterey and onto a serpentine highway of coastline trees and white-capped ocean views. When I had reception, I called Jaleel on my cell phone. He was already at the cabin. We'd been together almost every day for the last six weeks, yet it felt like we'd been apart for months.

"Are you getting hungry?" I said into the phone. "I stopped at a supermarket in Monterey." A bronze disc of sun was about to slip into the water.

"Starved. Haven't tried the kitchen yet, but the cabin's all set for us."

"How does spaghetti and meatballs sound? My mom gave me a great recipe a long time ago."

"Hurry. More than my stomach misses you."

The cabin wasn't far from where Henry Miller had lived toward the end of his life. That could only be good luck for a writer, we thought. I'd already seen photos. The interior was small but charm-

ing, with a fieldstone fireplace, a '50s-looking kitchen, a forest view
from the living room, and a pleasant front porch with a rocker. The
fireplace was a necessity. Even in summer, nights could be chilly.
Jaleel and his publisher had wrangled about the scope and theme
of his memoir. Jaleel wanted to call it *State of Grace*. He was less interested in writing of his escape from Peartree, surviving by guile and
luck, than he was in his permanent transformation.

"Are you sure?" I had said. I liked the publisher's concept. The survival story was soaked in adrenaline.

"You write that story, Alex. You know me better than anyone. I've
told you everything. Call it whatever you want."

"Really? You'd let me do that?"

"I insist," he said.

We had agreed to live together that summer with a few ground
rules. Jaleel would be left alone to work, and he would leave me to
my pile of art and history books, long walks, and private musings.
He would cook breakfast and I would prepare dinners. At five o'clock,
everybody had to stop whatever they were doing and break out the
tequila, wine, or beer for happy hour.

We didn't get around to my spaghetti dinner until after we'd made
love. The crackling from the fireplace was like a sonata. Jaleel told me
not to go outside at night because there could be bears, so I ended
upon rocking contentedly on the porch, wrapped in a sweater, thinking about the future. The aroma of the pines gave me a high.

Being in love was a new journey for me. I remembered when Agnes
said that she'd never been in love. Mom had piped up that it wasn't
too late. Agnes just shook her head, as if there were only so many opportunities, and you couldn't count on them coming along like subway cars. *Carpe diem.* One could certainly be happy without being
in love, but every time I looked at Jaleel, nothing else in my life had
made me feel the way I felt now.

I was sensitive to every whisper, glance, and touch between us.
When we talked, incessantly into the deep of the night, it felt like
stream of consciousness. We each had a lot of buried pain. It seemed
corny to write about my feelings in a new journal, like I was an ado-
lescent again, but I was compulsive about it. I showed everything to
Jaleel. Sometimes I sounded like a smitten ten-year-old; other times

I was like Agnes looking down on everything through the lens of wisdom. When you're in love, there's nothing that can embarrass or surprise you. Feeling safe and vulnerable at the same time, I just wanted to curl under Jaleel's arm and not move from it.

*   *   *

No matter how much I wanted to slow down time, our three months came and went as abruptly as a spring rain. I began to feel panic.

"What's going to happen to us?" I asked. My head was on his shoulder, lying in bed as we watched the morning sun scrub the walls. "I have this feeling." I left out the word "bad," but I was sure he heard it in my tone.

Much had gotten blurred in our three months—not just what would happen to us but also, at least for me, something as basic as who I was. All the anxiety and danger that Jaleel had endured had ultimately left him at peace. He knew exactly who he was and what he wanted. I was a bundle of questions. How would I hold onto my incredible happiness? Did I still want to go to graduate school and ultimately teach? How would I balance that with having a family one day?

"I don't know what's going to happen to us any more than you do," Jaleel admitted.

"Liar. You have everything figured out. You're much smarter than me."

"I don't have our future figured out," he said sincerely. "Maybe it would be different if I understood the nature of time. And you think I'm so smart?"

A bubble of laughter escaped my lips, but his words stung when I realized what he was saying. A long-term relationship was different than a summer of hope and infatuation. He wasn't ready to settle down. I knew, as well, that we had very different temperaments. I had inviolate opinions. My principles were rigid. I was a born skeptic. I was also practical; he was the dreamer. Unlike Jaleel, I couldn't always forgive those who had hurt me. Nor did I particularly care about being forgiven, other than by Jaleel for what I'd done to him in Toluca Lake.

"Are you okay?" he said, our faces inches apart.

"Don't I seem okay?"

"No."

"Well, I'm fine," I lied.

I took a long shower while Jaleel dozed in bed. My thoughts bounced between the cosmic and the mundane. How deep and permanent were my feelings for Jaleel—and would they transcend the great anxiety I felt at the moment? What needed to be packed in our cars? I wrapped myself in a towel and sat on the closed toilet seat, chin reposed on my fist like *The Thinker*. I wondered how I was going to give Jaleel the news.

At the end of July, my period had been late, but I was often irregular. By the middle of August—seven weeks without a drop of blood—I began to worry. Yesterday I drove to Monterey to see a gynecologist. Jaleel thought I was looking for butterflies in the woods. My reaction at the doctor's office was a fit of such epic disbelief that she gave me a mild sedative on the spot. I'd managed to return to Jaleel acting as normal as I could.

I put on a robe and sat on my side of the bed. Jaleel managed to open one eye, looking up at me.

"You were in the bathroom a long time." He studied my face. I had been crying.

"Zeus, in his mischievous wisdom, threw a lightning bolt at us," I finally came clean. "I found out yesterday," I said matter-of-factly, as if that would make the news less alarming. "I'm pregnant."

I wouldn't have blamed him if he wigged out. My roller coaster emotions made me want to jump in the VW and drive off into the sunset.

Instead, he was absolutely silent. Why couldn't he just fall into a void of despair like a normal guy and tell me I'd ruined his life. "Did you hear what I said?" I raised my voice.

"I heard. Come here."

When I didn't move, he sat up behind me on the bed, wrapping his legs around mine. He circled his arms over my belly.

"You make it sound like it's the end of the world." His voice was as gentle as leaves scampering over the ground.

"Well, isn't it? What do I do, have an abortion? I'm not sure I'm fit to be a mother right now. I don't want to go back to Stanford, walking around campus pregnant. Everyone would just stare and make up stories. It would be like being back at Valley." I wanted to kick or throw something. "It's my responsibility. I had a diaphragm. It's my fault," I declared.

"It's not anyone's fault, Alex." He didn't take his arms away.

All I could think of was my mother and Charlie. Could I possibly be as confused as her? "Yes, it is. I was stupid and irresponsible—"

"I'd like us to have the baby," he interrupted, as if the decision, for him, was already made.

"You don't know what you're saying."

"This is a gift. I don't want to turn it down. Tell me how you feel?"

"I just told you. This is overwhelming me."

"Why wouldn't you want our baby?"

"It's more complicated than that."

"We love each other. We'll love our child."

I couldn't stop myself. "What about getting married?"

I felt like a hypocrite. I'd readily admitted to Jaleel how different our temperaments were, and to myself that infatuation and hope weren't to be mistaken for a long-term commitment. But I wanted Jaleel. I wanted to be with him for the rest of my life. How could a hard-boiled, no bullshit realist like me be suffering a total meltdown? Rationality and calm self-determination were one of the great illusions of the universe, I thought. In the end, we were all ruled by our passions.

"Can we talk about that a little later? This is all such a big surprise to me," he said.

Disappointed, I felt like I needed a long walk. When I returned, Jaleel had fixed us coffee and lit some logs in the fireplace. I grew up more in the next few hours than I had in my previous nineteen years. Jaleel said quite quickly that he wasn't sure he was ready for marriage. He let me raise most of the questions. I was hard on myself. Did I really want to be a mother, or did I just want leverage to hold onto Jaleel? Why should I feel rejected if we didn't marry, because rationally I respected and understood our streaks of independence? And what about money? For now I had funds in my trust, and in the end a small inheritance had come from my father, But when I thought about the cost of a good education for our child, I had no confidence the money would last forever. And what if we decided to have a second child? Raising kids wasn't cheap. Yet I knew one thing for certain. If I had the baby, I wasn't giving him or her up for adoption.

"I think we're blessed," Jaleel said. "If we conceived a child together, I want to honor that. I want to show my love for you through our love for our child. Doesn't that make sense?"

I said, almost resenting him, "You have the gift of convincing people that everything happens for a reason."

"That's because it does. And it doesn't always matter that we don't know what the reason is."

While he didn't show it, Jaleel was just as emotional as I was. I put my head on his shoulder and cried for what seemed forever. Yet by the end of the day, we found comfort in talking ourselves through the challenge. For now we would live together without getting married. Not being married didn't mean a child couldn't be raised with unconditional love.

As I calmed down, the alchemy of turning an accident into an opportunity seemed less daunting. Before we packed and left the cabin, we made a plan for our baby. We would raise him or her together, but if Jaleel and I ended up apart, we would split domestic responsibilities. The child would be six months with him, six with me. Jaleel was confident we could work out the details.

Yet the more I thought about the idea, the less sure I was. Two parents raising an interracial child separately, could we anticipate the obstacles that might come our way? We each knew what it meant to be knocked off our feet by the unexpected. At the edges of my heart was an anxiety about all the things that could possibly go wrong.

~61~

We moved into a two-bedroom apartment in Oakland, not far from Toby's neighborhood. My disappointment in taking a temporary leave of absence from Stanford was blunted by the excitement of entering the everyday world. The real world. There was a decent supermarket and pharmacy down the block. A Crate and Barrel distress sale gave us basic furniture. We found a practically unused crib and bassinet at a garage sale. Our one piece of art—Jaleel's drawing of Peartree—was hung in the living room. From our fifth-floor unit, the view was mostly sky, but just below, several construction sites signaled urban revival. As my belly kept ballooning, I made Jaleel tell me that all this was really happening.

"It's all going to be good," he answered with his trademark smile. "Even your morning sickness. The end justifies the means."

"You promise?"

"I do."

I hadn't been in touch with my mother since taking the summer off with Jaleel. I called New York one afternoon and gave her the news, that in four months I was having a baby, and I was dropping out of Stanford for a while. "You remember Jaleel, Mom," I added.

"A baby?" my mother echoed as if she hadn't heard correctly. For a woman who'd had her last child out of wedlock, not to mention with a secret lover, I couldn't imagine that my announcement would alarm her. But I could hear her thinking: "Alex, you're only nineteen. And Jaleel is that black man, the one who just got off the hook with the D.A. What kind of father will he be?"

"I'm thrilled," I said in the deafening silence.

"Are you in love with Jaleel?" she asked.

"Yes."

"When did you get married?"

"We didn't. I don't know if that's going to happen."

"Why not?"

"Long story," I allowed. Not that she would have understood, even if I explained every nuance of our decision making.

"Aren't you going to be just a little supportive, Mom?" My voice rose in frustration.

"Well, of course I'm supportive, Alex. It's just all a surprise."

As we kept talking, she became more cheery. It finally seemed to occur to her that having raised a happy, successful daughter meant she'd been a successful mother on some level. By the time we hung up, things had calmed between us.

On March 25, 1993, George Washington Baten-Robeson thrust himself into the world, a gangly monster at ten pounds, seven ounces. We chose his name partly on a lark but with some seriousness too. Men named George Washington had made history for their leadership, hard work, and creativity. We wanted the same for our son. His nickname was G.W.

Holding a precious life in my arms, I had a new identity as well. "You're a mother," I whispered to myself more than once, as if there was a wall of disbelief to climb.

Agnes called and invited herself to move in to help with G.W. I wasn't about to turn her down. When I invited Mom too, she said it was a terrific idea and would get back to me. I asked again two months later. Her time was not her own, she apologized. She was dating some interesting men, and marriage was suddenly a real possibility. I listened for a minute, congratulated her, and hung up.

If it weren't for Agnes burping, feeding, and changing diapers at all hours, Jaleel's and my survival as a couple would have been seriously tested. Living a few months with Lucy in New Hampshire, I had some idea how much work this was, but day by day, it could grind you down. Sometimes, for fun, we called our son "Boy George" or "Mr. Washington," but in the end, G.W. stuck like a dart. He had my mouth and nose, Jaleel's chin, ears, and forehead. His coconut-colored skin, obsidian eyes, and curly black hair dazzled us. At five months, Agnes threw a Styrofoam baseball bat into his crib, should he share his father's athletic gifts.

Jaleel worked every day on his book, but we tried to make time for each other when I put G.W. down for a nap. Toby came over once a month to visit and play with his nephew. My brother was working his way up the Silicon Valley ladder as a coder, a high school dropout suddenly earning $200,000 a year. Technology innovations were taking over America, Toby said, but things were still in their infancy. G.W. was going to inherit a world that was impossible to predict.

It was emotional, if not traumatic, when Agnes had to leave for New Hampshire. I thanked her for everything, and we promised to keep in touch. On our own with G.W., Jaleel and I suddenly had more work, more planning, more stress. We had pledged to avoid arguments, but that was impossible. Gradually, we fell into a routine. I told Joyce and a few other friends that I was now a mother—a fate at age nineteen that no one from Valley could have predicted for Alexandra Baten. *Faber est quisque fortunae suae*, Joyce said in a supportive voice, but probably thinking I'd lost my sanity.

To others, getting pregnant by a black man who was not going to marry me was disturbing. Reactions varied from the racist ("I hear black men don't make good fathers") to the insensitive ("You should have gotten an abortion and called it a day, Alex"). After a while I stopped telling people.

Albert Einstein was never clear if he believed in time travel, but had he raised a toddler, he certainly would have. Days blurred into weeks, weeks into months. I had begun taking Stanford courses at home, doing most of the work as independent study. By the time I had my degree, G.W. was two and a half years old and had started day care. He was strong as an oak, and owned a smile that had Jaleel and me wrapped around his finger.

"Have you picked a graduate school?" Jaleel asked as the three of us sat for dinner one summer night. I had, but I hadn't told him.

"I've been accepted by the University of Chicago."

"That's a terrific school. Congratulations!"

"It's okay," I admitted, "but I can always change my plans. I want to be with you and G.W."

"If my book that just came out sells well, maybe I'll write another, and we can live anywhere. If it bombs, then I was probably meant to work in a church somewhere. I might end up preaching even if the book is successful."

"Wherever you have to move," I made clear, "I'll find a graduate program nearby."

"Don't you think you should go to the best school you can? If we end up not living near each other, we stick to our plan. G.W. lives half the time with me, half with you. We'll work things out. We always have."

"I don't want that," I said bluntly, willing to risk a fight.

"Why is it a problem if we have to live apart? It doesn't mean I don't love you or G.W."

"Forget me for a second. Raising a child who's going to be shuttled from one home to another, how is that possibly better that us raising him together?"

"It might make G.W. more independent," Jaleel said.

"Just like you?"

"Or you."

I didn't feel that way. Our interpretations of abandonment were different. I wanted to make sure G.W. always had the structure and support that had been taken away from me. Jaleel seemed to think that resilience and resourcefulness came as much from adversity as from nurturing. It was as if he was running back to his past as much as I was running away from mine.

"Do you know what Dirick told me?" Jaleel said as I lifted G.W. out of his chair and put him on my lap. "It was difficult for him to forgive his father for keeping him in the dark about his secret life. Yet when Dirick overcame his bitterness, he was rewarded with strength of character. That's what adversity can do."

"What does that mean? Just because I'm not the forgiving type, I'm not as enlightened as Dirick or you?"

"Not at all. But you're not very trusting of the process."

"What is the process? Don't you and I make the process? I'd like us to be together to raise an interracial child who may not have the easiest time. He needs both a mother and father, together."

"Love is important, but it's not everything, Alex. They're some things love can't do."

"That doesn't mean you throw it away."

"G.W. will get plenty of love from each of us. We'll be a team, even if we don't end up living together."

It felt like we were in the ring for a full fifteen rounds. There were no knockdowns, but Jaleel won the fight. He was a master of adaptation. Life's best lessons, he liked to say, came from the unexpected. I liked the unexpected as much as a fist between the eyes. I wasn't going to be able to stop him, I realized, from whatever he was going to do.

"And what about us?" I said.

"We'll always be close."

"Terrific," I whispered in a ghostly voice.

Jaleel came over and wrapped his arms around G.W. and me. Why I always waited to the last minute to bring up the most delicate and important subjects was a mystery. I was the early morning mouse who fearlessly explored to her heart's content—but there were moments when my nerve failed me. Even though we'd agreed at Big Sur that living together wasn't a contract, I wanted an extension. I would have brought up the subject of marriage again, but that would be like Sisyphus pushing the rock up the hill. Just when he got close to the top, the rock careened down and he had to try all over again. To the gods, there was no worse fate for a mortal than having an ambition that couldn't be fulfilled.

I kissed Jaleel on the lips and took G.W. outside in his stroller. We roamed down the sidewalk, nodding to neighbors, as I gathered my thoughts. Maybe things would be okay. They would have to be. I did trust Jaleel, and going our separate ways now didn't mean we wouldn't end up together some day. In bed that night, I whispered urgently, "No matter what happens with us, just tell me that G.W. will be okay."

Jaleel had the most reassuring smile in the world. "If you and I don't live in fear," he said, "neither will our son."

~62~

We departed Oakland two months after Stanford officially bestowed my bachelor of arts degree. I had graduated summa cum laude with a double major, but my abiding love was history, particularly twentieth-century American history. I hoped to have my doctorate in three years. Jaleel's memoir, which endured a slow start, gained momentum and scrambled to the top of best-seller lists. A number of churches, their ministers and congregants impressed with his story, were looking for a lay minister. Invitations were extended. The commitments were open ended, which Jaleel liked. For now, he chose a Unitarian church in San Bernadino.

I dreaded saying goodbye the entire week before our split. Agnes had come back to help us pack, and while Jaleel was off playing with G.W., I asked for her advice.

"Keep busy doing what you love," she said simply. "Both parts of that sentence are important."

"You once gave me the *carpe diem* speech. Something about love isn't like subway cars. Mr. Right doesn't come along every five minutes."

"Alex, I'm hoping for the best for you and Jaleel. But remember we also talked about colliding planets. Sometimes they bounce off each other and go into their own orbits. It's just the way it is."

I kept telling myself that I could be as independent as Jaleel or Agnes, but it felt like I was lying to my heart. Our last night together, Jaleel and I made love, both of us cried a little, and then a strange quiet descended over the apartment, as if we were in a cocoon separated from the rest of the world. We were at peace for the moment.

Jaleel wanted to drive the U-Haul all the way to Chicago for us, but I insisted that Agnes and I could handle the two-thousand-mile trip. G.W. packed his own toys. The three of us wedged into the front cab like pioneers in a covered wagon. We had a ball crossing half the country, stopping at motels with swimming pools for G.W., sampling old-fashioned diners, and talking to friendly strangers I would never see again. It reminded me of Jaleel's stories of traveling on the Greyhound bus.

In Chicago, I settled into a ground floor apartment a few blocks off Rush Street, a modest but quiet place where G.W. had his own room. With book royalties, Jaleel bought a small, tidy home with a big yard.

Our grand experiment of sharing our son fifty-fifty began. After six months in Chicago, G.W. and I got ready to fly to L.A. Between schoolwork and parenting, I cherished the idea of a break. G.W. was excited about exploring another part of the world. He had his own miniature suitcase on wheels, so at O'Hare he could feel "like a big person."

Jaleel picked us up at LAX, and we spent a week together as a family. It felt a little weird sleeping with him after such a long time. Something was missing. I pretended not to notice. I certainly wasn't going to ask if he was dating. He didn't ask me either. When I flew back to Chicago, I was already lonely. I didn't know who I missed most, G.W. or Jaleel. It felt like I had fallen into an immense void and couldn't scale the walls to get out.

There was one benefit to being alone, though. I suddenly had time for a social life. I worked all week, challenged by classes, but on weekends, some other grad students invited me to join a volleyball league. Afterward, there was time for a tequila bar, movie, or a comedy club. I dated a couple of guys, but there was no one I was drawn to, not enough to want to sleep with. Did I owe Jaleel an explanation if I did sleep with someone? It was all confusing. We emailed each other almost every day, trading stories about our sometimes-busy, sometimes-quiet lives. I kept thinking that any moment, Jaleel would come to his senses, fly back with G.W., and the fairy tale—the one my mother unfailingly believed in: the perfect family living in its private paradise—would come true for me.

When Jaleel brought G.W. back six months later, however, he stayed for only two days. We made love once. There were jokes about G.W. already accumulating a stash of frequent flyer miles, and by the time he was out of college, he would probably have enough to fly around the world a half-dozen times, first class. Jaleel apologized for not hanging around longer. He was well into his second book and had a deadline. Our embrace at the airport was hurried.

Sometimes I would catch him on a television talk show. His memoir had thrust him back into the spotlight, and provoked new discussions on race and class inequality. On TV, Jaleel was articulate and humble, yet passionate on his subject. Despite all the civil rights legislation over the years, he wanted to make clear, racism and inequality were hardly dead. He likened them to a fungus that grew in dark places, avoiding the light, and was all the more poisonous because you couldn't see it.

One weekend evening, Jaleel showed up unannounced at my doorstep. He said he was on a book tour in the Windy City. Whether it was G.W. or me who was the most surprised, and happy, was up for debate. "Daddy, daddy," G.W. kept chanting, running around his father, grabbing one leg for support when he got dizzy. Jaleel looked beyond handsome in a suit and tie, and his smile was always the same. I threw my arms around him and we hugged for a solid thirty seconds. After half an hour of playing with G.W., he told me to find a baby sitter. His publisher had made a reservation at the best French restaurant in Chicago.

"How many people will there be?" I had energy, but after working on a paper all day, not enough to endure a long dinner with a group of strangers.

"Just you and me. Are you hungry?"

"Just you and me?" I repeated, skeptical.

"If this is inconvenient, Alex—"

I shook my head. "No. I'll get dressed. This is a treat."

We took a taxi to the restaurant. A bottle of Dom Perignon was waiting at our table. Publishers never treated you to an expensive dinner, Jaleel quipped, until they'd checked your latest sales numbers. For Jaleel to have some money and celebrity seemed dangerous to him. It was something he said he didn't want to get used to or enjoy too much.

"Do you think we're spoiling G.W.?" I asked after using our first glass of champagne to toast him. I thought we might be overcompensating for parental guilt, or at least I was.

"Better than depriving him. There's nothing wrong with hearing a child say to a parent two things: 'I want,' and 'I feel.'"

I had to think about that a few seconds before I understood. Having your own voice as early as possible was the best way to begin navigating life.

I asked about Dirick and Rudy. They both still moved at a hundred miles an hour, Jaleel said, because their work was never done. We finished the first Dom and ordered a second. Our eyes kept meeting, but Jaleel was always the first to pull away.

"What is it?" I said at last. "You dropped by tonight for a reason. It's not just a casual visit."

He pushed away his food, trying to find the right words.

"You've met someone special, haven't you?" I said.

His smile was that of someone caught off guard. "If there were a prize for the most intuitive person I've ever known—"

"That's you, not me," I said. "This one's pretty obvious. What's her name?"

"Deborah Mungin. She's African-American. We met at church."

"Mungin," I repeated, curious about the name.

"It's a slave surname, taken from a plantation owner. Deborah is from Texas too, not far from Peartree, of all places. She never had the money for anything more than junior college, but believe me, she's smart."

At Jaleel's deepest level, despite the means and opportunity to choose whatever path he wanted, his roots dictated life's most critical choices. Maybe the black-white thing played a part. It was one thing to have an interracial child, another to be an interracial couple.

"I've told her all about you, Alex." He made me look straight at him. "And she'll be great with G.W. I can't wait for them to meet."

"Are you in love with her?"

"Very much."

"And you're getting married . . . ."

"Yes."

"Then I'm very happy for you." I meant it, but at the same time, it felt like my heart had been cleaved in two.

"Alex, you are not getting replaced. You're my oldest and most intimate friend. You're the mother of our child. I will always love you. But we figured out a while ago there wasn't a future for us—"

"I didn't know that. I thought we were still trying to get together. Or was that just me?"

I brushed away a tear with my finger. I could be disappointed, but I had no right to be surprised, I thought. If I were gracious, I would have said that I looked forward to meeting Deborah. One day, I was sure I would. But at the moment, I felt a wall go up around me. I remembered my father, and how a stepmother could have her own agenda. "You're sure this is going to be okay for G.W.?"

"He's the most important thing in the world," Jaleel said. "I will always look after him, and I know you will too. Nothing is going to change in our arrangement."

"I have to be certain." If I had to, I was going to defend my son against even someone I adored and who was above suspicion. I no longer took anything for granted.

"The world would have to break into a billion atoms before I abandoned you or G.W."

But you already have, I thought.

Our conversation drifted. I could see Jaleel's gaze pivot inward. The real Jaleel, the one I loved most, could make himself vanish for long stretches of time into some unreachable depth. Whatever he was dreaming about, or reliving, if he didn't want to talk about it, you couldn't pull it out of him.

"This is pretty hard," I finally said. "I'm not sure I'm going to get over you."

"People don't always mean to inflict pain. I wanted it to work for us, Alex. I really did."

If his eyes weren't so honest, our pasts so connected, our love for G.W. so unbreakable, it would have been easy for me to spring from the table and call a cab. Instead, I reached out and took his hand, wrapping our fingers together.

Alex:
The Present

~63~

My mother charms the hostess into giving us a window booth at Bistro Louise. The air conditioning is welcome. The New England streetscape is another perfectly groomed Legoland, where single-story, clapboard buildings mix with old brick-faced granaries and dry goods stores. But things can change in a wink: Starbucks, gelato shops, Abercrombie & Fitch, Domino's Pizza, Chipotle. I think of Jaleel's drawing of downtown Peartree, of black people crossing the street while whites bunch together separately. I've never been to Peartree, so I have no idea what it's like now. In my town, there's a universal lassitude in summer, people of all colors moving through the molasses heat, looking in common for relief.

"What do you recommend, Alex?" Mom scrutinizes the menu like it's as baffling as the Rosetta Stone.

"You said you wanted the lobster salad. I usually have the Cobb, or if I'm in a carnivorous mood, they serve a great Reuben."

"I don't eat meat, sweetie."

She asks our waitress for another minute. She forgets about the lobster salad and chooses the *insalata mista* with olive oil. I have the Cobb, with extra blue cheese crumbles.

"It's been nine years, amazing, huh?" I observe, suddenly feeling my throat close. By amazing, I mean Twilight Zone amazing. We just aren't connected. The last time I saw Mom was by accident, at Madison Square Garden. She and her husband were there for a Knicks game. It was George's tenth birthday. Jaleel and I invited everyone to a Times

Square deli afterward. I thought the five of us were comfortable with each other, but an hour later, it was back to separate universes, as if our get-together had been nothing more than the coincidence it was.

Mom keeps her dark glasses on, which annoys me. For a while, we talk about the classes I teach, what I'm going to do for my sabbatical next year (I have no idea), and if I'm dating anyone seriously.

"No, not at the moment."

"No prospects?"

"No, Mom." I'm not unlike Agnes, I tell her. I've had a couple of serious relationships over the years, but nothing jelled. I'm happy being single. I tell myself that no one quite measures up to Jaleel. At times I blame my parents' marriage. The thought of coming even close to repeating that disaster gives me chills.

"Tell me about G.W.," Mom says at last.

I hide my disappointment that she's waited this long to ask. "Sure," I say casually. "Your grandson is a sophomore at Princeton. Plays varsity basketball. Wants to be a medical doctor. He and Jaleel are in Europe for a couple of weeks. First time for George."

Except for holiday photos, Mom hasn't seen my son since the Knicks game. He calls himself George now, not G.W., I tell her. When he was much younger, they spoke on the phone once a month, but Mom always pushed away the idea of a visit. George finally accepted that she was too busy for him. "Not your fault, honey," I emphasized. "It doesn't mean she doesn't love you in her own way."

"How do you know that?"

"I don't. But there's a good chance," I said, trying to make light of the situation.

A smile hurried across his face, just like his father. We laughed together. George picked up the underlying truth: My mother is capricious, and wants to be the star no matter who else is on stage with her. She calls, or doesn't, when she wants. Long ago I wrote down a Lord Byron quote, and placed the card on my makeup table. I think the great poet had my mother in mind: *Self-love forever creeps out, like a snake, to sting anything which happens to stumble upon it.* I remind myself that narcissism's now a classified disorder in the DSM.

"Europe, whereabouts?" Mom says, as this is something she can relate to.

"Paris and Rome. Jaleel is doing research for a new book."

"They'll love both cities, especially Paris! Jaleel is doing well?"

I tell her that he's published seven books and gets decent royalties. Years ago, he went to Berkeley for his undergraduate degree in humanities, and later a master's and a doctorate in interdisciplinary studies. He's hardly rich, but he and Deborah are comfortable, and happy together. He pays more than his share of George's expenses, I make clear. It gives me a lot of happiness that Jaleel and I will always be the best of friends, even if we don't raise our son in one house together.

"What a remarkable young man," Mom says, processing my update on George. "I'm very proud of what he's done."

She offers the compliment, I think, to make up for her absence in her grandson's life.

"Mom, why don't you ever visit? What do you have against George? Is it because he's half black? Or something else—"

"I don't know what you're talking about, Alex. I'm not a bigot."

"Do you still think it was Jaleel who killed Charlie? Be honest, because this has been bothering me for a long time. Is that why you never want to get too close?"

"The police never identified the murderer," she answers, as if any further discussion is pointless.

"But you think it's Jaleel, in your heart—even though I told you at Agnes's house that he was innocent."

"I didn't come here to get in some fight over the past, Alex."

She digresses to the subject of Toby. My brother has a wife and two young boys, all of whom he adores, she informs me. Except with his family or a few friends, he doesn't go out in public much. She's okay with my brother being a semi-reclusive coder. Because he bought stock options in the right tech startup, he's richer that Croesus.

I tell Mom I know all about Toby, more than she does. I'm in touch with him all the time.

It's the smallest thing—her willful self-absorption—that becomes the biggest thing when it sets me off. It triggers an explosion. A secret that has been buried too long, eating a hole in me, worms its way to the surface, like a swimmer who can't hold his breath any longer.

"Just so you know, Mom. It was Dad who killed Charlie."

I can't see behind her glasses, but her voice quakes. "That's just rumor. And why are you bringing this up now?"

"It's more than a rumor. I can give you chapter and verse. Dad confessed to my face—twice, actually."

"Nonsense."

"Whatever."

"I'll accept that Jaleel is innocent, but I refuse to believe your father had anything to do with murdering Charlie.

"You wouldn't want that either, Alex."

Her tone is like a parent warning a child to stay away from an ocean with a vicious undertow.

"What wouldn't I want?"

"You don't want to think that your father killed Charlie."

I'm confused. "I don't think, Mom. I know."

"It's not healthy for you to believe it. I was trying to tell you at Agnes's house years ago. But telling you was too complicated. And then you and Agnes took Lucy from me. That was cruel. Do you know how hurt I was? After that, I swore I was never going to tell you the truth."

Our food arrives, but I don't touch mine. I want to reach up and take off Mom's glasses, to see her eyes.

"Giving the baby up for adoption was the only realistic strategy," I remind her. "You and Agnes talked about it for months. You signed a contract, remember? You were divorced and hadn't a clue about what you were doing."

"Oh, so you knew everything about my state of mind? You knew what was in my heart?"

"If I got it wrong, why don't you tell me?"

"Giving up the baby wouldn't have been what Charlie wanted. He would have wanted me to raise Lucy. That's why I changed my mind that last morning."

"Look, I know you were in love with Charlie—"

"Do you? Do you know how much? The subject always seems to embarrass you. You get furious about it. Sometimes I think you want to strangle me for having the affair. But you have no idea."

"Then tell me." My voice claws at her. I'm tired of her evasiveness. I want to know everything.

"I liked Charlie from the day Dad introduced us. When he was best man at our wedding, I danced with him. I couldn't get him out of my mind after that. Every man holds you a little differently. And the way Charlie held me—it's hard to describe, but there was something special about him." She tilts her head back, her mind somersaulting back to some moment of intimacy. "That was the beginning."

Anxiety stokes my memory—Dad and Charlie best friends since high school, inseparable at USC, best man at each other's wedding. The Batens and Diggses living half a mile from each other—vacationing, dining out, playing golf together.

"You were lovers for your entire marriage, is that what you're saying?" I'm almost choking.

"On and off," Mom answers.

As surreal and difficult as this is, I can't let go. My mind rushes in a new direction.

"How many times did Charlie get you pregnant?"

"That's ancient history."

"Maybe to you. I want to know."

"I'm not talking about this any further, Alex. I came to visit for a reason, to tell you about a wonderful man I plan to marry, a widower named Jack. He happens to be the most cheerful, upbeat person in the world." She adds, "Is there anything wrong with that?"

"Not for some people."

"Aren't you going to congratulate me?"

"This is your fourth marriage, isn't it? I can't even keep track."

"I'm going to send you an invitation to the wedding."

"Please don't."

A sigh bursts from her lips. I'm being hurtful, disparaging—not to mention ungrateful for all the great things she's done for me as a mother. Her chest heaves.

"How many times did Charlie get you pregnant?" I repeat. "You don't believe in abortion. I know that."

"Mom finally removes her dark glasses. Tears are welling in both eyes. "You don't want to ask that question, honey."

"I'm asking."

She looks as distressed as I've ever seen her, worse than when I caught her on the phone with Charlie, more defeated than on our living room couch the morning after the kitchen shoving match.

"Say it, Mom!"

She just stares, at me, through me, maybe back in time to the magical moment of conception. "Charlie got me pregnant once before."

"What happened to the baby?"

"My god," she says, her last warning for me to stop.

And then I know what she's going to tell me. It sounds like I'm on drugs I speak so slowly. "That's bullshit—"

"You asked, Alex. You're not the only one who can give chapter and verse."

I go a little crazy inside. I can't organize my thoughts, but some words spill out anyway. "You're saying that Charlie Diggs is my biological father?"

"Yes. That's exactly what I'm saying."

The word "yes" hits like an earthquake. What am I supposed to do now? "That couldn't have happened," I argue.

"I was happy to have a baby with the man I was in love with."

"But how?"

"Your father was away for a good while in Washington, D.C., dealing with the SEC for a client. You were born nine months and two weeks after the actual conception, but I told Louis you were two weeks early. Your father and Charlie had different physiques, but their facial features were similar. Louis wasn't hard to fool. You knew how arrogant and naive he could be.

Like me, I think she is saying. I drop into a hole that takes all my strength to crawl out of and think clearly.

"So you did? You fooled him, Mom. You fooled me too. Lucy is not my half-sister," I add. "She's my full sister."

She can't bring herself to admit her deceit. I feel an anger creeping up the back of my neck. My shock at Mom's confession comes at me in waves, until I'm nauseous. Then an impossible thought pops into my head, and I'm staggered again. It was my father who murdered my father.

"Excuse me," I whisper, levitating from the table.

Everything is in slo-mo. In the bathroom, I lock myself in a stall and push my head over the open toilet. My dry heaves are painful and violent. It's like I'm fifteen again, about to testify in front of the grand jury. I'm still getting caught in my parents' dramas. I can't escape them.

I douse a paper towel in cold water and press it against my face. Ever since my first encounter with the crinkly-haired, all-knowing Dr. Sheffield, something in me has rebelled at therapy. But I've read a lot. I know what a good therapist would say about Toby and me. My brother was the lucky one. He was such an oddball that neither Mom nor Dad had high hopes for Toby. I was the golden child who got sucked in. I didn't know when I was very young, but I wanted to do more than meet my parents' expectations. I lived to make them happy, fix their problems, and never let them down, except if something was a matter of principle for me. I was miserable with guilt when Mom grew resentful of Dad. I would do anything for him when she left for good.

I crumple the paper towel, throw it away, and march out of the bathroom. Mom's already paid the check, but I drop in the booth, unwilling to let her go.

"Did Agnes know your secret?" I ask. "She's my friend, but she never told me."

"You shouldn't be mad at Agnes. She wanted to tell you on your visit years ago, in the worst way. I wouldn't let her."

"Then why didn't you tell me about Charlie?"

"You were sixteen. Telling you would have devastated you."

"I think it devastates me more now."

Her eyes jump over my face before sliding away. She's like a child who knows she's been bad looking for a closet to hide in. "All right," she says, throwing her hands on the table in surrender. "If you want me to apologize, I apologize. It just made more sense to me to keep everything quiet."

"But you did tell Charlie—" I wasn't sure what I wanted the answer to be.

"Of course. He agreed with having the baby, having you. He wanted me to be happy. We made a pact that it would be our secret forever. He didn't want to jeopardize his friendship with Dad.

"Alex, I'm sorry if I hurt you," she emphasizes. Mom is as sincere as she can ever be. Her head and shoulders are preternaturally still, as she conjures up one last thought.

"Look at you, honey. Devoted mother to a wonderful son, head of the history department at a prestigious college, published author of scholarly papers—how much more accomplished can one be?

"Charlie—" she starts to add, but can't finish the sentence.

I think she wants to say, "Charlie would be so happy about your successes," or maybe, "Charlie lives on in you. You have his genes." Something like that. She'll always be in love with him.

"When I was young, before we moved into the Tudor," I say, "I remember how special you treated me. Was that because you believed I was special? Or was it because I was Charlie's daughter?"

"What does all this matter? I'm sure it was all of the above." She clutches her handbag, stirring in the booth as her eyes flash to the exit.

"Or maybe you just wanted me to adore you."

"I need to get back to New York," Mom says, scooting away. "Jack's waiting."

~64~

The drive back to my house feels like a trip through another galaxy. I'm so disoriented, feeling so weightless, that I imagine it's my seat belt that keeps me from flying out of the car. My mother, despite being in love with select memories, doesn't elaborate on Charlie. Nor does she ask how I'm feeling as I absorb the biggest secrets of her life. I think she wants me to focus on how lucky I am. Despite all her deceit and pretending, and everything that was taken from me by my parents' dishonesty, my life has turned out just fine. Can't I see that? I've no right to complain.

I spin my anger back on myself, as usual. For someone who doesn't like being in the dark, I've managed to miss one of the brightest suns in my universe. I calculate that I had at least a hundred conversations or visits with Charlie over the years. How could I have missed something right under my nose? Once he was murdered, I largely stopped thinking about him.

I never particularly liked Charlie, but I didn't dislike him, until I learned of Mom's affair. How would I have felt had I known he was my biological father? Would I have excused all the secrets because he and my mother were in love? Would I have gotten to know him better? Maybe he really was as special as Mom thinks. The night of the poker game, approaching me in our hallway, it's possible that his questions about my future weren't an act. I consider that he might have genuinely cared, and that I was a jerk for judging him too quickly.

My mother keeps her eyes on the road, but she can't help one last jab. "I know you're a success, Alex, and that's important, but I wish you could be happier."

"You just dropped a nuclear warhead on me."

"You know what I mean. You spend so much time pulling everything apart."

"Except for today, Mom, I've been pretty happy. I like getting at the root of things. I like being independent. What I dislike in anyone is running away."

Mom deflects my blow with a wag of her head, like I'm beyond clueless. "Before you judge me too harshly, may I tell you something? Someone's life starts out in one direction, and all of a sudden you're moving in another. You didn't see the turn. You don't know where you are, so you just keep going. You never end up where you imagined you would." Her gaze floats to me. "Just wait until you're my age."

We're suddenly in my driveway. That's fine with me. Mom doesn't shut off the ignition. We don't trade kisses. We don't even hug. I have no idea what she's thinking, other than that this trip has been a bust. Things didn't go as planned. I'm thinking, as a daughter and a historian, that my mother's attitudes and values belong to another era.

"Thank you for lunch," I whisper, and lever myself from the car. There's nothing else to say.

"You're welcome, honey." Her voice carries a tender, hopeless note, like someone talking to herself.

As she backs out of the drive, her wave hasn't changed. It's the same as when I left for sleep-away camp. A kind of fluttering wrist, some wiggle in the fingers. I watch as her car dissolves into the metallic glow of the afternoon. I doubt either of us will pick up the phone or send the other an email anytime soon.

I check on my two Jack Russells in the back yard, grab a couple of Aleve from the kitchen, and slip into my office. I attack myself with more what-ifs. What if I'd learned Charlie was my biological father after Dad killed him, would I have changed my mind and gone to the police? What if Mom had divorced Dad and married Charlie long ago? Perhaps two sentient beings—in lieu of Toby and me—would be walking the earth now. What if Charlie, while still best friends with Dad, had found the courage to tell him the truth? Dad would have been furious, but I like to think he would have loved me too much to do my birth father any harm.

I open the computer file that I've been working on forever, the book Jaleel asked me to write when we were at Big Sur. I'm still shaken by Mom's visit, but I feel an urgency to get everything down. The visit wasn't a total bust. The words flow more easily than I expect:

> *Sunday, July 6, 2014. My mother's car just pulled up across the street. The brunch is her idea—our private reunion after nine years. Her email insisted she has important news, but she wouldn't tell me details. All morning, I've distracted myself by rereading the memoir I can't seem to finish writing.*

* * *

Around midnight, my shoulders relax and my throat opens. I breathe in the pure oxygen of finishing a project that has taken me eighteen years. A few pages to begin the book, and two short chapters to end it. My mother struck like a lightning bolt today. If I publish my memoir, she might tell her friends it's just payback from an angry overachiever. But it's all true, every word. There's plenty of drama, but no anger anymore. I look at my story as I look at history. In our ever-changing universe, lives collide, and, like runaway planets, we just keep going.

The story continues. Alex and Jaleel
share the next chapters of their lives.

On Facebook
Alex: http://on.fb.me/1PKt1eH
Jaleel: http://on.fb.me/1TWERFo

And Twitter
Alex: http://bit.ly/1Xcmgqo
Jaleel: http://bit.ly/1TcGJWp

Michael French

Friends of Michael French describe him as a "hyperactive omnivore" (a charge he admits to), feeding on politics, art, capitalism, religion, history, travel, and popular culture. The late night college bull sessions of decades ago have been replaced by leisurely dinners at ethnic restaurants where conversations are kept at reasonable decibels. But the subjects remain pretty much the same. (OK, throw in the ever-expanding digital universe.)

Travel hooked him early, when he went from Hollywood High School to Switzerland as a foreign exchange student. As Mark Twain wrote, travel is fatal to bigotry and prejudice, and French's first trip abroad opened his mind "wider than the Grand Canyon."

After receiving an English degree from Stanford and a master's in journalism from Northwestern, he was drafted into the Army and became editor of the post newspaper—"a two-year, tuition-free education about bureaucracy and humanity." His first "real job" after that—making more than $1 an hour—was with a public relations firm in New York City, writing annual reports for Fortune 500 companies, "which was not as dull as it sounds. I learned about capitalism," French says, "the good and the bad."

He and his wife, Patricia, moved to Santa Fe in 1978, and started a real estate company and a family. Squeezing in writing time whenever he could, he published his first best-seller, *Abingdon's*, with Doubleday in 1979. "My father always said one needed a work ethic to be successful," French recalls, "and Patricia and I were fortunate we shared that trait."

They still found time to take their two children to Australia, Africa, Indonesia, and Europe. At some point, children become teen-agers and want nothing to do with parents or travel, but Michael and Pat persisted on their course and have now visited seventy-two countries.

For French, ideas for stories come at unexpected times—visiting a hill village in Myanmar, a seventeen-hour plane haul on which sleep-deprived hallucinations can briefly turn you into a genius, or sometimes just a bite on a blueberry muffin (Proust's madeleine). Ideas also come from listening to a friend describe his disintegrating marriage, a visit to a DeKooning exhibit at MoMA, or a late night screening of Fellini's *Juliette of the Spirits*.

The best writing ideas are never forced, French believes, and need to be strong enough to keep you going for long stretches of time. Shaping characters and plot into a meaningful read is often dark, clandestine toil, "like working for the CIA. Best not to tell anyone what you're writing—in many instances, they wouldn't get it anyway."

Sometimes, French admits, he doesn't understand why anyone is drawn to the craft as a career. "Think of a blackboard covered with a twenty-line mathematical equation, the kind Matt Damon solves in what feels like three seconds in *Good Will Hunting* but utterly mystifies and demoralizes the rest of us— 'solving' the many problems that come with completing a book is not so different. Many books are finished on a near-empty tank and with a flourish of masochism before there's a sense of satisfaction. Then you give your book to a literary-minded friend and ask for his opinion—really, don't do that. Stick it in a drawer for a while and have a rewrite or two, then show it to someone who can be honest while appreciating how much effort you've put into this."

French's work, which includes several best-sellers, has been warmly reviewed in the *New York Times* and been honored with a number of literary prizes.